A Walk Around
Cold Spring Pond

Mo —
Hope you like
it.

[signature]

A Walk Around Cold Spring Pond

Stephen F. Medici

Thea & Golf Publishing

A Walk Around Cold Spring Pond
Copyright © 2011 Stephen F. Medici
Published by Thea & Golf Publishing

For more information contact:
Stephen F. Medici at sfmedici@hotmail.com

Book design by:
Arbor Books, Inc.
www.arborbooks.com

Printed in the United States of America

A Walk Around Cold Spring Pond
Stephen F. Medici

1. Title 2. Author 3. Fiction

Library of Congress Control Number: 2010936805

ISBN 13: 978-0-9802289-1-5

Dedicated to
**Catherine, Anthony, Frank, Anne,
Rocco, and Angelina**
*(my parents and grandparents,
who taught me the most important stuff)*

ACKNOWLEDGEMENTS

I am privileged to acknowledge the contributions others have made to this work. First, an immense thank you to my wife, Colleen who is always the first to read my stories, the first to add human characteristics I was too obtuse to envision, and the last to criticize. Thanks also to Jerry DiCola for giving me the inspiration and life-experiences to create Doc, for his forty years of friendship, and for his critical analysis of the first draft.

Special thanks also to retired NYFD Battalion Chief Edward White for his insights about the explosive capabilities of various fuels and for being patient with me while I learned.

Many thanks also to John J. Burns, RPh., and Maureen Peters, RN BSN, who did the medical editing and guided me through the mysterious terminology surrounding cancer and pharmaceuticals. Thank you to my son Christian Medici, who did the technical editing of the poker table scenes.

Finally, a world of gratitude to Katie DaRin for her painstaking editing of the final draft. Her contributions helped make the finished product considerably more readable than when I handed it to her.

Summer 2008

CHAPTER ONE

Doc

The first time I ever saw Annie, the sun was in my eyes. I'd just started my morning jog and had turned down Lynton Lane towards the shimmering Peconic Bay. It was a particularly beautiful and bright August morning here in Southampton with just enough crispness in the air to remind me that Labor Day and the fall were just around the corner.

My name is Jerome Cafara but only my mother calls me Jerome; everyone else calls me Doc. It's a long story. Anyway, I bought the tiny cottage at the end of Lynton Lane three weeks ago and moved out here from the city last week. My hope is to get the roof to stop leaking so I can move in permanently. Or at least until I figure out where I really belong.

I fell in love with this part of the Hamptons a couple of years ago while renting a small place about a mile from here. It was on one of my morning runs that I spotted the for-sale sign and met the Mauros—the people who owned my dripping cottage before me. It had been in their family for two generations but the upkeep and constant barrage from mother nature became too much for the aging couple. Actually, at the closing, Mrs. Mauro confided in me that she was tired of cleaning the place after her four adult sons' weekend parties. Apparently they didn't inherit mom's zest for cleanliness. So thanks to Mrs. Mauro's sons, this triangular strip of land jutting into Cold Spring Pond became mine on July 18th, 2008.

Cold Spring Pond is a beautiful little inlet off the Peconic Bay—the water that separates the north and south forks of eastern Long Island. The pond is only about a half mile across and almost perfectly round. It empties into the Peconic through a narrow inlet less than a mile east of the Shinnecock Canal. In years gone by, it was a safe haven for boaters because of its tranquility even when the winds kick up on the open bay. Today, because it's so shallow, only clammers and windsurfers come into the pond. And that's why I love it. There's just about no one here.

The pond is ringed by no more than fifty modest cottages, each with their aging wooden docks. It's fed by several cold underground springs, hence its name and clear brackish water. The pond is home to a variety of shellfish but not many year-round people. Its adjacent marshes provide a safe environment for dozens of species of fish and birds, protected from man's reach. It's about as close to "untouched" as any place can be on Long Island.

So this morning, as I began my jog around the pond, the sun glistened on the still water. As I approached the end of Lynton Lane, I looked left and saw a couple of kids jumping rope in the street. Their golden retriever, Gustoff, who I'd encountered before, sat near one of the young girls twirling the rope. Rather than deal with Gustoff's joyous, but slobbering greeting, I decided to turn right on to Cold Spring Point Road. It's a narrow street that leads to the entrance to the Sabonic Golf Club and eventually all the way back to Route 27, the island's main artery to the Hamptons.

That's when I saw Annie. She was bent over and tying her sneakers in preparation for a run of her own. She had come out of one of the driveways leading to a bay-front home. These are the real houses—the genuine Southampton "waterfront" homes that line the sandy beaches of the Peconic Bay and start at seven million. The "bay-people" as they are known, tend to take a dim view of the diminutive cottages like mine; not because they leak, but simply because they're on the pond and not the bay. Hence, we're known as the "pond-people," and need to understand our subordinate position in Southampton society.

Annie was fifty yards ahead of me and had begun to run in the same direction; towards the golf club and parallel to the bay. I had a great view of the back of her Nike running shorts and all they contained. She had great legs. I decided to maintain my distance and enjoy the scenery for a while.

If I'd known then what I know now, I would have gone left and dealt with Gustoff. It would have saved me a lot of pain.

But I'm getting ahead of myself.

CHAPTER TWO

Doc

Cold Spring Point Road is a narrow one-lane path, only recently paved, and usually covered with blowing sand. It's a private road, owned by the Cold Spring Association, of which I am now a member. Because so few members live out here year-round, the road is often impassable in winter, either due to drifting sand or floods from the adjacent bay.

Today it's dry and relatively free of sand and there's a shapely young woman jogging about fifty yards in front of me. We're both running towards the east so the sun is hitting us directly in the eyes. But even with the glare I can tell she's in great shape; long thin legs and a narrow waist. From this distance and without seeing her face I guess she's one of the teenagers who summer in the big houses along the bay. I noticed several of them a few days before when I went down to the beach to take some shots of the sunset.

Now I'm not a very competitive guy, and usually when I run I like to be by myself, but for some reason, today I decided to catch up to the teenager and see if I could pass her before reaching the curve in the road at the golf course entrance. I was still well behind her so I needed to close the distance in about a minute. Maybe less. Like I said, I'm not usually competitive but I do like to set modest personal challenges for myself every so often and this seemed like a good one. What the heck. If I couldn't catch her before the curve, only I'd know it.

So I picked up my pace a bit and quickly realized that this was not going to be easy. There wasn't enough pavement left to make up the distance unless I sprinted all out. My need for a personal challenge didn't extend to pulling an under-utilized hamstring, so I backed off and resumed my jogging pace—about an eight minute mile. As I said, *only I'd know.*

The long thin legs in the Nike shorts ended her run at the golf course and turned to walk back towards her beach house. The sun was still in my eyes but as she approached me I could see she had not been a teenager for at least a quarter of a century, which could make us about the same age. Well, close anyway. I was still jogging and as she walked past me she lowered her water bottle to say, "Beautiful day, huh?" Her voice was soft and she sounded genuinely happy. Much happier than I usually am after a three mile run.

If forced to describe her, I would call her pretty. Not clas-sically beautiful like a Catherine Zeta-Jones but youthfully pretty like a Jenifer Aniston. Or more accurately, what Jen will look like when she too is on the sorry side of fifty. I suppose you could call her *'classically pretty.'*

"Great day," was about all I could huff out as I went by.

I continued my run to the curve in the road and still felt like I had a little left so I turned south on Sebonic Road and did the last half mile thinking about who else she looked like. She reminded me of Jenny, one of my secretaries from years ago and of my ex-sister-in-law who I really like and who now lives in Utah with my ex-brother-in-law who's an asshole. It's funny how divorce makes you a lot less tolerant of your in-laws' flaws.

I finished my run with a fifty yard sprint and felt pretty good about it, so I decided to walk back to the cottage the long way—along the beach. As I said, the beach is lined with some very nice homes and I never tire of admiring them as I trespass along the shore. Actually, as long as you stay down by the waterline you're not really trespassing because technically, those fortunate enough to own waterfront property in Southampton only own the sand down to the high tide line. That allows *pond-people* like me, and, I suppose even the poor land-locked, to walk along the shore whenever they want. And it drives the *bay-people* crazy. I can only imagine how the Southampton royalty, those who have inherited oceanfront property, must feel. But I find it hard to feel sorry for anyone with oceanfront property in Southampton.

To be fair, so far I've found the folks of the Cold Spring Association to be very cordial about the use of the beaches on the bay. Perhaps that's because there's so much beach and so few people. They might change their tune if bus loads of day-trippers from Brooklyn start arriving with their picnic baskets and coolers.

That morning, the beach was completely empty. As it usually does at low tide, the retreating water left behind a colorful assortment of shells and stones. They were still wet and glistened as the sun climbed higher on the eastern horizon. I like walking this section of the beach in the morning because with the sun on your back you can see forever. To my right lays the great Peconic Bay and across the way I could clearly make out the towns of Mattituck and Southold on the north fork. In front of me the beach stretched for miles in a prolonged arch that ends at the horizon. Along the way are huge cliffs of snow-white sand. On top of the cliffs sit some of Southampton's finest and newest Mc-mansions. The young Wall Street types who summer in those castles on the sand can see across to Connecticut from their kitchen windows.

I found a horseshoe crab at the waters edge that had been turned on his back by the waves and was now struggling to right itself before the birds noticed his dilemma or the strengthening sun got to him. Perhaps, because of the slope of the beach, this seems to happen a lot and I often wonder if I am disturbing the delicate balance of nature by flipping the crabs back in the water. I just can't walk by a struggling creature and not do something to help. They look so helpless with their many legs kicking in the air, trying desperately to grab hold of something—anything that will get them off their backs and back in the cool water. So mother nature will have to adjust because that morning I rescued three crabs.

The bay was as calm as a sheet of glass and I could see a few sailboats out near Robin's Island. Robin's Island sits directly in the center of the Peconic Bay and used to be owned by some friends of George Washington. It's only about 440 acres all in but has a colorful history and was most recently purchased by a Wall Street tycoon named Bacon for a mere eleven million. Someone told me he wanted to build a hotel on the island but the nature conservancy put the whammy on that in 1997 when they declared the whole place a conservation easement. So now the native deer and birds are having a ball. I wonder if they're card-carrying members of the nature conservancy.

I decided to sit on the beach for a few minutes and watch the sailboats. It appeared three of them were racing. They were about a mile off shore and I could tell they were beautiful vessels although they all struggled to catch a healthy breeze. At this time of the morning the bay is usually calm. The winds kick up later in the morning, and that's when the wind-surfers come out in full force. Dozens of them will appear on a weekend afternoon. Windsurfing is one of my regrets in life. I regret that I never tried it and know that my 55 year old back probably couldn't take the strain of trying to learn now. It's just one of those things I needed to discover when I was younger.

As I sat on the soft sand enjoying the warming sun and the view, I was overtaken by a shadow. Someone was walking towards me from behind and I could see from the shadow it was a woman. I didn't turn around but she must have stopped about six feet behind where I was sitting because I was now completely in her shadow.

"Gorgeous, aren't they?" The voice was soft and delicate.

I turned to discover it was the long legs in the Nike shorts. Once again I was blinded by the sun as I tried to get a look at her face.

"I haven't been on one of those in years but my dad used to take me out all the time when I was a kid." I assumed she was referring to the distant sails.

She was carrying a beach chair and a bottle of water.

"They'll need a little more wind if they're serious about racing," I said as I casually turned my attention away from her legs and back to the water.

She set her chair up on the sand right next to me. "My name's Annie. Annie Dunn-Weaver." Again her voice was so delicate if there had been any breeze at all, her words might have been carried away.

"I'm Doc. Doc Cafara. I just passed you on the road. You run pretty fast."

"Yeah, I know who you are. I just wanted to come down and finally introduce myself. You moved into John and Pat's house a few weeks ago, didn't you?"

"That's me, wet Cafara." Then I realized she wouldn't understand about the leaks, but before I could explain she went on.

"I was watching you unload the van from my window the day you moved in. I was going to come over and introduce myself as soon as I saw your wife but she never came out."

"That's because she lives in Toronto and hasn't been my wife for seven years. In fact, the nicest thing about being out here is that she doesn't even know I've moved."

"Oh, I didn't know you were divorced. Pat just said you had children so I assumed..."

"Who's Pat?" I inquired.

"Pat Mauro. The people you bought your house from. Pat told me they'd finally sold and that you were coming out here from the city now that your children were grown. She said you were an empty-nester so I assumed you were married. Sorry."

"No need to apologize."

"So what brings you out here?"

For some reason I felt a bit foolish sitting on the sand and carrying on a conversation with someone sitting in a chair. I'm not sure why—perhaps because it forced me to look up at her as we spoke. I noticed she was wearing a wedding ring. It was difficult to miss the size of the stone. Diamonds the size of grapes were not uncommon in Southampton. I think the people out here really like fruit.

"Well, it's kind of a long story but I've been renting further down the strip for a while and saw the for-sale sign when I was out jogging one morning. I realized there was nothing left to hold me in Manhattan so I'm going to give it a go out here this year. That is, if I can get my roof to stop leaking."

"I think the Mauro's were having trouble with the roof for quite a while."

That would have been good information to have at the closing, thank you. She continued. "Did you know that your house was moved?"

"What do you mean, moved?"

"I mean moved. Like when they pick up a house and move it to another spot."

"No kidding?"

"No kidding. It used to be right there next to our house." She pointed to a spot next to a huge Dutch Colonial. "About fifteen years ago the Mauro's moved it to the pond-side and sold the bay-front property to my dad. They put it up on huge timbers and rolled it down Lynton to where it is now. I think they liked the pond better because their boys were young and the water was safer for swimming for kids. I think I have a picture somewhere of the day they moved it. You can have it if you like."

The truth, I would later learn, was that Annie's father, Burt Dunn, a wealthy businessman, wanted an unobstructed view from his newly erected beach castle and made the Mauro's an offer for their land they couldn't refuse.

"That's very nice of you to offer. Thanks." I stood and pretended to need to stretch; something I would do anyway after a three mile run. At least now that I was standing, I didn't feel like Gulliver in the land of the big people.

Annie was wearing a pair of sunglasses on her head. She was still in her running attire and her shorts and top were still wet with perspiration. But she looked great. I mean, for someone who just finished a three-mile run, she looked pretty fresh and her petite figure was accentuated by the wet clothing. I later learned she was 51 but that day I would have guessed 41.

"So you're going to spend the rest of the summer out here?" Again that fragile wisp of a voice.

"Actually, I'm planning to live out here year—round. I've got an apartment in Manhattan that I'm trying to sell and once that's done, there's nothing to keep me in the city."

"Do you work out here?" The question caught me by surprise. It had only been a few weeks since I closed on the sale of my business and I wasn't prepared for questions about '*what I did.*' For over thirty years I defined myself by my work—a commercial real estate agent. The words themselves tell the story and usually require no further explanation. But now I am…dare I utter the word…retired. Annie is the first person to ask me about work since I left Manhattan.

"I'm sort of temporarily retired." That's the best I could

come up with and made a mental note to rehearse a more intriguing explanation the next time it comes up at a cocktail party or in an elevator.

"Well it gets pretty lonely out here in the winter. There are only four or five people that stay our here all year. The rest head back to the city come Labor Day. The older folks, the snow-birds, head to Florida as soon as the boats come out of the water—usually by the first week in November. It's desolate out here off season." She seemed to be speaking from personal experience, so I inquired, "Have you spent a winter out here yourself?"

"Never an entire winter but when my dad was alive he sometimes kept the house open year-round and we'd come out for a weekend or two. It's cold. Some days are incredibly windy and the bay can get really rough. One year it froze solid and when the ice started to break up with the heaving of the tides, it was beautiful. It looked like we were in Antarctica. I don't think I've ever seen ice look so beautiful." As she spoke she pointed out towards the bay.

I was excited to hear her talk of the bay frozen over with ice. That was one of the reasons I wanted to spend the winter out here—to photograph the natural beauty of all four seasons. I'd been looking forward to this for years. Now I'd actually have the chance to do what I'd been putting off since the girls left for college.

"I'm glad to hear…" I was cut off by the sound of a man's voice in the distance.

"Annie," someone was calling from the deck of the huge Dutch-colonial. He was waving his right arm over his head as if to say good bye. Annie turned in her beach chair and returned the signal.

"My husband's leaving for work," she said with noticeably little enthusiasm.

That was the first time I ever saw John Weaver. From a distance, he looked like any other husband going off to work. He was about my size and dressed in grey slacks, white shirt and tie, and a blue blazer. Around here, if you leave for work at 9:30 on a Tuesday morning dressed like that, I would have guessed lawyer, investment banker taking a half-day, or stock broker. And I would have been wrong. He was a doctor.

In retrospect, I never should have sat on the beach that morning. We all would have been better off and maybe all three of us would still be alive.

Chapter Three

"Son of a bitch!" he yelled as the last card was turned. "That's the third time tonight you pulled trips on the river." Ben Stockhouse, a rotund radiologist from Easthampton was sweating more than usual. The elite group sitting around the green felt table all knew he was the weakest player and weren't surprised by his poor showing tonight.

"Ben, you're just a schmuck for the flushes. You've got to stop chasing them. They'll kill you," John Weaver said as he reshuffled the cards. "You've got to play the percentages."

"Fuck off John. One lucky night and you're Chris-fucking-Moneymaker."

"All I'm saying is…" he didn't get to finish. Hank Alexander came through the door from the kitchen carrying a tray of steaming clams casino he'd made himself.

"Girls, girls, let's stop the fighting and have something to eat. If you don't eat these while they're hot you're going to miss something really special." Hank liked to host the games because it gave him a chance to fulfill his second great passion—cooking. His first great passion was ripping polyps out of colons. Actually, his real passion was collecting the $2,500 he charged to separate the polyps from their middle-aged male hosts. Hank was a gastroenterologist and did, on average, ten colonoscopies a day.

The other three players at the table were also from the medical profession; two surgeons and a psychiatrist. The poker games had started in June and became a regular Tuesday night event partly because Hank had a spectacular game room in his twenty-room Dune Road mansion, but mostly because of what he didn't have in the house—a wife. The current Mrs. Alexander was vacationing in Europe for the summer with their three children.

A colorful tiffany-style lamp hung over the card table. The table itself had been imported from England and the six armchairs were a perfect match even though they came from a trendy shop on Main Street in Southampton. Hank Alexander had spared no expense when it came to his game room. Basically, he felt since it was the only room in the cavernous house he got to design and decorate, he would go all out. At one end was a magnificent bar with mirrors that reflected the finest potent potables money could buy. Then, in addition to the card table, there was a nine-foot pool table with green felt to match the card table, a ping pong table, a dart board, and a sixty inch TV hanging on a wall crafted from mahogany planks that started their journey somewhere in South America. There was another smaller flat-screen hanging on the opposite wall, just so no one at the table had to miss any of the Yankee game.

Early on, the group agreed it was silly to rotate the site for the weekly games; what with Hank's game room, his penchant for fine cuisine, and his seven empty bedrooms. Often the excessive drinking that accompanied the poker would necessitate use of one of the bedrooms, and Hank was happy to have the overnight guests, even if his cleaning lady wasn't.

"How much fucking garlic do you put in these things?" John wanted to know as he slurped his third clam from its shell.

"You've got to use a lot of garlic my boy. That's the secret."

"There's no fucking secret. After eating these, everyone can smell you coming from Riverhead to Montauk." John chased the spicy mollusks with two inches of Johnny Walker Blue.

"Great. It's not bad enough you take all our money tonight, now you're insulting my hospitality." Everyone knew Hank was joking. Although John had won the last four hands and most of the other hands tonight, they all knew this was unusual. He'd had a pretty bad run of luck this summer.

The rules were simple; each player came to the table with $10,000 in cash. They played Texas hold-em from nine o'clock until one player had all the chips. Usually that took three or four hours. Then they'd divide the pot up: the winner got $40,000; second place took home what he came with, $10,000; third and fourth place took home $5,000 each. The players who came in fifth and sixth, the first two to lose all their chips, went home empty handed.

Now to most people, this may not have seemed like a friendly game of poker, but to these privileged gladiators of medicine, it was. Or at least it started out that way. The cash tended to flow back and forth most Tuesday nights; if you didn't finish in the money one week, chances were you would next week, or the week after. Unfortunately for John, he came in fourth, fifth, or sixth every week and was down a total of $95,000 for the summer. Tonight he drew a third queen on the last card, took Ben's final stack of chips and was going home the winner. A very drunk winner; but nobody begrudged him the victory. It just seemed ironic that he finally won on a night he had too much to drink and could barely hold his cards much less out-maneuver his able opponents and colleagues.

"Well I don't care what I smell like. These things are fucking great, Hank." John was slurring his words badly.

After the feast of clams, the six men pushed back on their arm-chairs and watched the end of the Yankee game. They drank, smoked cigars, and hurled complex expletives at the umpire who robed Jeter of a double after he clearly beat the tag. Ben and one of the surgeons had already indicated they had no intentions of driving back to East Hampton tonight and would be requiring two of Hank's extra bedrooms, so the drinking was a bit more intense than usual.

"How about you, John? You here for the duration?" Hank asked.

"Shit no! I'm fine. I'm going home." It sounded more like *"Shino, um finnnnne, um goin hummmmm."*

Ben gave Hank a questioning look. "Hey John, I'm pretty wasted and even I can tell you're more wasted than me. You better book a room here at Casa Alexander." But John ignored him and yelled something at the TV.

The subject came up again about midnight when Doctors Lewis and Mitchell, who had shared a ride in from Amagansett, got up from the table to leave. "All right gentlemen, we're out of here. See you next week."

"Take it easy on the driveway. Last time you left here, you took about forty feet of ivy with you. Joan had a fit when she heard you ripped up all that ivy. Did you know she got that in some high-end nursery on the cape? She had the stuff brought over and hand-planted by these two fags from Montauk. It took them over a week to get all those plants in the ground and you left tire tracks all the way down the right side." Hank barked from the door as the doctors sped away. "Assholes," he muttered.

He turned his attention back to the three remaining guests still sitting around the card table. He thought it ironic that he spent every Tuesday night for the past nine weeks with these guys and yet he knew so little about them. The only connection they had was Southampton Hospital where they all spent much of their time.

He'd known Ben Stockhouse the longest but had never been to his home, met his wife or ever saw a single patient referred by Ben. Hank was one of the few year-round surgeons on the east end of Long Island and he couldn't think of any patient any of his Tuesday-night crowd had ever referred. As he thought about that, watching them drink his scotch, with their feet up on his fine chairs, he tried to reflect on how he got involved with this group. After all, he wasn't much of a card player and they certainly weren't much in the way of conversationalists. So what did he get out of the weekly games?

Then he remembered meeting John Weaver at a medical conference out at Gurney's. John had introduced him to Ben, and maybe one or two of the others. After dinner and the requisite speeches, he invited them all back to his boat for a card game. John's boat, as it turned out, was worth the trip. He'd brought it to Montauk for the conference and kept it at a marina up by the fishing docks. It was a spectacular seventy-two foot sport-fisher he'd inherited from his recently deceased father-in-law. Apparently, John's wife never grew sea legs and wanted no part of the boat, so he was free to use it for occasional offshore fishing trips, hosting high stakes card games, which had become legendary in Southampton, and for entertaining pretty young women whose last names weren't Weaver.

"Anybody for a nightcap?" Ben twisted in his chair holding a bottle of Chivas and offering to share one more with any dry glass in the room.

"Yeah, what the fuck?" John leaned forward extending his glass. He took a half glass of the golden liquid and poured it down his throat like it was water. "Now I really have to go." He stood, steadied himself with one hand on the green felt, and stepped away from the table.

Hank was the first to say what was on everyone else's lips. "John, maybe you'd better spend the night. You look pretty fried. You don't want to drive home tonight." He hoped it sounded convincing. Too often, John left the games in this condition and it astounded Hank that he could even find his car no less drive the serpentine six miles back to Cold Spring Pond.

John stood still, staring down at the table and the cash he'd won. He held that position long enough for Hank and the others to think maybe he was considering Hank's advice. He seemed to be thinking about something. His eyes darted back and forth; first at the table top then at Hank, then back to the table.

Hank studied his colleague. Of all the players, John Weaver was the one Hank knew the most about. He'd heard through the remarkably reliable Southampton grapevine that John had married his wife just a few years ago and that she was the one that came from money. Lots of money. Her father, a guy by the name of Burton Dunn, had come from Ireland in the thirties and used his considerable family wealth to buy as much Manhattan real estate as the Morgans, Rockefellers and Vanderbilt's were willing to part with. Hank heard that at one point, John's father-in-law owned one in five properties south of Canal Street, including the site of the former World Trade Center.

Hank also heard that John was spending his wife's inheritance as fast as he could get his hands on it. Actually, the story around Main Street was that John was a bit of a rogue and liked to gamble. Unfortunately, he wasn't very good at it. But his wife controlled most of the money and John only had access to his own paycheck and the interest from one of his wife's trust funds. It seems old Burt saw John for what he was and protected his daughter and grandsons by rearranging his estate into several trusts. Trusts that controlled and preserved the family fortune for many years beyond his death and into the future.

This proved frustrating for John. When he married Annie Dunn, he assumed he was marrying into a life of considerable privilege. Although his own career and practice as an accomplished oncologist provided a comfortable living, John had anticipated far more than comfort. He liked the extravagances Annie introduced him to during their short courtship: the Mediterranean cruises on private yachts, the planes, the cars, and most of all the invitations to otherwise inaccessible parties and people.

Hank knew John was a people-snob. John would often arrive at the weekly card games and promptly drop the names of the Southampton elite with whom he'd recently dined. People that the rest of the group would never meet because, in Southampton, the super-rich seldom mingled with the merely-rich, and certainly not with the newly-rich. They tolerated them, but just having money didn't automatically translate into inclusion. You needed old money. Or fame. A lot of horses or a vineyard with your name on it sometimes helped.

Finally, John looked up from the table. He gathered up the cash and folded it into a small bundle that he shoved in the back pocket of his custom-made jeans. "I need to get home."

"John, I really think you ought to stay. You…" Hank didn't get to finish.

"No. I'm fine. I need to get home." It sounded a little clearer than the last time.

Hank knew from experience it was futile to argue with his colleague. John drank too much every week and had never stayed to sleep it off. Somehow he managed to get home without killing himself or anyone else. He walked John to the front door and made sure he drove down the long driveway without incident. The red taillights of the Mercedes disappeared around the corner of the massive stone pillars at the end of the driveway and onto Dune Road.

CHAPTER FOUR

Annie heard the car crawl over the gravel outside her bedroom window. She knew her husband was home and was grateful that once more, he was able to avoid an accident. She was aware of his drinking at the card games. It worried her, but like Hank, she knew her admonitions were fruitless.

She glanced at the clock on her nightstand. It glowed 1:48. "Not bad," she thought. Some nights, he didn't come home at all. Often, after leaving Hank's house, John would stop at the marina and sleep on her father's boat until daylight. Then he'd stop for a coffee at the Shinnecock deli and come in with a headache and an attitude. Those weren't good mornings. John's headaches were often the stimuli for prolonged periods of cold silence that echoed through the airy beach house. Sometimes the silence would last for days.

At those times, Annie was at a loss for what to do. Her previous marriage hadn't prepared her for this. She'd been married to Peter, the father of her two sons, for 24 years and never had to deal with anything like this. Peter was as even-tempered as a person could be. And he was gentle. But then, he didn't suffer from the migraines John had to deal with.

John's morning headaches, often brought on after a night of over indulgence, succumbed only to several hours of sleep. He needed to be alone and in a dark room. Nothing else seemed to help. Annie felt helpless but he assured her there was little she could do to help. "Just leave me alone for a few hours," was his usual request. And she would. Sometimes she'd go for long walks along the beach just to stay out of his way and out of the house for several hours and let him sleep. It was during those walks that she would reflect on the recent past: her first husband's tragic death, the loneliness she felt since her twin sons went away to college, and how she first met John.

In the beginning things had been wonderful. John Weaver was a successful oncologist with a busy practice in Manhattan. They met at a charity event at the Metropolitan Museum of Art, about three years after Peter's death. A mutual friend introduced them and Annie was immediately taken by John's sophisticated yet boyish good looks. He was charming and attentive. They started to date, usually just lunches and dinners at first, but it was only a few weeks into their relationship that John told Annie he had never felt this way about a woman before.

Then, soon after Annie's sons left for college, John invited her to accompany him on a medical conference in Bern, Switzerland. They spent their first night together in a castle-like hotel overlooking a beautiful lake surrounded by snow covered mountains. They spent the next two weeks touring Switzerland and France and visiting one of John's brothers in Paris.

When they returned to New York, John suggested they live together in his west side condo. They'd only known each other a few months at that point and Annie resisted. She had been living in the Park Avenue apartment she and Peter bought when they were first married, the place they raised their children and shared nearly a quarter century together. She wasn't ready to leave. It meant leaving behind more than just an address.

But by Christmas, Annie realized she loved the time they were together and hated the loneliness of her cavernous apartment. She wanted to be with him all the time. So when the boys came home for the holidays, she told them she was going to sell the only home they'd ever known in New York, and move out to her father's Long Island house; the place they'd spent most summers. The boys were fine with that.

Then, on New Year's Eve 2004, as they sat on a bench in Central Park, John asked her to marry him. Three weeks later they were married at John's golf club by an old family friend, who happened to be a judge. It was a simple ceremony. No friends or family were there, not even Annie's sons. She thought it would be too painful for them to watch their mom give herself to another man only three years after their dad's death. She was right.

Both her sons grew to despise their stepfather. They saw him in a clear but garish light that Annie could not. They suspected he was manipulating their mother's unresolved grief. From the start, they were suspicious of his motives. This made it very uncomfortable for everyone because the twins refused to live with Annie and John after they were married and had moved into John's condo. Instead, they choose to tap into some of grandpa's trust fund money and share a small place in Soho for the few months each summer they returned from college. Annie hated being apart from her boys.

Then about two years ago, Annie's father succumbed to a painful struggle with lung cancer. She had always been close to her dad, especially so since her mom died right after the twins were born. Burton Dunn had never remarried; never even looked at another woman, as far as Annie knew. Despite his wealth, after his wife's death, he began a slow and continuous descent towards the end of his own life. Almost as if he'd lost the desire to live without her.

It was around this time that John's headaches began. He assured her they were just persistent migraines and that, as a medical professional, he'd been through all the tests to rule out anything more sinister. But they got worse and came more frequently; especially when he mixed his anti-migraine medications with liquor. For the last two years the migraines had become a part of their marriage.

But tonight, other, more painful demons were about. For on the nights like this, when John came home filled with alcohol, his arrival triggered different fears in Annie.

CHAPTER FIVE

Doc

One of the really nice things about living alone is that I can eat pretty much whatever I please. When Kitty and Peggy lived with me in Manhattan, their leafy diets usually determined our evening meals. My two health-conscious daughters spent each summer vacation with me in the city, mostly because I was able to get them summer jobs at Bloomingdales, but I like to think partly because they loved their dad. Either way, they did most of the cooking and food shopping while we shared my three bedroom apartment, and I never ate a more balanced, healthful diet.

But a man can only eat so much lettuce, arugula, and tofu before he starts to lust after Central Park squirrels. For some reason, my twin daughters had both decided that meat was evil and that humans weren't meant to consume anything that ever walked, flew or hopped. I love my daughters dearly, but those three summers we spent together in New York nearly killed me. My stomach still hasn't forgiven me and it's taken four years for my colon to readjust to normal male consumption.

So now that I am on my own, I revel in the choices available to me. Sometimes I find myself thinking about what to have for dinner before I'm even out of bed. And why not? I enjoy shopping for, preparing, and cooking myself a delicious meal. Meats, stews, fish and pasta are my staples but any combination of the aforementioned is also terrific. I find myself sometimes speaking about food with adjectives usually reserved for fine art or a Beethoven concerto. Words like *magnificent* piece of fillet, or a *gorgeous* tilapia, or, once I even caught myself describing a plate of linguine and clams as *beautiful*. I love food.

And so it is, on this Friday morning, that I find myself at my usual haunt, a great little market on the outskirts of Southampton called Schmidt's. To be sure, Schmidt's is not Shop-Rite or Publix or King Kullen. Schmidt's is a fabulous little family-run throwback to days gone by when people actually cared about the quality and freshness of their food. It has creaky wooden floors and narrow isles filled with unusual and costly fruits and vegetables. They have cheeses hanging from the ceiling and a real butcher, complete with white apron and sawdust on the floor.

While out running this morning, I decided I would make something really special for dinner tonight. My good friend Bobby Bideaux is driving out from the city to spend the weekend and hopefully catch some striped bass tomorrow. So, anticipating a successful day versus the bass, I figured we'd be eating fish tomorrow night. That meant we'd both be happy with a good steak tonight; steak piziola to be exact, from my mother's recipe and her mother's before that.

I had just been handed a fantastic piece of rib-eye and, in return, handed Jimmy, the almost-famous butcher at Schmidt's, $62.75. Meat at Schmidt's is not cheap but it is worth it. You can't get prime meats at the supermarket and for a meal with Bobby, only prime will do. A little olive oil, a few red peppers, a tomato, and yellow onions will turn this into an excellent piziola. I told you food was important to me. Now where was I?

Oh yes…I was just walking away from the butcher counter when I spotted Annie in the next isle, trying to decide between two wedges of cheese. She was dressed in a yellow skirt and white blouse that hung off her shoulders and accented her tiny frame. Her dirty blonde hair was pulled back in a pony-tail. She had on no jewelry, not even ear-rings, and it wouldn't be much of an exaggeration to say she looked classy. Certain women, even without the jewels, look classy.

"I'd suggest the Reggiano if you're going to be drinking red wine with it." I thought I'd demonstrate my limited knowledge of cheese. She turned and seemed lost in thought.

"Oh, hi Doc. Doc...right? I was surprised she remembered.

"The Reggiano has a nice dry taste. The Ricotta Salata is more fruity and goes better with white wine. But they're both great with ice cold beer." I don't know why I felt the need to impress her.

"Well then it's the Reggiano because I only drink red and my husband only drinks beer."

I've been divorced for several years and have no problem striking up a conversation with most women, but for some reason I still don't understand, I didn't feel comfortable with Annie. It was the same way on the beach a few days ago. It's hard to explain. Maybe it was just because she was so pretty and seemed so innocent. I don't know.

"I haven't seen you running the last few days," she said.

"Oh, I've been out there every morning. I get up pretty early. I like to catch the sunrise."

"Well that explains it. I need a cup of coffee and my emails before I do anything in the morning."

"You check your email before you run in the morning? You must be a very important person," I joked.

"I like to see if my boys had anything to say from the night before. They're both in college and I'm usually in bed before they go out at night so they drop me an email just to say they made it home safely. But, not always." Her face lit up at the mention of her sons.

"You have two in college?" I asked the obvious question.

"Yep, twins. Frank's at B.U. and Nick goes to the University of Florida. They're great kids."

We were both making our way towards the checkout counter as we spoke and since I still needed to pay for my veggies, I slipped into line behind her. As I did, I noticed her smell. It was a scent I was not familiar with, sort of a light powdery smell. I liked it.

"That's funny. I've got twin girls but they're a little older, so no double match-making I guess."

"Really? How old are they?"

"They'll be twenty-six this January. Kitty's an ER nurse in Tucson and Peggy is a lawyer in the city. And they too, are great kids. I wish I saw more of them." I realized as soon as I said it, that I probably sounded like the pathetically lonely soul I'd become since they moved out. We are what we are.

"You don't look old enough to have twenty-six year old daughters." I knew she was just being nice. In fact, even though from the neck down I keep in pretty good shape, lately I've been noticing that parts of my face seem to be moving around, mostly southward. Not good.

"Well thanks." I knew better than to make a comment about a woman's age. Even one you intend as flattery could backfire. You never know with age. So I changed the subject.

"Do you always shop here?"

"Oh, yeah. My dad used to take me here when I was a kid and we'd come out for the weekends. It hasn't changed much. I think the only thing they've added is the sushi bar. I think this is the only place to buy good fruit anywhere on the south fork. This, and the farmers' stands."

As we waited on line we chatted about the history of Schmidt's, the weather, the up-coming election and our children. Our conversation continued past the cashier and spilled into the parking lot. It was a bright sunny day and Annie looked radiant. We stood and talked for fifteen minutes in the sunshine. I still found myself a bit fidgety but I kind of liked it. I mean, she was married so there was no reason to be nervous about the impression I left, but still, I wanted her to see the best side of me. Maybe some part of me understood what was to come.

After a while, she said, "I need to run. We're having a cocktail party tonight for some of John's partners out on the deck. I need to get a few things at Walbaums and get my hair done."

"I'm guessing he's a lawyer. M&A law perhaps?" I thought I'd show her I was intuitive as well as an expert on at least two cheeses.

"Why would you say that?

"I saw him wave good bye to you the other morning when we met on the beach. He looked like a lawyer and seemed to dress the part. Also, anyone who dresses that well and leaves for work after nine doesn't have your typical nine to five job— too late to commute into the city." I thought my deductive reasoning would astound her. I'm still not sure why I cared though.

"Nice try Sherlock but you missed some important clues."

"Like what?" I needed to know.

"Well for starts, the MD plates on his Mercedes."

"Oh, a doctor." I felt foolish

"Actually, John's an oncologist. He is part of a four-man practice in New York and Riverhead and he invited his partners over to show off the view from our deck. And their intolerable wives are coming. So I better shove off."

"Well if you ever get up early, perhaps I'll see you running."

Annie lingered at the door of her car then turned and said, "Hey, why don't you come over for a drink later? John would love to meet you and, like I said, it's just his partners and their wives and maybe a few locals. Very informal. You don't even need shoes. Beach wear is fine."

"That's very nice of you Annie..." I paused a moment to calculate if there was anyway I could tell Bobby to come a little later. No, he was probably on his way already. "...but I have a dinner guest tonight. But thanks anyway."

"OK then. Another time."

I opened the door of her convertible for her and lingered just close enough to steal one more whiff of her mysterious perfume.

I said, "Another time." And I meant it.

Chapter Six

Doc

My cell phone rang just as I fired up the gas grill. "Hey, I'm at the golf course and I remember you telling me if I see the course I went too far so I guess I went too far. What did I miss?" Bobby's voice was as strong as his massive arms.

"You missed the turn onto Cold Spring Point Road. Go back about two hundred yards."

"OK, I got it," he said.

I could hear his Mustang roar as he accelerated out of the golf course driveway. Bobby always liked muscle cars and would prefer a '68 Firebird or Camaro to just about anything built since the millennium. I've known him for over forty years and he's always driven something powerful and loud.

"See you in five minutes," I said and after flipping closed my phone I put two pilsner glasses in the freezer. Bobby loved wine but I knew him too well to think he wouldn't want an icy cold Coors Light after a two-hour drive from Manhattan. The wine will wait until dinner.

It was a perfect night for eating out on the deck. There was just enough breeze to keep the bugs away and it was warm for this late in the day. The sun was still hanging around the western horizon but in less than an hour, according to my almanac, we were due for a giant full moon to rise over the pond. The full moon in August, on a clear night, is something to see. And to see it rise, well that's something special. To do so from the deck of your waterfront house with a cold beer in your hand and your best friend at your side, not to mention two steaks from Schmidt's on the grill—well that's about as good as it gets.

I heard the Mustang grind on the gravel in my driveway and a minute later Bobby walked onto the deck with a case of wine under his huge arm. I could tell from the look on his face that he was happy to be here.

"Wow, this is some view." This was the first time Bobby had been to my leaky cottage by the sea. He and his wife Catherine had been busy the last few weekends and unable to come out to see my new home. And this weekend Catherine was consumed with her new baking business so Bobby was flying solo. All the better for a boys night out.

As he stood on the deck looking out on the pond, I studied my lifelong friend. Bobby has always been a big guy. He played linebacker back in high school and even at 53, he could still pass for a former NFL player. That comes in handy for a cop in the Bronx. His massive shoulders and barrel-like chest sometimes made it hard for him to find the right cloths. Yet despite his size, Bobby had the face and disposition of a choirboy.

"This is fantastic!" He put the case of Barolo on the round table near the edge of the deck. Making a motion towards my nearest neighbor's house, he asked, "How far does your property go?"

I explained that my third of an acre was a triangle with two sides facing the water. Ordinarily that would be an enviable lot; in my case, not so much. I was told that a good deal of the 300 feet of thirty year old bulkhead would soon need replacing. Then again, I was told that by a guy who installs state-of-the-art vinyl bulkhead at $400 per foot.

I showed Bobby around the house, pointing out all the places he didn't want to sleep if it began to rain. So far I was only able to fix three of the leaks. There were four more and they were the pesky ones. My problem was that the last four were over the areas were the ceiling was this great old knotty pine. I didn't want to start ripping that down unless I absolutely had to. Bobby agreed.

The tour concluded at the fridge were I revealed the two frozen beer glasses and the stuff to temporarily fill them. We sat on the deck, and like men often do, faced, not each other, but the object of our focus, the pond. Women will always face each other when they talk. Men prefer to stare straight ahead and converse without eye contact. It's better.

"So what's with the Barolo?" I asked. I knew Bobby had great taste in wine and that the case he brought must have set him back several hundred dollars.

"It's to celebrate your new place." He said as he smiled and took a long pull on his beer.

"It's a little extravagant, don't you think."

"Definitely not! When I come out here, and I expect to be invited often, I don't want to have to drink that shit you call red wine. I want you to promise you'll only bring this out when I'm here. I can't drink that shit you buy."

"Fair enough." I got us two more beers and brought out a tray of cheeses and olives.

"So what's this I hear about you spending the winter out here contemplating the lint in your navel?"

"First of all I told Catherine not to share that with you. Second, I said I wanted to be out here all winter because I want to photograph the pond in all four seasons and put together a book for the local market. You know; a cocktail table book of pictures rich people always have lying around."

We settled into a comfortable banter busting each other's chops through the third and forth beers. In all the years I've know Bobby, this was what I liked best about our friendship. Just being able to instantly catch up. We could go weeks without talking on the phone, then see each other and slip right back into the last conversation we had about the Mets' short stop. I guess we both figured that if anything important came up in the meantime, we'd call. Otherwise, let's assume all the important stuff was under control. Again, not the way women do it.

The evening air was warm and the steaks came out great. We went through three of Bobby's Barolos before agreeing on an acceptable time to begin our fishing trip. After the first bottle, we thought first thing in the morning sounded good. After two bottles, we decided to put it off until early afternoon. Bobby said the tides would be better but he really had no idea. After the third bottle we agreed to decide in the morning.

CHAPTER SEVEN

Doc

The top of his desk was covered with stacks of x-rays. John Weaver pushed back from the wooden desk and studied a report concerning one of his youngest patients, a six year old boy named Sami. For John, this was the hardest part of oncology—dealing with the families of children afflicted with one of the dreaded forms of his specialty. He hated it, and even more, he hated having to tell the parents how little time some of them had left with their children.

Sami's situation was especially sad because just three months ago, John had assured his parents that the pancreatic cancer was in remission—that the wonder drugs had worked their magic. Now, the MRI report showed evidence of more trouble on the other side of the pancreas, in a place that even the most skilled surgeons dared not go. It meant months more of chemo treatments. And in the end, John wasn't sure it would make a difference. Too many times in his career he'd seen a reoccurrence of this sort start the downward spiral. He was scheduled to meet with Sami and his parents in an hour.

He was shaken from his melancholy by the buzzer on his phone.

"Doctor, there are two gentlemen here to see you. Neither has an appointment but they told me to tell you Mr. Zucker sent them. Should I have them fill out background forms?"

John tossed Sami's file on his desk. "Shit!" He thought this might happen but was hoping he had another week. Suddenly Sami's family was the last thing on his mind.

He pressed the key on the intercom, "Judy, have them wait one minute. I'll be right there."

Zucker was a name John didn't want to hear. He was a loan shark from New York who fancied himself a private banker. Actually, considering his high-end clientele, he probably could be considered a private banker. He was a source-of-last-resort for many wealthy Manhattanites who didn't want the outside world to learn of their financial distress. Arnie Zucker was a way for them to "bridge" a temporary financial shortfall without the banks, credit score centurions, or spouses ever knowing. He provided short term financing to some of the biggest names on Wall Street. He was a respected businessman to those who sought his assistance.

But to those who borrowed from Zucker and didn't repay on time, he was just a loan shark; as ruthless as any other and worse than some. Because his clients sought anonymity, their transactions had no paper trail, no contracts, nothing at all in writing; Just a promise to repay the debt at the agreed time and at the agreed rate of interest. And because Arnie Zucker liked to think of himself as a legitimate private banker, he wore only the finest suits, belonged to only the most prestigious golf clubs, and dined with some of New York's most influential people.

Unfortunately for John, he was one of the people who had borrowed from Zucker and was now a little tardy on his weekly payments. Actually, it was the first time since starting to use Zucker several months ago, that John wasn't able to keep up with the debt. For the most part he would borrow $20,000 to finance his poker games and trips to Atlantic City and, even if he lost it all, (which he usually did), he could cover it within weeks from his medical practice. Annie never needed to know about any of it. And he never looked to Annie for cash. That would be too embarrassing especially; after all the shit he had taken from her father about living beyond his means.

Last week was the first time he had failed to wire his payment to the agreed account. Fortunately, he'd won at Hank's game Wednesday night and had planned to repay his most recent loan, plus interest, tomorrow. Arnie Zucker insisted all debts be settled or serviced on Saturdays. John never understood why Saturday. But he also didn't understand why someone from Zucker's "office" was here to see him. Couldn't this be handled over the phone?

"OK Judy, show the gentlemen in." He spoke into the intercom.

A moment later, Judy ushered in two well-dressed but large men. They introduced themselves as Ricky and Jimmy and without taking a seat, explained that Mr. Zucker was upset that he hadn't heard from John.

"Mr. Zucker likes to know that all his investments are doing well and when he doesn't hear from you, he gets worried." Ricky spoke like a Brooklyn street thug but looked like a banker; albeit, a large one. Jimmy nodded.

At first John was somewhat put off by the aggressive, yet so far polite nature of the visit. He settled into his chair and decided to push it a bit.

"If I recall, I borrowed twenty and agreed to repay it within two weeks with the usual ten per cent per week consideration. The money's not due until tomorrow, Saturday." He pointed at his calendar for emphasis. I plan to wire the full $24,200 tomorrow morning. Is there a problem with that?" He thought he'd throw a little attitude at them much the same way he did when playing cards. As in cards, it usually didn't work.

Again, it was Ricky. "Mr. Weaver, the problem is that you didn't make your vig payment last Saturday. You know the rules: all vigs paid by noon on Saturday. Mr. Zucker didn't hear from you and got worried. He wanted us to make sure nothing happened to you. Understand?" His tone was increasingly condescending.

"And to make matters worse, now you have to pay an extra week's vig to cover our traveling expenses all the way the fuck out here to Riverhead." This time Ricky didn't sound as friendly.

But John's testosterone picked a peculiar time to kick in and he responded, "You can tell Mr. Zucker that I'm fine and his money will be wired tomorrow. Now get the hell out of my office. I have a medical practice to run."

Apparently, that was not what Ricky and Jimmy wanted to hear. "You don't seem to understand Doctor Weaver. The penalty gets paid in cash. You pay us the penalty, now." His tone was now combative and John understood it was time to back off.

Ricky and Jimmy seated themselves in the two leather chairs facing John's desk. "Now we understand that it may take you a few minutes to pull together the $2,420 dollars, so we'll just wait here until you get it." This time Ricky's voice was deep and firm. "And then you can wire Mr. Zucker what you owe him tomorrow."

CHAPTER EIGHT

Doc

"Got it!" Bobby called back to me as he threw a line from the bow around the large grey cleat. We were traveling south through the Shinnecock Canal in route to the striped bass that awaited us just outside the inlet in the ocean. To get from the the Peconic Bay to the Atlantic Ocean we needed to pass through the canal and its locks. The locks were necessary to control the surging water as the tides changed, and since the tides were now going out, we, and several other boats, were tied to the bulkhead awaiting the uplifting experience.

The sun had come up with a menacing vengeance. At least that's the way it felt after a half-night's sleep and two and a half bottles of wine. We slept in until eleven and missed the incoming tide, the one you want on your side when you try to outsmart the bass. By the time we had coffee, picked up ice, and put the gear on my boat, the sun had reached its peak for the day.

And so we sat, waiting on my twenty-foot Grady White, for the lock gates to open so we could continue towards the inlet. The August sun was strong and felt good on my bare back. The digital display on my console told us we had 125 gallons of fuel, were floating in 15 feet of water, were facing due south, and listening to 104.3 FM. Although I opted for a relatively small boat, I didn't skimp on the electronics. I figured if I was going several miles off shore I wanted all the techno-help I could get. And I wanted a good sound system.

Sometimes when you're fishing, it's good to have an old Jethro Tull CD along in case the fish aren't biting.

Bobby was holding the bow line and I had one at the stern. As the huge gates began to creak open we pushed away from the bulkhead and headed towards Jackson's marina where we needed to pick up some squid and live eels. Striped bass don't just surrender. They have to be teased and that takes bait. The slimier and smellier, the better.

After we picked up the bait I said, "Bobby, you take the wheel. I'll cut up the squid on our way out. Just follow the buoys and head towards the bridge." I pointed in the direction of a tall bridge about three miles to our south. "The inlet's just before we get to the bridge."

I sat on a bucket near the bow and began to dissect and slice the squid into long slivers. The hope was that when we put one of these shinny slivers on the end of a hook, along with a live eel, our friends the Stripers would find this irresistible. In fact, this combination had worked for me many times before. I learned it from my father when I was a kid. Some things you just can't improve on. I usually volunteer to cut the squid because I'm good at it but mostly because it really stinks up your hands. I figured if my fishing guest showed up with a case of Barolo, he deserved to go home with some fish, but not the stink.

By the time I finished with the squid, Bobby had arrived at the inlet and was gingerly making his way through the narrow channel that leads to the Atlantic. You've got to take it easy going through the Shinnecock inlet because it's subject to significant shoaling which makes for some sloppy water as the tides change. Today it wasn't too bad.

"Head south-south-east and when you get to the last can head full south."

"How will I know when it's the last can?" Bobby needed to know as he increased throttle.

"You'll know from the noise. It's the only one with a fog beacon. It makes this really loud sound every ten seconds. I guess it's supposed to help you find your way back in if there's bad weather. But now-a-days, anyone with a brain has the electronics to find the inlet no matter how bad the weather is."

We cruised in the warm sun, and surprisingly calm water, for about ten minutes until we passed the noisy can and arrived at the spot I was confident would produce bass.

"How do you know this is the spot?" My good friend wanted to know.

I pointed at the depth-finder on the console and said, "Just as we pass from sixty feet to ninety feet on the screen. See? There's a ledge on the bottom. The bass feed along that ledge. And that, my friend, is where we will find our dinner. All we need to do is drift back and forth along the ledge."

The Atlantic is a beautiful thing. Even just a few miles off the south shore of Long Island, the water gets deep enough to turn a shade of blue you don't see anywhere else. It's so clear you can watch your line sink into the depths until it disappears at about thirty feet. When the surface is calm, as it is today, you are easily lulled into a sense of peacefulness. It's almost hard to believe that in a matter of minutes, with the right wind, waves could be breaking over your transom.

But today everything was great. The water was calm, the sun was shinning, and we had a cooler full of beer. Shit, even if we didn't catch fish, it was a great day. The plan was to bag a couple of big stripers, listen to the Met game and maybe catch a Saturday-afternoon nap after a few beers. You can't beat it. Everything was perfect for me and my best friend.

So why was I uncomfortable with the conversation we were about to have? Bobby had been my friend as long as I could remember. I could tell him anything. He was one of those people who listened well. Empathically, some would say. He was about the least judgmental person I ever met. He was the perfect guy to talk to when you had something big on your mind. And I did.

About a half hour and three Coors into our drift Bobby got a hit on his line. The spool on his reel began to squeal as the line ran and his fish took off with the hook. He jumped to his feet at the sound and braced the rod against himself as if he was going to wrestle a nuclear submarine off the bottom rather than reel in a 25 pound bass.

"Keep him on your side of the boat!" I called odut as I reached for the gaff.

"Feels like a monster!" Bobby was working hard to lift our dinner off the bottom of the ocean. Each time he pulled the rod back he reeled frantically and then did it again. To tell the truth, I was a little surprised my powerful friend was exerting so much effort. His massive arms bulged with veins as he gripped the rod. You wouldn't think a 240 pound man would have so much trouble lifting a 25 or maybe 30 pound fish through 90 feet of water. But then again, our dinner wasn't coming up willingly. It was fighting for its life. Bobby was just fighting for dinner.

After ten minutes of struggling, I could see a silvery blur rising from the blue depths under the boat. Stripers are beautiful fish. Bobby worked it closer to the surface and I could tell it was a big fish—at least 25 pounds. As it broke the surface it started to thrash.

"Gaff it!" He yelled and I could tell they were both getting tired from the battle.

I gaffed it and hauled it over the rail onto the deck where the magnificent fish continued to trash and leap. This is the part of fishing I always have trouble with. The fish is fighting for its life, gasping for breath, or whatever fish gasp for when they're out of water. It's an unfair fight and always ends the same way; so the most merciful thing to do is put him out of his agony quickly. After such a noble battle, he deserves no less.

I gave him one firm shot on the side of the head with the aluminum bat I keep on board and he went silent. It's the best and most painless way to kill a large fish. If he was a bluefish, I'd have no trouble with this. They're mean bastards and will snap at your ankles while struggling on the deck. But a striper is only concerned with survival—the very thing we deny him.

Bobby worked the hook out of the fish's mouth. "Well, at least he got the eel." The eel was missing but the strip of squid was still on the hook.

"Have you got a scale?"

The scale confirmed that Bobby's trophy was about 26 pounds and certainly long enough to make the minimum limit, so we had our first fish on ice and quickly decided this called for a celebratory beer. But not before re-baiting and getting both lines back on the bottom.

"Gosh, they're beautiful fish," Bobby said as he settled back into his lucky fishing position.

I told him I agreed. "Of all the fish around here, they're the most beautiful. Almost too beautiful to kill."

"Too bad for them they taste so good."

I studied my friend. He had his feet up on the transom and his NYPD cap pulled down over his face. Bobby, for all his strengths, was a gentle man; the kind of gentle giant who gave much thought to things. Once, when working a robbery in the South Bronx, he came across an eleven year old crack addict who just happened to be in a pawn shop when it was robbed. Or maybe he was just a kid in a pawn shop who happened to be a crack addict. It didn't much matter. Either way, the short young boy got in the way of a bullet that was intended for the pawn shop operator. His lifeless form was still lying in the corner when Bobby and his partner arrived. Blood covered the floor around his head. A look of disbelief still on his face.

Bobby had to walk the two blocks to where someone said the kid had lived. His job was to tell a young mother that her son was dead. As he walked, he tried to form the words. But his lips dried each time he prepared his speech. There were no words. There was no way to tell such a thing. By the time he got to the address he was given, a small crowd had already gathered in front of the old brownstone. News in the ghetto travels fast. Especially bad news.

In the center of the black crowd he spotted a young girl sitting on the top step of the stoop. She was crying and surrounded by other women, older women, trying to console her. By the time he got to the bottom of the steps, Bobby was crying like a baby too. The insanity of the situation—a 24 year old mother weeping for her eleven year old son, overtook him. The young mother wound up consoling him and walking him back to the pawn shop to identify her baby. All the time, she had her tiny arm around his waist and telling him, it was going to be OK.

I guess his heart and his compassion equaled every other aspect of him, huge. As strong as he was, he was gentle. As loud as he could be, he also possessed a softness. He never talked about firing his weapon. I don't think he ever did. In 26 years, I'm not sure he ever even drew his weapon. To look at him, you wouldn't think he'd need to carry one.

So why was I having so much trouble starting the conversation I'd gone over in my head so many times. Was it because I didn't want Bobby to think any less of me? Was it because I was afraid he'd see me differently? Was I just afraid that every-thing about us was about to change when he found out? Maybe in some ways, it had to.

Or maybe it was because I knew that as soon as I spoke the words aloud, they would be real. Up until this moment they were just thoughts in my head; never put into words. But a part of me knew that once I told someone else, there was no going back.

I reached in the cooler and pulled two beers from the icy water. I handed one to Bobby and said, "There's something I want to talk to you about."

CHAPTER NINE

Doc

Bobby propped himself up on his elbows and tipped back his cap so he could see my eyes. "Sounds serious," he said, "What's up?"

I took a long swig on my beer can and looked out at the tip of my rod. When I'm nervous I find it better to focus on a particular point rather than looking at the person I'm talking to. Even if it's my best friend.

"This is something I've been thinking about for a long time," I started. "I figured, now that I'm sure about it, I ought to talk to you first."

Bobby just kept looking in my direction.

"Bobby, do you believe in God?"

He looked at me for a moment of thought, and then said, "I'm not sure what the hell I believe in anymore but I'm sure I believe there's got to be a God. I mean there are just too many things I can't explain without God."

"Like what?" I really wanted to know.

"Like the beauty of the sky. Like the way a sunset makes such fantastic colors. That can't be just an accident." He went on. "Like a flower, or more specifically, like the massive array of different flowers that exists. Why would that be if not for some divine intervention? Why would there be so many different flowers if Darwin and Mendel were all there was? I mean if you buy survival of the fittest, then shouldn't there only be one sort of super plant that has kicked the ass of all other plants. Same for animals."

As I suspected, Bobby had also given this subject some thought over the years. He just came to a different conclusion.

"I used to feel the same way. I used to look at a baby and say, this can't be an accident of nature. There has to be some bigger plan. It's too beautiful. There has to be a reason why we're here. I used to buy into the whole Jesus thing; that he came to earth to show us how much he loved us and all that shit.

"You know me. We went to twelve years of Catholic school together Bobby. Shit, we were altar boys together. There was a time, when my dad was sick, I went to mass every morning before work because I believed my prayers were heard. Maybe I just needed to believe, but it really helped me get through a rough time.

"Now, I don't know what I believe. But I've been giving it a lot of thought. I've probably read twenty books on religion and faith over the last year. I just don't buy it any more. I can't put my finger on any particular day or event that made me feel this way. It just seemed to happen."

Bobby, in his usual calm manner, pressed a little more. He never looked away from his rod. "So, what are you saying?"

"I'm saying, I just lost faith. It's as simple as that. I no longer have something I used to have a lot of—faith. I no longer am willing to give the mystical the benefit of the doubt over science. I've just seen too many heartbreaking things to believe there is a plan. It just doesn't make sense any more. And in the absence of faith, I see no reason to believe a sunrise is anything more than a sunrise or a flower is anything more than just a flower."

Bobby seemed to study this for a thoughtful moment and then responded, "OK, so what?"

It wasn't the response I had expected. Although I'm not sure what I expected.

"What do you mean?"

"I mean, so what? What will change in your life if you no longer believe in God? Did your world come to an end when you stopped believing in Santa Claus? No, my friend, life goes on and you just need to realize that you'll be the same person tomorrow whether or not you believe. It's called growing up. Welcome to your fifties."

In a way I was relieved to finally have this off my chest. Bobby was my closest friend in the world. He was like the brother my parents denied me. He knew me better than anyone. So why was I so unsatisfied with his response?

"It's a little more complicated than that, Bob. First of all, in a way, it's like losing a friend; a close friend. I mean, I was never what anyone would call a holy-roller but I felt like I had a personal relationship with God. I talked to him everyday and every time I had a major decision to make. That form of prayer just came very natural to me. I would end every day with a few words to him in bed, just before I fell asleep.

"Also, not believing in God changes everything. I mean, if there's no God, then there's no heaven or hell, right? So does everything just come to an end when we die? Is it like the last episode of "The Sopranos" and everything just goes black?" Bobby just rolled a pretzel rod around in his mouth and seemed to give that some thought.

"And if that's so, then why be good? I mean, if there's no God and we are just like any other animal, then why behave better? Why not just behave like an animal? It's illogical."

"Now you sound like Mr. Spock."

"Well think about it. If there's no God and we're just some big accident, then why not do what all the other animals do? Why not just look out for number one. Our whole purpose here might be nothing more than to procreate and spread our seeds, just like a lion or a fish or an antelope. They do what's best for themselves and say '*fuck everyone else*', right? I mean that's what being an animal is all about—surviving and creating a few offspring to carry on your gene pool."

"I think it was Napoleon who said, *"Religion is what keeps the poor from murdering the rich."* In other words, without the fear of some hellish afterlife, we'd all be doing whatever we wanted."

Bobby looked away from his rod for the first time and gave me a look of impatience. "So what are you saying? That now that you've given up on God, which I still think you're wrong about; now that you've given up on God, there's no point to your life? Is that what you're telling me?"

To be honest, although I'd spent months thinking this through in my head, now that I was saying the words out loud, I could hear the cracks in my own logic. I didn't feel worthless because I no longer believed in a god. I was still a father to two girls and my life had meaning. At least I think I did. I'm just not so sure what that meaning is.

"You know what you need?" Bobby was about to tell me, and would have, but his rod jerked down and line began to spin off his reel.

"Hold that thought asshole; I need to deal with this monster of the deep."

CHAPTER TEN

Annie heard the crackle of John's tires against the driveway stones. She'd only been in bed a few minutes and it was just a little after eleven, so she hadn't expected him home so early. Usually when John called to say he was meeting some colleagues for a drink after work, he'd stay out late. Sometimes he would call from her dad's boat and say that he'd had too much to drink and was going to stay on the boat. And thankfully, on those nights, he wouldn't come home at all.

In many ways, that was better. She was too familiar with John after he'd been drinking or, as a result of the drinking, lost a bundle gambling. His anger became her pain. And lately, it seemed like the pain was happening more often.

She thought back to the first time John caused her pain. They were only married a few weeks and had taken a weekend trip to Atlantic City to see the Moody Blues at the Tropicana. After the concert, Annie went back to their room while John went down to the casino to play some cards. He promised to be up in an hour but the cards were falling his way and John had a thing about never getting up from a hot table. So seven hours later he staggered up to their room with thirty-five black chips in his pocket and a belly full of Maker's Mark.

Annie heard him come in but was too tired to even roll over so she let herself drift back to sleep. A few moments later she felt her husband climb onto her back. He was kissing the back of her neck; gently at first, but then a bit more forcefully. And when Annie didn't respond, he bit her neck just hard enough to startle her. She rolled onto her side.

"What are you doing?"

But John wasn't in the mood to talk. With one hand he rolled her onto her stomach and straddled her legs with his. It was at this point Annie realized he was naked. She also realized that he was forcing himself between the back of her legs, causing her more discomfort with each painful thrust. He lay on top of her and again bit the back of her neck, this time hard enough to draw blood.

"John, stop! That hurts!"

But he said nothing. He continued to force himself into her from behind and with each brutal, silent thrust she gasped as if the air was being pushed out of her. It had never been like this before and Annie's diminutive frame was suffering under the pressure and weight of her husband.

For a brief moment she thought perhaps the pain was her own fault. Maybe she was supposed to be responding differently, in some way she had not known before. After all, it was never this way with her first husband, Peter. He was a gentle lover and that was all she knew. Maybe she just didn't know how to adjust to John's forceful love making.

Then she realized this wasn't about making love. This was an attack. She was under attack by the man she'd married a few weeks ago. The same man who now pinned both her arms over her head with one of his hands while the other pushed on the back of her head. Her face was crushed into the pillow and she could barely breathe. And still the thrusting continued harder and faster until he was spent.

When he was though with her, he rolled onto his back and said flatly, "Not a word from you."

Annie continued to lie on her stomach, too afraid to move or talk. That was two years ago.

When she heard the car door slam tonight her eyes closed and she said a silent prayer. "Please, please don't be drunk."

CHAPTER ELEVEN

Doc

Ifelt better after the fishing trip with Bobby. It was as if I
was no longer carrying around this huge weight. Although
most people would consider their relationship with God a very
private matter, I needed to talk to someone about my recent
conclusions. And for me, Bobby was the right guy. Now that
I shared my new view of the universe, I felt somehow vali-
dated—as if my personal beliefs were now legitimate.

Anyway, I felt better and with my newfound energy,
decided it was time to take another shot at fixing my leaking
roof. If a lifetime in the commercial real estate business taught
me anything, I'd learned to always try to fix a leak yourself
because if I had called a roofing repair company, as my daughters implored me to do, I would wind up with a completely
new roof. And for some delusional reason, I was convinced I
didn't need a new roof.

So, armed with a claw hammer, some extra shingles and a
few roofing nails, I found myself on the roof of my waterfront
shack. I noticed immediately that the view from my roof was
much better than the view from my second story windows.
From up here I could see all the way to the Peconic Bay and
east to the Shinnecock Hills Golf Club. This would be a great
place to watch both the sunrise and the sunset. And even if I no
longer believed some deity was directly responsible for them, I
could still photograph them. I made a mental note to someday
either build a widow's walk on the roof or jack the whole house
up ten feet off its foundation. I recognized that neither was
likely to occur.

I had previously identified a couple of suspect shingles and went to work replacing them. To be honest, this was my first attempt at roof repair and I had no particular knowledge of the subject other than what I picked up at the hardware store when I bought the nails. I found this relatively easy project fulfilling, in a manly sort of way, and was feeling pretty good about my handyman skills as I descended the ladder.

"Good views from up there?" A woman's voice called out. I recognized the soft tones as Annie's. She was standing at the bottom of the ladder. She must have just finished one of her morning runs because she had on those really short shorts and was a little sweaty.

"As a matter of fact I was just thinking about how easy it would be to move my bed onto the roof so I could experience the sunrise without even getting out of bed."

"I could see you up there all the way from the beach. Doing some repairs?" She motioned to my tool belt.

"It's the ongoing saga of man versus rain. The Mauros never mentioned the leaks when they gave me the tour. But I've kind of grown to like it. I mean, it's nice to be able to hear the rain and feel it at the same time from the comfort of my soggy sofa."

Did I mention that Annie looked fantastic, not just because her nipples were protruding against her wet cotton running shirt, but because…Well, that was exactly why.

"You probably don't want to hear this, but everyone in the community knew about those leaks. John and Pat hosted a party last year on the fourth of July and we had to move it inside when it started to rain. I can still see the knotty pine ceiling dripping on us. We made a game of catching the drops in our drinks."

"I don't recall prospective buyers being invited to that party." I said with a friendly sarcasm. "Actually, it's more of an annoyance than a serious problem. I just need to make sure I don't leave my camera equipment where it can get wet. Maybe my car would be the safest place."

"Are you a photographer?" Annie asked.

"Just a hacker. But that's part of the reason I'm out here. I want to photograph the pond in all four seasons."

"I thought you were out here to hide from your ex-wife. Toronto, wasn't it?" She smiled in a delicious sort of way.

"That's just a happy dividend. Actually, my ex and I get along pretty well. Direct deposit and a well patrolled national border help, but we're civil."

As we spoke, Annie was doing her post-jog stretching which consisted of reaching for the sky, one arm at a time, and then bending over to touch her toes. She held that delightful pose for several seconds and I couldn't help feeling a little embarrassed when she caught me looking at her cute little ass.

"So you and the ex are on good terms?" She said while holding the toe stretch.

"Yeah, all things considered we're OK. She's moved on with her life and my money and I've started over. It could be a lot worse. I guess for the girls' sake, we keep it civil."

Annie was now standing erect with her hands on her hips and stretching backwards. "Listen, Pete Mitchell, the guy next to us, picked up a bunch of littlenecks over by Robins Island this morning so we're having an impromptu clambake tonight. Why don't you come?" She didn't wait for me to respond. "And bring a bottle of white wine."

And with that, she turned and continued her jog down Lands End Lane. "Come around six. Beach attire." She called over her shoulder as she disappeared around the bend of hedges.

Upon reflection, if my roof hadn't leaked, and I wasn't up on my roof that morning, maybe she wouldn't have noticed me and maybe I never would have been invited to the clambake. And if I'd never been invited to the clambake, maybe I never would have seen her in that black dress. Then maybe I never would have fallen in love with Annie. And if I'd never fallen in love with Annie...Well a lot of things would be different.

CHAPTER TWELVE

The fire John Weaver made on the beach had already settled into glowing embers by the time Doc arrived with a bottle of Pinot Griggio in hand. The sun was still hanging over a horizon filled with wispy clouds. It was a perfect night to be on the beach; just enough cool breeze to keep the bugs away but warm enough so the women congregating on the deck didn't need to cover their shoulders.

Doc had walked up the beach to arrive at Annie and John's fabulous bay-front home. He could see several women holding cocktails and chatting on the sprawling deck that surrounded the house. On the beach were an equal number of men, dressed in colorful shorts, some sporting whales or golf gear. An elderly man wearing a straw hat seemed to be in charge of cooking because he was the only one paying attention to the fire. The smoke from the coals drifted softly out over the glistening bay.

And then he saw her. Annie was on the deck serving something from a large silver tray. She had on a black sundress that hung on her milky shoulders and clung to her hips before loosely dangling to her bare feet. It was made of fine cotton and, even from a distance Doc could tell this sundress didn't have a K-Mart label. Her radiance drew him in like a moth to a summer light and he took the steps two at a time to reach the deck.

"Hey, I'm glad you came." Annie called out to Doc from across the small crowd.

Doc held up the bottle of wine and motioned as if to ask, "Where should I put this?" But Annie had already gone back to serving her guests and had her back to Doc.

"You must be Mr. Cafara." A strong voice from behind caught him off guard. Doc turned and faced his host. "I'm John, Annie's husband. Or, as she sometimes says, her current husband. I'm glad you could join us."

Doc realized that he'd never really met John before, even though he'd seen him from a distance the first morning he and Annie met on the beach. He was a big man. Doc guessed about six foot two. He reached out to shake his hand then realized he was still holding the bottle.

"I'll take that and thank you for bringing it." John took the wine with one hand and turned Doc around with the other. "Come down to the beach. I'll introduce you to your new neighbors."

Like a seventh grade dance, the men and women were at opposite ends of this party. All the women were on the deck and all the men, about ten of them, were on the beach standing around the bonfire holding bottles of beer. Most seemed to be in their forties or fifties except for the guy in the straw hat who was clearly the elder of the group. The guy in the blue shorts full of whales was holding court and carrying on about the price of oil and why he was sure it was going back to $150 a barrel. Doc listened on the sidelines for a few seconds before John introduced him to the group.

"This is the fellow who bought the Mauro place," John said with his arm still hanging on Doc's shoulder. "Doc Cafara I'd like you to meet your neighbors." He went around the group one by one and made the appropriate introductions: Jack the banker from Citi; Pete the old-timer who supplied the clams and was seeing to their proper steaming on the fire; Dick the longest homeowner in the association; Arthur the accountant; Felix the OBGYN; and so on. Doc did his best to try to remember as many names as he could.

After a half hour of conversation on the beach, mostly focused on the recent run of bluefish and how to best hook them, Doc took his bottle of Corona up to the deck in hopes of finding Annie and some of the pate she'd been serving earlier. He climbed the six steps to the deck and was greeted by three women all holding what looked to be their third cosmopolitan. The most coherent of the group, a faux-blond named Wendy who belonged to the guy from Citi, asked, "You must be the gentleman who bought John and Patty's house."

"That's me." Doc said as his eyes searched the area for the only person he knew to rescue him. But Annie was nowhere in sight.

"I understand you're a doctor. Is that right?" Wendy had to know.

"No, actually I'm a retired real estate broker and currently an amateur photographer and roofing specialist." The humor went over their alcohol soaked heads.

"Then why are you called Doctor?" Phoebe, who belonged to the gynecologist, asked politely.

Doc had to think for a moment. It had been so long since anyone called him anything other than Doc, he needed to reflect on the origin of his nickname. "It's because I used to have a great memory and some of my teenage friends started to call me 'doctor memory.' I was good at memorizing long strings of numbers or events from the past…"

"But why doctor? " Phoebe interrupted before he could get to it.

"When I was a kid, there was a character called doctor memory on a record. The record was called 'We're all Bozos on this Bus.' It was by a stoner group called Fireside Theater. Do any of you remember it?" Doc got three blank looks. "We listened to that record a lot and someone started to call me that whenever I would come up with some historical fact my friends had forgotten. Somewhere along the way, it just got shortened to Doc."

"So you're not really a doctor?" Phoebe and her cosmo were confused.

"Nope, but I'm always the first to volunteer CPR if a pretty lady stops breathing." Again the humor escaped the group.

And so it went. Doc met most of his new neighbors and, on the whole, he had to admit, they weren't a bad lot. Except for a few of the pickled wives, everyone seemed nice enough and happy to share with him the long history of the Cold Spring Pond Association. He learned that the first 'settlers' on the island were, in fact, a group of Irish doctors from Manhattan who liked to get away from the city on weekends and play poker in the small shacks they erected along the dunes. Most of them weren't married, or if they were, the wives weren't invited initially. Back in the forties, the weekends usually consisted of day-long card games followed by hours of heavy drinking. Somewhere in the fifties, someone realized this beach paradise would be good for something other than poker and booze and started building more substantial houses: ones with doors and windows and even electricity.

It wasn't until 1965 that anyone thought of this place as a year-round community. That's when several families bought land from the town of Southampton and built summer bungalows that, in the seventies were expanded and in the eighties became sought after summer retreats for the Wall Street crowd. The Association began in 1963 when six of the seven inhabitants decided to pool their resources and connect the houses with a gravel road that eventually became Cold Spring Point Road. To this day, the main purpose of the Association is the upkeep of the road which has remained private.

After dinner was served, Doc spent some time talking to John Weaver, who was the only person he met that seemed to have disdain for the community. He seemed to resent the familial spirit the residents held for one another. John explained that his wife had vacationed here for many years, first with her parents and then with her first husband and twin sons. He was a relative new-comer to Cold Spring Pond and he resented Annie's frequent reflections about her wonderful memories of the area. On the Fourth of July she would recount how her dad used to erect a huge bonfire every year. In the fall she would mention that she and her sons would take their kayaks along the edge of the pond and slide in and out of the golden reeds, sometimes startling a watering deer.

But there was more to John Weaver's open disdain for the pond and its people. It was as if John knew he would never fit in. Sure, he belonged here as much as anyone else. After all, he'd married Annie whose family had been part of the community for over forty years. And it wasn't as if he didn't have his own accomplishments. He was a successful oncologist with thriving practices in both Manhattan and East Hampton. He had his own credentials and apologized to no one for his success.

Doc couldn't put his finger on it but sensed that John's attitude had little to do with the geography and everything to do with family. He got the impression the doctor didn't approve of the way Annie coddled her sons. He certainly didn't seem to have much of a relationship with the boys himself. Doc tried to imagine how his daughters would feel about a stepmother, if that ever happened, and could empathize with John's predicament. Fitting a new woman into their lives would not be easy.

And then there was the money thing. Several times during their otherwise casual beach conversation, John mentioned the financial value of something or someone when it seemed inappropriate. He referred to a lovely old cottage along the pond as "That two point four million dollar teardown." And at one point he seemed to be ranking his guests not on how long he knew them or on their age or their standing in the association, but by their net worth. He seemed to take too much interest in how much people had accumulated and equally in how they accumulated it.

It was Annie who finally came over and interrupted them. She needed John up on the deck.

"John, the Wilsons are leaving. Come and say good bye." She motioned with sweeping arms that she wanted John to hurry so as not to miss this opportunity to be a gracious host.

"Nice talking to you Doc. I need to go kiss some wrinkled old-money ass." He said it so only Doc would hear then took his place on the deck to help usher guests out through the house.

Doc struck up a conversation with Pete, the source of the evening's feast, who was happy to wax eloquently about where and how to get the best littlenecks on the south shore.

"You've got to clam in the morning," he said. "And only while the tide is going out. Once it starts coming back in, you can forget it. The clams dig themselves about two inches deeper on an incoming tide."

"I didn't know clams were that smart," Doc said, partly to humor the old guy and partly because he seemed to remember from his high school biology that bivalves didn't have much of a brain.

"Pete will talk your ear off about clams and mussels if you let him." The words came from Annie who was now standing barefoot in the sand, her soft black dress blowing in the gentle breeze. "He can go on for hours but he sure knows how to find them." She gave Pete a peck on his cheek. "That's why we keep him around." Then she turned her attention to Doc.

"Thanks again for coming. Sorry we didn't get a chance to talk." She seemed sincere.

Doc guessed that the party was breaking up and this was his cue to leave as well. It was only about nine and the sun was barely down but most guests had already left.

"I guess I better be going."

"Hey, are you running tomorrow? Her voice was soft music to Doc's ears.

"Yeah, I probably will. I need to go into town in the afternoon so I'll run early."

"How about I come by around 7:30 and pick you up. We can run together and we can talk then. That is if you don't mind running with someone who sweats as much as I do."

Doc didn't want his enthusiasm to be too obvious. But he also didn't want to blow an opportunity to spend some time with Annie. There was just something about her that made him want to be around her. And tonight, silhouetted against the fading glow from the fire, she looked beautiful.

"7:30 it is. And sweat as much as you want."

He walked home along the beach, the same way he'd come. His hands were in his pockets and he was feeling great. He just didn't understand why yet.

Chapter Thirteen

Doc

To this day, I don't understand why I felt the way I did that morning. It reminded me of the many mornings I used to get dressed for high school knowing that Anita Marafucci, the ninth grade bombshell in the tight cable sweaters, might sit near me on the bus. I needed to look just right, smell just right and, above all, say just the right words. Usually, Anita just walked past and sat in the back of the bus with the older kids. But once in a while, her friends wouldn't be there and she'd look for a seat amongst us awkward goons sitting just behind the driver. Twice she actually sat next to me and I can still smell the *Heaven Scent* perfume that followed her everywhere. Those were the days.

Oddly, the morning I was to meet Annie for a jog, I felt much the same. I found myself paying unusual attention to my choices in running attire. I made sure to give myself a healthy dose of *Right Guard* after my shower. Why shower before running and even if you do, why put on deodorant before running? I never did before.

I brushed my teeth and used mouthwash. I combed my hair. I even splashed on a little Aramis, just in case the *Right Guard* didn't do its job. As I stood in my bedroom admiring the complete package in the mirror, it occurred to me that this was ridiculous. I was going running. If I tried to keep up with Annie, we would probably run about five miles and within fifteen minutes I would be dripping from head to toe.

Why was I so concerned about impressing her? Maybe it

was because she was a little younger. But, she was married. She had two grown children and a successful husband and a huge beach house. She'd given me no indication she was looking for anything more than a running partner for the morning. Perhaps she was even bringing along other people she runs with. Why did I care?

I don't know. But I did care. I wanted Annie to see the best side of me, and at 7:30 AM, that was increasing difficult for someone my age to pull off. I guess some of it was because I hadn't had any recent validation of my masculinity. I mean, since the divorce I'd dated several women, but most were people I knew professionally or a friend-of-a-friend. Upon reflection, I realized that since signing the papers that turned my wife into my ex-wife, I'd been out with only five other women and not more than three dates with any one of them. I never really got to know any of them very well and I certainly didn't let any of them know much about me. My sister from Michigan says I'm strange and afraid of commitment.

I glanced at the clock on my dresser: 7:26. I wanted to seem casual when Annie arrived. I certainly didn't want her to sense I'd been up for over an hour stretching, and primping for her benefit. I went down stairs onto the deck. The sun filled the sky with its August heat and the boards were already warm. The steps to the beach gave me a good place to sit and put on my socks and sneakers and if I hadn't been watching a white heron stalking its breakfast in the reeds, I might have noticed Annie coming across the lawn.

"Good morning neighbor. Ready to run?" Her voice was as soft as ever.

"Just putting on the wheels." I said and rose to greet her.

She was holding two bottles of something blue. "I brought you a Vitamin Water, but maybe we should save them for when we're done." And with that she let herself into the house and put the two bottles in my fridge. I followed her, noticing that from the back, her shorts looked even better.

"Gee, it's amazing you have enough energy to walk no less run. There's nothing in here but beer and cheese."

"The two staples of a heart-healthy life."

"No, really. Do you ever eat at home? There's nothing in here." She was still gaping into my rather barren refrigerator.

"Actually, I eat at home most nights. I'm a pretty good cook. And like most good cooks, I like to get what I need fresh each day. So I make a daily trip to Schmidts where I sometimes help damsels in distress choose the proper cheese."

She smiled. I think she was pleased that I remembered our meeting at Schmidts.

"Do you really cook for yourself a lot?"

I didn't want to sound like the lonely pathetic hermit I was rapidly becoming. I mean, after all. I did come out here to get away from the world, to take pictures of a pond, and to think about my relationship (or lack thereof) with God. Why did all that suddenly sound so miserable? So I decided to put a little spin on my response.

"I like to entertain at home and cooking's a great way to spend time with people you're trying to get to know. I just find the restaurants out here too noisy until after Labor Day. You can't talk." There, that said it all. I implied that I was cooking for guests, female guests by extension, and therefore I was not a pathetic hermit.

Annie was already on her way out the door. "OK then, let's get going."

I was a little disappointed she didn't want to hear more about my imaginary dating life, but before I could say anything else, she was jogging down my driveway. I let the screen door slam shut and followed. Although the view from a few feet behind was better, I felt the civil thing to do would be to jog next to her and maybe try to carry on a conversation while we ran.

But Annie was all business at first. She ran a lot faster than I was used to and by the time we turned the corner onto the main road around the pond, I was struggling to keep up. I think she sensed my fatigue because our second lap around the neighborhood was a bit more to my lungs' liking. And by the third, she settled into a comfortable jog.

"So, really Doc, what are you doing out here?"

I wasn't sure if she meant, *"Why are you running with me?"* or if she was exploring the bigger picture, *"Why did you really move out here?"* I decided to answer the latter. I explained that after I sold my business, there was really nothing and no one to keep me in Manhattan. Both my daughters lived elsewhere, my mom still lives on Long Island, my sisters all live out of state, and most of my friends were beginning to retire and heading south. Florida isn't for me and I got a great offer for my apartment on Second Avenue so it seemed like the right time to make a move. My mom's in her eighties and needs a little looking after so I didn't want to go too far. Southampton seemed like the perfect place.

After renting a place down the street for the past two summers, I fell in love with this tiny secluded community, and when the Mauros decided to pass their leaks on to an unsuspecting newcomer, I jumped at it.

I decided to leave out the part about needing to be alone to determine my place in the universe and all that. Instead, I focused on my desire to photograph the area, specifically the pond, in all four seasons and possibly use the photos to create a book about the area's wildlife and natural beauty. After seeing some of my black and whites, a friend had already offered to put together an exhibition of my pictures at his gallery in East Hampton.

"So are you completely through with the world of capitalism? I mean, do you plan to go back to work at some point?" And then she said the most beautiful six words in the world, *"You look too young to retire."*

I didn't know if proper etiquette would be to simply say *"thank you,"* or if I should explain that I view myself as temporarily, partially retired. The way I see it, I'm just taking off some time in between major life phases. Anyway, I informed her that I teach a photography class at Stony Brook University and am currently acting as my own general contractor on the slow reconstruction of my newly acquired shack of horrors. Other than that, yeah, I guess I'm retired. But at least she thought I looked too young!

We were both huffing pretty good by now and had been running for about thirty minutes. Annie was starting to display that delightful combination of sweat and fatigue. She looked great in both. Her face glistened with perspiration. It actually made me take notice of her gentle features—skin that hadn't yet succumbed to gravity but was softly wrinkled in just the right places—eyes that reminded me of the comic strip character Dondi—and lips that were thin but very sexy. I could tell she had been really cute as a young girl and would age into a stunning beauty by the time she picked up her first social security check. Right now, she was perfect.

She must have caught me staring because as we rounded the pond for the home stretch, she asked, "Is something wrong?"

"No, I'm good to go another twenty laps." I deflected the question with humor.

We sprinted the last hundred yards towards my house, and I had no chance at keeping up which, I might have already mentioned, has its advantages too.

We finished the sprint at my car and we both leaned on the Jeep as we caught our breath. Oddly, she had hers a lot sooner than I, and walked straight into the house to retrieve the two bottles of blue Vitamin Water. She tossed me one and motioned for me to join her on the pond side of the deck where the breeze would keep things cooler. We settled into two white plastic chairs facing the pond.

I found the run exhilarating and sitting there with Annie was the perfect way to complete the event and ease my heart rate back to normal. Everything about her seemed easy and almost carefree. She spoke of some of the neighbors and gave me a little social history of the area. She told me that the young couple who lived to my right had bought the place about a year ago and were now locked in a nasty divorce and fighting over the house so no one ever came out anymore. Each time she mentioned a family, she went out of her way to say something nice about them and never said anything derogatory about anyone. Not even about old-man Miller who was sort of the neighborhood curmudgeon.

She told me about her first husband and her father. Clearly, she loved them both. She wasn't embarrassed by the tears that welled up when she mentioned each man. I could tell she really missed them. Then she lit up when she talked about her sons. Both Frank and Nick were at college and she talked about an upcoming event when they'd all be together for a long weekend reunion. I got the impression, the boys weren't nuts about her current husband, John and chose to stay away more than Annie would have liked. It was the only regret she mentioned—that John and the boys didn't get along.

I found myself getting lost in her stories and thoroughly enjoyed the time we spent on my deck that morning. Even if she wasn't so pretty, she'd be the sort of person any guy would like to have as a friend. She was just that nice. But I must admit, it was the toxic combination of her sincerity and beauty that made me want to sit there and listen to her all morning.

Then it happened.

She leaned from her chair towards mine and put her hand softly on my arm as she said, "There's some other reason you're here Doc. It's not just to take pictures, is it? You don't have to tell me, but if you ever do want to talk about it, I'd be happy to listen. I really like talking to you."

Then she leaned in further and kissed me on the cheek before she jumped up and said, "I need to get moving. I'm going into the city this afternoon. Thanks again for the company. I really enjoyed it."

Then she added, in a slightly softer and more inviting tone, "I hope you did too."

Chapter Fourteen

M iranda wasn't his favorite, but she was certainly a regular. The diminutive twenty-two year old was always happy to earn a little extra money, so John usually asked for a little extra service. As long as she could get back to the city in time for her eleven AM class tomorrow, he could do pretty much whatever he wanted. It was just a job to her.

Her short dark hair was tussled gently by the evening breeze. Miranda loved the aft deck on John's boat. They'd met here several times before, and each time she marveled at the luxurious appointments on the fifty-foot vessel. John didn't tell her the boat actually belonged to his deceased father-in-law, and, by rights, now to his wife. He didn't tell her he was a doctor or where he lived. He didn't even tell her his real name but none of that mattered to Miranda. The escort service paid her eight hundred dollars to take the train from Manhattan to Hampton Bays and John never failed to be there waiting for her to step off the platform. She understood the game and the game paid her tuition.

"Do you want to take a ride?" He asked. "It's such a nice night."

She took a sip of her Absolute martini. "No, let's just stay here at the marina and look at all the beautiful lights."

And beautiful it was. The Hampton Bays Marina provided a safe harbor to many of the *rich and famous'* water toys. At night it was a crystal illumination of sleek white fiberglass hulls and polished chrome reflected in the still water. The boats belonged to those privileged enough not to care about the cost of maintaining or fueling them. They just wanted to keep their toys in the Shinnecock Canal for easy access to both the Atlantic Ocean to the south and the Peconic Bay a few hundred yards to the north. And, of course, to be seen by the other *rich and famous*. The least impressive of the toys could be exchanged for a pleasant three-bedroom condo on Manhattan's upper west side. The biggest yachts were built in Europe and Hong Kong and the instrumentation alone could pay for the same condo.

Miranda gazed out over the marina. From her perch on the stern transom, she could see hundreds of these floating palaces. There was nothing like this anywhere near 125th Street, where she grew up. The lights shimmering on the water was what she found most beautiful. Thousands of them—all white. She couldn't imagine anything so beautiful unless she'd seen it herself.

Ironically, the late Burt Dunn's yacht wore the name "*Annie's Pleasure*" on its transom; ironic because since his death, Annie hadn't seen the boat or even been to the marina. It had become John's playground. Occasionally, he'd take some of the doctors he shared office space with out for a day of fishing, but for the most part, what had once been Annie's father's pride and joy had become John's game room. He hosted high-stakes poker games in the large parlor on the aft deck; games that usually extended into the next day.

But, for John, the real value of the "*Annie's Pleasure*" was that it allowed him to feign what he most sought—the appearance of indifferent affluence. It pleased him that most of his marina neighbors thought the boat belonged to him. Only those around long enough to remember Burt knew otherwise.

And the boat gave John a place to entertain and to be entertained. Tonight he was to be entertained. He looked over at his guest. She was a beautiful girl, all five-foot-nothing of her. Had she been a little taller she could have won beauty pageants. She had that golden Latino glow, that firm tight figure, and eyes as wide as the moon which now shined down on both of them, reflected by the still water.

"OK then. What shall we do?" he asked with a bit of boyish charm.

"I'd like to sit here and finish my drink and watch the stars. Then I want to go below, and find out what color boxers you've got on." Miranda knew how to play him. She knew he liked to be teased and flattered.

"Sounds wonderful."

"Let's talk a little Jack." It was the only name she knew him by.

"What would you like to talk about?" he said as he joined her on the transom and gazed up at the stars.

"Tell me what you did today," she said without removing her drink from her lips. John knew Miranda was an easy drunk. Two martinis and she was just about incoherent; but still a lot of fun. Three and she was useless—sound asleep.

He thought about telling her the truth. That he spent the morning seeing patients and the afternoon playing golf with another doctor who was fortunate enough to have been born into a family that belonged to Shinnecock Hills. But the truth would only complicate their relationship. John knew that he and Miranda were just two people in need of what the other had, and was willing to give. It didn't have to be more than that for either of them. And to him, she was just the flavor of the month. Maybe next month he'd go back to Asian or one of those crazy eastern Europeans.

"I had a busy morning at the office and I played golf in the afternoon. But I was thinking about you all day and looking forward to seeing you tonight."

For her part, Miranda knew how to play the game. Ask no probing questions, and pretend to believe everything he said. She didn't have a 3.8 GPA at NYU because she was beautiful. She understood the rules and didn't want to risk ruining what had become, a good thing.

"What did you do today?" John actually wanted to know, more out of curiosity than any real interest in her life.

"Well, when I was sitting in my International Finance class this morning all I could think about was being here tonight with you in this beautiful place. I day-dreamed about us being on the boat, but the boat was somewhere else. I think it was somewhere in the Mediterranean because the water was really blue and the buildings came right down to the water like they do in postcards of France or Portofino." Miranda had been to neither.

John knew that when she did this—talk about her day-dreams, it was her way of letting him know she was ready for bed.

"We were lying on the cushions on the front of the boat and we were both naked. It was day time and the sun was really warm on my ass. You were rubbing oil on my back and on the back of my legs and I was getting wet just thinking about it."

"Maybe we should see if we can rekindle the moment." He took the second martini from her hand and tossed it overboard. She slid into his grasp, her face barely reached his chest. John put his arms around her waist and lifted her off the deck to kiss her. It was a long, hot and deep kiss. Miranda sucked on his lower lip a little harder than he would have liked.

Then he slid his hands down the back of her bare legs. "Is this where I was putting the oil on you?"

"Ummm," she whispered into his neck.

"How about here? Did I put any oil here?" He asked as he

ran his hands up her legs, under her dress and onto her naked ass. Miranda never wore panties for John.

"Ummm." She moaned.

As his fingers began to explore the dampness between her legs he could feel her going limp in his arms. Then he felt her hand going down the small of his back a lifting his shirt.

"Let's take this inside."

They descended the four mahogany steps from the aft deck into the cabin without Miranda's feet ever touching the ground. He knew she liked to be carried. He knew a lot about what she liked. But tonight wasn't about what Miranda liked. She knew the game and it was progressing just as it always did.

The main stateroom was spacious and luxurious. The queen size bed in the center of the room was covered with a puffy white satin spread that looked like fields of drifting snow.

Miranda fell back onto the bed and pulled her tiny dress over her head, tossing it onto the corner chair for retrieval in the morning. Then she spun around on her back so that her head was at the foot of the bed, just where John was standing.

She reached under her back, unclasping her lacey black bra and let it slip to the floor. John looked down on her naked body. He was surprised by her tan lines. Her breasts were whiter than he remembered.

She reached over her head and grabbed the back of his legs, pulling down his Dockers as he unfastened the belt. He tossed his shirt and stood there for a moment in just his powder blue boxers. John enjoyed watching her like this, and the feel of her hands on the back of his knees sent a shiver up his back.

Then, as always, he knelt down at the foot of the bed and kissed her on the top of her forehead, then the nose, and gave her a long deep kiss on the lips. Their mouths were one and seemed to fit together in this up-side-down arrangement. She put her arms around the back of his neck and nudged him up onto her. He lifted his weight onto his elbows and his lips found her aching nipples. He was careful not to put the weight of his body on hers as he licked the firm tips then sucked hard on one until Miranda moaned her pleasure. She arched upward and licked around his naval.

John could feel his hardness as Miranda pulled his shorts down his legs. Her outstretched arms were too short to reach his feet so he kicked them off the last few inches and they fluttered to the floor at the foot of the bed. He continued his descent running his tongue from her nipples, down the center of her soft smooth belly, past her tiny naval and into the warmth of her wetness. His tongue and lips feasted on the darkness between her outstretched legs and he knew this was as good for her as it was for him.

Again, he was careful not to put too much of his weight on her. Although his face was buried deep inside Miranda, his body hovered over her. He shifted his weight to his elbows and knees, then came up for air and licked the front of her thighs. That's when he felt her holding him with one hand and taking him in her mouth. He held his aching torso over her so she could work her magic with her lips and the inside of her mouth. Back and forth, up and down, sucking harder and harder until he exploded and collapsed on her, his teeth biting into her left thigh.

Sometimes they would fall asleep like that. John would roll over and lie at her side and sometimes he would continue to lick her legs and knees until they fell asleep. Neither of them ever made an attempt to lie together face to face. And in the morning, usually at dawn, she would get dressed and leave without saying a word.

CHAPTER FIFTEEN

Doc

I'm not even sure when it actually happened, but now that I've come to the uncomfortable but conclusive decision that I no longer believe in god, I find myself longing for the companionship that was always his. I miss talking to him. I miss asking his advice. I even miss thanking him for all the wonderful blessings I'd assumed were gifts and now realize were probably just random events.

In the past, as I walked down Third Avenue in the mornings, on my way to work, I'd have a rather one-sided nonverbal conversation with him. We'd chat about whatever was on my mind or consuming my life that day. Usually it was just the mundane events that we all have to endure but I always felt like I'd had a chance to vet my thoughts before having to commit in the real world.

Now it's different. It's totally different.

I've lost the most intimate of friends. I've lost my ultimate confidant. I miss him. And the frustrating part is that he didn't give up on me. I gave up on him. I left him. My loneliness is of my own doing. That's what hurts.

So now when I look up at the stars on a beautifully clear night like this one, and I'm tempted to talk to him, I can't. It just seems wrong somehow. I used to get great comfort in looking for his face in the distant stars. It's hard to explain the lonely feeling I have now. It's like losing a friend, but worse. It's like voluntarily ending a lifelong friendship for no good reason, and then wishing you hadn't every day of your life.

Earlier tonight I watched the Mets crush the Braves. When I watch a game on TV, I take full advantage of the modern miracle called the remote control. Between innings I flip through the 278 channels offered by Cablevision. I came across a show about a family in Chicago who'd lost two children in a house fire. The kids were about five years old and the mother was weeping openly as she talked about the day of the fire and how she could hear them calling for her though the thick smoke.

What struck me as odd was the father. Holding the hand of his wife, he looked into the camera and said, "I know my girls are with God now and they're in a better place."

He seemed so sure of it. It wasn't just words. He really seemed to believe it. In the face of such a horrible tragedy, this guy still had faith in the very God that had just burned his daughters to death. How could that be? How could he still believe? Why wasn't he bitter?

The sad part for me was that I found myself envious of that man. I envied his faith. I really wish I could have such blind faith as that. This would all be a lot easier. I realize that it just comes down to that; I no longer have faith. I no longer have faith that there is a supreme being. I no longer have faith that there is anything spiritual going on around me. And, if that's the case, then I can no longer believe in an afterlife.

That one really scares me because for fifty-five years now I was sure that someday I would see my dad again; that there would be some sort of reward for the good deeds and that bad deeds would be punished; that this entire mystery would be revealed to me and that somehow I would find an understanding of it all.

But now, now that I've turned my back on my friend, I don't have the right to believe in any of that anymore. Now, if I apply my logical and reasoned rationale for denying the existence of God, I must also deny the hope of an afterlife.

And that is frightening because it creates a ticking clock on my existence that wasn't there before. Now, even if I live to be ninety, there are a finite number of Christmases, springs, sunrises and sunsets that I will get to experience. Because after that, there is nothing more.

It's sad for me to have to think about it that way, but, if I am to be truthful with myself, I can come to no other conclusion. Someday I will draw my last earthly breath and that will be it. Nothing else lies ahead. No heaven. No reward for a good life. No day of reckoning and no face of God waiting for me.

Sometimes I think that when I started my questioning of God, if I had realized then how lonely and finite my conclusions would make me feel, I would have stopped questioning.

Chapter Sixteen

Felix T. Brown didn't start off looking to become one of Mr. Zucker's collectors. He didn't enjoy the violence and he preferred intimidation to physical coercion. But he probably should have thought of that when he was cutting classes in the seventh grade and getting high with his older cousin Levon. Without a diploma, his choices were limited. Besides the NFL, there weren't many employers looking for a 295 pound black man who can lift the rear end of most cars a foot off the ground.

So when Levon introduced Felix to a guy, who knew a guy, who knew a guy who worked for Arnie Zucker, he jumped at the chance to move up a few pegs on the street. Nobody fucked with anyone associated with Arnie Zucker, although probably no one from Felix's block in Hollis had ever actually met Arnie Zucker. Or ever would.

This morning Felix and Levon were visiting a fifty-eight year old man who made the mistake of falling behind on his loan payments to Mr. Zucker. Jack Crowley lived on a quiet street in Tarrytown, just a thirty minute train ride to his office at JP Morgan in Manhattan. Jack, a VP at the bank, was in charge of all administrative services for its domestic locations and earned between $350,000 and $450,000, depending on his bonus each year. He and his wife both drove late model Mercedes: SL 550's to be exact. They owned their home, valued at two point three million, free and clear. They took lavish vacations to Europe, usually twice a year, and belonged to three golf clubs, including Sleepy Hollow, where Jack was chairman of the rules committee.

Felix didn't know why Jack owed Mr. Zucker money; he didn't even know how much he owed. All he knew was that he and Levon were supposed to *"remind"* Jack of the importance of making regular payments. After four years, Felix knew what *"remind"* meant and when he spotted the pudgy, bald guy, in the Zegna suit coming out his front door, he quickly developed a distain for his wasteful excesses. They had been here before to *"familiarize"* Mr. Crowley. *"Familiarize"* meant to intimidate without physical force, but to be very clear that Mr. Zucker was growing impatient. They were here a few weeks ago for that and it seemed to Felix, the fat little fuck had gotten the message. Apparently, not.

As Jack reached the driver's door of his sleek blue Mercedes, Felix called out, "Mr. Crowley, we need to have a word with you before you leave."

The sight of the two large black men walking up his driveway didn't seem to concern Jack. All the same, he opened his door and tried to get in before they could travel the twenty steps to reach him. And he almost made it but Levon moved faster than Jack and jammed an aluminum baseball bat into the car door preventing its closure.

"We really need to talk, for just a minute, come on now," Felix said as Levon held the bat in place.

"I have nothing to talk to you two about. I'll wire the payment as soon as I get to my office. In fact, I plan to make two payments today." Crowley was admirably defiant in the face of his predicament and seemed sincere. But that wasn't of concern to Felix.

"That's good. That's good." Felix said as he helped Jack out of his car. "Weez just wants to chat for a minute and remind you of the importance of prompt payments."

Before he realized what was happening, Levon was behind Jack and, using the bat, had him in a choke hold. He spun him around and Jack's face smashed into the roof of his car. Levon held him there while Felix continued.

"Weez just needs to be sure you don't forget. That's all. So, later on today, when you gets home from the hospital, you makes sure you remember to send the money."

With that, Felix opened the driver's door and grabbed Jack's left arm, forcing his hand into the door jam. This seemed to get Jack's attention.

"Look, I swear, I'll send the money as soon as I get to work."

"I know you will." Felix slammed the door. The sound of metal shattering bone, was quickly followed by the guttural scream of a man.

"We just wanted to *remind* you." Felix said as he and Levon walked back down the driveway to their car.

Chapter Seventeen

Annie looked out the window from the fortieth floor conference room where she'd been waiting. Below she could clearly make out the Statue of Liberty and most of Battery Park and in the distant haze, the Verrazano Bridge stretching towards Staten Island. It was a fabulous view and each time she'd been here in the past, she made a point of asking for this particular conference room for her meeting.

She reflected on the last time she was here. Her dad had just died and the family attorney, Franklin Montague asked her to come in to review some details of his will. Frank, as everyone called him, had been a close friend of her father ever since they served together in the Navy. After the war, they went to the same college, dated the same circle of girls, lived just a few blocks apart and stood as Best Man for each other when it came time to settle down. Annie remembers calling him Uncle Frank when she was young and can still see the tears rolling down Franklin's face as they stood around Burt's casket at the cemetery.

"Annie, you look wonderful," he said as he came through the door. He gave her a long fatherly hug that they held for several seconds. Both were thinking about Burt and getting nostalgic.

When they separated Annie said, "You look great too Frank." But she really thought he was getting too thin and could use some time in the sun. His 82 year old frame was beginning to sag and his skin seemed thinner than when she last saw him. It occurred to her that because Burt had died in his late seventies, she'd been spared the pain of witnessing his physical atrophy. It was so sad to see a man, who she remembered as so vibrant, barely able to fill out the collar of his loose fitting button-down shirt.

They exchanged several minutes of social pleasantries and stories about the children and grandchildren before Frank suggested one of his assistants join them. The young assistant looked to Annie like he was no older than her twins but Frank assured her Jimmy had graduated from Cornell law the previous summer and was specializing in Estate and Trust law. "Jimmy's completely up to date on your trusts as well as the ones Burt set up for Nick and Frank."

Annie settled into one of the overstuffed leather chairs around the table and got right to it. "The reason I wanted to meet with you Frank is that I remember you telling me about the boys' trusts and that certain things happened at certain ages but I don't remember the details. The boys will turn twenty three next spring and I thought that was one of those ages you said something has to happen." She looked at the elderly lawyer. "Am I right about that?"

"Yes, Annie, you have a good memory. Burt was very cautious about the trusts for your boys. I recall the two of us sitting in this very room about three years ago writing these things up." As he spoke he leafed through the large file Jimmy had brought in and settled on a particular section.

"Here it is." He put on his reading glasses and took a few moments to refresh his memory about the trusts. When he was finished he leaned back and again, Annie could tell he was thinking about her father.

"Burt was a very cautious man. He knew he was sick when he last updated his will and these trusts. Even though Peter had left you and the boys comfortable financially, he wanted to make sure you would be protected. At the same time, he wanted to protect the boys from themselves. Remember, at the time, your sons were teenagers and Burt, knowing he wouldn't be around much longer, didn't want them to inherit the money before they were ready to handle it. So he set up a trust fund for each of them. As you know, when your dad did pass, a little over four million dollars went into each of their trusts, and the balance of his estate, about 160 million, went into a trust for you."

For the benefit of his young assistant, Frank walked through the reasoning and motives of his old friend. He turned in his seat, more towards Jimmy than to Annie and continued. "To be honest, Burt didn't like or trust Annie's current husband John. Annie knows all this. Burt insisted that I structure his estate so that Annie would have access to whatever she wanted from her trust but that only the interest would be distributed to her for each of the next four years. You see, Burt was afraid John wouldn't have Annie's or his grandsons' best interests at heart and he wanted to make sure John had no control over the money. So we set up a series of by-pass trusts. Most of Burt's estate went into a trust for Annie and will pass to the boy's trusts when then reach twenty three." He looked to Annie to acknowledge she had remembered correctly.

"Oh, that was clever." Jimmy offered. "And because the money was obligated to pass to the trusts of the children, it was never part of Annie's marital property."

"Correct. And in the event Annie and John should ever divorce, her only assets are the interest payments from the body of the trust and whatever money she inherited from her first husband, Peter."

"So when the boys reach twenty three, all the money in Annie's trust moves to the boys' trusts?"

"No, Annie keeps two million in her own name outright

and her trust dissolves. The other..." Here's where Frank needed to look on the other side of the file for the current balances..."The other...210 million goes to the boys evenly. There are restrictions on their trusts that prevent them from accessing principal until they are thirty five years old. Burt figured that if they weren't financially responsible by then, they'd probably never be. Anyway, Annie is co-trustee for both of them and, as such, retains practical control of the money."

Now it was Annie's turn to ask a question. "Frank, I just want to be sure..." She hesitated for a moment and glanced towards Jimmy. "I just want to be sure that in the event of a divorce, at any time, John has no right to come after the boys' inheritance."

"Is that something you anticipate?" Frank asked with fatherly compassion.

Again, Annie hesitated. "It's a long story Frank but I haven't been happy for some time now and I just wanted to be sure. Just in case." She felt embarrassed by the words.

"I understand. And I think your father would be proud of your prudence to come and check. There are several things I know for certain about my friend Burt. He worked very hard to accumulate his wealth and even though he gave about half to charities before he died, he wanted his daughter and grandsons to enjoy the fruits of his work. I also know he didn't want the money to ever be an issue for you and John because, well, like I said, he just didn't trust him."

"So there's no way John can come after any of dad's money? She wanted to know for sure. She needed to hear her trusted Uncle Frank say the words.

"No honey. When the boys turn twenty three, as long as you still want them to get the money, that's where it goes. Only you can change that. The pre-nup that you and John executed supports your right to do whatever you want with your trust. He knew the deal going in."

"How'd you get him to agree to that?" Jimmy wanted to know even if the question seemed a bit distasteful.

Frank shot his assistant a stern look before answering. "John is a successful physician and has assets of his own. He understood before they were married that when the boys reached twenty three, the value of Annie's trust would drop to two million dollars. He knew that going in. If I remember correctly, at the time, John had about six million dollars of net worth so the pre-nup protected him as well."

Annie looked out the window at the harbor below and thought of the days when she and her father would ride the Staten Island ferry just to catch a cool breeze on a hot summer day. She always felt safe when she was at his side. Much the same way she felt safe when Peter was alive. Oddly, it was the same feeling she got when she was with Doc.

Chapter Eighteen

Annie wanted to get back to Southampton before the Labor Day weekend traffic began clogging the Long Island Expressway, so after leaving her lawyer's office she decided not to do the shopping she'd planned and headed straight for the tunnel. It was a typical hot, humid August day and she left the top of her convertible up to take full advantage of the air conditioning. If she could hit the LIE before 3:30, she had a chance of beating the traffic.

The two hour ride would give her a chance to think and reflect on what Frank had told her. She had a lot on her mind and the last few days she was having trouble concentrating at home. She hoped the monotony of the drive would free her to think things through fully.

First, there was John. She already regretted not telling Frank more about her problem. Perhaps she would have if they'd been alone. But she was increasingly certain that she would leave John at some point, so the question about divorce would have to come up again. His physical abuse was becoming more frequent and his drinking only made it worse. She felt sorry for him because she knew the migraines were real, but she was growing apart from him at the same time. It was as if there was a tall brick wall that separated them and she could hear him suffering on the other side, but she didn't want him on her side either.

She also sensed that John was no longer focused on his practice. He seemed to be spending less time at his office and more and more time either on the boat or traveling to Atlantic City, or anywhere other than home. In a way, that was good, but it also meant they did very few things together. No more walks on the beach. No more quiet dinners in the village. She couldn't remember the last time they sat together on the sofa and watched TV, and they'd been at the beach house all summer.

Annie was certain she was miserable with John but she wasn't ready to admit she'd failed at her marriage, and that made her look for any hope of working things out. A part of her still wanted to try; to give him the huge benefit of the doubt, to forgive the attacks, to forgive the infidelities she was sure were going on. She'd wanted to give it all she had. At least up until now.

And that was the other thing that kept clouding her thinking—Doc. He seemed to be everything John was not, in both good and bad ways. Although she had spent very little time with Doc, she felt a sincerity in his words that her husband hadn't shown in a long time. She sensed a kindness in him and a gentleness. She felt a deep current running beneath Doc that he hadn't yet spoken of but was there just the same, and she wanted to know more about it.

Annie knew that Doc wasn't from the same social background that she enjoyed—or used to enjoy. She knew he was a much simpler and far less complicated man than her husband, and that he had never had to deal with the burden of wealth. The more she thought about him the more she realized how little she really knew about him. Why did his first marriage end? Was it his only marriage? What were his dreams? Was he seeing anyone? Who were his friends? Aside from fixing up that old shack, what did he do?

In many ways he was still a stranger to her. He seemed like the kind of person who would make a great friend, maybe even a great lover. But even if he was in a serious relationship, he'd still be a nice person to have as a friend. He seemed intelligent and well read. He cared deeply about his daughters and had already mentioned his ongoing responsibility for his elderly mother. He had run a successful business but seemed neither impressed by nor concerned about finances.

On the other hand, John measured almost everything with a dollar sign. Although his practice had been successful for many years, he always seemed to be scraping together a new "deal" of some kind with his partners. He reveled in fiscal details and could spend all Sunday reading the Times business section and the Economist. John wouldn't wear a suit that retailed for less than $2,500. He took two year leases on his Mercedes because he felt it beneath him to drive anything older than that.

As she turned off the expressway and onto Route 111, Annie thought about the last time she and John were together, two nights before. He'd only been home a couple of hours and announced he was going to bed. It was barely 9:30. Annie was finishing a James Paterson novel and would have preferred to linger but she knew that was not what John wanted.

As soon as she stepped into their bedroom he was on her, tearing at her blouse like a wild animal. There was nothing romantic or even sexual about it. It was an attack, and as usual, she was the victim. And, as usual, it ended with Annie stretched facedown over the hassock at the foot of their bed, feeling like she'd been torn apart and with tears in her eyes.

That night, as she lay in bed, she decided to call Franklin Montague.

CHAPTER NINETEEN

Doc

As the Saturday of Labor Day weekend rolled around and I had no particular plans, I decided to call a few friends from the city. I figured those who weren't already committed to barbeques or events in town might like to drive out for an "end of summer" get-together. Most of my city friends had not yet seen my still-leaking, but beautifully situated shack and the weather report was fantastic for the next three days. Actually, it occurred to me that my only visitor had been Bobby and that was a couple of weeks ago.

Strangely enough, the first six people I called had no plans for Sunday and quickly agreed to come. I stopped there because they all had significant others and I didn't want this to turn into a circus. What I had in mind was a sunny afternoon of close friends swimming, lying on the hammock, or stretched out on the deck sipping frozen margaritas or icy Coronas. I planned to put together a few choice delicacies for the grill, maybe one fish, one beef and big tomato salad. That's all. Nothing complicated. I really just wanted to show off my new home and spend some time with people I used to hang with back in my cosmopolitan days.

I thought it would be appropriate to also invite a few of my neighbors, particularly those who had invited me to their homes or the ones who had dropped off *"welcome to the neighborhood"* gifts my first week here. And of course, I wanted to invite Annie and John, although I felt sure they would already have plans. And so, I took a walk around the neighborhood, stopping at the chosen few to see if they wanted to come. Tom and Marion, who lived next door, were the only ones who didn't already have plans and Tom insisted on bringing an assortment of the calms and oysters he so patiently cultivated along his bulkhead.

Annie's was the last house I stopped at and I didn't expect to find anyone home because there were no cars in the drive way. But John answered the door dressed in his usual Brooks Brothers catalog best.

"What's up neighbor?" He seemed surprised to see me.

"Hi John. I'm having some friends over tomorrow afternoon for a barbeque, and was hoping you and Annie were free. I know it's short notice."

"Oh, sorry buddy. I'm going back to Manhattan in a few minutes and won't be back until Friday."

I hope my disappointment wasn't too obvious. I was really looking forward to seeing Annie again. I hadn't run into her since that peck on the cheek after we ran and, I must admit, I'd been thinking about her a lot.

"But I'm pretty sure my wife will be around. She's not coming back with me and I don't think she has any other plans. Actually, that would do her a world of good. She hasn't been herself lately. I think she's been overdoing the running because she always seems tired. It would do her good to just relax for one day."

Well, that could work out just fine. I was going to be the only one at my own party without a companion anyway. So why did I suddenly feel guilty?

"Okay, great. Let her know it's bathing suit casual and to come around two."

"Leave me your phone number. I'm sure she'll want to call you to see what she can bring." John was amicable enough but seemed to be rushing me. Maybe I had caught him on his way out. So I left my cell number and headed back to Casa Leaks to cut the lawn and prepare for tomorrow's soirée.

I spent a good part of Sunday morning roaming the narrow creaky aisles of Schmidts, searching for the perfect red peppers, cuts of beef, cheeses, and a beautiful piece of yellowtail for the grill. Then I did the pedestrian thing and went to King Kullen for beer, mixers, and a few bags of ice. Annie hadn't called me so I was sort of hoping to run into her in town, but I noticed her convertible in front of her house on my way home and my heart sank a little. I was really hoping she'd come.

Then, as I was dumping the ice over the beer waiting on the bottom of my cooler, my cell rang and I felt like a kid in high school, wishing it was Annie. It was.

"Hey stranger. I hear I'm invited to a party." Her voice was as soft and sweet as always. At least it was to me.

"I was beginning to think you weren't around." I didn't want to sound foolishly anxious.

"I'm sorry I didn't call you last night. I didn't feel well and wanted to wait until this morning to see if I bounced back. I'd love to come. What can I bring?"

"Nothing. I just got back from Schmidts and I'm good. Just bring a towel and come around two."

"Who's going to be there?"

"Tom and Marion from next door and about a dozen friends from the city."

"All right, but I have to bring something so tell me what you need."

"Actually, I'm a little low on white wine so if you have a bottle lying around bring one. But don't go into town to get one. Just if you have one already."

Then I asked, "Did you run today?"

"No. I've been kind of run down the last couple of days. I've been taking it easy."

"Okay then. Plan on taking it easy this afternoon on my deck. I think you'll like my friends; at least the ones who don't drink too much."

"All right then. I'll see you in a few hours. Looks like you've got a beautiful day. You sure there's nothing else I can bring?"

I assured her I was all set, then said, "Sorry John can't make it."

There was a pause, then Annie said, "No you're not. And neither am I. See you at two."

<hr>

My guests started arriving just before two. Bobby and Catherine were first and, as usual, Catherine had made an assortment of her legendary cookies. While I was showing her around, four of my friends from work arrived in a BMW that looked like two racing jockeys would have trouble getting comfortable in. As they pealed themselves from the little car, I saw Annie walking up the driveway. She had on a pale yellow sun dress that was so shear there was no secret she had on a green floral bathing suit underneath.

I did introductions all around and herded the group onto the deck. Within minutes everyone else pulled up toting bottles of red wine and tequila. By 2:15 we had a bona fide party going and Bobby and a couple of the guys from work were already in the water throwing a plastic football.

It occurred to me that this was quite an eclectic group I had assembled. We were all pretty close in age, except for my neighbors Tom and Marion, but that was about the end of any common ground. There were only sixteen people, but just about every conceivable political and ethnic group had representation. My friends from work, Atul and his live-in girlfriend Shioban, were of British decent but originally from India. My former secretary Pat liked to joke that she wasn't really black; just from the southern most reaches of Italy. Her husband Curtis, couldn't let you forget he was black. And the people who lived across the hall from me in Manhattan, Steve and Arlene, were proud to be your typical yuppie Jewish lawyers. They had the market cornered on both lawyer and Jewish jokes and told both frequently.

I noticed that Annie had struck up a conversation with Atul down on my dock so I wandered over to see if I could get them something to drink.

"Have you got any decent white wine?" Atul always gave me shit about my lack of good taste when it came to whites. The rhetoric went way back and actually, I have sometimes gone out of my way to buy absolute crap just to get back at him.

"As a matter of fact, I grabbed a case of white Thunderbird just for you. Or I could pour you a glass from the bottle Annie brought. And by the way, you can take a lesson from her. If you want good white wine at my house you have to bring it yourself." I winked towards Annie, then continued, "Or you could pretend to be a straight man and have a beer."

"Well if her wine is as lovely as she is, I'll have to try Annie's." Atul said in his tick British accent.

I turned to Annie, "And for you my dear?"

"I'll try one of your margaritas, but don't make it too strong."

"Coming up," and I scurried away to tend bar. By the time I returned several others had joined them on the dock, most with their feet dangling in the cool water. It was turning out to be just the sort of afternoon I'd hoped for; warm, sunny and relaxed.

I suppose I'd underestimated the effort involved in feeding

sixteen hungry people, some of whom were already pleasantly buzzed, because I spent most of the next two hours in the kitchen or mixing drinks. From the window over my sink, I kept my eye on Annie and watched her drift from group to group. She seemed very comfortable with everyone, and everyone with her. That wasn't a total surprise. She struck me as the type of person who has enough self confidence to fit into any conversation and enough genuine interest in others to be an excellent conversationalist.

At one point in the afternoon, I joined her and several others in a discussion about the upcoming presidential election. As I said, we had just about every conceivable political persuasion covered, so I wasn't shocked to hear two guests of opposite points of view going at it. One was going on about how John McCain was out of touch with the modern world and was carried along by his former POW status. The other was quoting chapter and verse from the Senator's position on fiscal controls, something the current administration didn't seem to care much about.

When asked her thoughts on the subject, Annie answered in as eloquent and diplomatic a fashion as I would have expected from such a charming lady. She said, "Although I don't agree with most of his politics, I have all the respect in the world for someone who cares enough to express theirs and tries to make a difference."

Later, I delivered a round of frozen drinks to a group sitting on the beach near my hammock. Again, Annie was in the middle of things but this time the group was playing some sort of drinking game. Each time a person failed to answer a question about pop music correctly, they were obligated to chug whatever it is they were drinking. This group was beginning to slur their words and I watched from a distance so as not to be drawn in.

"Who did John Kaye sing for?" was the question posed to Annie by her adversary Bobby.

There was a temporary silence in the group. Lots of eyes rolled back in deep thought as everyone tried to conjure a visual of John Kaye. But Annie just looked Bobby square in the eye and screamed "Steppenwolf!" as she threw her arms over her head and did a little celebratory dance at Bobby's expense. It was the first time I'd heard Annie offer anything more than a whisper and I wasn't sure if it was the alcohol or just the fact that she was having a great time.

After dinner, we all sat around and watched a beautiful September full moon rise majestically over the pond. By 7:30 it was completely dark; a sad reminder that summer had truly come to an end, if not officially, then just because it was the first day of September. The air, which had been warmer than usual during the day, was rapidly cooling as night fell.

Those who had to drive back to the city lingered long enough to sober up before saying their goodbyes and heading west. I waved to each as they drove away. Bobby and Catherine were talking to Annie when I came back onto the deck. They were the last three and showed no sign of being in a hurry to leave.

"Well, Mr. Cafara, that was a great way to end the summer." Catherine said.

"You couldn't have asked for a better day." Bobby added and took a long sip of his Sambuca.

Somehow, Annie sensed Bobby was my closest friend, or maybe she'd been told, but she could tell I was glad they were still here. What she didn't know was that the reason I was glad was because I wanted them to experience Annie. To see if they thought she was as terrific as I did. Weeks later, Catherine would confide she thought Annie was wonderful and would be perfect for me, if only she wasn't married. Catherine was always trying to terminate my bachelor status. I think she thought I was a bad influence on Bobby.

The four of us sat and talked for another round of drinks and by the time Catherine said it was time to leave, the moon had climbed directly over us. Catherine, the wiser of the two, seldom drank when she and her husband socialized because she knew she'd be the one driving home. Tonight was no exception.

"Come on lover boy, we have to get going. Your brother and his hateful wife are coming tomorrow. I need to get home and put out the crosses and garlic." Catherine didn't care for her sister-in-law.

I gave Catherine a kiss and Bobby a hug and their Mustang disappeared into the night.

"Let me help you clean up." Annie said. "You've got a lot of glasses and dishes to do."

"Let's sit and have a nightcap." I offered instead.

"I've got no place else to be and it's a short walk home, so that sounds good."

I poured two generous Sambucas, threw in a couple of coffee beans, and we headed for the deck. The pond was still and shimmered in the bright moonlight just enough to remind us it was there. We settled into a pair of side-by-side lounge chairs facing the pond, just at the edge of the deck. It was like being on the back of an ocean liner looking out on the vast expanse of blackness, except we were the only ones on this ship. I couldn't have imagined a more perfect setting.

After a few minutes of pleasant silence, Annie was the first to speak. "Your friends are really interesting; especially Atul. I can't believe how many places he's lived."

I was getting pretty mellow and could already feel the warm comfort of my second Sambuca. I began to get a little reflective. "I've been very lucky to have met so many wonderful and interesting people in my life," I sighed.

"How did you meet Atul?"

I had to think back a long time. It was a pleasant memory. "I hired Atul to open our London office back in 1995. I met him at a golf outing at Sunningdale, a place inappropriately named because it is almost never sunny and wasn't on the day of our outing. I can remember it was pouring buckets and yet these crazy Brits thought it was wonderful. Some of them played two rounds in the rain. I struck up a conversation with Atul while we were both waiting at the bar in the clubhouse. We hit it off right away. He ran a commercial real estate office in the heart of London and I needed someone to open ours. It all worked out and we've become great friends. Now he lives in the Village with Shioban and their son Max."

Annie asked me about how I wound up in London and about all the places I've visited. It seemed as though she wanted to know all about my life before coming to Southampton. I deliberately left out the details and pain surrounding my divorce and probably spent too much time talking about my two favorite subjects; my daughters, Kitty and Peggy. But Annie seemed enthralled by my stories and was genuinely interested in my relationship with the girls. It felt like she was trying to validate her belief that I was a decent guy.

Our conversation drifted from family to politics and back to family again. We touched on some of our more colorful neighbors, efforts to keep the pond clean by prohibiting commercial clamming in the summer, and how far away the moon really was, although it appeared to hang just over my leaky roof.

I refilled our glasses two more times and when I returned the third time with the almost empty bottle, Annie had moved to the hammock. Her fragile sundress was blowing in the gentle breeze as she lay on the sagging rope hammock and she looked beautiful. I was glad her husband was in Manhattan. I was glad I had her all to myself. But most of all, I was glad I'd met her. If we never became anything more than good friends, I was still glad I'd met her. She was a breath of fresh clean air in my life; a life that had become cynical and doubting. A life that had lost direction.

"No more for me." She said when she spotted the bottle in my hand.

"I'm afraid there's no more for anybody. We finished it and I think it was full when Bobby opened it."

"So does that officially make us drunk?" She asked as she tried to turn towards me.

"I think it does."

"Then come and lie next to me and tell me what that red and blue thing is in the sky." She pointed her empty glass skyward spilling the last few drops of Sambuca on her neck. Annie stretched out on the hammock in a way that most men would interpret as a "come hither" pose. I didn't need any encouragement but it just didn't seem right. She was a married woman and to be honest, in my whole life I've never helped anyone cheat on their husband.

Then, as I stood next to her delicate body stretched and inviting, I remembered the conversation from a few weeks ago with Bobby; the one where I questioned the need for a moral life if there is no God—no afterlife. If we're all just one genetic step up from Lassie, why not behave like animals? Do what satisfies our most basic needs. Take from the feast that which is set out before us. Revel in opportunity. Steal another man's money, food, house, or wife? If there is no God, why not do whatever makes us feel good?

Maybe it was just the alcohol, but Annie was inviting me in. It's not like I was banging on the door, forcing my way in. Her body language, hell, her very words, were an invitation. And I had just enough alcohol in me to push aside any ethical dilemmas that followed me here.

I knelt down in the sand next to the hammock and put my face just above hers. "What lights?" I said as softly as I could.

She seemed to ignore how close we were, or maybe it was just what she expected, but she kept here gaze on the moonlit sky and said, "Those blue and red lights, over there. About that far from the moon." She made a motion with her hand to indicate the distance.

It made no sense to me, perhaps because I wasn't looking at the sky. I was staring at her eyes. To be precise, I was staring into her eyes. I will remember, as long as I live, how sad her eyes seemed to me. It seemed as though there was a deep sadness inside her that was trying to get out through her eyes. And yet, they drew me closer.

"You're not looking at my colorful star." She now realized I was staring and only a few inches away.

I held my position but said nothing. Frankly, I had no idea what to say. But I'll tell you I was a little surprised when I felt Annie's hand on the back of my neck drawing me closer yet. Now she was looking into my eyes and if I saw sadness in her eyes, I was afraid what she'd find in mine. It felt as though she was looking into the back of my eyes, right into my head.

Then I felt her hand pulling me down onto her until our lips met. It was the most gentle kiss I've ever felt. Our lips barely touched at first, just lingered over each other for what seemed like minutes. I could taste the Sambuca on her lips.

"Kiss me, please." She whispered.

Well, what could I do? She did say please.

I kissed her. And then I kissed her again. And then I gently kissed her neck for a while on my way down to her chest. I kissed and softly licked whatever skin wasn't covered by her dress and I could taste the Sambuca she'd spilled on herself, and it tasted wonderful. She tasted wonderful.

Then I felt her other hand on my back, under my shirt. Her

fingers played a symphony in swirls of motion on my skin. I was still kneeling next to the hammock and I wasn't sure how to climb aboard without breaking contact with her. She solved my dilemma.

Annie twisted herself to the right until she was thrown from the hammock and directly onto me. We fell back together onto the sand and she climbed on top of me, her legs straddling my hips. When I looked up at her face there was something in the sky just to her right. It was the red and blue light she had been talking about.

"I see it." I said.

"What?" She replied in a voice that told me she was confused by my sudden interest in astronomy.

"I see the lights you were talking about. I think it might be the space station."

Every time I think back to that night I can't imagine why I cared about that blinking object in the sky; cared enough to interrupt what was rapidly becoming a very sensuous roll in the sand. To this day I don't get it. But we both seemed relieved to lay there gazing up at the unknown object rather than taking our passion to the next level. We lay in the sand for almost another hour, just watching the sky and holding each others hand. I think both of us were afraid to say anything for fear of it being precisely the wrong thing. The enormity of the darkness above us, with its vast emptiness, seemed the perfect silence.

And so, in a way, we listened to each other.

Fall 2008

CHAPTER TWENTY

Doc

Anyone who's ever lived on Long Island knows that the first real day of fall occurs, not when the calendar or some solar alignment with the equator would have it, but rather, the first real day of fall occurs on that first morning at summer's end when you wake up with cold, dry sheets. On this particular morning, I was freezing and grabbed the only blanket in the room, one my mom had crocheted many years ago. For me this marks the official end of summer; the end of the humid dog-days of August, and, when I was a kid, usually, the first week of school.

Today, it just seemed like a very cool morning with a crisp dry breeze blowing through the windows I'd left open the night before. A night that already seems like an eternity ago.

I walked Annie home around three in the morning after she woke me. We'd both fallen asleep in the sand next to the hammock. Ambien's got nothing on a triple Sambuca.

As we stumbled through the darkness towards her house, the thought occurred to me that we could come upon her husband. Even though she'd assured me John was not returning to Southampton until Wednesday, stranger things have happened. And in this case, that would have been really embarrassing for both of us. Maybe even more than just embarrassing.

Although every fiber of my body was ecstatic with the near giddy feeling that comes from realizing someone else in the universe cared about me, my head was throbbing like a jackhammer. Annie, on the other hand, seemed to awaken from the sand without missing a step; almost refreshed, and was in a chatty mood as we approached her drive way.

"Doc, you need to know that I've never done anything like this before." She paused. "I mean, I've never been with another man since I married John."

I didn't know what to say. Actually, my brain wasn't even doing a great job of processing the incoming sounds, let alone making any intelligent ones of my own.

Annie continued. "I probably shouldn't be telling you this, but then again, who else would I tell?" She looked down at the small blue driveway stones that crunched under our bare feet.

In the faint remnants of moonlight that try to hang on as dawn approaches, she looked more beautiful than at any other time I'd been with her. A bit of sand stuck to her neck, probably because of the spilled Sambuca. I gently brushed it off as I looked deeply into her eyes. She looked back into mine and everything seemed right.

It suddenly didn't matter to me that I was with a married woman. I was falling in love with her. It didn't feel wrong. It didn't feel dirty as I expected it might. It felt like we were the only two people in the world at that moment and everybody and everything were a thousand miles away. It felt so right. It felt wonderful.

Then she leaned forward and kissed me. Her kiss was as soft and gentle as her frail voice, and yet, it was a lustful invitation to so much more. So much I wanted to do.

And then, just as softly, she pulled away and again looked into my eyes.

"I know it sounds crazy but I think I'm in love with you." She turned away as she said it.

"And that's why I have to go."

"Go? Where? Where do you have to go?" I was shaken like a prize fighter who'd just been hit with a five punch combo.

"Back to New York. I need to go back to New York with John at the end of the week. Please don't ask me any more about it. I just need to go back and see how I feel."

I stood there with all the air punched out of me. Didn't she just say she loved me? Isn't that the best thing that could have happened? So why was she leaving?

"Annie, I love you."

"And I think I love you. But I am still married. At least for now, and that matters. It matters."

She let my hand drop from hers and turned to climb the steps to her door. When she reached the top she looked at me and said, "I'll talk to you again before I leave."

The door closed behind her before I could respond.

The woman I fell in love with just told me she loved me. Nothing she said after that mattered.

CHAPTER TWENTY-ONE

The Sea Grill restaurant sits one story below ground in the middle of Rockefeller Center in the heart of Manhattan. From its linen covered tables, diners can view the famous ice rink in winter and the flowered promenade in summer. Its menu, dominated by local seafood, attracts the city's rich and famous. On any weekday, celebrities from the nearby NBC studios can be seen enjoying lunch. Today, Ann Curry, Matt Lauer, and two of their producers are discussing an upcoming special over trays of sushi and maki rolls. At the table behind them, John Weaver and two of his partners were just finishing their lunch.

Herb Keller, the senior physician in their group practice had called the meeting. Although there were several other partners in the group, usually, John, Herb and Eric Kaplan, the third doctor at the table, made all the decisions for the partnership. It was these three men who'd started the practice fifteen years before. The younger doctors deferred to their experience and business savvy if not to their medical prowess.

Herb, a short, bald and stubby man in his sixties looked more like a plumber than a cardiologist. But he knew how to dress. His taste for Armani helped disguise his portly appearance and his Princeton education gave him command of the language in a way few plumbers could hope. Today he was using the latter to persuade his colleagues towards a financial opportunity he felt warranted the groups' attention.

"So just run this by me again Herb. How is it that we can write this off?" Eric wanted to know.

"It's just like any other equipment we buy for the practice. We can expense this over the expected working life of the machine, which, in this case, is eight years. That way, we spend the $640,000 today and can both expense it over eight years and depreciate it at the same time. Our accountant tells me this is what many LLC's do now. The IRS doesn't look twice because they have no idea what a SPECT does anyway. In a way, we're almost getting the new equipment for free." Herb waited for a response from his partners.

Both Herb's colleagues understood the need for maintaining the most modern equipment in their three offices. They just didn't want to go to their pockets again so soon after the MRI enhancements had been done. Being the senior partners also meant most capital improvements came out of their paychecks.

John needed more information. "So what will this cost us over the next few months if we don't finance it?"

Herb filled them in on the accountant's proposed plan which meant each senior partner would forgo about half their pay for the next three months and in return they would have the latest release of the single-proton emission computerized tomography (SPECT), a tool used for 3-D tissue analysis. From a business point of view, he knew it was gold. Each test done on the SPECT could be billed at over six thousand dollars and even if the insurance companies only reimbursed them the $3,500 they had committed to, the machine would pay for itself in less than two years.

"Jessie says we'd be crazy to finance it. So I say let's listen to our accountant and do it right." Herb was growing tired of the persuasive arguments he'd made over lunch and was now repeating.

"So we're agreed then. Let's get this done," Eric said. "And if I can't get by on thirty grand less each month, I know who to talk to."

Herb was so glad to have the conversation resolved, he let the comment go. But John couldn't.

"Eric, please tell me you haven't been into that little prick from Brooklyn again. He is not a guy you want to fuck with."

John knew that, much like himself, Eric liked to live well beyond his means and sometimes that meant temporary financing from Arnie Zucker. He knew he'd introduced Eric to the fruits of Mr. Zucker several months ago but thought it was a one-time event. Recently he found out that his partner was using Arnie to bankroll a couple of jumpers Eric bought for his wife, an avid, if not talented show jumper. Such horses, John knew, could cost hundreds of thousands.

"Hey John, we all don't have what you have. Some of us have to work for a living." Eric was referring to the commonly held misconception that John had access to his wife's money. Outwardly, it appeared that way to most. And that's just the way John wanted it.

The waiter came to bring Herb the check and return his credit card. As Herb paid for lunch, John shot back, "Eric, just be careful with this guy. He and his goons are serious. This isn't a game for these guys."

"Gee, thanks dad." Eric returned with mocked appreciation. "I've met the goonies. They're harmless. Besides, I've got to be one of Zucker's best customers. I always pay on time. The little fuck makes a fortune off me."

Herb finished his paperwork and looked up at Eric. "So why don't you just go to Citibank for Christ's sake?"

"Herb, you've seen my balance sheet. I've mortgaged everything I appear to own. Like most of America, it's all a house of mirrors and cards. It's all about image to my wife. If she can't have whatever she wants, when she wants it, well, things get ugly at the Kaplan house.

"You need to grow a pair and get control of your wife." John said.

"Again, easy for you to say."

"Yes," John said. "It is."

CHAPTER TWENTY-TWO

The sheer white curtains floated in front of the open windows overlooking the Peconic Bay. From her bed, Annie could see across the glistening bay to Mattituck and Southold. Although she'd awoken in this bed hundreds of times since her childhood, this morning was somehow different. It wasn't the bay, the landscape or the clear blue sky that were different. It was Annie herself.

It hurt to leave Doc standing in the driveway. She was torn between wanting him to stay the night, and running alone to the sanctuary of her childhood. In the end, she ran.

But not before pouring herself one more drink and sitting alone for hours on the rooftop deck from which her father used to say, *"you could see forever and even beyond forever"*. Annie, fortified with a blanket and a brandy, sat cross-legged on the deck thinking about Doc, her dad, her first husband Peter and her current husband, John, until the sun began to peak over the eastern treetops. She reflected on how, other than her sons, in her entire life only these four men had touched her heart.

She was emotionally mature enough to understand that she'd canonized her father and Peter only after their deaths, but could still feel the love and the warmth from both, long after they were gone. She understood too that the love she held for them would never fade. Not even after meeting John, did she love Peter any less. He was gone, but the love affair continued. And, if she was to be truly honest with herself, she

came to understand that John felt this too. That he was com-
peting for his wife's love with two ghosts.

And then there was Doc. She'd only met him a few weeks
ago but she saw something in his eyes; something peaceful yet
haunting. It was as if he could see her pain, the pain she'd
not spoken of. Yet somehow he seemed to understand, much
the same way her father always understood her when she was
frightened or worried about the boys. Doc was, in many ways,
very much like her father. He was gentle and kind. He was
funny, in a self deprecating way. And he cherished his daughters and his friends; all qualities she admired in her father.

Although she had a brutal headache she seemed to
remember telling Doc she loved him. Or did she say she thought
she loved him? Either way, she'd had too much to drink and
needed to explain to Doc that she may have been confused by
the circumstances. After all, how long had it been since John
had gently stroked a hair off her face and softly kissed her forehead? How long since he told her she was beautiful? How long
since they'd done anything together that didn't involve at least
twenty other people or somehow promote John's standing in
the community?

She may have been simply caught up in the moment just
because Doc treated her like any woman would want. Annie
tried to tell herself her feelings for Doc may be nothing more
than a misplaced desire for the kind of relationship she used to
have with Peter. Could it be that simple?

Or was she confusing her need to get away from John with
a desire for Doc? Shouldn't she really sort out the first before
pursuing the latter? She'd been working up the courage to
leave John for months now. It took so much conviction just to
talk to Frank Montague and to even mention the term divorce.
She agonized over just that for weeks.

Annie threw back three Tylenol with a glass of orange juice and tried to focus on the scene outside her kitchen window. On the beach she could see several summer people preparing themselves for the end of summer. It happened every Labor Day. The city people who only rented for the season had to make the mass migration back to Manhattan on Labor Day. Beach chairs needed folding, inflatables needed deflating, and children's' sand toys needed to be gathered and stowed for the ride back west.

At least this mornings' weather was bright and sunny. Too often, such packing had to be done in the first cold rain of the new season. Annie could recall many such miserable mornings when the boys were young and needed to be back in the city for school the day after Labor Day. She and Peter would round up all the toys, bikes, and tennis rackets while her dad kept the twins occupied in the house. Even memories as simple as these, could bring her to tears when she was lonely for Peter and her father.

Her headache wasn't yielding to the Tylenol this morning. Actually, she thought about how many mornings the past week had started much the same; a blinding pain behind her eyes and a touch of nausea that subsided after a bowl of Cheerios. She hadn't thought much about it because the two or three days before her period were usually filled with unpleasant surprises.

And she wasn't a person who quickly ran to the medicine cabinet. In fact, the only pills Annie ever took were a daily dose of Synthroid for her underactive thyroid and an occasional Tylenol.

As she sat at her kitchen table waiting for the pounding in her head to subside, her thoughts drifted back to Doc and the previous evening. Yes, she loved having him lick the alcohol off her neck and chest. Yes, she loved lying with him in the sand and holding him and looking up at the stars slowly rotating towards the west. Yes, she loved feeling so important to someone so wonderful. She loved it all, but did she love him? Or had it just been so long since she felt this way?

She wasn't sure. What she was sure about was that she had to get away from Doc and back to the city. If there was to be any relationship with Doc, first she had to confront her demons. She needed to be sure that her decision to leave John wasn't being propelled by her feelings for another man. She needed to be certain that she was about to do the one thing she'd dreaded for only the right reason. And the only way to do that was to go back to New York and confront John.

The thought alone was painful. She knew John would react badly. Even more troublesome was the thought of telling her sons that she was leaving John after just three years. To Annie, this meant she'd failed. For her, divorce was always synonymous with failure, and she didn't want to fail in front of her sons. She was afraid they would see her actions as an easy way out of a bad situation. And it was anything but that. Although the boys never really liked John, they tolerated him for her sake. Annie had never told them about the attacks. She couldn't.

And then there would be the practical issue of where to live after letting John know she was leaving. She couldn't stay with him a single day after he found out. She was afraid to.

Chapter Twenty-Three

The Tropicana isn't the newest or nicest casino in Atlantic City. In fact, it's one of the original hotels built along the boardwalk and had become somewhat run down and dated. But it was one of John Weaver's favorite places to play cash games of no limit Texas Hold-em. And the Tropicana was very good about flying their high rollers down from New York even if it was just for an overnight.

John and Ben Stockhouse, one of his poker buddies from the Wednesday night games, had flown down in the Tropicana helicopter along with several other players from Manhattan. Once they got to the casino, John and Ben went separate ways. In fact, John hadn't seen Ben since midnight, about the same time he had to dig into his jacket pocket for another stack of hundreds. He'd lost over fifty thousand dollars in less than three hours but came back a bit in the last two hands.

His game of choice was a private game, arranged by the casino to accommodate cash players who didn't flinch at the $250-$500 blinds. Usually there were two such tables in a private room near the back of the hotel. The Tropicana was happy to provide the room, food, alcohol and a dealer. After all, they took a handsome cut of every pot for their trouble and to provide security. There was a lot of cash in the room.

Tonight, only one table was being used and the six players had thrown their jackets and briefcases on the chairs folded over the empty table nearby. The air was getting stale from the cigarette smoke and over-reaching testosterone. No one had entered or left the room in over an hour, not even a barmaid.

John glanced at his watch as the dealer started a new game: 4:25 AM. He'd been playing about five hours and had won two big pots, both with pocket pairs. He had about thirty thousand dollars in chips stacked neatly in front of him, but he was still low man in the table chip count.

He looked at the faces around the table; three middle-aged Asian men, a black guy who looked like he couldn't afford to buy lunch but who'd come to the table with a hundred thousand in hundred dollar bills, and a white kid who couldn't have been more than twenty-five who started some sort of computer company that booked business travel. He knew some of them from previous nights at previous tables. What he didn't know was that all of them came to the table with bigger bankrolls than he did.

What they didn't know about John was that the sixty-five thousand dollars he brought to the game had been borrowed from Arnie Zucker the previous afternoon.

John limped in on the next hand before the flop then took one bluffing a flush all the way to the river, the last card dealt. It was getting late and he was tired. He decided to cash in at five and grab a few hours sleep before jumping on the noon chopper that had already been arranged. At this point he would have been happy to steal a few more medium pots and head back to New York with most of Arnie's money back safely in his jacket.

The dealer, an attractive young brunette who claimed to be in law school, dealt a new hand. John looked as his cards only after they'd both slid to his end of the table. A jack and queen, both hearts. No one seemed too enthused about their hands and the ante stayed at the big blind so John hung around for the flop. The dealer flopped the three of spades, queen of spades and jack of diamonds. John's heart jumped just enough but not so much that anyone noticed. The bet was to him.

"Twenty-five hundred," he said trying to sound disinterested. Actually, he was very interested. His two high pairs were strong and he was hoping someone at the table would take the bait.

The black dude folded but the computer geek and two of the Asians saw his bet. The third Asian, a short guy named Eddie, looked at John a long time. He studied the cards lying in the center of the table then ran his tongue over his drying lips.

"Let's see if you're full of shit again doc." He counted out two stacks of black, thousand—dollar chips. "Make it eight thousand."

John tried not to reveal his pleasure. He assumed Eddie was holding either a queen or a jack, giving him a decent pair. He knew the odds of him having two pair as well, were low. If Eddie had either a pair of queens or a pair of jacks, John was going to make this very expensive for him. And he wanted to do it right away, before more cards came out that could muddy the waters. He needed to act now and go big. But he didn't want to drive Eddie out. He just wanted to take a little more of his money.

John pretended to be concerned about the bet and played with his chips while looking around the table. The other Asians and the geek seemed apathetic but that's what you're supposed to do.

"Your eight," he said as he pushed eight black chips into the center, "And ten more." John made a point of dropping the chips so they splattered over the flop cards. His intention was to drive out the other players and go one-on-one with Eddie.

The two Asians folded and tossed their cards towards the dealer. But the geek hesitated. He stared at his hole cards then began to clean his fingernails with the edge of one of his cards. "Call," he said as he counted out eighteen thousand in clay spheres and pushed them in.

This was an unexpected treat for John. He hoped to take Eddie for one more decent bet, but now he had two lambs to toy with before the slaughter. And that meant a lot more chips, especially if the pasty geek had a pair as well. He did some quick math in his head and figured that after this pot he'd be up about forty grand.

Now it was Eddie's turn to play. With no emotion at all he said, "Call. And I still think you're full of shit."

With that, the dealer turned another card...the three of hearts. That changed everything, and John silently cursed himself for not betting more to drive out anyone hanging around just to see the last two cards. Now, there were other permutations to consider. If either Eddie or the geek had a three underneath, their three threes would be the best hand. Suddenly the testosterone shifted. But to whom? It wasn't immediately apparent from the players' faces.

It was up to John to start the betting and he knew he had to make an important choice. Either he would bet big, probably all his remaining chips, in an attempt to convince the others he had set a trap and was now ready to spring; or he would check and see who had the nuts.

He glanced at each player, slowly studying their hands, their eyes and their lips. Lip movement sometimes gave away concern, a sign of weakness. But if he was going to make the big bet he had to do it quickly or it would lose its definitive statement.

"I'll check to the raiser," he said, referring to Eddie's last raise.

Eddie wasted no time bringing out the big guns. "How much have you got there?" He looked at John's stack and tried to calculate how many chips he held. This could be either just a scare tactic or the real deal. In this case he meant it, so, without expending too much effort, John estimated he had about thirty-five thousand in front of him.

"Looks like about thirty-five." Then he added, "Have you got the nuts?"

"Maybe not, but I do have the cards. Let's make it thirty-five thousand." Eddie carefully counted out seven stacks of five thousand each and pushed them just a few inches in front of his position. It left him with only thirty thousand more. He looked at the geek. "Up to you young fella. Have things gotten any better for you?"

"Call." It was all the geek said and it was sufficient. Now all eyes turned to John.

He knew he had to see it through. It would take trips to beat his hand and he was counting on both players having only a pair; two pair at best, but that would still guarantee him a chopped pot—an even split between the two players who might both have a pair of jacks and a pair of queens. It was either going to be the best poker night of his life or one more really bad one.

"Call," he heard himself saying even before he was sure it was the prudent move. He counted out the chips and found that he had twelve hundred dollars left. Inconsequential at this point.

"Pot's right," said the dealer. She knocked her knuckles on the table and said, "Good luck gentlemen." And then she turned over the last card, the river card, the most beautiful card John had ever seen. As it fell into place at the end of the line of five common cards, John could see it was a picture card even before it hit the felt. The queen of clubs! John had a full house; three queens and two jacks. Even if one of the other players had a pair of jacks underneath, giving them a full house with jacks over queens, John's was the better hand.

He tried to be cool. It was almost impossible even for a seasoned player. He was about to pull in over one hundred and fifty thousand dollars. And it could be more if these two assholes weren't done betting.

"Well, I've gone this far." He picked up the three chips he had left in front of him and tossed them onto the impressive pile. "Twelve hundred. And then I'm going home."

Because the bet, relative to the size of the accumulated pot, was insignificant, and because he wasn't about to let John walk away without showing his cards, Eddie threw in his twelve hundred.

"Call," he said with a controlled contempt. Then he looked toward the geek.

The geek made no move toward his chip stack. His right hand was resting on his down cards and his left was in his lap. "Somebody's got to show me two more ladies or I'm taking your money." As he said the words, he turned his cards...a pair of threes.

John had been beaten by four threes. He felt as if someone had kicked him in the chest. He couldn't suck in enough air to even curse. He was breathless and speechless. He stood and glared at the kid.

And he owed Arnie Zucker another sixty-five thousand.

CHAPTER TWENTY-FOUR

Doc

Annie had promised to talk to me before leaving but I hadn't seen her all week. I made a point of jogging each day around the same time she was usually on the road, but I never saw her. I even took a couple of long walks along the beach, passing in front of her house like a love-sick school boy, but she was nowhere to be seen. In fact, her car hadn't moved from its usual spot in two days.

Ironically, I'm not sure what I would have said even if I did see her. I mean, she was right. She's a married woman and I have no right to expect anything from her. Even if she was as unhappy in her marriage as I thought, or hoped, Annie was the kind of person who would deal with that first and not the sort to be blinded by passion. She would make sure one relationship was over before even thinking about starting another one.

So what could I expect? Nothing really, I just wanted to see her again before she left for the city. I just wanted to smell her one more time and hear the soft whisper she called a voice. Like that love-sick school boy, I just wanted to be near her.

Since I couldn't find her by running the neighborhood or by walking the beach, I decided to bury myself in work. I still had two major leaks to deal with in my roof so I headed for the local hardware store, a quaint place right in the middle of Main Street called Herricks Hardware. The main street in the village of Southampton is actually called Main Street and, to me, it is the quintessential town hub. In addition to Brooks

Brothers, Saks, London Jewels & Vilroy & Boch, the street has been the home to many authentic local merchants for as long as anyone I know can remember. Next to Brooks Brothers is the best little bookstore you'll ever need. Across from Saks is a bakery, run by an octogenarian named Tessie, whose oatmeal cookies should be illegal.

There are dozens of great places to eat that cater to both the summer people and the year-round locals with the same politeness and interesting food. There are places to buy diamond rings worthy of a sultan's wife and places that make fantastic pizza and homemade cheeses. What you won't find on Main Street is any franchised fast food. Not a golden arch or a KFC in sight.

I'm not sure why, but on Main Street everyone parks diagonally. Maybe it's a better way to show off your Bentley or Rolls, if you have one. To me and my Jeep, it's a pain in the ass. But today being the first Thursday after Labor Day, town was empty and I found a spot right in front of Herricks. I picked up a roll of tar paper, a small bundle of shingles, and some roofing nails and was back at Cold Spring Pond before lunch, which is good because there are too many temptations in town at lunchtime.

I spent most of Thursday afternoon on my roof trying to figure out where the rain was getting in. Before starting, I checked the weather forecast: clear skies until the weekend, then a significant storm making its way up the east coast was due to bring in a lot of wind and rain. I needed to get this done today. So I peeled away a large swath of shingles just under the living room skylight. The plywood was damp but not yet rotten so I decided to take the easy way out and patch with new tar paper and shingles. If nothing else, the coming storm would tell me if my efforts were valid.

Unfortunately though, I saw nothing on the roof that

indicated the location of the remaining leak. All the flashings looked good. The shingles were a little worn but showed no sign of leakage. I'd have to wait and observe from inside when the weekend rains arrived.

Before gathering my tools and descending the ladder, I glanced towards the bay. From my rooftop I could see over most of the other homes, even the large, bay-front houses, all the way to the bay and across to the North Fork. It was quite a view. I'd be lying if I said I wasn't looking in the direction of Annie's house, and I'd be lying if I said I wasn't disappointed to notice her car wasn't in her driveway. It was gone.

I sat on the peak of my roof and wondered. I wondered how she could leave without even a good-bye. Had our night together meant so much more to me than it had to her? I knew how I felt but maybe she just had too much to drink and was now too embarrassed to face me. Maybe she just saw it as a terrible indiscretion; one that should be quickly and quietly forgotten. Maybe she just wanted to get back to her life the way it was before I moved out here.

But, no. She told me she loved me, hadn't she? Or was that just the after effects of the alcohol too?

And here's the funny thing. Sitting there on my roof, feeling pretty alone and miserable, the first thing I did was what I always used to do when I was in trouble. I started to talk to God. I wanted to ask him for advice. I needed to ask for help; to let someone know how I felt and what I hoped would happen.

But I wasn't three words into my divine soliloquy, when I realized he and I were no longer on speaking terms. Or, more to the point, I was reminded that I had turned my back on his existence, and if I denied he existed, how could I find comfort in speaking to him? It almost felt hypocritical. I mean, if I no longer believed in God then I couldn't have it both ways.

I couldn't deny his existence but talk to my former, now non-existent, friend just because I used to.

If I was learning one thing about atheism, it was that those of us without faith are lonely. I wanted so much to believe, not because it made sense to me but because I needed my old friend back. He was always my confidant. He was always there when I was in trouble. Now I really felt alone. Totally alone.

I stared out at the pond from my lofty perch and tried to think of a way to replace the relationship I missed so much. I needed to believe in something. It was always part of who I am. After all, it isn't me who changed. I just stopped believing. I didn't change. But then, who did?

My self-reflection was broken by the sound of car tires on my driveway pebbles. I turned and almost lost my balance. Even though I was sitting, I was sitting on the roof peak and when I turned to see who was in my driveway, I slipped backwards.

Then I heard it; the sound so sweet I wanted to fly off the roof. Annie was calling my name.

"Doc. Are you up there?" I guess she spotted the ladder.

I struggled to regain my balance and my composure. "Up here."

By the time I got to my feet and headed toward the top of the ladder I heard Annie's footsteps on the bottom rungs. She was climbing my ladder. When her face cleared the roofline, I offered her my hand and helped her step from the ladder onto the roof.

"How's the leak situation?"

"I think I got one. One to go, but I'll have to wait until the next rain to figure out where it's coming in."

"Wow, you can really see a long way from up here." Annie said as she straightened and stood at the peak, gazing at the pond and all the surrounding rooftops.

I wasn't sure what to say. After all, she'd obviously been avoiding me for the last three days. Shouldn't I expect some form of explanation? And what the hell was she doing up here on my roof?

"Yeah, it's amazing how much more you can see from up here than from my bedroom window." That just didn't come out right.

I decided I should break the ice and just say what I hoped we were both thinking about a lot during our three day hiatus. "Look, Annie, I'm sorry for Sunday night. I never should have…"

She cut me off in mid sentence. "There's no need to apologize. I'm fifty-one years old and can look out for myself. I had a little too much to drink but I don't have any regrets. I am responsible for my actions. No one else." She paused for a moment and looked down at her sneakers. "Doc, I think I'm falling in love with you, and whether you feel the same way or not, I've thought about this a lot over the last few days."

Did she say something after, *"Doc, I think I'm falling in love with you?"* Because if she did, I didn't hear it. The sound of those nine beautiful words was drifting through my head and nothing else was getting in. I didn't want to speak. I wanted to listen to her telling me she loved me again and again.

"Ever since Sunday night, or I guess it was Monday morning, I haven't been able to think of much else. There's so much I want to say. So much I want to tell you. I'm feeling things I haven't felt in…" she paused quietly, then continued, "well, in a long time. You've awoken something in me. That's the best way I can describe it."

This was all sounding good so I continued to keep my mouth shut.

"I loved the way you kissed me. It was so…so gentle. I loved the way you tried to look after me with your guests and introduced me to your friends. I can tell you have some great friends and that speaks a lot about who you are. And I loved the way you held me when we were lying in the sand."

We were standing face to face on the ridge of my roof, about thirty feet in the air. Annie must have realized how ridiculous this was and said, "Can we sit?"

"Sure." And we both sat on the ridge facing the pond.

She took a long breath and continued.

"But I've never been unfaithful to John, and I can't start now."

What happened to "I love you Doc?"

"Although we haven't spoken about it directly, and you're too much of a nice person to ask me, I'm sure you've been able to figure out that I am not happy in my relationship with my husband. I haven't been in a long time. In fact, it's probably just the fear of being totally alone that's kept me with him this long. Ever since the boys went off to college, and then my dad dying, well, I've been really lonely. I guess John fills that void for me. Or maybe I'm just afraid. I don't know."

I decided it was time to say something. I touched her chin and said, "Hey, you don't have to have all the answers. It's OK. I get really lonely too. Everybody does sometimes." I thought about my recent feelings of loneliness brought about by my new religion—that being none.

She was starting to cry, just a little. Annie cried as softly as she spoke.

"I know. I've just been so confused. I think about why I married John and I can't come up with any good reasons. The best I can do is that maybe I just needed to be with someone. You know, so you feel like you're a part of something. My father was sick and we knew he didn't have long. I guess maybe I was more scared of the future, a life without any of the men in my life, than anything else. Peter had only been gone about three years."

"And you didn't want to be alone. That makes sense to

me." I tried to say something supportive although I'm not sure I believed what was coming out of my mouth. I put my arm around her and nudged a little closer to her on the hot shingles.

"Well, I guess it really doesn't matter now. I just want to end things with John."

The look on her face told me she was as surprised by the words as I was. Perhaps she hadn't fully thought this through and it just slipped out. It seemed like she regretted the statement already, but, at the same time, was relieved that she'd finally said it aloud.

"All I know for sure is that I need to go back to Manhattan and work something out with John. The sooner the better. And once I tell him, one of us will have to move out because…well, one of us will just have to move." The crying had stopped and she was wiping her eyes with the back of her sweater sleeve.

I thought about saying something really stupid like, *You could stay with me*. Fortunately, I didn't because the next words out of her mouth caught me off guard.

"Doc, I need to go back to the city to get away from you." She looked me right in the eyes for that one.

"I don't understand."

"I can't make rational decisions about my marriage because of you. I have to do it because I'm in a lousy marriage, not because of someone else. You only complicate things. I'm sorry, but I think you can understand that."

We sat on my rooftop for another forty-five minutes just talking. Actually, Annie did most of the talking. I think it was somehow cathartic for her. I was trying to think of things to say to convince her that seeing me while she sorted out her life might actually be helpful. But, in the end, I knew she was right. My feelings for her, and hers for me, would only confuse the real issue; she first needed to get away from John. And if that took a few months, well, I'll still feel the same way.

I hoped she would too.

I helped her down the ladder and we said good bye at her car. She agreed to call me as soon as she split with John but she didn't know if that would be a few days or a few weeks. I gave her my email address and asked her to email me if she ever needed to "talk" without really talking.

Annie gave me a kiss on the cheek then drove out of my life. At the time, I didn't know if I'd ever see her again.

CHAPTER TWENTY-FIVE

As she opened the front door to their apartment, Annie resisted the temptation to turn and run back to Southampton. She'd thought about it all the way back to Manhattan. That would be the easy way out of this. Instead, she opened the door.

She and John had shared this apartment since they were married. Her sons, Frank and Nick, had never lived with them. Their feelings about their stepfather were never a secret and John was just as glad they wanted no part of him. He wanted no part of their lives either. Although Annie insisted a bedroom be dedicated to each, neither had ever slept at the posh Fifth Avenue address. Instead, on breaks from college, they rented a small loft together just north of Little Italy.

So this apartment really was 'home' for Annie and John. In their three years of marriage they'd hosted several lavish parties here, usually for associates of John, but once for the museum group Annie supported. And this was where they had a luncheon for friends and family the day Annie buried her beloved father Burt. But other than that, all they really did here was eat and sleep. It certainly wasn't a place of love. It was just a place to live.

Or were all these feelings just coming out now because Annie had finally made up her mind to leave? Did she always feel so apathetic about the place she lived? She didn't think so. In the beginning she must have been excited to be here, to share a home with her husband. Or was she? She just couldn't remember feeling happy here.

Looking out the oversized living room window at the Thursday traffic below, she thought about the task in front of her. Telling John that she was leaving would be the most difficult thing she'd ever have to do. Not because she thought he'd be hurt by the abandonment, but because she wasn't sure how he'd react. To be fair, he'd only hit her a few times and always after drinking, but this was sure to be different.

On the other hand, maybe he felt the same way. She had suspected his infidelity for some time. Perhaps John would be just as glad to be done with a loveless marriage. Maybe he had someone he'd rather be with too.

In any event, Annie had decided, on the drive back to Manhattan, that she would talk to John on Sunday afternoon. First she needed to tell her sons about her decision. She planned to call both of them in the morning. She also needed to line up temporary living arrangements. It would be impossible to stay with John after she told him. She hoped to book a small suite at the Essex House, then look for a modest apartment on the west side of town for a longer term solution. Eventually maybe she'd buy something for herself and the boys. And she always had the house in Southampton. Her father had been careful to put that in a trust for the boys so it was always seen as Annie's place; probably another reason John never felt comfortable there.

Her plan was to book a place on Friday and move some things out on Saturday while John was at work. She'd pick up some of the household necessities at Crate and Barrel: sheets, dishes, glasses, towels, etc. John would freak if she ever took things from their apartment. She didn't need to give him one more reason to go nuts.

She would suggest an afternoon walk in the park. Earlier in their relationship, this wouldn't have seemed strange. They walked in Central Park all the time, especially in the fall when the colors were spectacular. But lately, the only times they'd walk together were when John was trying to 'walk-off' a migraine and those weren't pleasant times.

Annie wanted the open, public space as the forum for her discussion with John because she felt safer. Somehow, being surrounded by a city full of passing strangers gave her a comfort level she wouldn't have in the privacy of their apartment.

She planned to tell him she wasn't happy; that she resented the physical abuse and wanted to find love again, and that she thought they both deserved to be happy. She'd tell him she would move out and had already booked a place for the short-term. She would make it as painless a process as possible. Actually, as she thought about it, she couldn't think of a single way John's day-to-day life would really change.

And they were both aware that they'd planned for this day even before they were married. Their pre-nup was very clear about the financial consequences of divorce. Each party would exit the marriage with exactly the assets they entered it. In John's case that meant his practice, his interest in his partnerships, his apartment, and his bank accounts remained his. And he retained all his club memberships and the two cars registered in his name. Likewise, Annie's assets, although significant, remained Annie's and subject to the provisions of the arcane trusts established for her by her former husband and father.

So, unlike divorce for many couples, theirs would be relatively uneventful financially. The only thing Annie could foresee a problem over was her dad's boat; a toy that John cherished and Annie had seldom seen since her father's death. John would want the boat, and although he had no legal claim to it, he might make a stink about it just to have something to torture her with. She'd already decided if it came to that, he could have it.

Then there was the issue of Doc. She promised to call him when she was ready but when would that be and what would she say? She wanted to make all decisions irrespective of Doc. He shouldn't cloud her thinking or impact her decisions about her future. If, later on, something came of it, something wonderful, well, that would be great. But for now, she was focused on herself and ending the miserable relationship she was already in.

Yet, she missed him already. She missed his tender touch, a touch she wanted to feel more of and in deeper places. He had awakened feelings in her that had been dormant since Peter: feelings she should have had for John but that never had a chance to grow because of his brutality. For the first time in many years, she found herself fantasizing about a man; one she barely knew but felt she knew so well.

But before any of this—before the apartment hunting, or shopping, or moving out, or talking with John or calling Doc, or anything—she had to see Franklin Montague.

Chapter Twenty-Six

The alarm on her clock radio blared at 6:30 AM. Annie rolled over and slammed the sleep button. She'd planned to spend a busy day looking for an apartment, but John called her cell phone the previous evening and told her he was taking a late flight to Atlantic City with Ben Stockhouse. He wouldn't be back in New York until Monday morning and then had to go straight to work. He promised to be home Monday night and to take her to dinner.

So the urgency to move out was put off for a few days. Since she wouldn't see John until Monday night, she decided to wait until Monday to check in at the Essex House. She now wasn't sure when she could have the conversation she dreaded. She didn't want to have it in a restaurant and certainly not in their apartment. It would have to wait. In a way, she was relieved. At least she had more time now to sort out her next steps.

She made an appointment to see her family lawyer and old friend, Franklin Montague latter that afternoon. He insisted on taking her to lunch so they met at Tresta's, a trendy but quiet place on Second Avenue, not too far from Annie's apartment. They settled into a booth near the back of the small dining room and Annie got straight to the point.

"Frank, I need to leave John."

The sage advisor didn't seem surprised. He knew about Burt's apprehensions. Annie had told him how her sons stayed away because of John. And then there was Annie's question about the boys' trusts a few weeks ago when she'd come to see him. She wanted to be sure the trusts were secure in the event of a divorce, which they were.

"Annie, I am so sorry, but not too surprised. You haven't seemed happy since...well since Burt passed away."

Over lunch they discussed Annie's plans for a quick separation, her exit from the apartment, and the reason she feared staying there. Franklin was shocked at the news that his goddaughter had been subject to such violence and that she kept it to herself for so long.

"Normally, I would never advise someone to leave the home. You could later be accused of abandoning the marriage. But under these circumstances, I think you're right to get your own place immediately. You have to get out of there."

Franklin reminded Annie about her pre-nup and how prudent it was to have such a document. "Not only are you both protected, but because you have no children from the marriage, it leaves just about nothing to argue over." Then he added, "Do you have any bank accounts or brokerage accounts in common? I mean accounts that are in both your names?"

Annie nodded. "Just one checking account at Citibank. We use that for day-to-day living expenses. That's where the monthly interest payments from my trust funds get directly deposited."

"OK, after lunch, stop at the bank, open a new account in your name only and have all future direct deposits go there." Franklin was making a list of things he wanted Annie to do and handed her the piece of paper on which he'd been writing. "I want you to check with your credit card companies to be sure John's not on your cards and go through your papers to make sure you've never co-signed anything with him."

Annie was glad she had Franklin. Since her father's death, and even before, he was like a second father to her. She always found comfort in his eyes and in his thoroughness.

"Thanks Frank. As always, you make everything right."

"Don't kid yourself honey. You're in for a rough couple of weeks. The little I know of John tells me he will try to make things difficult for you. Don't let him. You owe him nothing except honest answers to his questions about the marriage and any assets you have in common. Leave all other conversations to me."

His concern caused him to make one last suggestion. "Annie, I know this has been on your mind for some time and it's obviously taken a toll on you. You look really tired. Make sure you take care of yourself. You look like you've lost some weight since I saw you in August. Make sure you're eating."

She appreciated the fatherly concern and smiled. "Thanks. I have been really tired the last few weeks. This has been on my mind for almost a year now and I guess it's just catching up with me."

When they stepped out into the cool afternoon sunlight they embraced and Annie hung on to Franklin for just an extra moment. "You're a good friend Frank."

CHAPTER TWENTY-SEVEN

After her lunch with Franklin, Annie went to Citibank and made the changes he'd suggested. She then took a cab down to Saks and picked up a bottle of her usual perfume, the one Doc commented about. Saks was the only place she knew that carried Le Vainqueur by Rance, and she was just about out. She crossed Fifth Avenue and picked up a paperback she'd been meaning to read at Barnes and Noble.

It was a beautiful day and Annie decided to walk back uptown. She hadn't been doing much running lately and felt a little guilty about that. But, as she told Franklin at lunch, she'd been unusually tired the last two weeks and, although running usually helped clear her head, she just hadn't felt up to it. Even after the nineteen block walk to her apartment, she was considerably fatigued.

Back in her apartment, Annie looked through all her documents and couldn't find anything she and John had co-signed. That didn't surprise her. They'd done so little together the past few years.

She was determined to take her mind off her marriage so Annie made herself a pot of green tea, settled into her favorite chair and began to lose herself in the pages of her new paperback. The weekend storm everyone was expecting arrived just about on schedule, and rain beat against the window next to her comfortable warm chair. By the time her tea was cold, she'd read ninety pages and the world outside her window had gone dark.

Annie was conscious of her loneliness but tried to escape into her book. It worked for a while but by the time she got up to make something for dinner, she was seeing Doc's face in just about everything in her apartment. She missed him terribly. But she wasn't sure if she missed Doc or if she just missed being loved. The two were closely linked, but could be very different.

And she missed not just love, but making love. The cold loneliness of her apartment was a chilling reminder of how long it had been since she could even remember making love. The brutal and one-sided assaults from John were, well, assaults. Certainly nothing like the tender love-making she enjoyed with her first husband. Her skin yearned for the gentle touch of a man.

She was wearing a comfortable old pair of flannel sweat pants. The soft grey cotton fell loosely around her thin legs and she pulled an afghan around her shoulders to ward off the chill. Again her thoughts turned to Doc as she settled back in the plush chair. She wondered what he was doing. She wanted to call him but knew she shouldn't; that it wouldn't be fair to either of them.

Yet, under the blanket she ran her hand along the inside of her thigh, stroking it softly, like a lover might. She closed her eyes and thought about the night she and Doc watched the stars from under his hammock. She imagined him stroking her leg slowly, with innocent swirling motions so as not to seem too forward. At least not until she responded by spreading her legs just a bit, which she would. Then his hand would slow even more and linger on the inside of her thigh just long enough to send a shiver through her.

In the blue twilight of her room Annie found, for the first time in years, the safe feeling she used to know. It was warm and deep and soft. She found herself moaning quietly as she surrendered to the fantasy.

CHAPTER TWENTY-EIGHT

"Gee Dad, sometimes you're such a dork."
"It's not that simple Kitty." Doc defended himself to his daughter. "It's complicated."

"What's so complicated? You just spent thirty minutes telling me you met an unforgettable; that was the word you used, unforgettable woman. And now you won't tell her how you feel. You've done this before you know. Remember, about a year after you and mom split, you were dating that teacher from New Jersey. What was her name?"

"Wendy."

"Right, Wendy. Same thing. You started to get close and then just didn't take it to the next step or even try to see if there was a next step."

He could hear the frustration in his daughter's voice. They'd been through this before and he knew she wasn't entirely wrong.

"This is different Kit. Very different."

"It doesn't sound so different from this side dad." Her voice softened. "Why can't you tell Annie how you feel?" What's the downside, other than the possibility of getting your ego shaken?"

From the moment he dialed her number, he knew the conversation would go this way. Although he always looked forward to their Friday afternoon calls, Doc sometimes didn't know how to assure Kitty she couldn't protect him from Tucson. She always tried. Of his two daughters, Kitty was the more outspoken and protective of her father. And she desperately wanted him to be happy. To her, that meant married again.

Although he wasn't sure why, he didn't want to tell her Annie was married. The idea of telling your daughter you're hot for another man's wife, a neighbor no less, just didn't seem consistent with the values he'd hoped she'd taken west with her when she left for college. He wanted her to think he was better than that.

He thought about all the other things he hadn't told his daughters.

"I told you Kit, she's gone back to New York anyway. It's out of my hands."

"What kind of a lame answer is that? Don't do this Dad. You're using the excuse that it's no longer in your control to justify your lack of action. "Call her. Or, better yet, go into the city and surprise her."

Doc thought about how impractical that would be. "I can't do that sweetie."

"Why not? Why can't you jump in that crappy Jeep and drive into the city and sweep her off her feet? Take her to one of your good places, Il Cortile or maybe Po's. Both of those places are really romantic. Come on Dad, you can do this." Her voice was filled with a daughter's love.

"Look honey, I'm sorry I even told you about Annie now. I should have waited until things sorted themselves out." He tried to change the conversation. "So what's up with you and the med student? Last time we spoke, you said you were on date number three."

"Dad, you're avoiding the subject."

"Just trying to let you know I don't want to discuss it anymore." He said with some contrition.

"Dad, I've never heard you say you thought you loved anyone before. Not since mom. When you were describing Annie to me you sounded so happy. I could feel it through the phone. She sounds wonderful. Please don't walk away without finding out. I want you to be happy."

"I know sweetie. I know. Just give me a little more time."

"Dad you're fifty-five years old. I don't want to have to worry about you forever from three thousand miles away. I do. I worry about you, especially now that you've moved out to the boondocks."

"Southampton is not the boondocks. We actually have running water and flush toilets." As he said the words he looked out at the beautiful pond twinkling in the late afternoon sunlight. "You'd actually like it out here. It's really pretty."

"Dad," she said with a tone of exasperation. "People don't go to the Hamptons because it's pretty. They go for the action, the nightlife and the celebrities; none of which, I should remind you, you're interested in. And what are you going to do all winter? I've seen the pictures of your shack. It doesn't even look like it's insulated. It's going to get mighty cold out there in January."

"I told you. I want to use the time for my photography and for some reflection." He realized he hadn't yet said anything to his daughters about his recent conversion to atheism. That was not a conversation he looked forward to.

Kitty asked him to hold for a second while she answered her call waiting. When she came back on the line she said, "Look Dad, I've got to meet Billy in a few minutes so I'd better get going. But please promise me you'll talk to Annie before our call next week. You really should."

"OK, I promise to talk to her before we speak again. I'll fill you in then."

"Great. I love you Dad."

"I love you too honey. Have a good week."

Doc had no intentions of calling Annie in the next week. But he was hoping she'd call him.

CHAPTER TWENTY-NINE

John Weaver's luck at the poker table wasn't getting any better. He'd been playing three hours and was down almost ten grand. He hadn't slept since he left New York the night before. The other players at his table, all women, were hitting some brutal long-shots on the river and John was about to call it a night.

That's when he peeked at his cards and saw the pair of tens. He decided to play one last hand, then get some sleep. Miranda had accompanied him on this trip and was waiting for him in their room. She'd never been to Atlantic City, and was happy to travel with John for the long weekend. They'd agreed on a fixed price for the three day engagement and he knew she'd be comfortably tipsy after three hours alone with the mini bar.

The woman to his left started the betting with four ten dollar chips, twice the big blind. Three of the other ladies folded, then the blond from Delaware raised to a hundred dollars. John saw the bet but didn't raise. He, like the other two women, wanted to see the next three cards, the flop, before putting a value on his hand. And he had to be cautious because he was down to his last five thousand of the twenty he got from Arnie Zucker on Thursday.

He settled back in his chair and assessed his two adversaries. One was an overweight black women from Brooklyn who already had too many of John's chips. The other was the blond who couldn't stop talking about her son the med student. Neither seemed to be particularly adept players, yet they had bigger stacks then John. He hoped to change that with one good hand.

The dealer, the only other male at the table, turned the next three cards and brought a huge invisible smile to John's face: ten – six – ten. John had four tens but causally rechecked his hole cards to give the impression he had only a passing interest in the game. He knew he had the best hand but it would only pay off if one of the other players had a pair underneath and wanted to get into a pissing match. This could get him back in the black. It had been a long time since he hit four of a kind and he didn't want to waste the opportunity to cash in big on this.

The corpulent black woman started the betting with a hundred dollar bet. This told John she was either trying to steal the pot or she had enough to want to go a little further. He watched her as she rechecked her hole cards. Sometimes this simple act would tell John something about the strength of his adversary's hand. This time it didn't tell him much.

The blond saw the bet but seemed reluctant. John needed to decide when to lower the boom. If he went big too soon he could scare them off. If he let them see the next two cards it was possible one of them could get lucky and come up with quads of her own, although that was unlikely.

He decided the best bet was a moderate raise; one that would give them both a chance to do something stupid like re-raise. Then, he'd have them. He glanced at his stack of chips. It was shorter than he would have liked. Then he glanced at their stacks and did some quick math to calculate how much he could win with this one hand. He figured maybe as much as sixteen grand.

"Three hundred," he said as he tossed in three black chips.

"Baby, I think you got yourself a ten in there." The black

woman said pointing at his hole cards. She threw her cards into the center of the table. "Not me."

John tried desperately not to show his disappointment. He nodded his head as if to say, *"I understand your logic."* Then he feigned a lack of concern and looked towards the blond. She was studying her hole cards. But she was also watching John. There was a pause that seemed to last for days but was actually only a few seconds. She fingered her chips, counting out enough twenty-five dollar discs to see the bet, but John was hoping for a big raise.

"Not this time." She said as she tossed her cards. "And I had a pair too."

John was furious. This could have been a great hand but now it was nothing. A great hand is only great if it has someone to play against. He lashed out.

"How the fuck do you lay down a pair on a hand like that?" He didn't expect an answer, he just needed to shout. "Fuck you all, I'm out of here." And he grabbed his chips and stomped away from the table.

When he was a safe distance from the group, the blond said, "I guess he had the ten, huh?"

CHAPTER THIRTY

Doc

I spent most of the first Saturday after Labor Day doing the things all people with summer homes at the beach have to do each year as the days grow shorter. I put away most of the outdoor furniture that had been scattered on my deck and on the sand. I was determined to get my mind off Annie, and the otherwise mundane chore of hosing salt off the chairs before tucking them in the garage for the winter seemed to help.

I deflated the two air mattresses the girls gave me for Father's Day, but decided to leave the kayaks on the beach. There were still plenty of warm days ahead and I intended to use a kayak to get some shots of the reeds as they transformed from light green to brilliant gold. My neighbor Tom told me that October was the best month for bright colors around the pond. The maple, oak, and evergreens reflected in the still water with the golden grasses along the shore. He said it was quite spectacular.

Having completed my housekeeping, I decided to drive into town and pick up a few vegetables for a soup I wanted to make. By the time I got back to the shack it was already getting dark. A light drizzle was starting to fall so I brought some firewood in from the garage and prepared myself for a cozy evening, alone at home. If all went well, I would turn out a respectable pasta e fagiole, get a good fire going, and read another fifty pages in my DeMille novel; all before my roof started to leak again. That was my plan.

To my great surprise, I was beginning to enjoy being

alone out here. I missed Annie, but I was comfortable with my solitude. When I first decided to spend a winter out here, my greatest fear was that I'd be lonely. My daughters live in different time zones, most of my friends are all in the city, and my closest friend is more than an hour drive to the west. In general, I don't like time by myself. But I guess this was one of those 'face your demons' things because there's no way spending a winter on Cold Spring Pond was going to be a social extravaganza. I knew that when I made the decision to live out here.

To be honest, I needed to be alone out here. I wanted time to think. Although I'd intellectually accepted my loss of faith, I needed to test it. And the best way to do that was by doing something I had seldom done before: sit and listen. I wasn't exactly sure what I was supposed to be listening for but my dad always said, "*You can't learn anything while you're talking, so shut up and listen.*" So, my plan was to shut up and listen to the natural world around me; the world I'd rushed past and pretty much ignored during most of my working life.

I guess that means I'm supposed to silently watch the deer grazing at the pond's edge in the morning, or stare for hours at the clouds drifting by, or sit cross-legged, which I can't do, and study as many sunrises and sunsets as I can. Maybe it means I'm just supposed to appreciate the beauty around me. And even I can tell there's no shortage of that around Cold Spring Pond. Everywhere I look I see something beautiful here. Anyway, there'd be plenty of time for listening.

With a little help from my friend Duraflame, I had a nice fire going. My dinner was simmering on the stove and I was about half way through a bottle of Bobby's Barolo. I stretched out on my sofa with the DeMille book on my lap, but rather than reading, I found myself lost in the flickering flames.

Even as a kid, I loved watching a fire. I drifted back to the many evenings I'd sit by the warm hearth at my grandfather's house; the smell of espresso filled the small room. I was eight again and my grandfather was giving my dad a haircut on a stool in the kitchen under a single light bulb hanging from the ceiling. My grandmother sat in a soft chair near the fireplace crocheting a decorative edge on a napkin. I leaned against her legs and warmed my feet by the fire. I don't think I've ever felt more safe.

I realize now that I was flirting with the most dangerous demon of solitude—getting stuck in the 'good old days.' Friends warned me about this. Actually, they warned me about it because of who they knew I was. I guess when you're a guy who thinks—no believes, that you've had a great life, and that just about every experience in your past has helped to make you stronger, people are afraid you'll revert back to the *good old days*' the first time you take the time to actually reflect on your life. Maybe they're afraid I'll finally see something in myself I've ignored or denied up till now.

I ate my soup sitting at the kitchen counter. The Barolo was beginning to have its intended effect. I could say it was the fireplace but I know it was the wine that warmed the night and protected me from the cold drizzle hitting the window in blowing sheets. I threw a real log on the Duraflame and it erupted, giving the room a pleasant glow. All in all, considering the weather, it wasn't a bad evening. I hoped to knock off another fifty pages in my book before surrendering to the alcohol.

More than anything, I was pleased with myself for making the adjustment from a hectic, urban routine to this semi-catatonic pace of retirement. Originally, I wasn't sure I could do it. After all, I'd been working fourteen-hour days in Manhattan and traveling to London on a regular basis for the last eleven years. That all stopped abruptly less than five weeks ago when I sold the only business I'd ever owned.

Friends and colleagues advised me to "force myself" to take some time off before jumping into another business. They said someone like me couldn't sit still for long but that I really needed to take some time to relax and enjoy the life I'd been flying over for so long. And I believed them. I couldn't envision myself doing anything other than working hard. It was all I knew and I thought it defined who I was.

Well, I guess we were all wrong about me. Only a few weeks into this, I seem to be able to relax just fine. Here I am, stretched out on my sofa, in front of a roaring fire and doing something I previously only had time for on forced vacations—reading. And I was actually looking forward to the solitude of a winter here at the pond, surrounded only by my thoughts and the natural beauty of it all.

Yeah, they should see me now.

I decided to change into a pair of old sweat pants and a sweat shirt from Kitty's alma mater, ASU. It was one of the two $170,000 sweat shirts I have to show for the twin's collective educations. I also decided another bottle of Barolo was in order, although I was beginning to think Bobby wasn't kidding about saving it for when he next visited. I was down to the last six bottles. I'd just poured myself a full glass when I heard the gravel on my driveway crunching under the weight of car tires.

CHAPTER THIRTY-ONE

Doc

I certainly wasn't expecting any visitors so the sound of a car door slamming and footsteps on my deck startled me. I lifted myself from my comfortable slouch, put down my glass and started for the door. I keep a Louisville Slugger next to my bed in the unlikely event of an intruder but that was upstairs. The only possible defensive weapon between me and the door was a fireplace poker leaning against the pile of wood I'd brought in earlier. I squeezed it in my right hand just as there was a hurried knock at the door.

"Who's there?" I said it in as masculine a voice as I could muster. There was a pause. No response from the other side of the door. Then....

"Doc, its Annie, and I'm getting drenched out here. Open up."

I swung open the wooden door and, sure enough, it was Annie. And she was pretty wet. She pushed her way in and hopped up and down in an attempt to shed some of the rain.

"What are you doing here?"

"Well, it was such a lovely night, I decided to take a drive," she said with extreme sarcasm.

We stood staring at each other for several moments. Even dripping wet, she was beautiful. I couldn't take my eyes off her, but to be honest, after a bottle of wine, my eyes were having a little trouble focusing properly.

Finally, she said, "Can I come in?"

I was shaken back to the moment. "Yes, yes, of course. Come in." Then, "What are you doing here?"

"How about I get dried off first, then you can have your inquisition?"

"Yeah, yeah, come in. Let me get you a towel." I scurried around the corner of the kitchen to grab a towel.

"A dry shirt would be nice too." She was all business while I was tripping over myself.

As she dried herself off, I ran upstairs and pulled the first shirt I grabbed from my closet. It turned out to be one of my plaid flannels. At least it was clean.

Before I stumbled back down the stairs, I caught a glimpse of myself in my bedroom mirror. I checked my teeth to be sure I wasn't sporting a piece of parsley from dinner. I felt ridiculously incompetent in the presence of her perfection.

"There's a bathroom over there. You can finish drying off and put this on in there." I was practically stammering.

"Are you OK?" She asked with a confused look on her face. But she didn't wait for an answer before heading for the bathroom.

As the bathroom door closed behind her, I turned and scanned the house for further evidence of my stupidity. The kitchen was full of dirty pots I'd planned to deal with in the morning. There was a pile of unfolded laundry lying on the dryer, two days of unopened mail on the kitchen counter, and the two Barolo bottles; one empty, one about half full. Clearly, I wasn't expecting guests.

Annie called out from the bathroom, "And what's with the fire poker?" I realized I was still clutching the potential weapon in my right hand. Now I felt completely inept. I put it back near the fireplace.

"You can't be too careful." I said to the door. "Nights like this bring out all sorts of crazies."

"Maybe in Manhattan. Out here, nights like this just bring out ducks." She called from behind the door.

As I waited for her to emerge from the bathroom, my mind

raced with possible answers to my own question. Why was she here? I jumped to the conclusion that she had come out to her house sometime earlier in the day. But why come here? The last thing she said to me was that she needed to get away from me and get things settled with her husband before figuring out how she felt about me. Even to me, that sounded like a prudent plan.

The bathroom door opened. Annie stood on the threshold for a moment. She leaned back against the door jam. Her hair was pulled back in a ponytail. My flannel shirt was enormous on her. The top three buttons were open but what drew my total attention was the length. The red flannel came all the way to her knees. But there was nothing below her knees. I mean, she had taken off her jeans, shoes and socks. The shirt drifted loosely around her shapely calves.

I swallowed hard. "You clean up pretty good Mrs. Dunn-Weaver."

She glanced at the bottles on the counter. "How about sharing some of that?"

It took a moment for the words to penetrate my head. You see my head was busy trying to imagine what else Annie had taken off in there.

"Aaaah, sure. One '97 Barolo coming up." I might have been drooling but I tried to say it with some level of suave.

Annie took the glass and sat cross-legged by the fire. "Oh, that feels wonderful," she sighed as the warmth of the fire and the grapes took hold. "I hope I'm not interrupting anything? I guess I should have called first, but to be honest, when I got in my car in New York, I wasn't sure if I had the nerve to come out here."

I sat on the sofa, about three feet from her, and extended my glass. "Salute. Here's to rainy nights and damsels in distress." We clinked glasses and she finished her wine with one long gulp. My kind of woman!

She held out her glass, waiting for a refill, and said, "So here's the plan. I'm going to get a little drunk then I'm going to make love to you until you beg me to stop. How's that sound Jerome?"

I thought about asking her not to call me Jerome but I didn't want to interrupt her otherwise perfect train of thought.

"Sounds like someone's already come to a decision about her home life."

"We can talk about that tomorrow."

Needless to say, her glass had already been refilled. "How do you know I don't already have a female guest upstairs?" I teased as I glanced playfully at the top of the stairs.

For a split second she actually seemed shaken. Then she decided to play along. "What's she wearing?"

Not wanting either of us to forget the aforementioned proposal, I needed to focus attention back to the real people in the room. I sat next to her on the floor and offered another toast. "To you, my flannel shirt and rainy nights." We clinked again and this time our eyes never left each other. In hers, I could see pain and yet a passionate longing. Not having much experience with that look, I wasn't sure if I should first attend to the passion or, if it was proper to at least make an inquiry about the pain. Even half way to drunk, I was a bit conflicted about this. I took the high road and hated myself for it even as the words escaped from my lips.

"Are you sure you want to be here?" *Please say yes.*

She said nothing. But she kept staring at me. Then she put her wine glass on the hearth and put her left hand on the back of my neck. She pulled me closer to her, our lips almost touching and her eyes still looking deeply into mine. "Any more questions?"

Annie kissed me and I kissed back. Her mouth was open and she used her tongue to pry open mine. It was a deep, delicious kiss. Somehow, through her lips and mouth, she was telling me that there was no place else she wanted to be. Ditto.

After several seconds we gently pulled apart but our lips were never more than an inch from each other. We held that pose for another few seconds, then Annie maneuvered me backward and onto the floor. She climbed on top of me and kissed me again. I ran my hands down her back, all the way to the bottom of the red flannel. It ended just below her ass and both my hands were now working their way up the back of her naked legs. I was right. She'd removed all her wet cloths in the bathroom. Joy!

The fire was crackling as we quickly got undressed right there on the floor. It was like something out of the movies. These things don't happen to me. They happen to other people.

But tonight, it was real. And it seemed so right. We made love on the floor by the fire, then cuddled with the glowing embers providing the only light in the room. Later, we went upstairs and made love again several times before the wine and raindrops blended together in a foggy but wonderful sleep.

We both slept soundly, or at least I'm sure I did, until close to nine. It was still raining lightly when I first opened my eyes which turned out to be a blessing. On most days, the sun screams into my bedroom like a freight train. That wasn't what I wanted this morning.

I lay next to Annie watching her sleep for almost a half hour before she stirred. It may sound strange but she was even more beautiful asleep than she was awake. Maybe it was because when she slept she didn't have to think about her troubles. But whatever the reason, sleeping on her side, facing me with her mouth half open, she looked beautiful and so innocent.

You wouldn't think the angel lying next to me this morning was the same person who, just a few hours ago, was making love to me like someone who hadn't had sex in years. Annie was a wonderful lover. She made me feel like I was the only person on the planet last night. She had a wild sort of enthusiasm, for lack of a better word, for my body, and her diminutive frame rapped itself around mine in a way that seemed almost perfect.

The sex was exciting. The passion was exhilarating. Annie came to me. She gave herself freely and certainly seemed to enjoy the evening as much as I did. So why was I feeling so guilty?

CHAPTER THIRTY-TWO

Usually, at this time of year on a Saturday morning, Dave Rosen would be getting ready for his son's football game. Luca Rosen had become one of New Jersey's most notorious running backs, and even as a high school junior, was closing in on the state record for most yards gained. 205 pounds of youthful muscle covered his strong bones making him the fastest back in the county, maybe even the state. Division One colleges were already sending brochures and letters of introduction handwritten by the coaches.

Dave thoroughly enjoyed his son's popularity and took pride in his accomplishments. He video-taped every game. He and his wife, Abi, were active members of the booster club. He never missed a game, even if it meant rescheduling a business trip until after the season. If he could get away from his job at the local Capital One Bank a few minutes early, he'd drive to the school and watch the team practice.

So it was unusual that he hadn't returned home yet. He'd driven Luca up to school over an hour ago. The team was already on the bus and on their way to Hamilton for an eleven o'clock game. Abi was beginning to get worried. Even if her husband had stuck around to watch the kids board the bus, he should have been home by now. She was concerned they'd be late for the game.

Actually, Dave did linger at the high school to watch the players get on the bus. He was leaning on the chain link fence near the yellow bus. The drizzle that had begun that morning had given way to clearing September skies and Dave pushed back on the fence, closed his eyes, and let the sun's welcomed rays hit his face. It was going to be another great day.

At least that's what he thought before he heard the pair of foot steps coming towards him. As he opened his eyes and tried to focus on his attackers, he felt a sharp pain on the left side of his face. He'd been hit with an aluminum bat.

"Why you make us come all the way down here again?" Even with the bat still ringing in his ears, Dave recognized the voice. He threw up his hands to fend off another blow, but none came.

Felix and Levon stood over him. "Dave, you gotta start keeping better track of your obligations."

"Holy shit! I think you broke my cheek bone." Dave was in pain but he didn't really think they'd broken anything. He just wanted the blows to stop. He hoped if they thought he was already damaged, maybe the goons would leave him.

"Look fool, you two weeks behind on your obligations. And we already come down to the ass end of Jersey to enlighten you once before. Why you make us do that?"

Blood trickled from his mouth as Dave spoke. "I swear to God, I'll have the money by Monday. Just give me till Monday. I can get the money."

Felix actually felt sorry for the poor slobs he was dispatched to *remind* about their obligations. He couldn't understand how white folks could get themselves into such trouble with all they had going for them. He just couldn't figure out how someone with a decent job and a big house could wind up owing money to Arnie Zucker. What the hell did they do with the money? What were they thinking?

But Felix wasn't a gambler. He'd never felt the rush they

got from hitting a number or watching a horse run faster than a bunch of other horses. He'd never bet on a football game or even been to a casino. It just wasn't his nature to risk money he worked hard to earn. Maybe it was because he'd come across so many sorry souls like Dave since starting to work for Zucker's collectors. He never wanted to be like them; on the wrong end of an aluminum bat.

"I know you'll do what's right, Dave." Felix's voice now had a hint of compassion.

"I swear, I'll wire the money from my bank on Monday. I swear." And he meant it too. Dave had borrowed ten thousand dollars from one of Arnie Zucker's people a few weeks earlier when he had a sure thing at Saratoga. But the mare ran second and the interest on the loan was causing him to make more and more poor choices. If he took the money from Lucas' college fund, his wife would…well, he was better off dealing with Felix and Levon.

Or so he thought.

His latest bad decision was to move the money from a dormant account at the bank to his. It would just be for a few weeks. No one would find out. He was, after all, the branch manager. He could hide such a maneuver as long as he needed to. He'd do it first thing Monday morning and get these monsters off his back.

Dave pulled himself to his feet using the fence. His right hand was grasping the top of the chain link and extended over the steel bar. He saw the blow coming but couldn't react fast enough. The bat came down on his thumb and three of his fingers crushing them against the bar. He screamed in agony.

"Do the right thing chump." Levon finally had something to say. Then he and Felix got back in their car and left Dave lying against the schoolyard fence.

When the football team emerged from the locker room and headed for the bus no one noticed the unconscious man bleeding and moaning on the ground just fifty feet away. They were too excited about their upcoming battle.

CHAPTER THIRTY-THREE

All the way back to Manhattan, Annie thought about the past thirty hours. She didn't completely understand why she'd broken her promise to herself not to see Doc. She hadn't intended to do it when she got in the car. Initially, she was just going downtown to have dinner with two friends who'd called her on Saturday afternoon and insisted on getting her out of her funk.

But as she drove down Second Avenue, Doc was the only thing on her mind and when she saw the sign for the Midtown tunnel, the direct path to Doc, something inside her took over. She knew John wouldn't be back until Monday. It would be no problem getting out of dinner with the Callahans. They lived downtown and were walking to the restaurant anyway, so her absence wouldn't put them out. She called them from the car and excused herself with a story about one of the boys coming home unexpectedly.

So why did her infidelity suddenly seem like the right thing to do? Was it just the loneliness? Was it the emotional roller-coaster of getting ready to tell John she was leaving only to have him leave town for a few days? Was it the depressing thought of explaining her failed marriage to her sons and friends?

Or was it just Doc? Was he just what she needed on a rainy September night?

Whatever it was, once she was on the Long Island

Expressway, there was no looking back towards the cold loneliness of New York. As the skyline silhouette disappeared from her rear view mirror, she thought about what lay ahead. Hopefully, Doc would be home and hopefully he would be alone. If not, well she would just spend the night at her house and drive back in the morning, a bit embarrassed but a lot wiser.

But he was home and they had connected in exactly the way Annie hoped they would. By the time she pulled into his driveway she'd fantasized about their evening several times. She was physically hungry for Doc and wasted no time getting that message across. Actually, she'd been surprised by how boyish he was. She expected more. Maybe a more aggressive lover. Maybe a more sophisticated performance from the man she thought of as pretty worldly. Maybe, after three years of John's abuse she just didn't know what to expect.

But now that she was on her way back to New York, she caught herself smiling in the mirror. The sex had been perfect. Doc was boyish, but in a good way. He was slow to move but once she initiated a move he was an eager learner. And most importantly, he let her set the pace. That hadn't happened in a long time.

Even without the wine Annie had been completely comfortable with Doc. His body was firm. They fit together well, both during the passion and after. It was all wonderful. It was so different, yet familiar. It reminded Annie of her life with Peter, a time when love-making was soft and gentle. She longed for those feelings again.

When they awoke on Sunday morning, they lingered in bed for a while. First, they made love again. Morning sex was always the best kind for Annie. Then, Doc brought her coffee in bed and they watched Charles Osgood and Chris Matthews on TV from under the covers. By noon it seemed safe to rejoin the world so they showered, dressed and drove into town for brunch at the Drivers Seat, Doc's favorite place for blueberry pancakes.

They spent the afternoon walking along the oceanfront homes on Dune Road. The previous day's rain had cleared the air. The sun glistened on the foamy white waves rolling from a sandbar about fifty yards off the beach. It was one of those spectacular September Sundays when it's just too nice to be indoors. They walked for hours, talking a little but mostly just holding hands and enjoying the moment. The post-coital glow had faded and been replaced by a warm, comfortable after-noon stroll.

Doc suggested they pick up a couple of steaks at Schmidts. The food shopping became an event and by the time they left the store, he'd purchased enough cheese, vegetables and bread to last two people a week. They spent the rest of the afternoon lying in the sand, drinking Barolo and eating cheese and thin strips of Italian bread Doc grilled with garlic and olive oil. As the sun retreated they followed it to the west side of the deck where they could see its final gasp on the horizon.

Then Doc made a salad while Annie curled up on his sofa in front of the TV. The Giants were losing but she really wasn't paying attention to Eli Manning. She was watching Doc maneuver around the kitchen, pouring himself into the dinner he was preparing her.

It was a perfect afternoon. It had been a perfect day. Annie put down her wine glass and looked at Doc. He was dicing something green and didn't seem to notice her stare.

Filled with a warmth she hadn't felt since Peter's death, she studied the middle-aged man dancing around the kitchen. He seemed as happy in the kitchen as he was in the bedroom. How wonderful she thought, to be so happy.

And that's when she knew it. She knew she was in love

with him. Not because she needed to or because he filled some misunderstood void in her life, or because she was so unhappy with John, but because he sang. He sang as he cooked.

She loved that. And she was now more sure than ever about what she had to do when she returned to New York.

CHAPTER THIRTY-FOUR

Doc

I have to admit, I didn't expect to feel this way about my weekend with Annie. Although we spoke on the phone briefly when she arrived home Sunday night, we haven't spoken since. On Monday, I picked up the phone three times, but never dialed. On Tuesday, I wanted so much to hear her voice, I was tempted to call and just listen to her say hello, before hanging up like a mischievous ten year old. But I had promised not to call and she promised to call me by Thursday with news about her conversation with her husband.

So, here it is Thursday morning and I can't wait for the phone to ring.

To take my mind off Annie, I went for a run around the pond. It was a beautiful September day, a little warmer than usual, but that was perfect for my plans. After my run, I bathed using the shower out on the deck. The previous owners had built walls around the shower from cedar planks and to me; there were few things you could do alone that were better than taking a hot shower under the sun. There is just something wonderful about bathing outdoors.

I decided it was time for me to get down to some work—the work I came out here to do. So far, I'd taken very few pictures and if I wanted to capture the essence of summer, I wouldn't get many more days like this. The trees surrounding the pond had yet to show any sign of autumn. Their leaves had resisted the temptation of the cool evenings and clung to their summery green hue.

With my camera and a good lens tucked safely in a water-proof plastic bag, I paddled my kayak across the pond to take advantage of the morning sun. The stillness was broken only by the gentle wake of the kayak. Most of the pond is less than four feet deep so I could watch the bottom sliding by through the clear still water. I made a mental note to figure out a way to get a shot of this at a future time with a macro lens. I could see blue claw crabs and scallops on the sandy bottom.

It took about twenty minutes to paddle to the far side of the pond. Now that I had the morning sun over my shoulder, I put the lens on the camera and started clicking. It was as if nature had waited for me to arrive before beginning its show, for as soon as I was in place, ducks, swans, even a blue heron jumped onto the stage. My zoom allowed me to get a few really fine close-ups of the wildlife before a wispy cloud blocked out the sun.

While I waited for the perfect lighting to return, I marveled at the natural beauty all around me. It seemed too spectacular to be random. The contrast of colors, the glistening water, the majestic birds, all seemed testimony to some higher order. Like someone had a very specific plan.

But who and how? While I'd gotten used to the notion of living my life without a god, I could see his hand in everything around me. I hadn't really thought about his relationship with the rest of the world—just mine with him. Or better put, my lack of a relationship with him. I had come to accept that there was no god for me. That made some sense to me. But even though I denied his existence, he seemed to go right on with the rest of his creations. The birds hadn't thought about god, they just swam in a pond and flew though the sky that came from somewhere beyond their thoughts.

Maybe I needed to be more like the heron; just take the pond for granted. Just accept the pond and the trees and the sky as things that are supposed to be there; things that always were there and would always be there. If I was more like the heron I wouldn't need to think about it any more deeply than that.

But I was thinking about it. I thought about all the books I read that explained, without the need for a god, the existence of our world and all the beauty in it. I thought about our ancestors who explained all the unexplainable events of their world by conjuring stories of angry gods or jealous gods, or gods who sent messengers to earth to screw with our simple lives. It seemed to me that whenever we were unable to understand something, we attributed it to God's whim. The flood happened because God was mad. The crops were plentiful because God was happy, or because we had sacrificed some poor creature at the start of the season to please God.

The more I'd thought about it, the more I came to the conclusion that we had simply invented God because we didn't understand what was going on around us. We didn't yet understand gravity, chemistry, physics, biology or atomic mass. We didn't understand bacteria, microscopic life or our place in the universe.

But now that we do understand all these natural occurrences, now that we understand our position, if not our place in the universe, why do we still cling to the notion of a god directing all this? I came to the conclusion it was because man is so egocentric. For some reason, man had to think himself more important than all the rest of nature. Man needed to have a special relationship with whatever was in charge, and in that, held dominion over all the rest of nature.

It all made sense to me. I was pretty sure I'd figured it out and that only people who could surrender to their frailty, their unimportance in the universe could accept what I had come to accept. That we're not special. That we're just what we are; fairly sophisticated, carbon-based creatures with ancestry going back to the bottom of the pond. No better or more entitled than any other creature in the food-chain.

But here I was, sitting in a kayak, in the middle of a shallow pond, and in awe of the creation around me. Just seeing, no not just seeing, experiencing the beauty of nature caused me to stop and, once again doubt my conclusions.

Were my beliefs as shallow as the pond? And were they as fluid as the currents that filled and emptied the pond with every changing tide?

I don't know. I wish I did.

Chapter Thirty-Five

He could hear the wall phone ringing in the shack even before he beached the kayak. Doc raced up the steps onto the deck and into the house grabbing the phone on the tenth ring. He was panting like a dog.

"Hello," he swallowed hard after getting it out.

"Where have you been?" came the soft reply.

"Hold on. Let me catch my breath." He stepped away from the wall phone and leaned against the kitchen counter to steady himself. Sprinting was never his strength.

"OK, I'm back." But still panting like Rin Tin Tin.

"Where were you?"

"I was out on the pond getting some shots of Mother Nature. God, it's good to hear your voice."

"Yours too. Except you sound like you're going to die on me any minute."

"No. I'm good now. Just ran up from the beach."

"Sounds like I need to come out there and take you running again young man. You sound awful. What do you say I come out Friday afternoon and we can work on your endurance?"

"That would be great and maybe we could go running."

"Very funny. I saw that coming. Seriously Doc, are you OK?" Her voice was full of genuine concern.

"Well, I'm very lonely and I really miss you Annie." He assumed that's what she wanted to hear.

"Excellent answer! You passed the quiz."

There was silence on the line for several seconds. Then Doc asked, "Did you have your conversation?"

"Let's talk when I get there." She seemed firm about that.

"That sounds great. What time can you be here?" His enthusiasm was evident.

"I have a doctor's appointment first thing in the morning, and then I'm getting my nails done so I should be there by two or three in the afternoon. Why? What have you got planned?" She tried to sound impish.

"Everything OK? I mean about the doctor." Now, he sounded concerned.

"Yeah, yeah. My annual physical was scheduled for November but I moved it up partly because, well you know. I figure I'll have a lot of other things to deal with. Also, I've been really tired lately so I wanted my doctor to check my lazy thyroid. He may need to kick my medication up a notch."

"You're probably tired from the stress of...well, you know." Doc didn't want to say the words "*impending divorce*". He didn't want to push it.

"Naw. She's had to adjust my meds a few times over the last few years. It's no big deal."

Then she said the words he wanted to hear more than any. "I'm really looking forward to seeing you Doc."

"How long can you stay?" He was hoping she'd already dealt with her husband and might say "*forever*". She didn't.

I have to be back in Manhattan Monday night. So I'm yours till then. That is, if you want me." Again, the impish tone.

"I'll plan something special. I really miss you." Having said the words again, he was afraid he sounded like a lost puppy.

"I miss you too sweety. I've got to run. I'll see you tomorrow."

As the line went dead and Doc heard the dial tone, he

turned toward the sliding glass door he'd entered from the deck. Looking beyond the door, and beyond the deck, he saw his kayak floating off shore about fifty yards. His three thousand dollar camera was on the kayak seat and one of Mother Nature's finest, a grey Canadian goose had landed on the kayak and was taking an unhealthy interest in the camera.

CHAPTER THIRTY-SIX

The white paper covering the table was sticking to Annie's legs. She never liked the open-backed gowns Dr. Weber insisted her patients use and she liked waiting for her doctor even less. Dr. Tomasue Weber had been Annie's primary doctor since the twins were born. Annie liked her casual style. She also liked the fact that they were about the same age.

The wall clock in the examining room was approaching 10:30, and Annie was about to call to postpone her nail appointment when the door swung open.

"I'm so sorry, Annie." The perky red-head in the white jacket hardly looked like a physician. More often, she was mistaken for one of her nurses or assistants. But the diploma hanging just behind where Annie sat told any doubters that Cornell University had been convinced of her credentials back in 1982.

"It's OK, but I was just about to bail on you."

"So, how have you been?" Tomasue leaned against the counter and looked at her patient's chart. "Looks like you're not due for your annual for a couple more months. Anything bothering you?"

Annie was tempted to share her recent life-events with her doctor but decided against it. Divorce is a sensitive and emotional topic and she didn't think it was right to tell Tomasue before she told her sons, or, for that matter, her husband. Instead, she stuck with the physical issues.

A physician's assistant had already taken Annie's blood

pressure, EKG, and two vials of blood. She'd been weighed, measured and probed. Now, after thirty minutes of tests, she could finally tell someone why she was really here.

"The last few weeks, I've been really tired. No other symptoms, just really tired. I kind of feel the way I did a few years ago before you discovered my thyroid was on the blink."

"Are you still on the Synthroid?" Dr. Weber checked her chart again. ".075 milligrams, right?"

"Yep." Annie produced the bottle of pills she'd been taking ever since her thyroid condition surfaced, and checked the dosage on the label. "Yep, .075 milligrams it is." She handed the doctor the bottle for further inspection but Tomasue was already writing in her chart.

"Anything else going on? Dry mouth? Any fevers? Any trouble sleeping?"

Annie thought about her recent bedtime activities as a smile crossed her face but it went unnoticed by her doctor who was still writing notes.

"No. Everything else is pretty normal. I just feel like I did before I started taking the Synthroid. I'm just tired all the time."

Tomasue now looked up from her chart at her long-time friend and patient. "Everything OK with the boys?" She asked, probing for any other causes of the fatigue.

"Yep. Frank is dating some socialite from Baltimore, and Nicky just set some new school record in the 400 meter relay. They're both doing great at school. I'm still sorry they didn't go together."

"Most studies say twins are better off going to separate colleges. I agree. They've got to be independent at some point."

Annie nodded.

"How about at home? Everything OK with hubby?" Tomasue knew Annie had remarried after her first husband's death, but had never met John and couldn't recall his name.

Annie thought for a moment. She wanted to purge herself of the torment John had caused her but it just didn't seem right. Not before she told her sons.

But the pause wasn't lost on Tomasue. The concerned doctor pushed a little harder. "Annie, it's OK to talk to me if something's bothering you. It might have something to do with your fatigue. Very often, a distraction in one aspect of life can..."

Annie cut her short. "Everything's OK. Every married couple has their issues from time to time." She gave Tomasue a glance that said, "*That's all I have to say about it.*"

Tomasue Weber had been practicing medicine for over twenty years and knew when a patient was lying to her about symptoms or causes of them. It frustrated her because often she believed she could help if only she were allowed. But she also knew when to back off.

"OK. Let's see what the blood work tells us. If it is your lazy thyroid, we can up the dosage a bit and see if that helps. I should have the results tomorrow morning. I'll give you a call."

"Actually, don't." Annie thought about her weekend with Doc and didn't need any interruptions. She explained, "I'll be out in Southampton this weekend. I'll call you on Tuesday when I get back."

"Good for you. It's supposed to be a beautiful weekend. Al Roker says it may even hit ninety on Sunday. Probably our last bit of summer." Dr. Weber was writing as she spoke.

"I'll talk to you next week."

As Annie dressed, she thought about the upcoming weekend. She didn't know what plans Doc had made but she looked forward to the adventure, whatever it was. If it was half as wonderful as the previous weekend, it would be great. And, just like last weekend, John would be away until Monday so she could postpone the difficult conversation she needed to have with him. But there was something about the anticipation that bothered her.

Last weekend, she drove out to see Doc on the spur of the moment. She hadn't planned to see him. In fact, she was resolute in her plan to not see him again until she'd talked to John. But this time she was reveling in the anticipation of a lovely weekend with Doc; three days and nights of warmth and love and being held gently in the arms of the man she wanted so much to better understand. And, she was surprised by how much she looked forward to the sex. Doc had awakened in her a desire that had been all but extinguished since Peter.

But this time she was planning her actions. This time she was consciously deceiving her husband and looking forward to being with another man. For the first time in her life she wrestled with the morality of doing something that felt so right, but others might deem so wrong. For the first time in her life she was about to do something—planning to do something, that she would have been ashamed of if her father were watching.

For a moment she considered calling Doc and explaining that she hadn't yet talked to her husband; that it didn't feel right being so happy with Doc while she was being untrue to her marriage. She wanted everything with Doc to be right. She wanted everything in their relationship, if they were to have one, to start from clean, firm ground. She didn't want anything about their relationship to be tarnished.

If she'd known everything in her life would be different four days later, she might not have left the doctor's office at all.

CHAPTER THIRTY-SEVEN

The loose driveway gravel announced her arrival more clearly than a hundred trumpeters. Doc was watering his hydrangeas on the north side of the house when he heard the car door slam, and saw Annie walking across the lawn holding what he hoped was a well stuffed overnight bag. She looked adorable in a pair of yellow shorts and white cotton v-neck sweater. It was the perfect outfit for what he had planned for the afternoon.

He wasn't quite sure what the appropriate greeting should be for someone you slept with the previous weekend, but have no authentic claim to. *Darling? Great to see you again? I've missed you?* None of them seemed to fit.

"Hey sweety!" She said as she ran the last few steps towards him and threw her arms around his neck.

"Wow, it's good to see you." That was the best he could come up with.

"Oh, you too." She buried her head in his embrace and whispered into his sweater, "I missed you so much."

"Same here."

They held the embrace for several minutes and, for a moment, he wasn't sure if she was crying into the fold of his arm. The sun was already high in the sky and warmer than usual for September, and he was happy to stand there all day if that's what she needed.

When they pulled apart, he could tell she had had some sort of emotional moment. Her eyes were wet and she sniffled just enough to whisper, "I really love you. And I love it when you just hold me like that."

"Well then, I'll have to do it more often."

He led her into the house and took her bag up to his bedroom while she hit the bathroom. When he returned downstairs she shouted through the bathroom door, "So what have you got planned for me today, Mr. Cafara?"

"I'll tell you when you get out." He shouted back as he poured two glasses of wine. He'd already prepared a plate of fruit and cheese which was waiting for them under the over-sized green umbrella on the deck. Actually, he'd planned out every aspect of the weekend, or at least his vision of how it would turn out.

First, some refreshments on the deck, then a boat ride to his favorite place in Sag Harbor for lunch. Then, because the weather forecast was just about perfect, they'd take the boat another twenty miles out to Montauk for dinner at Gossman's on the water, then stay over at a tiny resort just across from the docks. On Saturday, they'd take the boat back to Southampton and bike to the ocean beach for a day in the sun. On the way home, they'd stop at some of the local farms to pick up fresh vegetables to compliment the salmon steaks he planned to grill. Sunday was wide open.

When Annie joined him under the umbrella, he couldn't help himself. She looked like she belonged in exactly this setting. Behind her sprawled the glistening pond. The sun sparkled in her wine glass and he wanted to say something profound to match the moment, but came up dry. She stretched out on one of the deck chairs with her bare feet on another. He handed her a piece of green apple to accompany the wine she was already finishing.

"So here's the plan." He was anxious to share with her his weekend plans, hoping she would be impressed by his thoughtful attention to detail. "First, we'll take the boat to…"

Annie cut him off. "No, I want to be surprised. I'm sure it will be wonderful as long as we're together."

"Oh, we'll be together. Don't worry about that."

"That's really all I care about. I just want to be with you. I want you to hold me like you did when I got here. I want you to kiss my back like you did last week. And I want you to bring me coffee in bed again. That was wonderful." She said it like a child on Christmas morning.

"I think we can fit all that into my plan." He was racing mentally to figure out how he could get her coffee at the Montauk motel. Doc wanted the weekend to be perfect for her.

They sat together, each facing the pond. After Doc opened the second bottle of wine, Annie shifted in her seat and looked at him. "Doc, I need to talk to you about John."

She explained that she had not yet told her husband she planned to leave him. That twice during the week, she tried to begin the conversation only to have John's beeper go off summoning him to the hospital for the rest of the night. She explained to Doc that she knew exactly what she was going to say and how she planned to do it in a public place to avoid a scene. She had it all worked out. She even had a suite reserved at the Essex House starting Monday night for her retreat.

Monday night would be the night. She and John had arranged to have dinner at a small place right on their block. She would move some things over to the Essex on Monday afternoon so she wouldn't need to go back to their apartment after delivering the blow.

"The funny thing is, although I think I know how he'll react, I really don't have any idea how he'll feel. Isn't that strange? I mean, after you live with someone for three years, you'd think you'd have some idea. But I honestly don't know what to expect."

"What do you mean?"

Annie was quiet for a moment, then looked out at the pond

and said, "It's just that I don't know if he'll care. I mean, I know he'll care about the money. That's for sure. But I don't know if he'll care at all about not having me in his life anymore." She looked at Doc. "Isn't that sad. I just don't know if I matter at all."

Doc wasn't sure what to say. To be critical of a man he knew so little about just didn't seem right. And there was still that tinge of guilt. After all, he was the *"other man"* in all this. He was sleeping with another man's wife. It seemed a less than honorable position.

When he didn't respond, Annie turned back to the pond. "I know one thing's for sure. I'm not going to let him hurt me again. Ever again. I feel ashamed I let it go on as long as I did, and I can't explain why."

This was the first time Annie had spoken of the physical abuse to anyone. She wanted to be completely honest with Doc but didn't want to drag him into something he could do nothing about. She was also embarrassed. She didn't know exactly how she could explain the brutal sex without somehow seeming tarnished by it. She feared giving Doc the mistaken impression that there was any part of the aggressive hedonism she enjoyed. She didn't want him to think of her like that.

Doc sensed her embarrassment. He wanted to say something that would ease her pain but no words seemed right. Again, it wasn't his place to enter the bedroom of another man's wife. He said nothing but extended his hand and gently stroked her cheek.

"Someday, I'll tell you all about it." Her gaze never left the pond. "But not now. I don't want to think about it now. I just want to think about us."

"OK. To us then." He raised his glass in a mock toast she didn't see.

The weekend went pretty much the way Doc had planned. They loaded the Grady White with their respective overnight bags, a small cooler, and a couple of beach towels. The ride to Sag Harbor was smooth and they were at the town dock in less than thirty minutes. For twenty bucks, a well-tanned college kid took the line from Doc and secured the boat in an open slip. Sag Harbor keeps a dozen small slips available at the public dock for boaters who come to town for dinning or shopping and it provides summer employment for a few of the town trustees' teenagers.

Because it was already late afternoon, the usual Friday lunch crowd at B. Smith's had thinned out and Doc and Annie dinned alone on the waterfront outdoor terrace. The sky always seemed bluer than normal from the tables at B. Smith's. Doc thought it was because of the stark contrast between the azure sky and the many brilliant white yachts that called this marina home for the summer. At any time you could count vessels from Bermuda, Naples, and places most people never heard of, among the seventy to ninety foot class visiting Sag Harbor. Most over ninety feet were registered to places in Europe and the Middle East with flags of completely unfamiliar colors. It was truly a millionaire's playground.

Which made the public dock appear almost comical with its twenty-foot runabouts arranged in orderly fashion that seemed to mimic their larger cousins just a few yards away. The irony was that most of the enormous vessels were empty, save for their constant crews. The owners might fly in once or twice over the summer for a party or fund-raiser but seldom left the safety of New York or Boston, both an eighty-minute helicopter ride away.

"This place is beautiful Doc. In all the years I've been coming out here, I've never come here for lunch. I didn't even know it was here. My dad used to take me shopping in Sag Harbor but we never came down here near the water. It's quite impressive."

"I'm glad you like it." Doc really was glad. He wanted everything for Annie to be perfect this weekend. "Do you want to take a walk through town and do some shopping?" He added, just in case she wanted to stroll down some fond childhood memory of her and her father.

"No I think we better stay here and make sure none of those big boats eat yours." She smiled as she motioned towards the tiny Grady White bobbing in the sea of giant fiberglass.

After a delightful lunch of B's signature crab cakes and a shared berry tart, they cruised slowly out of Sag Harbor, past Shelter Island and eastward towards the eastern-most part of Long Island, Montauk. The sea was still calm so the ride was smooth and the late-afternoon sun was warm on their backs. Curious gulls followed their wake until convinced there'd be no fishing spoils thrown from this boat.

Once out of the harbor, Doc pushed the throttle and the 225 horsepower outboard thrust them forward, faster than Annie had ever traveled on the water. Her dad always owned a boat, but the type that slept eight, not one that skipped across the surface like a flat stone. She found the speed and the force of the wind in her hair exhilarating.

Doc turned north for a few moments, to get far from the shore, then back to the east. Annie looked back at the white foam in the serpentine wake shimmering in the sunlight. Surrounded on all sides by water and standing next to Doc, she suddenly felt very safe; as if nothing John could do could hurt her now. She wasn't sure if it was due to the wind in her eyes or the beauty all around her, or the warm sun on her shoulders, or just being with Doc; but tears were running from the outer edges of her eyes.

Annie reached over and put her left hand on Doc's hand which was firmly on the throttle. Slowly, almost unnoticeably, she began to pull back on the throttle and the speeding boat slowed a bit. Through the wind and noise, Doc shouted, "Too fast?"

She said nothing but continued to exert pressure on his hand and the boat continued to slow until it was flat in the water. Momentum carried them forward a few more moments but when they came to a complete stop, she reached over and turned the key off. Instantly, there was incredible silence.

Doc looked at her to see what was wrong, but he said nothing. Annie moved around the center console to the bow and sat on the forward bench, her face directly in the sunlight.

"Isn't this beautiful? It's so quiet. It's so peaceful. There's nobody within miles of us."

He had to admit, until she stopped the boat, he was more concerned with navigating than with sightseeing. But, she was right. It was beautiful. The water was a deep clear blue. With the sun sinking on the horizon, its rays shined on the calm surface like a silvery oil.

There was an unusual stillness to the moment; a peacefulness only achieved when you are alone yet in touch with the nature around you.

"You're right. It is beautiful." Doc looked to the horizon. There wasn't another boat within sight, not entirely unusual for late September, even on a beautiful day like this.

Annie motioned for him to join her on the forward cushion. "Come here sailor."

He sat next to her and put his arm around her shoulder. They sat with their faces in the warm sun for several minutes, not a word spoken. Then Annie twisted around and kissed him on the neck. It was a soft kiss but as she concluded, she gave him a playful bite to let him know she was in the mood for more.

"What's on your mind Mrs. Dunn-Weaver?" As soon as he said it he regretted using the word Mrs. It was a garish reminder that they weren't supposed to be here. Not together, and not on their way to a weekend of adultery, Annie's intentions notwithstanding. But it didn't have the same effect on Annie. She seemed not to hear. Her focus was directly on Doc. Her gaze was straight into his eyes and nothing else existed for the moment.

Doc took the cue. He stood and lifted Annie's tiny frame with him, her back against his chest. Then he ran his hands around her waist and slowly pulled her sweater up and over her head, dropping it on the boat's deck. He hesitated a moment to give her a chance to protest. There was none.

His hands got back to work, softly rubbing her bare belly, working their way up to her bra and its contents. He gently caressed her breasts and she arched her head back towards him and sighed. Her eyes were closed but Doc took a moment to scan the horizon for any new boat traffic coming their way. Still none.

Encouraged by their solitude, he kissed her neck. Annie continued to express her approval with another long sigh, then brought her hands behind her, between them, and unclasped her bra. She stretched further back and put her hands behind Doc's neck, interlocking them tightly. Again she sighed her approval.

Doc continued kissing her neck; by now it was one, long, gentle bite. Annie moaned and slowly moved one hand from the back of his neck to let her bra fall to the deck. Then she used her hand to guide Doc's up to her breasts. She was completely oblivious to anything other than his touch. The rest of the world had disappeared for Annie. She was completely lost in the moment and its rapture.

Doc, a bit more aware of his surroundings, kept one eye on the lookout for potential passers-by. Still no one in sight. He cupped and rubbed her breasts until he could feel the hardness of her nipples. Again, a moan from Annie.

It didn't take them long to completely undress and fall onto the forward cushion. Like the previous weekend, Annie was proactive and maneuvered Doc onto his back before climbing on top of him. They were both ready so she took him inside her and began to rock, slowly at first, almost in cadence with the natural motion of the boat, then faster and harder until they both climaxed. Her eyes were still closed tightly and Doc wasn't sure if he'd caused her some pain or if she was simply extending her moment of shivering bliss.

Bliss it was, and she collapsed onto him and hugged him tighter than he'd ever been held before. They lay in the sun, holding each other, for fifteen minutes. As wonderful as this all was, Doc was aware of two realities that needed to be addressed. The first was the sound of another boat's motor approaching but still at some distance. The second was that the sun was sinking in the west and they still had close to an hour to travel before reaching Montauk. They needed to arrive before darkness because he was unfamiliar with the Montauk harbor.

"I hate to spoil the moment," he whispered, "But I think there's a boat coming at us. I want to be the only sailor who sees your cute little ass today, so we'd better get up."

"Not interested in seconds, sailor?"

In a move he was sure he'd regret the rest of his life, Doc persisted and eventually got Annie off him and back in her clothes.

Chapter Thirty-Eight

The sun's rays pierced the old-fashion venetian blinds that hid the charter fleet of Montauk from those inside the Nortic Motel. Doc looked toward the night table next to their bed and learned they'd been asleep for ten hours. It was nine o'clock, Sunday morning. He remembered stumbling back to the room after lobsters and two bottles of McManis merlot at Gossman's, but not much after that. Annie was next to him and naked so he assumed the best. He was right.

He dressed as quietly as he could and sneaked out without waking her. He was determined to find Annie a good cup of coffee but as he glanced up and down the street, he realized he was in for a challenge. Without a car, which he didn't have, there was just about nothing open for business on a Sunday morning. He remembered a pancake place near the docks and resigned himself to the half-mile walk.

It appeared to be another spectacular day but through his squinted eyes, he couldn't be sure. There was still too much light coming in and his head was pounding. The walk along the glaring sidewalk was painful, but he made it to the pancake place, got two large coffees and a blueberry muffin, and was back to the motel in under thirty minutes.

Now, he just needed to remember the room number. Like most motels, the Nortic used only plastic, credit card-type keys that don't have room numbers on them. He stared for a moment at the long row of green doors shining in the morning sun. They all looked the same. After an embarrassing visit to the front desk, he did recall the number 104.

Annie was still asleep and didn't even stir when he opened the blinds. He sat on the edge of the bed admiring her naked back. He felt guilty having an unobstructed view of her ass, so he pulled the sheet up just enough to cover her cheeks. And still she didn't stir.

He gently rubbed her back and whispered, "Annie, you've got coffee waiting for you." And still she didn't move.

Doc realized it had been a while since he shared a home with a woman and maybe some women need more sleep than others. His ex-wife might have been unusual for all he knew, but she couldn't sleep a wink once the sun was up. Maybe Annie was just a very sound sleeper. He decided to give her a few more minutes while he showered and shaved, all the while a bit worried that she was so still.

When he emerged from the bathroom, to his relief, Annie was sitting on the side of the bed wearing a Florida Gators tee shirt. She looked like she was still asleep but she was sitting up with her feet on the floor.

"I was beginning to worry about you."

She groaned, "What time is it?"

"Almost ten –thirty. There's coffee on the table." He made a hand motion toward the small table next to the window.

Annie squinted and shielded her eyes from the harsh morning light streaming through the blinds. "Wow, I hope we had a good time last night because I don't remember much of it." She stretched her neck and arms in an attempt to escape the desire to go back to sleep. "I remember having dinner and you ordered those raspberry things for dessert, but that's about it."

"Well, if it makes you feel any better, I don't remember much past that either. Perhaps we should remember not to have martinis before two bottles of wine. Or maybe…"

"How long have you been up?" She stood and walked toward the bathroom like a zombie.

"About an hour. It's another beautiful day in the neighborhood," he tried to sound like Mr. Rogers.

Annie slid one foot in front of the other until she reached the bathroom door. "If I'm not out in ten minutes, call the fire department."

Doc was relieved when he heard the shower running and the usual sounds of motion coming from the bathroom. Feeling a little guilty, he tried to recall just how much Annie had to drink. There was the apple martini before dinner and several glasses of wine with dinner. After that, things got blurry, but he didn't think they'd gone anywhere else after dinner. Perhaps it was just that she was keeping up with a 190 pound man drink for drink. Annie couldn't weigh more than 120, tops, but he recalled he was a terrible estimator of women's sizes and weights.

Annie emerged from the steamy bathroom looking considerably more alive. She was wrapped in a towel that was too small even for her petite frame. She ordered Doc out of the room while she dressed and prepared for the hideous sunlight waiting beyond the green door. He obliged and passed the time outside the motel by tossing pebbles across the parking lot into the bay.

Perhaps because he raised two daughters, he felt responsible for Annie. Not an ultimate responsibility for her happiness or well-being, but a fatherly obligation to protect her; and certainly not to cause her any harm. Was he irresponsible last night by letting her drink so much? A pang of guilt flushed through him as he recalled his pleasure at the dinner table when Annie ordered a martini before dinner. The first thought that came to mind was that this could only help make his evening more enjoyable. If Annie got drunk the love-making could produce some new and more erotic behavior. Not that she'd been inhibited before.

He thought about his own daughters and how he had so little information about their personal lives; their sex lives. He knew his daughters were pretty open with his ex-wife and could recall times when the ex had refused to share the girls' confidences with him. He assumed that was because she knew he'd react like a father rather than a parent. But the image of either of his twins doing with a man anything like what he'd done with Annie just a few hours ago ran a cold shiver through him. How do daughters go from daddy's little girls to sexually alive women? Where had the years gone?

His trip down parental memory lane was cut short by the sound of Annie's voice from the motel door. "OK, I'm decent. Come on in."

"You OK?" He was sincerely concerned.

"I don't know what happened. It was like I couldn't wake up. Like I was in a dream that I was here, in this bed, but no one could hear me. I felt like I was under a hundred pound blanket and just couldn't wake up."

"Maybe it was a dream."

"Could be, but it was really weird. This happened to me one morning last week at home. I didn't get out of bed until almost noon. I'm just really tired lately."

"You sure you're OK now?"

"I think so. I mentioned it to my doctor yesterday. She thinks my thyroid meds may need to be increased. She's done it before, but I take a pretty high dosage already." She was packing her overnight bag as she spoke.

"So what's on the agenda today Jerome?"

"Please don't call me that. Really, no one calls me Jerome; not since I was in eighth grade." He said it in a very nice way but he was serious and she picked up on the tone.

"OK, Doc it is. So, what's up Doc?" She said it using her best Bugs Bunny voice.

"How about a little breakfast, then we'll take the boat back to Southampton and spend the day on the beach. It's supposed to hit ninety today."

≈≈≈

On the ride back to Southampton they decided to take bikes to the beach, about a five mile ride from Doc's house. Annie had a bike in her garage and met Doc in front of her house, saddled and ready to go. Doc's bike was a rusty old Trek the previous owners decided wasn't worth removing when they handed over the keys. After adding some air to the sagging tires and throwing a beach towel and bottle of water into his backpack, they made their way through Southampton towards Dune Road and the ocean beaches. They peddled without much effort down Halsey Lane, past driveways that disappeared behind meticulously manicured privet hedges. Someone once told Doc that the standard used to measure true wealth in the Hamptons was whether or not your house could be seen from the street. If it could, unless you were directly on the ocean, you obviously didn't have enough property.

Parking a car near the ocean beaches in Southampton is almost impossible, but the town leaves lots of room for bikes. They left the bikes leaning against a sign that spelled out the multitude of rules applying to beachgoers and walked down to the ocean. Doc spread the oversized towel on the sand about twenty feet from the shoreline. Annie pulled off her tee shirt revealing the top of a very skimpy yellow bikini. She plopped herself next to Doc on the towel.

"You want to go in for a swim?" He hadn't thought to wear a swim suit under his shorts.

"Later. First let's just catch some sun. This may be the last hoorah for summer. Let's enjoy it."

Doc started to tell her a story about the time his dad buried him at the beach many years ago, but half way through he noticed Annie was already asleep.

Chapter Thirty-Nine

As wonderful as the weekend had been for Annie, she knew the next 24 hours were likely to be some of the worst of her life. She was right. She just didn't know why yet.

As she drove back to New York, she rehearsed the conversation with John she dreaded. It would be easier, she thought, if she hated him. But, despite the mistreatment and shallow relationship they called a marriage, she didn't hate him. She actually felt sorry for him.

Was it really his fault he was the kind of man he was? She knew John had a strange and segmented childhood. His father abandoned his mother and his three brothers when John was in kindergarten. His mom had remarried when John was a teen but drank herself into an early grave and at seventeen John was an orphan. His oldest brother, who had married well, took him in and insisted John go to college despite his interest in the navy.

When they first met, he often spoke about his mother. Usually, it was to blame her for one of his many flaws. In that way, John was a fatalist. He often told Annie he didn't feel in control of his own life; that his genetic porridge determined his limitations and potential. It was always someone else's fault.

So it didn't seem fair to hate him for the pain he's caused. Even the physical abuse was probably programmed into his life long before he ever met Annie. She was just the closest available victim, and ironically, the victim felt sorry for the demon.

Annie was shaken back to the moment by the sound of her cell phone humming on the passenger seat. She put the earpiece in her right ear without diverting attention from the road and silently hoped it was Doc calling.

It wasn't. It was better. Her son Nick was calling to check in—something he did at least three times a week since moving to Boston.

"Hey, Mom. Where have you been? I've left you a couple of messages at your apartment."

Annie wasn't ready to tell her son about Doc, or her plans to leave John yet. She owed it to her husband to talk to him first. "Hey baby. I rode out to Southampton on Friday afternoon. It was such a nice day here I wanted to..." She thought for a moment. "I wanted to do some cleaning at the house while John's away. You know how he hates when I clean."

"Is everything OK? You sound funny?"

"Yes, yes. Everything's great. I'm just driving back from there now. I'm on the expressway."

"How come you haven't answered your cell until now? I left you a couple of voicemails there too."

She realized she'd turned her phone off when she pulled into Doc's driveway two days ago and hadn't thought about it since. Rather than lying to her son, Annie changed the topic.

"How's school? Have you gotten any marks yet?"

"No. Nothing yet. But my Quant Analysis prof is a pretty cool guy. He's taking us to his office tomorrow to see what a trading floor looks like in action."

"Do you think it's..." Annie was interrupted by the sound of another call. "Hold on a sec. I have another call. Let me see who it is and I'll get rid of them." She was hoping it was Doc and she'd call him right back.

"Hello."

"Mrs. Weaver, please." The voice was unfamiliar.

"Speaking. Who's this?"

"This is Gloria from Doctor Weber's office. The doctor would like to speak to you. Please hold for Dr. Weber."

Chapter Forty

The sign said "Queens Midtown Tunnel" but Annie's mind was miles away. She'd forgotten to call her son back after the call from Tomasue Weber. The last forty miles of her drive were a blur of "*what ifs?*" and the mental gymnastics that people do when they can suddenly no longer take their health for granted.

Her doctor's words were deliberately neutral and vague, but her tone worried Annie even more. Dr. Weber had confirmed Annie needed to increase the dosage of the thyroid medication but said other tests left her concerned. Something about unusually high calcitonin levels and lower than normal range TSH. Whatever it meant, it was important enough that she wanted to see Annie right away and rerun the blood tests, although her words were, "*It might just be a bad reading from the lab.*"

As the ribbon of lights on the tunnel ceiling raced by, Annie thought about her dad. Wasn't this the way it started with him? Wasn't it a routine check up that revealed the cancerous demon destroying him from within? It all started with a blood test that came back "*unusual*".

She parked her car in her building's underground garage then walked the seven blocks to Dr. Weber's office. The fresh air did her good. As she walked, she tried to think about what was really most upsetting. Was it the thought that she might be sick herself, or was it the awful memory of the last few months of her father's life? As painful as her husband's death was for her, Peter died instantly in an accident. He didn't suffer the agonizing atrophy of lung cancer over fourteen months. And Annie's grief was sudden and shocking, not the type that comes from watching the slow inevitable downward spiral she helped her father endure.

Two other patients were sitting in Tomasue's waiting room, both casually leafing through magazines. Gloria, the receptionist, buzzed her boss and was told to have Annie come in and wait in one of the examining rooms. One of the PA's took two vials of blood from Annie's arm, weighed her and was about to take her blood pressure when Tomasue entered the room.

"That's OK, Lauren, I'll do the BP." Tomasue said to her assistant and took the BP cuff from her. "I want to talk to Annie anyway."

When the PA closed the door behind her, Tomasue leaned against the counter and began. "I'm sorry if I alarmed you when I called this afternoon. I wanted to make sure you came back today so we can rerun the blood work. Some of the results on the first sample were very *unusual*."

Annie was struck by the choice of words. Her doctor didn't notice and continued.

"As we both suspected, your chronic fatigue may be caused by your lazy thyroid. I'm going to give you a prescription for twice the dosage of Synthroid. You should start the new meds right away and let's see if that makes a difference. If not; if you don't feel better in a couple of weeks, we can up it a bit more, but I like to take it in steps." She looked at Annie to make sure she understood, and then went on.

"The underactive thyroid could be the cause of the fatigue, but I want to be sure there's nothing else going on." She paused to check Annie's chart.

"How's your appetite been?

"Normal, I guess. I mean I haven't noticed any change." Annie tried to think about her meals the pass few days with Doc. "If anything, I've been eating a little more than I usually do because I've been eating out a lot lately."

"Any change in bowel movements; any blood?"

"No."

"Unusual headaches or pain in your joints?"

"No. I'm just tired."

"OK. Let's see what the new blood work gives us and we'll take it…" Annie cut her off.

"Tomasue, you're not telling me what you're really thinking. What's up?"

For Doctor Tomasue Weber, the hardest part of her job was telling her patients when she suspects cancer. It's a word that paralyzes some people, like yelling 'shark' at the beach. And until the tests confirm her suspicions, she didn't like to alarm patients. But Annie was more than a patient, she was a friend, and Tomasue knew her friend was already thinking the worse because of her father's ordeal just a few years ago.

"Look, Annie…until I see the results of the retest, I don't want to jump to any conclusions. It may just be your body's reaction to the low levels of thyroxine because the Synthroid's not doing its job."

"Or it may be what?" Annie's tone was firm. She didn't want to play games and expected straight answers from her doctor and friend.

Tomasue hesitated, and then adjusted her position against the counter. "I don't like the high thyroglobulin count. When I see that with low TSH range, I look for thyroid cancer cells." She hurried her pace. "I'm not saying it can't be ten other things, but high thyroglobulin and low TSH are usually the result of a thyroid tumor or MTC. That's medullary thyroid cancer. It could be telling us your body's fighting some form of cancer." The word hung in the air while both women looked at each other for a full fifteen seconds.

"But, like I said, it could be lots of other things and it could also be just a bad blood test. Let's look at the second test tomorrow before we worry too much."

Annie put on her brave face and said, "OK. Let's see tomorrow. When will you get the results?"

"We should have them back first thing in the morning. Maybe even late tonight." Tomasue felt guilt about lying to her patient. She knew the results could be available in a couple of hours but didn't want to raise Annie's expectations.

"So, you'll call me when you've got them?" It was half question and half statement of what Annie expected.

"I'll call your cell as soon as I get the results. Let's hope for the best. In the meantime, get this prescription for the new Synthroid filled as soon as you can and start taking the increased dose right away. You take it in the morning, right?" Tomasue handed Annie the prescription.

"Yep. One each morning." Annie curled her lip as if thinking about something, then slid off the examining table and said, "You know, when I got up this morning I knew this was going to be a shitty day. I just didn't realize how shitty it could be."

CHAPTER FORTY-ONE

The clock on the microwave oven shined 4:45. John Weaver had been home most of the afternoon catching up on some reading. His weekend in Atlantic City proved successful; he came home with twenty two thousand dollars more than he brought, and Miranda had been excellent company. After dropping her at her apartment, he came home to find a note from Annie saying she'd be back from Southampton by three and had made dinner reservations for them at seven.

John thought nothing of the reason for Annie's trip to Southampton. He knew she drove out there often just to check on the house or to pick up some clothing she left behind. It never occurred to him that his wife could have a romantic interest. He just didn't think of her that way. Annie was his alone. He was sure the infidelity in this family went one way.

He fixed himself his favorite afternoon cocktail, a Maker's Mark on the rocks, and then hunted through the refrigerator for something to go with it. It appeared as though Annie hadn't been food shopping since they got back from Southampton on Labor Day. Only the bare essentials: coffee, orange juice, milk, and a couple of low-fat yogurts graced the top shelf. The others were completely barren.

As he settled into a chair at the kitchen table, he thought about the coming week. He tried to conjure a mental image of his weekly calendar, the one he kept on his desk at the office. He remembered correctly that Tuesday was a pretty light day. Usually, when he spent the weekend in Atlantic City, he left

Tuesday open in case lady luck was with him and he wanted one more day to have her shine on his cards. After Tuesday, he knew he had a few busy days coming up.

Since he had a few extra minutes, he decided to shower. Miranda had worn some heavy perfume and he didn't need Annie's better-than-average nose picking up on it. That happened once before and it erupted into a two hour argument about her lack of trust in him. Better to smell of soap than hooker. It caused less friction.

When he emerged from the bathroom he heard a sound in the kitchen. "Annie? That you?"

"It's me John. Sorry I'm late." She was carrying a small overnight bag and a very small paper bag.

"How's Southampton?" He gave her a peck on the check and Annie could tell from the strong smell of Dial soap that he too wasn't alone the last few days.

"Yeah, fine. I needed to pick up a few things and it was such a beautiful day yesterday I stayed over."

"What's in the bag?" John asked pointing to the paper bag.

"Oh, Tomasue increased the dosage on my Synthroid because I've been so tired lately. I picked up the prescription on my way back from her office."

"You saw her today?"

"Yes. She called me on my way home so I stopped there before I came home."

"Everything all right?" He seemed more concerned than she ever remembered.

"I think so. She didn't like something about the blood sample from last week so she asked me…"

"You saw her last week too? What for?" Now he seemed angry that she hadn't told him about a routine doctor visit.

"I just told you. I've been really tired lately. Apparently my thyroid's on the blink again so I moved up my annual physical a few weeks and I saw her on Friday before I went east."

John sat at the table. He was wearing just a bathrobe. "I thought you just said you went east on Sunday."

To her great surprise, Annie didn't care about being caught in the lie. It seemed insignificant considering the circumstances. Their mutual weekend infidelities notwithstanding, she was about to tell her husband she planned to leave him and she was waiting to hear from her doctor about what could be a serious illness. A little lie at this point seemed like small potatoes and wasn't worth the effort to cover up.

"No. I went out on Friday. You misunderstood me."

She really wanted to shower and change before dinner. She hoped John hadn't noticed that many of her clothes were gone; already moved to the Essex apartment she'd rented in anticipation of the break-up. Reflecting on his lack of attention to detail, especially when it came to Annie, she relaxed. But she was anything but relaxed about the conversation she planned to have with him in a few hours.

"I made a reservation at Dinoto's for seven o'clock. Is that OK?"

"Fine."

"I want to shower first, then take a quick nap. My head is pounding and I'm beat from the drive." Annie was famous for her fifteen minute power naps from which she could awaken completely refreshed.

"Yeah, sure. Hey, what was it about your blood work she didn't like?" John twisted around in his seat to face Annie.

"Oh, I don't know. Something was too high and something was too low. They took more blood and should have the results tomorrow." Annie really didn't want to get into it with John.

He was a respected doctor but after tonight, she didn't expect to be hearing much from him for awhile. She was surprised when he let it go at that.

"I'll be in the shower." But before she could leave the kitchen, her cell phone was vibrating in her pocketbook. She thought about letting it go to voicemail. It could be Doc checking to see if she got home safely. But she answered it, partly in open defiance of her husband. If it was Doc, she'd playfully fake a conversation as if it was a wrong number and he'd understand she couldn't talk.

"Hello." It wasn't Doc's voice. It was a woman. A familiar voice.

"Annie, this is Tomasue. Have you got a minute?"

"Sure." Annie glanced at John across the room and mouthed the words *"Doctor Weber"*.

He swiveled his chair around. Annie was standing, leaning against the kitchen counter.

"I got the blood work back. Annie, it's not what I had hoped. I'd like to talk to you about it."

Annie felt as if she'd been punched in the stomach. All the air rushed out and her legs buckled before she caught herself. John noticed her reaction and leaped to his feet to steady her. He got his arm under hers and moved her toward a chair. Her cell phone was still in her hand and John could hear a faint voice calling, *"Annie, Annie, are you alright?"*

He pried the phone from her grip and motioned to Annie that he would take care of it.

"This is Doctor John Weaver; Annie's husband."

"John, this is Tomasue Weber. Is Annie alright?"

"Yeah, I think you startled her. She's sitting down now." John looked at Annie to see if she wanted him to continue or if she wanted to speak for herself. Annie motioned for the cell phone.

"Hold on Tomasue. I'll put her back on." He cupped the small phone against his robe and said to Annie, "You sure you're up for this?"

She nodded and took the phone. "OK. Shoot."

Tomasue's voice was calm and reassuring. "Annie, I'm about to leave the office anyway. I can stop by in ten minutes and we can talk if that's OK with you."

"That's fine. Thanks. It's 115-10 Fifth Avenue. I'll tell the doorman to let you up. Apartment 18-A." Although they'd been friendly for years, neither had ever been to the others' home. "I guess I'll see you in a few minutes then."

When she flipped the phone closed she looked across the kitchen table at John. His left hand extended across the polished wood in a gesture of caring. "What's going on?"

Annie hesitated, then said softly, "She's coming over to talk about my lab results."

John knew his wife and Tomasue Weber had been friendly for many years; long before he met Annie. He knew they occasionally met for lunch and played tennis together a few times last summer. Even so, he thought it odd that she would come to a patient's home to discuss the results of a medical test. "She's coming here?"

"Her office is just a few blocks away. It's on her way home anyway." Annie said the words but her mind was already far away, flicking from one mortal thought to another. *It must be really bad news. Why would she want to talk to me so soon? I can't be sick. Not now. I have too much to do. I was just about to straighten out my life. Not now.*

John's concern was obvious in his voice. "What did she say? Exactly what did she say, Annie?"

Before she realized what she'd done Annie had reached for John's hand on the table. The thought of hearing bad news was hard enough; she didn't want to be alone. For the first time in many years, she was scared. And after all, John was a doctor. He could help interpret the words. Isn't this exactly when you wanted to be married to a doctor?

"I don't remember. It didn't seem important a few hours ago. Something was too high and something was too low. She thought it was my thyroid again." She looked at John with a desperation that said, '*You can fix this can't you?*'

They sat together holding hands across the table for several minutes. Finally, Annie said, "I want to use the bathroom before she gets here. I'll be right back."

It took Dr. Weber a few minutes longer to extricate herself from her office and by the time she arrived at Annie's building she realized it had been forty-five minutes since their phone conversation. The doorman, Leo, an Ed Wynn look-alike, showed her to the right elevator and reached in to push 18 for her. He said the apartment would be the one on the left as she exited the elevator, and the brass doors slid shut.

During the ascent, Tomasue thought about how difficult these conversations always were. This one would be especially tough because she really liked Annie. Maybe too, because they were so close in age and otherwise healthy women on the wrong side of fifty just aren't supposed to die. They're supposed to grow old and play with their grandchildren and meet for lunch and do volunteer work.

The doors slid open and, just as Leo said, there were only two apartments on the floor. She rang the bell in the center of Annie's door; the one marked Dr. J. Weaver.

CHAPTER FORTY-TWO

"Yes, we had a great time."

"Where did you go?" His daughter wanted to know all about his weekend.

Doc filled Peggy in on most of the details. He told her about their lunch in Sag Harbor at B. Smith's, one of his daughter's favorites. He told her what he could remember about dinner at Gossman's and their day at the beach in Southampton, their shopping and bike ride. He left out the boat ride details.

"Sounds like you guys had a great time." Peggy's enthusiasm was evident. Doc knew his daughter worried about him. Of the two, Peggy was the one who wanted him to live with her for a few months. She thought it would help him make the adjustment to retirement and she couldn't see him living alone in Southampton; not over the winter. The idea that her father had finally found someone made her very happy.

"It really was wonderful. We just enjoy each other." He thought he'd leave it at that. Doc considered himself a progressive father but wasn't about to have a conversation about his sleep habits with his daughter.

"I'm so glad for you. So when do I get to meet her?"

Doc was a long way from introducing Annie, still a married woman, to his daughters. He figured if Annie moved out of her apartment this week, as she'd planned, and got a place of her own, and was on her way to a formal separation and divorce, then maybe he'd arrange a dinner in the city in a few weeks. Maybe.

"Kitty will be in New York in the end of October. How about I try to set up a dinner for the four of us then?" He hoped that would appease her. "So what's new in the legal profession?"

"Not too much. I'm still working on that merger of the two software companies I'm not allowed to talk about. That's been keeping all of us pretty busy. The due diligence is a bitch."

Doc could tell that his daughter was at work, and if he wasn't going to divulge any juicy info about his new lady-friend, she was losing interest in the conversation. She probably needed to get back to work.

"OK, then. I'll talk to you over the weekend. Don't work too hard sweety."

"Are you seeing Annie again this weekend?"

The honest answer was that he didn't know. Annie hadn't said when she'd be out again. She just said she needed to settle things with John and then take it a day at a time. He knew she'd be busy with a new place but sort of hoped she'd want his help. Or maybe that wouldn't be appropriate; the 'other man' helping her move out on her husband.

"Maybe. We don't have plans yet."

"Alright Daddy, I have to go. I love ya. Talk to you in a few days."

CHAPTER FORTY-THREE

Tomasue and John had done most of the talking. Annie listened as if it wasn't her life they were discussing, but certain words stood in stark contrast to the otherwise professional dialog between the two doctors. She heard Tomasue use the word metastases several times when explaining why she was concerned about the elevated white cell count. Her husband, a professional oncologist, used the word carcinoma as casually as if he were saying headache. And they both seemed focused on the word, *metastases*. None of it sounded good.

"Annie, before we jump to any conclusions, we need to do more tests." Tomasue now turned her attention to her patient.

"I agree." John nodded. "We need to get you in tomorrow for an ultrasound profile of the neck, an x-ray, and an MRI. We can't know anything for certain until we see the lymph node metastases."

Annie needed a layperson's explanation. "Why? What will that tell you?"

John was the first to realize the conversation had been mostly in arcane medical terms that meant little to Annie. He tried to take a step back and slowly explained what Dr. Weber had said—that Annie's blood was filled with CEA, or carcinogenic antigen, usually an indicator of advanced stages of cell deterioration due to adenocarcinoma.

"Annie, it could be ten other things so let's not get crazy yet."

"But what you're telling me is that if it is what you think…"

Tomasue cut her off. "I didn't say I've come to that conclusion yet."

Annie pushed ahead. "…if it is what you think it is, then I've got cancer in my thyroid that may have already spread." She turned her attention to her husband. "John, please don't lie to me about this. I remember the words they used when my father got sick. It took months before anyone gave him a straight answer at North Shore. I want to know what's going on here."

Tomasue glanced at her watch. She felt like she was now the unnecessary third wheel. Annie's husband was a noted oncologist. If their fears about the lab results were confirmed, he would be infinitely more qualified to oversee Annie's diagnosis and treatment plan. He would be the one to try to save her life. As her doctor, he would be the one to determine how aggressively they should fight. As her husband, he would be the one to sit at her side when she was ravaged by the chemicals he would prescribe.

"Annie, John is right. We know nothing for certain until he runs those tests. Don't torture yourself needlessly." Then, in an attempt to extricate herself from the room, she said to John, "Will you call me when you have the results? I'd like to go over them with you if you don't mind."

"Sure. Of course. We'll know a lot more tomorrow." He recognized that Tomasue wanted to leave them alone. "I'll get the elevator for you."

When John walked into the hall to summon the elevator, Annie shot Tomasue a look of desperation. *"How can this be happening?"* They hugged. Annie held on tightly and Tomasue returned the embrace.

"I'll talk to you tomorrow. Let's hope for good news."

Annie watched her friend disappear into the hall and dropped her head. She took a seat at the kitchen table and waited for John to return. She could hear them speaking in muffled tones near the elevator but made no attempt to understand the words. She'd heard enough.

When John returned he closed the apartment door and put his hands on her shoulders. He attempted to calm his wife with a gentle massage and the words, "Hey, we don't know anything yet. Let's take this one step at a time." Then he sat next to her. "You know I'm here for you, no matter what. Right?"

But Annie's thoughts were already on others. If this was the same horrible demon that had taken her father, what she dreaded most was not the suffocating pain she watched him endure; it was not the nausea and sickness that always followed the chemotherapy, it was not the slow agonizing death she witnessed helplessly. It was the terrifying thought that she may have passed this villainous fate on to her sons. The thought that her boys might have already inherited this damaged gene scared her more than whatever fate awaited her.

CHAPTER FORTY-FOUR

It hadn't taken John very long to line up the tests he pre-scribed. Everyone at his office leaped into action when they heard it was for Annie. The ultrasonography was set for eight o'clock the next morning, followed immediately by the chest x-ray and the MRI. They could all be done within the practice at John's New York office although he wanted the ultrasound performed at the Sloan Kettering, a few blocks away, because they were the best. It took only a few minutes and two phone calls for him to get it set up.

Annie had taken a shower and was dressing. She still had trouble believing this was happening. Tomasue had been gone less than an hour but the words were already blurring. Annie's mind was racing in the shower, mostly trying to recall the terminology used when her dad was diagnosed. *Did they say cancinoma right away? Or did that come later? How long was it until he really got bad?*

She was confusing the facts of her case, the few they knew, with what she remembered about her father's illness. She needed to calm down. She needed to do what John had said, *"Take it one day at a time."*

As she stood in front of her closet trying to decide what to wear, she remembered the dinner reservation she'd made. This wasn't the time for a heart-to-heart with John. How could she even think about it now? She needed to know what tomorrow would bring. She needed to know if she'd even be alive a year from now. Separation from her husband now seemed trivial in light of the information she'd been given in the last few hours.

If she was sick, if she needed to fight the fight of her life, wouldn't she need John at her side? Wouldn't most people, faced with such a crisis, be grateful to be married to a talented doctor who specialized in fighting cancer? He'd saved so many others; wouldn't he be exactly the person you'd want trying to save you? John was renowned in his field. In matters relating to stage four cancers, John Weaver was one of the few specialists in New York to whom the sick were usually referred by their primary care physicians.

No, if there was ever a time she needed John, it was now. She would have to push thoughts of divorce and separation from her head. As most do, Annie always took her good health for granted. Suddenly, all her priorities were thrown upside down. Now, she needed to focus on the information she didn't have twenty four hours ago when she was lying in the arms of another man. The thought suddenly made her flush with guilt.

Less than a full day ago she was with another man, Doc; someone she had no right to. Not yet. She stared at herself in the full length mirror which hung on the back of the open closet door. How did she become that woman? How did this thing with Doc happen? She didn't go looking for it. She wasn't the kind of person who cheats on their husband. She was a devoted mother and daughter. She was the one who endured, not the one who requires endurance. How did this happen?

And then, suddenly, she began to weep. Standing there, wearing only her under garments, she sobbed with no clear understanding of why. Was it the illness she dreaded, or was it the shame she felt? Or was it because either reason would have caused her father, whose approval she needed even after he was gone, to look away in disappointment? She didn't know, although she suspected it was all these as well as the betrayal of her husband. She wept without understanding.

John heard the sobbing from the kitchen and rushed to the bedroom. He saw her standing in front of the mirror, half clothed and weeping uncontrollably.

"Hey, we'll get through this." He put his arms around her in a tight embrace.

Annie's embarrassment and shame were only amplified by this unexpected and unusual show of concern from John, the man whose touch usually caused her to flinch. Perhaps he still possessed the kindness she once saw in him. Perhaps they just needed to need each other. Maybe this would be the force that moved them towards each other. How ironic that she'd planned to leave him in just a few…

"Oh my god! John, I made dinner reservations." She said through the sobs although the significance of the realization was lost on him.

"One thing at a time, honey." He hugged her from behind. "Let me take care of everything for you for now. Let me take care of you."

"Oh John. I'm so frightened." The sobs were subsiding.

"One thing at a time."

CHAPTER FORTY-FIVE

Doc

Ordinarily, I wouldn't have thought of photographing rooftops on my own. My plans for a pictorial of the area included wildlife and scenes of natural wonder; not man-made intrusions. It wasn't until going through some images on my computer last night that the idea came to me. After uploading all the new shots from my camera to my laptop, I began to delete those that were obvious "throwbacks".

Earlier in the afternoon, I happened upon a flock of Canadian geese resting on the pond. After creeping to within fifty yards of the majestic birds, I snapped on a telephoto lens and switched settings so my Cannon EOS would take multiple exposures with a single click. My plan was to capture, in a series of motion shots, the moments the colorful flock took flight and follow them skyward.

For the most part, I was successful in that I got a few good shots of the first few seconds of flight with the afternoon sun over my shoulder casting a perfect light on my subjects. Three consecutive frames were good enough to make it to my "could be" folder which stored any shots I felt warranted further consideration. Displayed in succession, they might make a nice two-page layout in the book I hoped to publish next year.

Toward the end of the geese series, when I tried to follow their flight path higher in the sky, I was missing more of the fast moving Canadians then I was getting. But, in the process, I noticed I had captured several shots of the nearby rooftops with a clear blue sky as a backdrop. Because I was standing on the ground, shooting up, the angles are what really caught my eye; a roof corner here, a window and shutter there, and one shot of bright green soffit and fascia protecting a pale yellow house at the ponds edge.

Most people would see these shots for what they were; a series of missed opportunities. But it gave me an idea. Perhaps a section of my yet-to-be-fully-developed book could contain photographs of the homes around the pond; not the entire house, just a colorful window or a particularly attractive ceramic planter. I once saw a book in Borders that was hundreds of pictures of doors; mostly front doors on homes of significance, but some humble ones too. So why couldn't I add some shots of the places the *'people of the pond'* lived in?

And after giving it more thought, I decided my quirky approach would be to photograph only the corners of rooftops with skies of varying colors in the background. If nothing else, the few dozen people who lived in those homes might have fun trying to guess which corner was a part of their house.

I began my morning walking around taking odd shots of the corners of all the homes' rooflines. The high wispy September clouds provided a great backdrop for my first crack at this rather unusual endeavor. First, I took shots from the beach, looking back at the beachfront homes. Then I walked through a bunch of my neighbors' yards to take advantage of the morning sun's low angle. Finally, I got in my kayak and paddled around the shoreline of the pond to get shots of the back of most of the pond-front homes. My odd behavior bothered no one because, at this time of year, there are only a handful of people out here anyway.

All this kept my mind off Annie from whom I hadn't heard since she left on Monday afternoon. I knew she was planning to lower the boom on her husband at dinner Monday night, so I was surprised she didn't call me on Tuesday. I must say, I felt a bit guilty having advance knowledge of the event. I mean, it's sort of like knowing a guy is going to get whacked at a certain restaurant and not saying anything to warn him. Well, not exactly the same, but I felt guilty regardless. After all, I was in love with the guy's wife. Perhaps that's where the guilt comes in.

Anyway, I was a little worried about her. I could see how nervous she was on Monday morning when we had breakfast on the deck. She was distracted and jumpy, not usually her profile. When I asked her about it, she confided that while she had no doubts about what she needed to do and had given this much thought, she was concerned about her husband's reaction. He had a tendency toward violent outbursts when angry and she was pretty sure this news wasn't going to make him happy. That's why she chose to do it in a restaurant, with lots of other people around. That's also why she'd already arranged an apartment for herself at the Essex House. She didn't want to spend another night with him after she told him about her plans for a divorce.

As I paddled back to shore, I thought about the fact that Annie had chosen the Essex House for her sanctuary. It made me wonder, for the first time, just how wealthy she really was. I mean, the Essex House has got to be one of the most expensive places to live on Central Park South. And Central Park South has got to be one of the most expensive streets in Manhattan to start with. I'd probably need to sell my Jeep to afford a park-view room there for just a weekend.

Annie had seldom spoken of money. She said only that her father had left her twin sons *well provided for*. She also mentioned that her former husband, who she spoke of with near reverence, had been an investment banker. You don't see many of those guys driving five year-old Jeeps. And then there was the soon-to-be-extinct John, a respected and successful oncologist with offices in Manhattan and East Hampton. I wasn't in danger of tripping over him at the Jeep dealership either.

So, I'd just assumed that Annie wasn't lying awake at night worrying about paying the mortgage—if she even knew what a mortgage was. I suppose the six-bedroom bay-front house in Southampton could have been a clue too.

In fact, the only time I remember Annie mentioning money at all, was once, while we were running. She said she felt like John resented her for the wealth she inherited, while he had to work so hard for his standard of living. She felt that John expected a very privileged life after marriage; one, that by most peoples' standards, he already enjoyed. But he was disappointed to find that Annie's family wealth was tied up in complicated trusts her father set up shortly before his death. He would have been further put off if he knew that Burt Dunn had set those trusts up precisely so John would never get his hands on the money. Apparently, even while dealing with cancer, old Burt saw John for the social climber he was and insulated the wealth he intended for his only daughter and grandsons by setting up generation-skipping trusts. In doing so, a generous but not lavish allowance was doled out annually to Annie but the real money was safely in the trusts for Nick and Frank, only once they reached twenty-three.

Anyway, it seems Annie has no trouble living within her allowance—I assumed that meant interest and dividends—but that John was hoping for a more lavish lifestyle and perhaps, an early retirement. According to Annie, he also liked to gamble, but she left it at that. From the one time I met him at the barbeque, I also had the impression he liked to drink; not that I would be the first to cast stones on that minor personality flaw.

I wanted to call Annie. I wanted to hear her soft voice and

just know that she was OK, but I decided against it. She said she'd call me when she could and seemed firm that was the way it should be. Also, although I was deeply infatuated with her, loved her, our relationship was young and I didn't want to seem pushy or, more importantly, I didn't want to seem desperate. After all, we met less than a month ago and, aside from the last two wonderful weekends, we'd spent very little time together. The thought occurred to me that perhaps I was just a bridge for her; a bridge from one relationship to whatever comes next. Divorce can be a frightening prospect for people. It certainly was for me, and maybe Annie's feelings for me have been fueled by her fear of being alone after leaving John.

Then again, she told me she'd decided to leave John long before she met me and that our relationship had nothing to do with the timing. My ego doubted that but good sense told me to believe her. And anyway, we hadn't spoken about a future together. We've sort of just been living and enjoying the moment, but I know we would be great together. She's as relaxed about most things as I am. She doesn't seem to need the finer things but enjoys them particularly when she can do so with others. We both love good food and red wine. We have completely different tastes in music but can appreciate the other's tastes and I could learn to tolerate her Enya CD. We both have two grown children that we don't see as much as we'd like, but we seem to have good relationships with them.

We both planned to vote for Obama in the upcoming election. We both like reading the Times on Sunday and working on the crossword over cocktails in the afternoon. We both like Chris Rock, Robin Williams and the Godfather I and II, but hate Rosie O'Donnell, Hillary, and Al Sharpton. On the latter, Annie was emphatic.

We are compatible on many levels; certainly all the important ones. At least that's the way it seems so far. So, I think we would be great together. I could see us as two old people sitting on the deck years from now, watching our grandchildren playing in the sand.

The one, really big one we've yet to discuss is religion. I know she was brought up Catholic, but so was I and that didn't seem to stick. Once, when we were lying in bed, of all places, I wanted to ask her if she believed in God. I think it was in response to her saying something about her father and husband being in heaven and that they'd be looking down on us approvingly. Aside from how much that creeped me out, it presented an opportunity to see if she really believed in an afterlife, or if like many people, she just said things like that on blind faith and wishful thinking. Because I couldn't shake the image of Burt and Peter—two people I've never met—sitting on a cloud and watching our post-coital cuddling, I didn't ask.

But I wanted to. I honestly couldn't care less what her beliefs were, but I was concerned that my recent conversion to the "church of the non-believers" might be important to her. To tell the truth, I am torn. On the one hand, it would be great if my soul mate, the person I can see rocking on the deck with me thirty years hence, felt the same way I did. I would draw strength from knowing someone else close to me had also lost their faith and was completely OK with a world without God.

On the other hand, it would also be nice if Annie had strong feelings and beliefs about God. I would certainly respect that and never say anything to disparage her views or try to change her mind. If her faith was strong enough, maybe she could change mine. That would be wonderful too.

Chapter Forty-Six

Annie needed to talk. She needed time to catch her breath and talk to someone who wasn't wearing a white coat. For the past six and a half hours she'd been shuffled between examining rooms and testing areas, probed, stuck and x-rayed. She was beginning to feel more like a specimen than the wife of one of the senior partners at this practice.

And yet, it was John who was dutifully overseeing every aspect of her ordeal. He'd gone in to work early to arrange time slots for all her tests; tests that might otherwise have taken weeks to coordinate at several different medical facilities. He called each specialist and radiologist at home the night before to be sure they, and not some second-stringer, would be available to run the needed tests on his wife. From her bedroom, Annie could hear him on the phone with each person, carefully explaining the information they had from Dr. Weber and the protocols John wanted in place the next morning.

"I don't want my wife sitting in the waiting room for hours between tests." She heard him shout into the phone at one of the radiologists who was trying to clear time for her unexpected visit. On another call she heard him confide to one of his partners, "Doug, I don't know what I'll do if... please just get this done for us tomorrow. I can't go another twenty-four hours without knowing for sure."

Tests that would otherwise take days or weeks to schedule anywhere else in Manhattan, had all been done in a few hours. The only procedure that wasn't done at John's office was the ultrasound. For that, John insisted they use the machine and technicians at the Sloan Kettering, only a few blocks away, because they had the highest resolution ultrasound equipment in the city. John walked Annie to the hospital and waited while the test was done.

And now she was sitting in John's office waiting for him to come back from a consult with one of his associates. It occurred to her that she'd probably only been there once before. As a rule, he didn't like her to drop in unexpectedly during the day. John had always drawn a clear and prominent line between his professional life and his marriage. When he was here, he was Dr. John Weaver, noted oncologist. He took his medical ambitions seriously and didn't see overlap between his career and his wife.

She glanced around the room. She knew this had been John's office long before they met but was still surprised there wasn't a single reference to their marriage; not even a picture of the two of them. The smartly decorated office was well lit and comfortable but retained a professional aura. Certificates and diplomas hung in expensive wooden frames, filling one full wall. The other wall held a large back-lit screen for viewing MRI films.

It was approaching five in the afternoon. She'd under-gone seven tests and was tired. John promised they'd know the results today but he insisted they not discuss any of the individual tests until he had all the results and radiological write-ups in hand. Some of this was his compulsive nature, but Annie assumed it meant John was expecting the worst from the tests. Hopefully, when taken together, he could find some reason to be hopeful.

He'd been gone only ten minutes but in that time, Annie made a mental list of what she needed to do if the news was bad. First, she had to call her sons. If it was the news she feared most, she wouldn't tell them the whole story right away. Better to break it to them gradually. Nick would want to rush home and interrupting his senior year wasn't going to make her any less…

The office door swung open. John and another doctor, a woman in a white coat, came into the room. Annie rose to greet them and extended her hand to the other woman.

"Annie, this is Deborah Cox, Doctor Deborah Cox. Deb is our chief hematologist. She's the best blood specialist on the east side."

Dr. Cox took Annie's hand. "Hello Mrs. Weaver. It's nice to finally meet you." Then she sat on the edge of John's desk while John motioned for she and Annie to sit on the leather sofa a few feet away.

"Annie, I asked Dr. Cox to join us because she's been doing a lot of research in the area of genealogical recessive trait RET mutation. She's gone over your blood work and the results we had faxed over from Tomasue's office."

Annie felt the air rush from her again and steadied herself against the arm of the sofa.

"Annie, it's as bad as we feared. Your blood shows advanced medullary thyroid carcinoma. This means your body's been fighting the cancer cells for a long time, probably years." John turned and faced her directly. "The MRI is pretty conclusive." He regretted the word as soon as it left his lips. "Actually, they are very conclusive."

Dr. Cox could see that John was having trouble saying the words to his wife he'd had to say so often to his patients. She wanted to spare him the pain. "Annie, your body's been fighting cancer for some time now. This has been metastasizing for several months, maybe a year. I wish I had better news but generally when serum calcitonin counts are this high, there's nothing else it can be."

John held Annie's hand. "Annie, we're going to fight this. We can beat this."

Annie looked down at the oriental carpet. Her mouth was dry and she felt light-headed but she needed to ask the question that meant so much when her father was diagnosed. "Where is it?"

The room was silent. She gazed up from the floor and saw the two doctors looking at each other. They seemed to be searching for the words. She knew that wasn't good.

Finally, it was Dr. Cox who explained, "Annie, the cancer probably started in your thyroid. That's the area with the most carcinoembryonic antigen. But it's also in your lymph nodes and your right lung. We can't be sure of the extent of the cell damage until we do a biopsy, but my recommendation would be the same no matter what. We need to start a program of chemo therapy and targeted radiation right away."

For a moment, the room went dark. At least for Annie it did. The words chemo and radiation echoed in the darkness over and over until the noise was deafening. She covered her ears and put her head in her lap.

"Annie, are you all right?" John was holding her from falling forward onto the floor. He was afraid she had passed out. Then, from within the bundle that had been his wife, came the words, "What about surgery?"

The question was muffled by her skirt and John had to ask "What did you say honey?"

But Dr. Cox understood and offered the kindest words possible, the truth.

"Annie, maybe the biopsy will tell us more but right now it looks like the cancer has spread too far to be operable." She paused to be sure the words got through, then added, "We could probably remove the thyroid but I'm not sure what that buys us."

Annie sat up. Her eyes were red and her nose was running. John handed her his handkerchief and rubbed her back. He didn't know what else to do.

Annie held back her sobs. "John, I want to go home."

Chapter Forty-Seven

As the taxi slugged its way through rush hour traffic, Annie and John sat in silence. He held her hand, a gesture so unusual that Annie actually felt worse because of it. She couldn't remember the last time she enjoyed John's touch. Had she drifted so far from him? How did that happen after only three years of marriage?

She glanced out the cab window as Fifth Avenue and Central Park crept by. The tops of the Park's ancient trees were beginning to show signs of the changing season. The cool nights had already transformed much of the green to yellows and golds. Annie could see her reflection in the cab window, silhouetting the Park and wondered if she would ever see another autumn or if this would be her last chance to walk through the leaves as she loved to do when she was a child.

Neither John nor Dr. Cox had mentioned a timeline. And Annie resisted the urge to ask, *"How long do I have?"* But now, seeing the leaves falling in the Park, she had to know. There was so much more she wanted to do. There were so many things she'd put off that now seemed unlikely to happen. She wanted to see her sons graduate, marry, and become fathers themselves. She had taken them so far and put so much into their lives, now to miss seeing them turn into men seemed such a cruel twist of fate.

And then there was Doc. Though she hadn't thought about him much in the last forty-eight hours, it was just a few days ago that he was her future. When she drove from Southampton on Monday, she'd planned to leave her husband and return to Doc by the end of the week. She hadn't thought much farther ahead but going back to see Doc seemed like the right place to start; perhaps, to start the rest of her life. Now, the rest of her life was starting in a cab and had a very uncertain end.

"John," she turned her gaze from the park to the man sitting next to her. "I need you to be honest with me. I need you to tell me what to expect here."

"What do you mean?"

"I mean, is the chemo and radiation and whatever else they want to do to me, is all that going to really matter; or is it going to be like Dad—just a way to make the time I have left miserable?"

John put his arm around her shoulder and pulled her close to him. "I told you, we can beat this. Don't start thinking like that. You've got to keep a positive outlook. You've got to believe you have the power within you to push this bastard out of you; to be strong again and go back to living your life. Annie, we have so much more living to do, you need to be strong, for me and for your sons."

The words sounded so strange. Annie couldn't remember a time John showed concern for her sons or talked about their life together. A chill of guilt ran through her as she recalled that less than twenty-four hours before she was plotting to leave her husband to be with another man. Now it seemed that she needed to rely on her husband like never before; perhaps for the first time.

"I'm going to be there for you Annie. We'll do this together, every step of the way. And a year from now we'll look back on this cab ride and laugh about it. We'll mark this as the beginning of our second life together. And it will be better, I promise." He kissed her forehead and pulled her even closer. "It's going to be much better."

Chapter Forty-Eight

The rain fell gently on the pond and everything around it. It was one of those soft rains, almost a mist, and Doc hoped to get some pictures later in the day when the light would be from the west. It was the stillness he wanted to capture. There wasn't a ripple on the pond, not a hint of movement. It could make for some great shots if he could get the right light before the tide changed and the calm waters began to flow slowly back to the bay.

He'd been working on his laptop all morning, preparing inquiry letters to dozens of potential publishers. His friends had been right; they warned him how difficult it would be to find a publisher willing to take a chance on an unknown and amateur photographer. Even so, he'd sent over a hundred letters already seeking some level of interest in his project. So far, it had netted him about fifty polite rejection letters, most saying it sounded like a noble effort but wasn't a project for them.

As he sat at the glass table, looking out on the pond, Doc reflected on how different this was from the way he'd earned a living for almost thirty years. Then, he was constantly on the go, either showing clients properties or traveling in search of new ones. People were a huge part of his day, and he genuinely enjoyed the social nature of his business, especially when it introduced him to interesting new people. Commercial real estate had its ups and downs over the years but whether times were good or bad, he was always busy. During slow markets,

Doc used his time to develop new contacts and worked on projects in London and Asia where business was brisk. He was always moving and always around lots of people.

So how is it that such a social creature could suddenly enjoy the complete silence of a day alone on Cold Spring Pond? Here, his only visitors for days might be the giant swans who glided silently across the pond. It had only been a few weeks since the summer people left for the season but he already knew he was going to enjoy this lifestyle. He found, much to his surprise, that he liked working in the peaceful quiet of an empty house, without the distractions of radio or television in the background. Silence, once feared, had become his welcomed companion.

He leaned back from the laptop and thought about why he was there. Sure, his years in business had secured him financially, but that wasn't why he left the city. Though he missed seeing more of his friends, he'd decided to live a hundred miles east of them knowing once Labor Day came, few people saw a need to drive to Southampton. Most Manhattanites probably thought the Hamptons closed down between Labor Day and Memorial Day, and if he was going to maintain a winter relationship with his old friends, he'd need to visit them in the city.

So what made him think this was the right place to be at this point in his life? He surely didn't think being in Southampton would help him find female companionship. Meeting Annie had been such serendipity. He wasn't running from anything, at least nothing he was conscious of. He would never do that again. He understood now that that's why he'd spent so much time in London during the most empty days of his marriage; he was hiding. Sure, there was plenty of work to be done opening a new office in a foreign country, but he could have sent someone else.

No, this time he wasn't running or hiding. This time he wanted to be precisely where he was to face a fear; a fear that had been with him for years but always in the background. Like a gladiator who must walk alone into the center of the arena to face his unknown adversary, so too had Doc Cafara come voluntarily to this lonely shack on the edge of a quiet pond to face his fear; the fear that for most of his life he suppressed; the fear that everything he'd been taught about his existence had been a lie.

Although he couldn't now remember what it was, he knew he'd read something that provoked him to take action. It might have been something in a magazine or in a book, it didn't really matter; the article talked about confronting fears. And Doc figured the best way to confront his greatest fear—the fear that the god he believed in all his life didn't actually exist—was to go someplace quiet and listen. Listen to the voice of God. And if he was really honest about it and really open to whatever happened, he knew, at least he tried.

So his intention was to test his loss of faith; to defy the god he no longer believed in, to talk to him, to send him some sign that he'd been wrong. To look for any proof that would lead him back to the way he'd always thought about his place in the universe.

He was there to listen.

CHAPTER FORTY-NINE

The wall clock in her kitchen said it was almost time to leave. They were supposed to be at the Hospital for Special Surgery at ten and it was a fifteen minute walk from her apartment to the prestigious medical facility. John was in the bathroom shaving. He'd promised to take her for her first chemo treatment even though it meant cancelling every appointment he had scheduled for the day. He did it without question or pause.

Annie had been ready for almost an hour. She knew she wasn't supposed to eat anything but that wasn't a problem— food was the farthest thing from her mind. It might have been mind over matter, but ever since she learned of her condition she felt a little nausea; just enough to stay away from food but not so much that she feared vomiting. It reminded her of the way she felt a few years ago after riding the roller coaster at Hersey Park with her sons—sort of dizzy and queasy but not really sick. This time it wasn't going away.

Her left hand was flat on the wooden table, her right held the cell phone she'd been thinking of using for the last fifteen minutes. She wanted to call Doc. She owed him an explanation for not calling sooner but wasn't sure what to say. Now with John in the bathroom using his electric razor, she saw an opportunity to make the call she hoped would be brief. She dialed, not knowing exactly what to say and hoping it would go to voicemail.

"Hello." The sound of his voice was a refreshing breeze in what had become a very stale room.

"Doc, it's me."

"Annie? I was beginning to think you forgot about me," he said to keep things light.

"Doc, listen. I have something of a family emergency going on here. I'll tell you all about it when I see you but I can't come out this weekend."

"Anything I can do to help?" He was genuinely concerned. Then he remembered that she was supposed to give her husband the bad news on Monday night and grew worried that perhaps things had gotten out of control.

"Are you OK?"

"Listen Doc, I can't talk right now. I'll call you over the weekend. Please don't call me. John might pick up my cell phone calls." She was thinking ahead—thinking that she may be knocked out from the chemo treatment and the last thing she needed was John picking up a call from Southampton.

"Are you at the Essex house?"

She'd forgotten all about her suite at the posh hotel. "No. I decided to stay here for awhile. It will be better this way."

"Annie, now I'm worried about you."

"No, I'm fine," she lied. "I just need to straighten some family things out before I come back. I'll call you on Sunday and see when I can get out there. I have to go Doc."

She flipped the phone closed just as the electric razor drone ended. Tears were running down her face and onto the table top.

"Did you say something, dear?" John called from the bathroom.

She wiped her nose and eyes with a napkin. "No honey. We should be going soon."

"Don't worry. They won't start without you." He stuck his

head into the hallway. Hey, I know you didn't eat anything this morning but did you take your vitamins and Synthroid? It's OK to take those. In fact, as you go through this, make sure you keep taking your meds. You've got to stay as strong as possible."

He'd told her what to expect from the treatments. Not that she didn't remember the hell her father went through while he was being "*saved*". But a lot had been learned about chemo therapy in the last few years, particularly about dosages, and John didn't expect her reaction to the treatments to be as violent. He told her that many people don't react badly at all, aside from some fatigue, and that there was a good chance she wouldn't lose her hair.

All the same, as they left the apartment that morning, she wasn't sure she wanted to spend what could be the last few months of her life, fighting nausea and diarrhea. Maybe there was a more dignified way to die.

And then there was the question: *If I only have a short time left, who do I want to be with?*

Chapter Fifty

Doc

After talking to Annie I was even more concerned than when I was waiting for her to call. The longer she didn't call the more I began to think maybe she'd had second thoughts about her decision to leave her husband. After all, things had moved along very fast for us. Maybe she decided to put some space between us and take a fresh look at the marriage. I wouldn't blame her for doing so. It seems like the mature thing to do.

We're coming at this from very different places; she from the midst of a three year marriage and I from the depths of self-inflicted solitude. I had nothing holding me back; nothing I was walking away from to be with Annie. She was leaving her husband and with that, perhaps many of their social acquaintances. I know how that works. No matter what your friends say before the divorce, they all choose sides sooner or later and you never see the ones who take your ex-spouse's side again. And I knew Annie's social network was important to her. She'd mentioned some of the charities she and John supported. Maybe Annie had second thoughts about walking away from that life.

Currently, my social network consisted of the three swans from the pond, Jose, the kid at the deli where I got the Times each morning and swapped Mets-Yankees barbs, and Jimmy K., the bartender at Café Seventy-Five in the village. On nights I don't feel like cooking, I go into town and have dinner at the bar at Café Seventy-Five. They always have a game on the big

TV and the seafood is great, especially when Jimmy tells me what the owner caught or dug up that day. So, if my dream reality played out and Annie actually left her husband and came to live in purist squalor with me, my guess is Annie's social circles would get a bit smaller.

She said she was fine but had to deal with a *family emergency*. I wonder what that means. On the one hand, it didn't sound like John had given her any trouble on Monday night. In a way, I was relieved to just hear her voice. My ridiculous consternation before her call was that he had gone wild when told she was leaving and was now driving around Manhattan with Annie in his trunk.

But a *family emergency* can't possibly be a good thing. If it was something about her sons, she wouldn't have said she was fine. And she hadn't gone to the Essex House as she'd planned. So something probably came up that delayed her conversation with John and that reasoning brought me back to the apprehension that she'd had a change of heart.

Whatever happened, there was nothing I could do about it. I had no choice but to accept her explanation and wait for her to call. She said she'd call me on Sunday, three excruciating days away. I decided to see Jimmy K. The Mets were starting a weekend series against the Cardinals.

Chapter Fifty-One

His calendar had been cleared for the day but John Weaver stopped by his office to pick up some files while his wife was across the street. Annie had tolerated the first chemo treatment well and was resting in one of the hospital's recovery rooms, so John ran across the street for a few minutes. He knew the worst of her reaction would probably come tonight or tomorrow. Given her slight frame, he expected her to react poorly until she got used to the toxic chemical concoction.

He used the time to return a few phone calls and emails then review some radiological reports on two new patients he was due to see tomorrow. His desk was covered with films and files, each representing the illness of another unfortunate cancer victim.

On the left side of the desk was a green file with the name WEAVER on the label. He'd gone over Annie's file again to be sure he hadn't missed anything. Always fastidious about his paperwork, John wanted everything about Annie's file to be checked and re-checked. It had to be perfect. And when he was sure it was perfect, he'd have Dr. Cox take a look or maybe another oncologist from down the hall. The more specialists that signed off on the diagnosis, the better he'd feel.

He was due back at the hospital to pick up Annie at 3:30 and was on his way out when his receptionist Lucy asked him, "Doctor Weaver, are you on schedule for tomorrow?"

Except in the summer, on a normal Saturday he would see fifteen to twenty patients in the morning, then be on his way to Atlantic City by early afternoon. Tomorrow, he needed to catch up on the patients he'd put off from today's schedule so there'd be no AC junket this weekend. Besides, he needed to be around for Annie.

"Yeah, I'm here all day. That reminds me. Can you stick around a little later tomorrow? I've got patients up till around four."

The exceptionally attractive brunette had heard about Doctor Weaver's wife; all the office help knew about Annie's illness. Seeing so many others have to deal with cancer, she felt sorry for him and what he and his wife were about to go through. Working an extra half day seemed the least she could do. "Sure, I'll be here."

"You're a doll Lucy. I'm going back to the hospital to pick up my wife and then heading home. Direct calls to the service and I'll check in later." He was already through the door and into the corridor waiting for the elevator. He called back, "I'll see you in the morning."

He pressed the down button and waited. It seemed that everyone in the office had heard about Annie's condition and had kind words of encouragement but he didn't want to talk about it anymore today. When he spotted one of the radiologists from down the hall coming towards him, John faked a cell phone conversation to avoid a real one. The good-natured tech in the white coat gave John a whispered "Hey John," as he went by and disappeared around the corner of the corridor.

The elevator ride down to the lobby gave John a chance to reflect on the last few days. So far, Annie was taking it all surprisingly well he thought. He had expected more of a hysterical reaction. After all, the news was devastating. Despite Dr. Cox's comforting words, the prognosis wasn't good and having gone through this with her father, Annie had to know what horror lay ahead.

He was surprised Annie hadn't called her sons yet. He'd expected that would be the first call she'd make after learning of her diagnosis but four days had passed and, as far as he knew, she hadn't told anyone yet. Typical denial phase he thought. He knew it would be best for everyone if she let people know. The sooner the better. She could start to deal with it rationally, and others could begin to prepare for the inevitable.

The elevator doors began to crack open as they reached the lobby. Daylight from the glass atrium and the afternoon beyond flooded into the cubicle. Through the glare John could see the silhouettes of two men waiting to enter the elevator. He couldn't make out the faces, but the voice was unmistakable.

"Hey, doc. We were just on our way up to see you." Felix took a step forward and Levon positioned himself in the doorway so that the only place for John to go was back into the elevator cabin.

"Take a ride with us doc. We needs to have a chat." Felix was already pressing a button and the doors slid closed leaving the doctor and his two huge black friends alone. John didn't protest. Despite their intimidating size, he didn't fear the thugs. He knew the drill. This was all business.

"Mr. Z says you missed your payment last week doc. Mr. Z's come to expect that wire every Saturday. He asked us to make sure you don't forget today-now that you already a week behind and all." His tone wasn't threatening. It was surprisingly business-like for a guy who looked a lot like a pissed-off Lawrence Taylor.

Annie's illness had thrown John's normal routine upside down. The money he'd won last weekend at the poker table was still in a brown envelop in his desk. He'd planned to deposit it on Tuesday then wire the usual payment to Zucker, but Annie's unexpected news and the resulting chaos had changed all that.

"Give me a break guys." The words seemed inadequate. "I'm on my way across the street to the hospital. My wife's getting treated for lung cancer and I lost track of the days. I'm good for it. Tell Zucker he's got fifty coming back on Monday. Let the rest ride for another week."

"You sure about that?" Felix looked over his sunglasses in a way that conveyed his skepticism.

"Absolutely. Fifty on Monday." John's tone was level and controlled. There was none of the panic Felix had come to expect. And for that reason, he believed him. But whether he believed him or not, the result would be the same. This was just a courtesy call. They'd been here before and Dr. Weaver always seemed to come through without the need for another "reminder". He was the kind of client that made Felix look good to Arnie Zucker. He got the job done.

The elevator doors opened on sixteen and a pair of attractive women got in. They rode back down to the lobby with the three gentlemen without saying a word. John and the ladies got out at the lobby but Felix and Levon stayed in the elevator.

"We got other business upstairs. Sorry to hear about your wife doc," Felix said as the doors closed.

CHAPTER FIFTY-TWO

Annie woke Sunday morning after a fitful night of nightmares and cold sweats. The sheets, wet with perspiration, were entangled around her to the point her arms were pinned against her. Earlier, after thrashing about for a few hours, she'd told John to sleep in the guest room. There was no point in them both struggling. He left the room around one A.M.

The digital clock on the cable TV box told her it was 9:34. The window, overlooking Central Park, told her it was raining. Her headache told her she hadn't had enough sleep and the nausea reminded her of the ordeal she'd gone through on Friday. Life since then had been a blur of vomiting and sleeping pills. Mostly she just felt weak and exhausted. After only one treatment, she was already beginning to doubt her resolve.

She untangled herself and shuffled into the bathroom. Maybe a shower and some toothpaste would help. She could tell from the towels and clothes on the floor that John had already showered and dressed. Before turning on the shower she heard him rattling around in the kitchen. On the rare occasions when he was home on a Sunday morning, John liked to cook them a big breakfast. She hoped that wasn't what the noise was about today.

The hot shower did more than just cleanse her, Annie felt a bit of rejuvenation as the water cascaded off her head and down her back. She was leaning against the shower wall to steady herself when she noticed the black and blue bruises on her left arm. She gingerly washed the wounds recalling the trouble the technician had finding an acceptable vein on Friday. To her, the ugly bruises were a stark reminder of her father's ordeal. For months, both his arms were covered in similar wounds as he endured his futile battle with cancer.

She still wasn't anything close to hungry, but she knew she had to eat something. The previous day she got by on ice chips and a few crackers with a smidge of peanut butter. John had been at work all day but Rose, the Columbian nurse's aid he'd retained to help out, had insisted she keep trying to eat. Rose was diligent about her charge and stayed with Annie until John returned.

"Coffee would be wonderful," she said as she walked into the kitchen. John was seated at the table with the Sunday Times spread all over the surface. He seemed surprised to see her.

"Hey, welcome back to the land of the living. I expected you to be in bed all day."

"Well, the day is young, but for now I don't feel too terrible. The shower really helped."

He began work on her coffee and gave her a kiss on her forehead. "Glad to see you up and around. How was Rose? Was she a help yesterday?"

"Yeah, she was great. I wasn't much company, but she helped me try to keep some food down. I assume it wasn't you that cleaned up the bathroom so she's also pretty good at housekeeping."

Annie was able to eat a small bowl of oatmeal and half a cup of coffee—a major success over the previous day. The small progress gave her hope that maybe she'd be able to bounce back each week after the treatments. She could endure twenty-four hours of nausea once a week if it could save her life. At least that's how she felt today.

By the afternoon, she was feeling a lot better. The feeling of weakness disappeared and she was beginning to think about eating something real for dinner. Maybe she just needed to sleep a lot more. She took a nap while John went for a run in the park, then watched the second half of the Giants game while nibbling on Saltines.

She was aware that she needed to call the boys and tell them at least a little about what was going on. She thought she'd start by telling them she'd been really tired lately and was going for a bunch of tests. Then, next week she'd break it to them that it looked like cancer, but that the prognosis was excellent and that John was taking great care of her. That would be their first concern—who's going to take care of mom? She knew Nick and Frank had no faith in their stepfather. She didn't want either of them leaving school to be with her.

Usually, she called the boys on Sunday nights. This week would be no different and perhaps, the normalcy of it might help her sell the watered down version. She'd keep it short and upbeat and try to make the boys believe, at least for now, that it wasn't a big deal.

But first, she needed to call Doc. And she needed to call him before John returned to the apartment. She just wasn't sure what to say. It was worse than that. She wasn't sure what she wanted to say. In so many ways, Doc's upbeat attitude about everything could make this all so much more bearable. Knowing him just a few weeks, she sensed he'd be a comforting soul when you needed one.

But that was crazy. She needed to be in New York. She needed John's expertise and the armory of world-class medical weapons available within a few blocks of their home. This was a time to be certain; to circle the wagons and do the right thing. This was not the time to follow your heart.

Annie didn't want to break the news of her cancer to Doc on the phone. It needed to be done in person. She owed him that. Though their passion for each other had been brief, it was passion none the less and she felt a connection to him she hadn't felt in a long time. She loved him, maybe enough to push him away. She certainly didn't want him to suffer along with her. She knew how horrible it was to watch someone you love succumb to the ravages of cancer; to get their hopes up every time they went to the doctor for another test, only to hear the same dreadful words, *"No sign of improvement yet."*

And perhaps there was another reason she needed to tell him in person. Maybe she just wanted to see him one more time.

The phone rang three times before he picked up. "Hey, I've been waiting for your call all day." He sounded genuinely thrilled.

"Listen Doc, I can't talk long. John's out running and will be back soon."

He could hear the distress in her voice. "What's wrong Annie? Are you all right?"

There was no point trying to deny something was wrong. "No, that's what I need to talk to you about."

"OK, tell me what's wrong. I want to help."

His voice was so innocent, so sincerely willing to help, that she broke down and started to sob. "Oh, Doc." She sniffled back. "I love you so much. I wish I was there with you." The tears were flowing freely.

"Then talk to me. Tell me what's wrong." His tone conveyed infinite patience.

Still breathing through the sobs, "I can't. I mean, I can't tell you now." Then she thought about her chemo schedule for the week ahead. She needed to be back at Sloan Kettering on Wednesday morning for another round so that left just Monday or Tuesday for a trip out to Southampton. Afraid that she wouldn't feel up to it on Monday, she said, "I want to come out and see you on Tuesday. Is that OK?"

"Of course it's OK." He was elated that she was coming to be with him. He felt that if he could just hug her, he could help make her problem, whatever it was, go away. She needed to be in Southampton. He needed to see her. "I'll make you dinner and we can have…"

She cut him off when the sound of a key turning in the apartment front door startled her.

"I have to go. I'll be there for lunch. I love you. Bye."

John walked into the kitchen holding a bouquet of mums and lilies. "Hey, looks like you're feeling a little better." He kissed her on the forehead. "I saw these at Benny's and had to get them for you."

A thousand emotions swept over her, but mostly she was overcome with feelings of guilt. The tears rolled again.

Chapter Fifty-Three

Tuesday morning couldn't come soon enough for Doc. Annie's call on Sunday afternoon left him confused and worried. On the one hand, he was ecstatic that she was coming to Southampton to be with him. To him, it meant she hadn't had a change of heart about their relationship. It meant she loved him. She said so on the phone on Sunday. When he heard the words, *I love you so much,* he was transported back to the day he first met Annie running on Cold Spring Point Road. Looking back on their first conversation on the beach, he could now understand the strange feelings he had that day

On the other hand, Annie was clearly very upset about something. Doc assumed it had something to do with her husband. Although Annie had always been careful not to disparage her husband, she'd said enough for Doc to understand the marriage had lost its warmth long before she met Doc. And if the marriage was lost, what could John have said or done that would make her so upset? Had he hit her? The thought made Doc's blood boil.

Maybe he threatened her with a prolonged and contested divorce. After all, money and access to a certain kind of life seemed to be fundamentally important to John. The thought of losing them could cause him to react in an ugly way.

Or, worse yet, maybe it had something to do with one of her sons. Maybe one of the boys had been in an accident or was involved with drugs or dropping out of school. Doc had never met Annie's twins, but she talked about them all the time. If something happened to one of them, she would be devastated; of that he was certain because he knew how he'd react if anything happened to one of his daughters. He and Annie had often empathized about their two sets of twins.

Whatever the problem, he was sure he could help. She just needed to fold into his arms and allow him to hug her and make everything better again. He was sure he could lessen her pain by sharing it with her. In a strange way, he welcomed the chance to demonstrate his love for her; to do something selfless to ease her burden.

Twenty miles away, Annie sat in the back of a black Town Car being driven by a good-looking young Jordanian man named Joseph. She'd decided not to make the drive herself. Although the nausea had gone, she felt a bit dizzy and didn't want to take any chances on the long drive to and from Southampton. So she called the same limo company she and John had used a hundred times before and asked that she be allowed to pay the $650 fee in cash rather than adding it to the family's monthly tab.

On the ride out of the city Joseph tried to make small talk with his pensive passenger. Two years of carting around New York's elite taught him a little pleasant conversation went a long way towards a better-than-average tip. It also helped assure his unfamiliar customers that not everyone from the Middle East is a terrorist. But by the time they reached the Long Island Expressway, Joseph could tell Annie was in no mood for idle chatter about the suddenly cooler temperatures. She just wanted to stare out the tinted window. To Joseph, she looked like she was deeply in thought—perhaps preparing for a big presentation or speech.

And in a way, she was. She knew there were two distinct conversations to be had today. The first and more straight forward, was simply to tell Doc about her cancer. As devastating as that news was, it was a matter of fact, science, and medicine—things a man could understand, even a man as close to it as Doc. Bad news is bad news and the sooner you get it on the table, the sooner you can deal with it. In a way, she hoped that by telling him, she would feel a burden lift from her shoulders. She hadn't told anyone yet. It felt like she was carrying around a heavy dark secret that needed to be let out.

The second conversation was going to be more problematic, mostly because she didn't have a clear idea of how she wanted it to end. She needed to tell Doc that she didn't want to see him again; that John was her husband and that he would be the one to help her through this ordeal. As much as she thought she loved him, Doc couldn't be a part of this next chapter in her life—maybe the last chapter, because if it was to be her last chapter, shouldn't she be surrounded by her husband and sons, the people to whom she belonged?

Then again, maybe she was wrong. Maybe his reaction would be totally unexpected. Maybe, upon finding out about her illness, he would run for the hills, thanking his lucky stars that she found out when she did. A few more weeks and it all might have been his problem. That would be just like a man; a couple of weekends playing slap and tickle and then disappear when the real world presents itself. Why had she assumed he was different?

And even if he did want to be a part of the next chapter—even if he did want to be there, to be the person holding her hair as she vomited into the toilet, why should she do that to him? She wasn't his problem. And she didn't want to be. Not like this.

The limo was approaching their turn and Joseph would need instructions.

"Please make a left at the next light—the one that says Sabonac Road."

"Yes ma'am."

"And then make another left onto Cold Spring Point Road."

"Got it."

She was running out of time. They would be there in a few minutes. She had so much more thinking she wanted to do. She wanted to be better prepared. She didn't want this to end badly, but they were turning into the dead end that led to Doc's house. She was running out of time.

And then she realized how true that was.

CHAPTER FIFTY-FOUR

Doc

I must admit I thought I was prepared for just about anything Annie could have said that day—just not for what she actually said.

I was on the deck putting the finishing touches on the lunch I'd prepared—grilled vegetables, assiago cheese, crispy Italian bread and one of the last bottles of Bobby's Barolos. I'd just taken the vegetables off the grill when I heard the sound of my driveway pebbles crunching under car tires. Her timing was perfect I thought.

As I came around the corner of my house, I caught a glimpse of a black car driving away and Annie was standing in my driveway. I noticed immediately she wasn't carrying any sort of overnight bag. That wasn't a good sign.

"Where's your car?" As soon as I said it I knew that wasn't the correct greeting. *Idiot!*

"Hey, sailor. Want to buy a thirsty girl a drink?"

We hugged and probably held the hug for a good sixty seconds. I was at a loss for what to say so I said nothing and in the silence, I heard Annie gently crying into my shirt. Without pulling away, I said, "It's going to be OK. Whatever it is, it's going to be OK."

I put my thumb under her chin and lifted her head until our eyes met. "I promise, it's going to OK. I'm here now."

Well, all that did was start the crying all over again. So I asked her to come with me to the back deck and poured her a glass of wine. Annie sat at the table looking out over the pond, the wine glass in her hand. The crying had stopped which was a good thing because I am useless around sobbing women. I just feel helpless, and I knew that's not what she needed from me.

She took a long sip of wine and without taking her gaze from the water said, "So how have you been Doc?"

I sat down beside her and reached for her hand. "I've been worried about you. Very worried."

"I'm sorry. I didn't want you to worry." She turned towards me.

"So, are you going to tell me what's wrong or do I have to ply you with alcohol?"

She actually smiled. "Remember I told you I'd been really tired the last few weeks?"

I said yes, but to be honest, all I remember is that she was really tired the last weekend we were together out at Montauk. But so was I.

Annie paused as if she was deciding to go on. It was only a moment but the silence seemed to last an hour. She turned back toward the pond and emptied her glass, then continued.

"Well, I went to my doctor to have a check-up and the blood work came back with some really bad news." She paused again. I could sense she was about to say something very difficult and was trying to muster the conviction to do so.

"Doc, I have cancer."

Pow! I didn't see that coming. I guess I'm not good at hiding my shock. I realized my mouth was hanging open.

"It's in my lungs and thyroid and maybe in the lymph nodes too. According to the tests they did last Tuesday, it's pretty far along; stage four in the lungs and follicular in the thyroid. It's so far along that surgery's not an option." She was speaking slowly and calmly.

My mouth was still open and I hadn't moved—not even blinked.

"So, I started chemotherapy on Friday. One of the doctors in John's practice is overseeing my program but it looks like I've got five weeks of treatments—chemo and radiation. And they may want to try this thing called Sorafenib which is a new drug that attacks the cancer cells by blocking some kind of protein the cells need to grow."

I guess I couldn't reconcile the words I'd just heard with the beautiful person sitting in front of me. Annie looked great, as usual; maybe a little tired but that was the look I'd come to know. How could this vibrant young woman be so sick? It just didn't make sense to me. What my eyes could see just wasn't lining up with the words my ears were hearing. Or maybe my mind just refused to do the math.

I did everything wrong. Instead of comforting her, I did what men do; I analyzed the problem in search of a solution. Instead of seeing her fear, I looked for ways out. Instead of validating her feelings of loneliness, I began the inquisition.

"Have you had a second opinion? Have they rerun the tests? When will you know if the treatments are working? Then what do you do?" I was astoundingly stupid.

And in return, Annie was amazingly patient. She filled me in on all the details of her ordeal thus far, starting with the call from Dr. Weber on Monday while she was driving home from Southampton. She told me about how great her husband has been and how he moved heaven and earth to get all the tests done the day after they talked to her doctor, and about Dr. Cox, the hematologist, who ran the tests a third time. She told me about her reaction to the chemo and how she'd slept for most of the weekend. It all sounded horrible. It was too much for someone so small and frail to have to endure in one week.

Annie held out her empty glass and said, "I'm probably not supposed to be drinking but what the hell."

I poured half a glass and felt a pang of guilt at even that. "So your husband is a cancer specialist?" *Why did I ask her that?*

"Tragically ironic, isn't it? Actually, John's an oncologist but his specialty is renal disease. He had others from his office confer on my situation."

I must admit, I was more than a little pissed off that the guy she was about to divorce just a few days ago is now her savior; or hopefully, he will be her savior. And if John does pull off a medical miracle, where does that leave me? I mean, it sounds brutally self-centered, but I find myself feeling quite jealous of him. I now have to root for his success. And if he is successful, then what? Clearly, Annie would feel differently about the man who saves her life.

Shit! I felt so selfish. How could I be thinking about myself? But having already crossed the threshold of self-indulgence, I needed to know. "Annie, where does this leave…us?"

I could tell she knew the question was coming. Her stare went immediately back to the pond and the horizon beyond. She put the wine glass down on the table, got up slowly from her chair and walked to the wooden railing. Her eyes never left the water.

"That's why I came out today, Doc. I needed to see you. I needed to have this conversation face to face. The phone just didn't seem right."

When I heard the words, "*this conversation,*" I already understood what she'd come to say.

"Doc, I know how I feel about you. I love you. And eight days ago, I saw my future with you. I even pictured us living in your little shack here," she pointed her thumb at my house, "and spending the winter together out here like Doctor Zhivago and Lara. And we'd cook and make love in front of the fire and take long walks on the beach. You'd work on your book and I'd try to get my life back together. And in the spring, we'd decide where we go from there, but it would have been a wonderful winter no matter what we decided."

She was crying again. I offered her my handkerchief and stood next to her at the rail. I was trying to decide if this would be a good time to say something but before I did, she continued.

"I have to stay in New York. Sloan Kettering is one of the best hospitals in the world and if I wasn't John's wife, I wouldn't have gone to the front of the line. If I wasn't married to him, I'd still be running around Manhattan trying to get the tests done. The radiologists at his practice are great and they care about me because I'm not just another patient—I'm Dr. Weaver's wife. I have to say, I feel like they care if I live or die. I can't say the same thing about the doctors who took care of my father. To them, he was just another old man who had cancer."

Okay, I have to agree. She'll probably get the best care in New York. It's funny though. When you get sick, it doesn't matter how rich you are. Oh sure, money will get you access to the best doctors and the best hospitals, but that doesn't mean they'll give a shit about you. Unless you're someone's mother, or sister or daughter—someone they know personally—you're just another patient in the waiting room.

Annie had a good point. She was scared and fighting for her life and she wanted to call in every chip she had. If being married to John got her access to the best technology and to medical professionals who actually cared about her, then she had to stay there. And that meant she had to stay married to John.

"Doc, I don't want to die. Not yet, anyway."

I put my arm around her. "I know," was all I could say before a couple of salty tears trickled down my cheek. We were both still looking forward, directly at the pond. I think we were afraid to look at each other. I know I was.

"I want to fight this. John says the treatments could buy me another five years and who knows; in that time maybe someone will come up with a better treatment or a cure. I have to try. I have sons who need me."

Now I had to look at her. "Of course you have to try. You can't just give up."

"Well, actually, that is exactly the alternative. Dr. Cox says that if I refuse the treatments I might have six or eight symptom-free months before the cancer gets so bad that there's no turning back. She says, I can live a relatively healthy life for another six to eight months but expect to be dead in ten or twelve."

Just hearing my beautiful little Annie say the word "*dead*" sent a dagger through my heart. I realized I didn't have the stomach for this. She was so much braver than I.

"I gave that alternative a lot of thought," she said. "I mean, it would allow me to take control of the rest of my life and to live it the way I want, and with the people I want to be with."

For a moment I thought she was going to tell me she wanted to spend the rest of her short life with me, doing all the things she'd never done, trying to squeeze a lifetime of enjoyment into six months. I thought she might say she wanted to rent a yacht on the Mediterranean and sail around with me for the next six months, stopping in a new port every night, eating fabulous Italian food then retiring back to our ship to make love until the sun came up. Then doing it all again the next day.

But that's not what she said. She said, "But that wouldn't be fair to my children and I want so much to see them grow into men—to be fathers on their own. I have to try, even if it means dealing with the pain along the way."

"Of course you have to try," I lied.

"I'm not as brave as people think I am, Doc. I don't want to die yet. I'm afraid to die." She looked down at her feet. "Wow, I've never said that before. But I am. I'm afraid to die because I don't know what comes next."

Now I had to hold her. She was so vulnerable. She just needed to be held tightly. I could sense it. But I certainly had no answers for her—not on the subject of *'what comes next.'* That was way out of my area of expertise.

"If I knew, for sure, that on the other side of death my father and mother and Peter were waiting for me, I'd feel a lot differently. I mean, if I was sure about that, I'd take the six good months here, then an eternity with them. I'd feel safe. That would be OK. You know?"

No, I had no idea. What I did know was that I really loved this trembling lady and didn't want to lose her; not to death, nor to John, nor to the ghosts she thought might be waiting on the other side of some puffy cloud.

Unfortunately, Annie's *"You know?"* wasn't a rhetorical question. She really wanted to know what I thought. She needed validation and boy, did she come to the wrong guy.

"Do you think that's what it's like when you die; that you're united with the people you most love?" For the first time, she was now looking me squarely in the eyes.

I thought about lying to her and telling her that that's exactly what will happen. I wanted to comfort her and if that belief gave her comfort, then what's the harm. She could enjoy her last days on earth and die with the peaceful thought that she would be embraced by her family on the other side. If she was right about the hereafter—great! I'd be happy to be dead wrong about this. And if she was wrong, then she'd die peacefully expecting her father's embrace and she'd never know it didn't happen.

But I couldn't lie about this. I'd be doing it for selfish reasons. This wasn't the time to examine our beliefs. So I told her a version of the truth.

"I don't know." That was certainly the truth. "I was brought up to believe exactly what you do. I guess, as adults, we need to decide for ourselves." That wasn't a lie either.

"There's got to be something after this. I mean, what's the point of all this if there isn't? God has to have something planned for us, don't you think?" Annie's face was red from crying. She actually wanted know what I thought about this. I could see it in her eyes; she needed me to agree with her.

"I always thought there was a purpose to life. I'd feel very lost and alone if I didn't believe that." What I didn't say was that that's exactly how I feel—lost and alone. But my words seemed to give her comfort and that's what mattered right now.

"That's what I think too. He wouldn't have created us just to live and die like cats or dogs, or fish," she said pointing out to the pond as if she knew precisely where the fish were hiding beneath the surface. "He had to have a more significant plan."

That's exactly what I used to think. That there was just too much wonder in the world to be an accident. I used to think the spectacular diversity of animal life on our planet was evidence that a supreme being must have given this all some thought. Otherwise why were there so many different types of butterflies, insects, plants and fish? Wouldn't natural selection have culled out just a few hardy survivors? Did our planet really need thousands of different kinds of creatures? And why did a sunset need to be so beautiful?

Surely some form of divine providence had to be at work.

But the older I got and the more I studied science and watched nature, the more I thought it could just be an accident. Maybe we are the one-in-a-trillion aberration in the galaxy that became a planet capable of sustaining life. Maybe all of man's beliefs about God were created by man simply to justify our self-centered view that we are something special when really we're not.

But that's not what Annie wanted to hear right now, so I told her, "And that's the challenge of life for each of us; to figure out what the plan is." I didn't say "*His*" plan. I said "*The*" plan. So I still wasn't lying.

We spent another half hour talking about just about everything but her illness. By now we'd sat down again and I asked her if she was hungry, the grilled vegetables were waiting in the kitchen. But she said no, she wasn't eating much these days due to the chemo. She told me she wasn't sure she could take another six weeks of the treatments, especially after the way she reacted to the first.

I offered, "I had a friend who went through this a couple of years ago, Annie. She was about your age actually and had stage four lung cancer. It came out of the blue. She was the sort of person who got regular check-ups every year and none ever gave her a hint anything was wrong. Then she was told she had cancer and started an aggressive program of chemo. But I remember her saying that they loaded a lot of the drugs into the first two treatments. She said they start off strong, then back down on the dosages so her reaction to the first two was pretty bad but after that, things got a lot better. She never even lost her hair."

"Yeah, John told me the same thing," she said. "They have the dosages so well defined now and so pin-pointed that a lot of people don't lose their hair. So, how is your friend doing now?"

"She's in remission for now. That's all they'd promise but hey, that's pretty good. It's been almost six years now." Now I was lying. My friend died fifteen months after being diagnosed, but Annie didn't need to hear that.

We tried talking again, about happier thoughts. There weren't too many. After another twenty minutes, she excused herself to use the bathroom. I brought the wine glasses into the kitchen and was about to put them in the sink when I noticed the black limo in my driveway. Apparently, Annie told the driver to come back in two hours and here he was.

I made the assumption that she hadn't driven herself because she didn't feel up to it and the thought of it made me realize how sick she really was. It hurt. It reminded me of how I felt the first time my father was too old and weak to do something he always used to do for himself—in his case it was shoveling two inches of snow. It was a devastating realization for me.

When she came out of the bathroom I said, "Your car is here." And I didn't try to disguise the disappointment in my voice.

"I do need to get back to the city Doc." She put one hand on my shoulder. "Listen, I'm not sure when I'll see you again. I promise I will though. That's a promise."

"So I guess that means you've made up your mind about the treatments. I mean, it sounds like you had your mind made up before you even came out."

"Yeah…I did. I have to try. I have children. You'd do the same thing."

"I'm not so sure about that but I think it's the right thing for you." I lied.

We walked out to the car together and she asked the driver for a few minutes. He was happy to sit in the car and wait while Annie and I leaned on the trunk and said our good byes.

"Why do I have the feeling that I'll never see you again?" It's how I felt so I said it.

"Doc, I promise I will see you again. No matter what happens, I'll see you again." And then she seemed to brighten and added, "Maybe even in the next couple of weeks."

"Is there anything I can do to make this easier for you? Would it help if I came into the city? I could take care of you."

Annie shook her head. "Doc, I have a husband. I need him now, and having you around would only make things harder for me. Please try to understand that."

I understood that she was stuck in the middle of two men; one she said she loved and wanted to be with, and one she was married to and needed to be with. But she was right; I would only make things harder for her. It's just a shame that this tragedy had to happen precisely when it did. A month later and she would have been rid of her husband and I could have taken care of her. A month earlier and I probably never would have met her.

I told her I understood and that I would wait for her call. "But please call me often and let me know how you're doing."

"I've got another treatment on Wednesday and another doctor appointment on Thursday so I'll call you on Friday."

And then she said the words that stuck like a steak knife in my chest.

"And Doc, please don't call me." She looked down as she said it. "It will only make this harder for both of us."

Anything I said after that would have only made things worse. I kissed her on the forehead and opened the limo door. This was really painful and as much as I didn't want her to leave, the sooner she did, the sooner the pain would ease a little. At least, that's what I hoped would happen, but I've never been very good at predicting my own feelings about things.

She got into the back seat and looked up at me with sorrowful teary eyes. "I love you Doc."

"And I love you. Get better." And then I had to turn away because I was about to explode with tears myself and didn't want her to see me like that.

So I closed the door and stepped back from the car.

She lowered the heavily tinted window. "Good bye Doc. I love you."

And then she was gone.

Chapter Fifty-Five

The air in the conference room was stale, but it was the discussion that bothered the occupants most. John Weaver, Eric Kaplan, Herb Keller and three other senior partners in their practice had assembled for a briefing from their accountant. Jessie Chou had been handling the financial affairs for the practice for the last six years and was a trusted advisor on all things not directly related to medicine. His tall, thin stature made it difficult for many to guess his age. Most would say fifty-five to sixty. Jessie was a worn out forty-two.

Such meetings were routine. Jessie insisted on delivering a short presentation every two months; this was the financial snapshot of the practice as of August 31, 2008. Often, his audience was only Herb and Eric. Most of the other physicians considered the lectures about revenues and expenses mundane and a distraction from their real means of generating revenue for the business; seeing patients. It wasn't unusual for the meetings to last less than ten minutes.

But today was different. Jessie had forewarned Herb that he wanted to discuss the disastrous year-to-date performance of their pension plan assets and that seemed to get everyone's attention. Herb let his partners know he expected them at Jessie's presentation and to come ready to make some tough decisions.

When everyone was seated, Jessie began by reminding the doctors that they'd established a pension plan three years earlier for the benefit of all employees but designed to heavily favor the higher paid employees—the physicians. In effect, it was a way for the partners to shield money from taxation while putting away for their retirements. For most of them, other than their homes, it was their primary asset. Or, at least it had been.

"So what you're telling us Jessie, is that we need to put in another $450,000 this year, in addition to what we've already put in. Have I got this right?" Herb wanted to make sure everyone understood what he already knew all too well.

"Yes Herb. Your firm contributed almost $388,500 in January and this would be in addition to that." Jessie Chou never tried to quote a number unless he was completely certain of its accuracy.

John had been quiet up until now but leaned forward in his chair and asked, "And this is all because of the stock market performance so far this year?"

"No. The equity side of our portfolio would have been OK, relatively speaking, had we not had such a large exposure to the bank stocks. Recall that in February, you decided to invest heavily in the banks; Citi, Merrill Lynch, Wachovia—they've all gotten killed this year. That's where we took a bath."

John resented Jessie's use of the term "we," since it wasn't Jessie's money that had suffered the dramatic decline. In fact, he remembered Jessie advising them that the banks looked very attractive because of the high dividends they were paying. It was on his recommendation they had transferred so much of their pension assets into the bank stocks. Now it looked as if that brainstorm was going to require another significant contribution to the plan and no one was pleased about that.

"Don't get me wrong. These are solid companies. They're going to come back. Hell, as a group they're down 24% from where they stood on March 1st. A lot of people think they're undervalued now—that now would be a great time to buy them." Jessie always tried to show both sides of any situation.

"What do you think Jessie? Would this be a good time to be buying the bank stocks?" Herb asked.

"I think that part of the new contribution should go into the bank stocks, yes. And if they rebound, even just back to their March levels, we'd make enough back that we'd probably not have to make another contribution until mid-2009."

Before he left the physicians to consider the advice, Jessie reminded them that the new contribution needed to be made by the end of October—just five weeks away. No one was very interested in the reason why this was so, just that a lot of money had to be raised quickly and that they didn't have it on hand. That meant another partner assessment directly on the heals of the one to purchase the EMG equipment. Because he did all their personal income taxes as well, the accountant knew enough about their personal affairs to know this was going to be tough for most of men sitting at the table.

Herb Keller closed the door behind the accountant and walked slowly back to the conference table. "Well gentlemen, that's the story. We need to raise some big cash fast."

Of the group, Eric Kaplan was the most financially savvy. He'd been the one dissenter on the decision to invest in the bank stocks several months earlier and he needed to make a point of reminding everyone of that. "Well boys, maybe now's the time to see what we're made of. If we put this money in the plan now and it does well, and shit, the market's got to come back—it's been in the crapper all year—then we don't have to put anything in again until next February. I say we put half the new money into the same bank stocks we have already. They've got to come back. Shit, Citi's trading under twenty. It was over thirty just a few months ago. Banks like Citibank don't lose a third of their value overnight."

This was precisely the direction Herb had hoped the

conversation would go. "I agree with Eric. I also think, in light of this unexpected expense, we need to rethink our decision on the EMG; not whether we buy it, but how we pay for it. Looks like we need to finance it." He turned to John. "What do you think John?"

"I agree. I can't afford both expenses right now. We need to finance the EMG and let's spread it over as long a period as possible." John seemed sure of this. As a result, the rest of the group fell in line and resolved to take a loan on the equipment and make the pension contribution with half going into the depressed bank stocks. The other half would go into the general equity funds.

"Eric, work out the financing with Jessie, will you?" Herb asked.

"I'm on it. Now let's get back to slicing up patients and making some money."

The meeting adjourned. No one in the room could have foreseen the dramatic collapse in the banking industry that would take place over the next few weeks. Nor would they have known they'd just made a disastrous financial mistake.

Chapter Fifty-Six

"I don't understand, Daddy. You said you really liked her."

"I do baby. But she's got a lot to work out so we decided not to see each other for a while." Doc tried to satisfy his daughter's curiosity with as short a lie as he could.

His daughter Kitty usually wouldn't have let him off the hook quite so easily but she was on a break at the hospital and needed to get back to her desk outside the busiest O.R. in Tucson by three-thirty. She had just worked a twelve hour shift and was subbing an eight for a friend.

"Listen Daddy, I have to go but I want to hear all about it on Sunday when you call me."

"I'll talk to you Sunday Kiddo. Go save the world."

"I'm not kidding. I want to hear all the details on Sunday. Gotta go Dad. Bye. Love ya."

How could he give her any more details than he already had? How could he tell her the truth: that he was involved with a married woman who told him she was going to leave her husband and now had cancer? It had all happened so fast, he wasn't sure he believed it all himself. And he certainly didn't want his daughter to know he might be responsible for breaking up a marriage.

He was torn about it. On the one hand, he saw nothing morally wrong with what he'd done. Doc saw no ethical problem in his relationship with Annie. She was an adult, responsible for her own decisions, and it had been her decision to pursue him. On the other hand, he was ashamed to tell his daughters anything close to the truth about Annie. For reasons he didn't understand, he didn't want his daughters to think of him as anything other than the pillar of integrity he always tried to be for them. To show them a lesser side of himself would be failure.

Besides, he'd just had his heart broken and still wasn't sure what was really going on. He needed to back up and reassess. In his usual analytical style, Doc tried to piece together what had happened. The one thing he was certain of was that he loved Annie. He was ready to make a life with her; marry her, if that's what she wanted. The pain of her being taken from him by a disease—one he couldn't help her fight, was killing him. He wanted to be there to comfort her. He knew he could be so good at it because he'd love doing it.

What he was now less certain about was Annie. While he didn't doubt the authenticity of her illness, three scenarios danced around in his head. First, if Annie really loved him, perhaps she said she wanted to be with John just to spare Doc the pain of watching her die a slow and painful death. After all, if you really love someone, you'd do anything not to have them suffer along with you. So maybe, as a definitive sign of her love, she had to leave Doc to spare him the pain of her illness. Maybe she loved him that much.

Second, perhaps she'd just gotten cold feet. Maybe, upon learning of her cancer, she came to her senses and saw the folly in an affair with another man. Maybe cancer, lethal or not, was the bucket of cold water in her face that brought her back to the reality she'd become accustomed. Perhaps it was enough to cause her to doubt her feelings for Doc—to attribute them to the lustful passion of a bored middle-aged Manhattan socialite, rather than real love. Maybe she got back to the city and said, "What the hell am I doing?"

Or third, maybe she was just scared. Maybe knowing she'd be getting the best care in the world from the doctors and hospitals to which she'd have entre as John's wife, made her realize "*he's my best shot at life.*" And she was right, having Doc in her life now, especially if he went into Manhattan, would only cause her more stress and anxiety. Maybe she still wanted to leave her husband but couldn't now that he was her lifeline.

If he knew for certain he could move on, he could take the next few steps toward whatever he decided to do. But this was an excruciating limbo. He didn't know enough to make a decision. He was frozen by his inaction which was in turn, caused by a lack of solid data. It left him between two worlds: one in which he would wait for his love to return, no matter what they might have to endure together, the other in which he would move on and not look back.

He'd always been a person of action. He needed to do something. But if he could have foreseen the events of the next few weeks, he would have been too frightened to act.

CHAPTER FIFTY-SEVEN

Annie's hand was trembling as she put the phone back on its cradle. She'd just finished talking to her son Nick. He didn't take the news of her illness well and saw through her veiled attempts at keeping the full horror from him and his brother. Annie had called Frank a few minutes earlier. He insisted on coming home for a few days. Boston University was closed on Friday anyway and he had no classes on Thursday so he told Annie he'd be on the early train Thursday morning. Maybe he could take her to her afternoon doctor appointment. He wanted to help.

Sharing the news of her cancer with Doc and now Frank and Nick, somehow made the whole thing seem more real. Tomasue warned her about that. She said that sharing the information openly would be difficult, but was important in the healing process. Otherwise, she warned, patients feel isolated and sometimes retreat into a morose self-fulfilling spiral toward death. Having family to share the burden lightens the patient's load and allows them to focus on getting better.

Annie hated to drag her sons into this. She didn't want to see them suffer along with her the way she suffered with her father. She'd been his primary caregiver. She had no siblings to share the burden. But, she never thought of it as a burden. It was something a daughter does for her parent that demonstrates her love and appreciation for all the parent had done for her. It completed the circle and it just felt right. In some way it gave her a closeness with her father that didn't exist before.

But Frank and Nick were so young—a few months short of twenty-three and about to graduate from college. They had their senior year to focus on and all the pleasant youthful rituals that are supposed to accompany that time in their lives. She didn't want them at her bedside. She would insist they finish school. There'd be no argument about that.

Still, it would be good to see Frank. She thought about her son and what a fine young man he was becoming. She marveled at how it seemed like yesterday she and Peter brought their newborns home from the hospital, having no idea how to deal with twin baby boys. She remembered the first time Frank rode a two-wheeler in Central Park. He wore a Michael Jordan jersey that came down to his knees but was able to break free of her assistance and pedaled off toward the boathouse all by himself. Peter captured the whole thing on his video camera and they watched it dozens of times in the weeks that followed.

Where had the time gone? Now, seventeen years later, Peter was gone, her father and mother were gone, and she found herself alone with a husband she wanted to leave for a man she just left standing alone in his driveway. It didn't make sense. She recalled a line from a John Lennon song that always made her smile: *"Life is what happens while you're busy making other plans."* It sure is.

But Annie knew she couldn't sit there all morning reminiscing. She had to get to her second chemo treatment. John promised to meet her there to drive her home afterward. She certainly couldn't get herself home after a treatment but it made her feel guilty every time he did something kind for her. It wasn't his nature to be so kind and nurturing and she wasn't sure how to respond to it. Could this be his way of making amends for all the mistreatment? Could she have been wrong about John? Maybe the migraines were the cause of his aggressive behavior after all.

It was all so confusing. For now, she needed John's help and professional expertise. If that meant she was using him, so be it.

She called for a cab to take her to the hospital.

Chapter Fifty-Eight

New York was enjoying an Indian summer and the streets were alive with activity. Although the afternoons ran out of sunlight earlier than in summer, this particular Friday afternoon could have been mistaken for the beginning of the Fourth of July weekend. Teenagers played stickball on Sixty-Fifth Street, yelling to their teammates each time an oncoming car or taxi approached. Dog-walkers were in tee shirts. Street venders did a brisk business peddling sodas and ice cream sandwiches. And above it all, peering out an open window, Annie gazed at the yellowing trees in Central Park. The warm fresh air felt great.

She hadn't left the apartment since returning from chemo therapy on Wednesday afternoon. She'd been so sick on Thursday she had to cancel the appointment John scheduled for her with another oncologist. She couldn't remember the last time she ate but she felt as if it had been weeks. Even the Zofran, prescribed by Dr. Cox, wasn't having much impact on the violent vomiting. Any time she lifted her head from the pillow, the room would swirl and her stomach would do cartwheels. It had been a horrible forty-eight hours.

Now, for the first time, she was able to sit up and take in the fresh air near the open window. She felt weak, understandable after vomiting for so long. She knew she needed to keep some fluids down or she'd become dehydrated. John had warned her that dehydration was a major danger for chemo patients.

Potassium levels fall off quickly and begin to manifest their absence with cramps and dizziness. He was right.

So for the last half hour she'd been chewing on small ice chips Rose left for her before leaving for the market. Originally, Annie told her to take the weekend off. Now she was grateful John insisted on her staying with Annie at least on Saturday, and depending on how she felt, maybe Sunday too. John wasn't going to be around.

That morning, John reminded Annie of the Saturday fishing trip he had scheduled long ago with three of the younger doctors at the office. They were looking forward to getting out on Burt's boat and trying to get some late-season stripers. At first he told her he was going to cancel. They'd certainly understand. But Annie reminded him that her son was due to arrive today and that between Frank and Rose, she didn't need John around. She insisted he keep the date with the young doctors.

John was due home in a few minutes. He called Annie before leaving his office to say his 4:30 appointment had cancelled and he was coming home to check on her. His plan was to drive out to Southampton after dinner, sleep at their beach house, then meet the other guys, the fishermen, in the morning at the dock. She knew he was looking forward to it. The last two weeks had been really tough on him too. And the weather forecast was perfect; nothing but sunny skies for the next few days. She was glad he was going.

She was also glad Frank was coming. Although her motherly instinct was to protect her son from pain, she knew Frank wouldn't rest until he saw her. He was the type of kid that needed to be reassured about most things, but especially when it came to his mother's well being. Of the two, he was the worry wart. She was hoping he'd feel better after seeing her and spending the weekend. And it worked out perfectly that John would be away most of the weekend. Not that there'd be any open animosity between them, just an uncomfortable coexistence.

The apartment door opened and closed. Annie could hear John talking to Rose in the next room.

"Has my wife been taking enough fluids?"

"Yes, doctor. She no sick since this morning. I give Mrs. Weaver ice. She finish all of it. But she drink no much water."

"Has she been running a fever? Is she still sweating?"

"No. No too much. Mrs. Weaver a little better today."

"Wonderful. Thank you Rose."

Finally, Annie yelled out from her seat by the living room window, "John, I'm in here. Why don't you just ask me?" She was trying to sound upbeat and positive so he could go to Southampton without feeling guilty about leaving her.

"How's my favorite patient today?" John said as he walked into the living room.

"I better be your favorite patient. And yes, I've been sucking on the ice chips all afternoon. I think I'm ready to try some Gatorade and go for a run in the park."

"Very funny. No, really. Have you been keeping down enough liquids? It's important Annie." When John wanted to, he could sound very sincere.

"Actually, I was just going to get up and get some Gatorade. I think I'll be OK. The dizziness has lightened up, and I'm only seeing visions of Elvis every other hour."

"Come on. Be serious," he sounded genuinely concerned.

"I'm OK. I will try some Gatorade if you'll get it for me." Then she added, "How was your day?"

He gave her a peck on the cheek and disappeared into the kitchen to fetch the drink.

"My day was going along great until about an hour ago."

"Why? What happened?" She yelled toward the kitchen.

John came back carrying a bottle of red Gatorade with a straw protruding for Annie and a glass of Jack Daniels for himself. "Cheers," he said as they clinked drinks in mock celebration. He swallowed half of the JD then took a seat on the ottoman next to her.

"Jimmy Roth, one of the guys I was supposed to be fishing with tomorrow, called me on my cell as I was leaving the office. He's got to fill in for a surgeon tomorrow. He cancelled on us. I was so pissed off, I dropped my phone near the elevator, the battery comes out and goes into the crack between the elevator doors."

"You're kidding!"

"No, and it gets better. The battery is stuck between the elevator and the rim, you know, by the opening. The doors start to open and down it goes; right into that little space, and disappears forever. So now I have no cell phone and no fishing trip."

"Why can't you go fishing without him?"

"Because when I went back to my office and called Stuart, to see if he could get another guy on such short notice, he tells me if Jimmy's not going he'd rather take a rain check too. So now it's just me and Hank and you need three guys to fish for stripers."

"Why three?"

John gave her a look that said '*You're sweet but so stupid.*' Then he remembered he was talking to someone who'd spent the last twenty-four hours with her head in a toilet and toned it down a notch.

"Because, you need a driver, a spotter, and someone to hold a rod. We were going to troll. When you troll for stripers, you need at least three guys." Then he tried to cheer her up. "I don't suppose you'd like to go fishing tomorrow."

"That sounds great. I could provide all the chum you need as I'm puking over the side."

In the scheme of things, not being able to go fishing didn't seem like the end of the world, but she knew how much he was looking forward to it. She also knew he'd never ask her son to go with him because he already knew what Frank's answer would be. Frank and Nick used to love fishing with their father on their grandfather's boat, but that was a long time ago and Frank would rather cut himself up as the chum than spend a day with John.

"I'm sorry honey."

"Me too. I need to call Hank back and tell him the bad news."

Annie sipped some of the sweet red liquid through the straw. It felt like it would stay down, at least for now. She decided to give her husband a comfortable exit from an uncomfortable situation. "Frank should be here in an hour." Then she added, "But I'm sure he wants to spend the day with me tomorrow. After all, that's why he's coming."

John understood what she was doing and was a bit embarrassed he'd forgotten about her son's visit. He knew it was important to Annie.

"Well, we both know Frank doesn't want to go fishing tomorrow. Like you said, he came to visit you, not me."

And at just about the same moment, they both realized Frank and John would now be together in the same apartment for the whole day tomorrow. That wasn't going to work. On the rare occasions her boys would visit her in New York, they made a point of staying away from the apartment if John was around. It just made things easier and avoided any confrontation. She usually met them at a restaurant or wherever they were staying. Sometimes, they'd just agree to meet in Southampton.

"Why don't you just go with Hank and fish for something else—something that doesn't require three people?" She knew it would be better if John wasn't around if Frank was going to be here. That wasn't lost on her husband.

"I don't know." He seemed annoyed. "Maybe I'll just go out east and see if I can find someone out there at the dock. Someone's gotta want to go fishing."

She was trying to help. "Anyone still out in Southampton? What about Ed Pisani? I wonder if they're still around or if they've left for Florida already."

"You'd know more about who's still out there. Those aren't my people." John was referring to the well known fact that most of the Cold Spring Pond folks had been friends of Annie's father and husband long before he came into the picture. The locals considered John an outsider—someone who wasn't there for the right reasons. To them, you spent the summer around Cold Spring Pond to get away from precisely the kind of things many others flocked to the Hamptons in search of—the lavish parties, the celebrities, or just to be seen at one of the trendy shops.

Then he remembered a conversation he had on the beach at their clam bake a few weeks ago. It was with that new guy—the guy from New York who bought the Mauro house.

"Hey, what about that new guy? The one who moved into the Mauro house in July. I remember him telling me he loved fishing. I think he has a small boat and was going to stay out there all winter. What was his name?"

Annie froze. Whatever bile was left in her suddenly made its presence known again in her throat. She swallowed hard.

"I remember…the guy I ran with a few times. His name is Doc something. I don't remember his last name." The ease of the lie frightened her. She hoped that without a last name it would be impossible for John to get in touch with Doc.

"Yeah, it's going to be beautiful tomorrow. I bet he'd love to do some trolling offshore."

Annie underestimated her husband's resourcefulness. Before she knew what was happening, John was digging through the drawers in his roll-top desk. "I bet he never changed the phone number at the house. He probably still has the Mauro's number. I just need to find my list of association members from last year." He was now sitting at the desk looking through piles of forgotten pages. "I know I must have it."

Annie was trying to think of a reason she could offer to persuade her husband to abandon his search. The thought of Doc and John spending hours together on her father's boat turned her stomach. What if Doc slipped and said something? What if he said something even as innocent as, *"I'm sorry to hear about your wife's illness."* How would he explain how he knew about her illness? The convoluted thoughts gave her a headache to go with her miserable stomach.

Then there was the other possibility; the chance that somehow, John already knew about she and Doc and was just baiting her. It would be like him to torture her this way if he ever found out. But how could he know? She'd been so careful and John was always away.

Was it possible that someone who knew them spotted her at the restaurant in Sag Harbor? Could they have been seen in Montauk? Or biking through Southampton? It had never occurred to her that someone might have seen them and reported it to John. After all, John did know a lot of people in town because of his privileges at Southampton Hospital. Someone might have walked right past them on the beach and she never would have noticed. How could she have been so stupid?

"Got it!" John pulled a few stapled pages from the bottom of the center drawer in his desk. "Mauros, right? That was their name, right?" He was excited at the idea of salvaging his fishing trip.

"Yeah, honey. But don't you think it's strange to call someone you hardly know?"

"Here it is. 631-8554…What did you say his name was, Jack?"

"No, I said his name was Doc. It's a nickname, I guess." Now Annie was frantic for a way to delay the phone call her husband was about to make. If he was insistent on inviting Doc, she needed to call him first to warn him. Caught off guard, there's no telling what Doc might slip out. But how could she stall him?

It was too late. He already had the phone in his hand and was punching the numbers into the handset. He leaned back in his desk chair. "If this guy is anything like a real fisherman, he'll jump at the chance to do some trolling tomorrow."

Annie said a silent prayer that Doc was out somewhere. Anywhere. From where she sat she could see her husband, but was too far away to hear anything coming through the phone receiver.

Time seemed to stand still. John seemed to be waiting for someone to pick up. He glanced over at Annie and gave her a facial expression that seemed to say, *What?* She must have looked anxious.

Then she saw him straighten in the chair as if someone had just come into the room.

CHAPTER FIFTY-NINE

Doc

I have to admit, I almost shit myself when I heard the voice say, "This is John Weaver."

The only thing I could think of to say was, "Who?"

"John Weaver. We met at our clam bake on the beach a few weeks ago. I think you've run with my wife, Annie."

I was still panicked. My first thought was that something had happened to Annie and he was calling to tell me she was dead. But why would he call me? Unless, maybe Annie had confessed about us rather than die with a guilty conscience. So, out of sincere concern for Annie, all I could come up with was, "Is everything OK, John?"

"Yeah, everything's fine." I guess he forgot that his wife had lung cancer.

But I was relieved he wasn't calling about Annie, or to tell me he knew I had slept with her.

"Have you got a minute, Doc?"

I told him, "Sure, what can I do for you?"

He explained that he had a last minute cancellation on his striped bass trip tomorrow and wanted to know if I was interested in filling in. He even said that I was his first choice because he remembered what an avid fisherman I was. I think he was full of shit on that one but I was happy he invited me. And also a little confused. I mean, after all, this guy knows a lot of people that must have been above me on the list. Why me? So I asked.

"Why me?"

"I told you. I remember how you talked about fishing when we were standing around the fire. I just thought you'd enjoy it. Give us a chance to get to know each other too."

I'm not usually a skeptical person but my bullshit antenna was up on this. But to tell the truth, I was torn between trying to come up with an excuse not to go, and wanting to spend a day on the water in the company of like-minded sportsmen.

He told me they were planning to leave the dock at eight AM and gave me the exact location of the boat. He even mentioned the tide would be going out starting at around nine-thirty; perfect for trolling offshore. It all sounded too good to turn down.

Then, while he was going on about the size of the fish they caught on his last trip, my mind drifted back to earth and the thought of Annie. Actually, the image of Annie that came to mind wasn't one of her lying on a gurney with chemo running into her. It was a vision of her lying on her side next to me in bed, completely naked and asleep. But he didn't need to know that.

Before I could think, I said, "Sure. I'm in. Thanks for thinking of me."

We made the final arrangements and I agreed to meet him at the boat at eight the next morning. It felt really strange and I wondered what part, if any, Annie played in this.

"OK then. I'll see you in the morning. And Doc, don't bring any tackle. I've got everything on board. We'll pick up chum at Jackson's on the way out."

Before hanging up I wanted desperately to ask how Annie was, but thought that might seem odd.

After I hung up I checked my phone to see the number of the last call received. He'd called from their apartment. I wonder if Annie was there. I needed to talk to her—to find out what the hell was going on. But I didn't dare call their apartment and if she was there, I couldn't very well call her cell.

I've got to tell you, this really had me spooked. I imagined every weird scenario. My imagination was in weird over-drive. Maybe he found out about us and was taking me six miles off shore to kick the crap out of me. Maybe the other guy coming with us was a professional crap-kicker. If that was the case, I was screwed.

Or, maybe he found my phone number written on something Annie had left around and called just to find out who the number belonged to. Maybe the whole fishing thing was just bullshit.

Or, maybe he really just needed someone to fish with and Annie suggested he call me. Wouldn't that be ballsy of her?

I ate dinner watching Jeopardy. After my stomach was full of linguine I was thinking more clearly and realized my imagination was getting the best of me. It was probably all as innocent as he made it sound; just a couple of guys getting together to catch some stripers.

It's just that in this case, one of the guys was in love with the wife of the other guy.

Chapter Sixty

Doc was slouched on the couch and reading an issue of Fortune when his cell phone rang. He pulled the phone from his pocket and stared at the number. It was Annie!

"I'll bet you didn't expect that call, buster." Her voice sounded soft but also a little weak.

"Annie? Oh, it's so good to hear your voice. Are you OK?"

"No, asshole. I have cancer. You, however, are brutally stupid. How could you agree to go with him? What were you thinking?"

"Whoa. Whoa. Slow down. I gather from your tone that you don't approve. What's this all about anyway?"

"It's just what he said. I was in the room when he called you. He needs one more guy to go fishing and you're the only guy he could come up with on short notice."

"So he doesn't know anything? I mean about us."

"I have no reason to think so. Then again, he did pack his shotgun. Do you need a shotgun for fishing, Doc?"

For a second, the sarcasm eluded him. Then he smiled and said, "How are you feeling Annie? I've been worried about you. It kills me that I can't call you."

The honest concern in his voice melted her heart. "I've been better. The second dose was worse than the first, but they told me to expect that. I just feel so weak. I haven't had any solid food since Tuesday night. In fact, except for a half bottle of Gatorade I just drank, I haven't had anything since Tuesday."

Then she softened. "I miss you Doc. I wish I was there with you so you could take care of me."

The despair in her voice broke his heart. "I'd take great care of you. You know that don't you?"

"I do." There was silence for almost a minute. Both of them just wanted to take in the moment and pretend they were leaning against each other.

Then Annie broke in. "Listen, I just wanted you to know I had nothing to do with this. John got your phone number from the association directory. He looked up the Mauro's old number. I was hoping you wouldn't be home."

"So all he wants is a fishing buddy?"

"No. He's already got one of those. All he needs is ballast. You're the crucial third man in his three-man attack on the poor stripers."

"I'm glad to hear you still have your caustic sense of humor."

"Yeah, I'm a barrel of laughs. But seriously, Doc, watch yourself tomorrow. As far as John knows, I haven't been in Southampton in a couple of weeks. So don't say something stupid like you ran into me at King Kullen or something like that. You haven't seen me since Labor Day weekend. Got it?"

"So I shouldn't mention our boat ride to Sag Harbor then, huh?"

"That seems like a long time ago." She said it with noticeable regret in her voice.

"Next summer we'll have to do it again."

"Sounds good to me. I tell you what. If I'm around next summer, you can take me to Sag Harbor again."

"I'll count the days."

"Listen Doc. I can't talk long. My son Frank is coming in from Boston. He'll be here any minute. I just wanted you to know that I had nothing to do with this. I didn't tell him to call you."

"I understand. I'm glad you called though. I needed to hear your voice."

"John's driving out there tonight with his buddy Hank. They're going to stay at the house. Try not to say or do anything dumb tomorrow, OK?"

"I'll do my best. Hey, enjoy your son. Is he staying long?"

"No. He has classes on Monday afternoon so he'll get a train back on Monday morning. But it'll be great to see him."

"Well, you enjoy it. And I'll try to stay out of trouble tomorrow." He paused, then added, "I love you Annie. Please get better. I need you to get better."

CHAPTER SIXTY-ONE

Doc

On the drive over to the dock I couldn't help but feel I was making a huge mistake. Something about going fishing with the husband of the woman you're in love with just didn't seem right. After I hung up with Annie last night, I sat on the deck thinking about this a lot.

In the old days, before I lost my faith, this would have been one of those times I talked to God, hoping that he would show me what to do. It's not that I would talk out loud. My conversations with him were always in my head but they were real, and the solitude of the pond at night would have been the perfect place to talk.

I miss those talks. I gained some sort of inner strength from them. And even if I came away from one without a clear answer, I always felt that by talking it through, my problem was more manageable—that some how he was sharing my problem with me. All I know is that last night, without him to talk to, I felt a loneliness that I've never felt before—a self-imposed loneliness.

Even as I pulled my Jeep into the marina, something told me not to get on the boat. I suppose it was my conscience. Freudian analysis would have a field day with this one—the need to confront one's demons and all that. I just think I wanted to be around anything or anyone connected to Annie. In some odd way, being on her father's boat and in the company of her husband, made me feel closer to her.

But there I was, standing at the top of the gangway that led down to the row of yachts most men only dream of owning but never do. I was about five minutes early but could see John and another man removing the canvas from a gorgeous white sixty-foot Bertram. The name on the transom was *'Annie's Pleasure.'* She'd told me a little about the wonderful times she enjoyed on this boat with her father, husband and sons. Apparently, they all loved to fish and would take overnight trips out to Montauk with the young boys, then return with a box full of fish.

"There he is." John Weaver yelled from his perch on the boat's swim platform.

I decided to play the role of the dutiful mate. "That's quite a vessel you've got there captain. But can it find stripers?" I yelled back while descending onto the dock.

John made the introductions. His friend Hank, also a doctor, was a pudgy little guy, around my age and seemed to know his way around a boat. In less than ten minutes we were easing out of the slip and on our way down the canal to pick up chum and fuel at the same marina I use. Although, I must say, it's a bit different when you pull in to Jackson's in a sixty-foot Bertram than it is in my boat. For one thing, two deck-hands fall all over themselves to throw you a line and help make your docking experience go a little more smoothly. Another difference an extra forty feet of boat will make is that one of the deck hands comes on board to actually pump the fuel for you while the other wipes down your windshields. When I pull up, I have to go looking for someone to unlock the pump so I can do it myself. If I had a windshield, I doubt anyone would want to clean it.

I later learned that it's not so much the size of your boat that matters to the college kids on the dock, it's the twenty John pressed into each of their hands as he came out of the boathouse with a huge bucket of frozen chum. The lesson learned was that for forty bucks, I too could be a big shot to these kids.

The Bretram swallowed almost four thousand dollars in fuel before the twin tanks were satisfied. Second lesson learned: never offer to pay for gas when asked out on a rich guy's boat. Fitzgerald was right, *"The rich are different."* John never blinked as he signed for the tab. I guess when you have big toys you'd better be ready to keep them full of gas, or in this case, diesel.

It took almost an hour for us to cruise down the canal and through the Shinnecock Inlet into the open waters of the Atlantic. John said the guy in the boathouse told him the fish were running in about 150 feet of water which meant we needed to head due south about eight miles. I did some quick math and figured that it cost him over $300 in fuel just to get to the fish.

As we headed away from the Long Island coastline—something I don't like to lose sight of when I'm in my little boat, John flipped on an array of electronics that made his flying bridge look like the control room in a nuclear submarine. There were five separate computer screens all flashing colorful messages and charts. My friend Bobby would have loved this.

I sat up in the bridge with John while Hank rigged up two rods down in the cockpit. He seemed to know what he was doing because he had the massive spoons—a huge hook at the end of a shiny piece of steel that swivels through the water mimicking a fish, connected to six feet of piano wire and then to the line on the huge rods and reels. The line was then fed through the outrigger, a long fiberglass pole on each side of the boat. Another quick calculation convinced me that John probably spent more on his fishing equipment than I did on my entire boat. Again, if you're gonna have big toys,...

The farther we got offshore, the bluer the water seems to

get. At 150 feet, it was a beautiful shade you don't see in any of the bays. I suppose it's just the depth that causes the fantastic color but its something to behold. It's such a deep blue, you forget there's a bottom down there at all.

John gave me a few instructions while we traveled out to "The Ledge" as it's known—the spot where the bottom suddenly drops off from about ninety feet to over 160 feet. According to John, the stripers travel along the ledge in large schools feeding on the smaller fish that, in turn, feed on the plants that grow on the sloping bottom. Our job was to travel slowly along the ledge with two of Hank's tantalizing rigs trailing three hundred feet behind the '*Annie's Pleasure*', put out a slick of chum, and use the space-age technology on the bridge to find some stripers. If we were fortunate enough to come across a school, chances were good that both lines would attract a fish at the same time and we'd need to stop the boat to reel them in. This, I was told, is why you need three people to troll for stripers—two to fight the fish close enough to the boat so that the third could gaff them and haul the thirty to forty pound monsters on board.

Being the new guy, my job was to slop the chum over the side using a soup ladle. I was reminded of the scene from the movie Jaws, where Sheriff Brody is doing precisely the same thing the first time Spielberg decides to show us the shark. And don't think I didn't consider the possibility of just such an occurrence.

The water was calm and the sun was high in the sky. We had about a mile of chum floating behind us as John maneuvered the boat on long sweeping arches along the ledge, all the while watching his screens for signs of fish beneath us. It almost didn't seem fair. I mean when I fish, I drop a piece of bait over the side, let it sink to the bottom, and hope a fish comes along. This seemed more like a well-planned, high-tech massacre.

And yet, an hour went by and nothing happened. Nothing except we'd just burned through another six hundred dollars in fuel and I'd dished out ten gallons of fish heads. All the while, John held his position up on the flying bridge, carefully monitoring the electronics, while Hank and I talked about the Jets and what an asset Bret Favre was turning into. Since we were in the stern, our football conversation was over the din of the twin three-hundred-fifty horsepower engines.

Actually, I was glad that I didn't have more face-time with my host, the husband of my lover. I knew more about football anyway. And it gave us all a chance to do what men do best—just coexist quietly, even with the roar of the engines. Besides, if I was to keep my promise to Annie and not do or say something stupid, I was better off keeping my mouth shut.

"I've got something on the screen boys!" John yelled down from the bridge. "Looks like a small school. Could be blues but it might be stripers. Stay awake."

And just then the starboard outrigger heaved back and released its line with a whipping sound. A few seconds later the port outrigger did the same and we had two fish on the lines.

"You take that one," Hank screamed to me pointing at the port-side rod. He had the other rod on his belt already and had begun to reel furiously.

John heard the commotion and shut the engines. The sudden silence was wonderfully refreshing to my ears. John stayed high above us up on the bridge, shouting directions down to both of us.

"Let 'em take some line Doc. They need to run. Just don't let him under the boat. If he goes under the boat, reel hard."

"You got it Captain." I just felt better calling him Captain. I guess it helped me forget who he really was.

"Hank, how much line does he have?" He shouted from the bridge.

"I'd say there's still about three hundred feet out. I didn't give him any when he hit. I've been reeling like a bitch." Hank was already beginning to tire.

"Just take it slow. You'll get him up."

And John was right. It took both of us nearly fifteen minutes to get our fish close enough to the surface for John to gaff them, but we did it. And they were both good sized Bluefish; not the breed we were looking for, but a lot of fun to catch. Unfortunately, our captain didn't share my enthusiasm.

"Fuck me! You've both got Bluefish," were his exact words. "What the fuck are we going to do with Bluefish?"

I assumed it was a rhetorical question. So we brought them on board and threw them in the cooler. "At least we won't get skunked today," I offered, hoping to brighten his mood by reminding him at least we're not going home empty-handed. From the expression on his face, I realized I should have kept my mouth shut. John didn't consider Bluefish worth catching and actually treated them with surprising disdain.

"How about some lunch before we put the lines out again, John?" Hank was tired and looked like he could use some food and a beer. Actually, it was a good idea. Though it wasn't noon yet, we were all hungry, so we took a break and broke out the turkey heroes and Coronas. The three of us sat on the transom and swapped fishing tales while we ate.

As long as the conversation stuck to tales of '*big ones that got away*', we were just like any other three guys out fishing. Once he had a couple of bites of his sandwich and a beer, Hank was a pretty funny guy. He told a few fisherman jokes and regaled us with the story of his trip to Cabo and the giant tuna he '*almost landed.*'

We talked about the baseball playoffs that were about to start and the most recent SNL on which Tina Fey did a great impersonation of Sarah Palin. The funny part was Hank's imitation of Tina Fey. By the third Corona, his crew was beginning to lose interest in fishing and John had to remind us we still needed to put some stripers in the cooler. I guess that was his way of saying, "*Lunch is over.*"

As we were cleaning up the deck, which amounted to throwing the empty bottles and sandwich wrappers into the bucket previously holding the chum, Hank asked John, "Hey John, how's your wife doing?" From the way he asked, I got the impression Hank didn't know Annie very well or maybe not at all, but that he knew of her illness.

"Not well I'm afraid. The cancer has metastasized and is in her thyroid and lymph nodes as well." And then he added, in a doctor-to-doctor sort of way, "And you know what that means."

Fortunately, my back was to both of them or they would have seen my eyes close in pain at the words. I felt as if I'd been punched in the chest and lost all my air. Worst yet, I wasn't sure how I should react to the news. Any normal man would have responded with something like, "Gee John, I'm sorry to hear that. I didn't know your wife was ill." But I wasn't a normal man. I was the man who'd spent two weekends in bed with his wife. I was the man who, four days earlier, tried to convince her to leave him and live with me.

My quandary was—should I feign ignorance and ask what they were talking about, or should I keep my mouth shut. Acknowledging Annie's illness was out of the question because, as she said, "*We weren't supposed to have seen each other since Labor Day weekend.*" There would be no way I would have known about her illness unless I spoke to her.

But to remain silent would have seemed strange, even among guys. You don't overhear that sort of news about some-one's wife and say nothing. I had to respond with something. Then, just as I was formulating my faked ignorance, Hank saved me.

"John, I don't know how you do it. Your wife's in stage four lung cancer and you still keep pretty much a normal schedule at work and can make time to be out here with us."

"Well, it helps having my office so close to home and to the hospital. And Annie's son is with her this weekend so I thought I'd only be in the way. They don't get to see much of one another." John then looked at me and said, "I'm sorry Doc. I guess you didn't know about my wife's condition. How could you?"

I said I was sorry to hear about it and told him to relay my good wishes to her, hoping we could leave it at that. But John pressed on. "We only learned of her condition a few weeks ago and it looks like the cancer is very far along. Her doctors aren't hopeful, and neither am I, but they're going through the usual protocol—chemo and radiation to try to suppress it and maybe buy her a little more time."

It hurt to hear the words spoken so calmly. But I suppose when you're a doctor, you tend to look at even your own wife's situation through the callused eyes of a clinician. I didn't have to fake my concern. "I'm so sorry to hear that." I said.

Hank asked, "What do the WBC numbers look like John?"

"They're off the charts. I don't know how her GP didn't spot this at her annual physical last year. The leukocyte count had to be elevated then. You can't have that much white cell activity and not see something in the blood work."

"And she felt OK up to now?" Hank asked.

"No, not really. She's been showing symptoms for months now. We just never put two and two together. She's been unusually tired all summer and hasn't had much of an appetite. If we'd spent more time together I would have noticed the change but our schedules kept us apart most of the summer. She was out in Southampton most of the time and I commuted a lot between both offices. I just didn't see her enough." John seemed to be blaming himself for not diagnosing Annie's cancer earlier.

But it seemed like his emotions were confusing the facts. The Annie I met in early August ran a six-minute mile every day. She never seemed tired. In fact, I remember marveling at her energy level. And her appetite seemed normal to me. Right up until we went to Montauk she kept up with me in the food and alcohol department. In fact, the first time she ever complained about being tired was that Sunday morning in Montauk, and that was after a night of drinking that could have put college kids to shame.

I wanted to tell him he was wrong—to let him know that Annie was fine up until about ten days ago. But obviously, I couldn't.

Then the bombshell.

"What's the prognosis from Cox?" Hank inquired delicately.

"Weeks. Not months. I doubt she'll make it to Thanksgiving." John looked down as he said it. His voice was shaky.

I took another blow to the chest and one to the guts. I thought my knees were going to give out. The first thing that crossed my mind was that Annie had lied to me to spare my feelings. That would be like her. The second thing that crossed my mind was how much I suddenly felt sorry for John. Whatever his faults, the poor bastard was about to lose his wife. I felt his pain.

Then it occurred to me that maybe she didn't know. Maybe, because of the special relationship John had with her other doctors, they hadn't yet told her how bleak the picture was. She told me on Tuesday, her doctor said she could have six good months before the effects would be debilitating. And with the treatments, there was even a chance for remission. Had they been lying to her? Or was she shielding me from the reality she chose to face without me?

The rest of the trip was a blur to me. I was so shaken up by the news about Annie, I was sort of sleep-walking through the remainder of the day. We did catch three good-size stripers and Hank and John seemed to be happy about that, even celebrating with a Corona toast with each catch, but I was miserable. I pretended to drink with them but secretly poured most of my bottle overboard when no one was watching. I just wasn't in the mood. Also, I was afraid of what I might say if my tongue was loosened by a few more beers.

It was surreal. I was heartbroken by the news about my beautiful Annie. She was way too young to die. And at the same time I felt genuinely sorry for John, the guy she was supposed to dump for me. An odd mixture of guilt and pity simultaneously ran through me every time John would say something. I wanted to say, "I'm sorry," but I wasn't sure if that meant I was sorry his wife was dying or that I was sorry because I'd been sleeping with her. Despite the gorgeous weather, it was one of the most uncomfortable afternoons of my life and I couldn't wait for us to get back to the dock.

Finally, John announced it was time to call it a day and Hank and I stowed the fishing gear while he piloted us back toward shore. After the rods were hosed down, Hank decided to filet the fish we'd caught so I went up to the flying bridge and took the seat next to John. For nearly twenty minutes we both sat in silence watching for the first sight of approaching land and occasionally turning to watch a seagull dive for the fish parts Hank was tossing overboard.

To this day, I don't understand why I did it, but I started chatting with John. Maybe there was a part of me so riddled with guilt that I hoped to get caught in a lie and exposed for the adulterous bastard I was. Or maybe there was a dark part of me that wanted to gloat about being the last person his wife would ever make love to. Or maybe I just felt sorry for the poor prick. It's hard to remember now—now that I understand what really happened.

We kept the conversation mostly about boating and fishing. I made it known how impressed I was with his boat. He liked that. We talked about other ways to fish for stripers and how I do it on my boat. I told him about my last trip with Bobby and how we used small diamond jigs while drifting within sight of land. He seemed in pretty good spirits for a guy who would likely be attending his wife's funeral in the next few weeks.

Oddly, John seemed to like me. I got the impression he didn't have a need for many people in his life and was, by no means, a social butterfly; but for some reason, he seemed very comfortable with me. Maybe it was the beer, but by the time we were heading back up the canal, approaching the dock, he was insisting we fish together again. He said he'd be back out to Southampton for his regular Wednesday night poker game but that he wouldn't have time for fishing until the following weekend and asked it that worked for me.

To my complete surprise, I not only said yes, but suggested we take my boat and try my jigging method. I wasn't sure if rich people cared about reciprocity but it seemed like the right thing to do. After all, he'd just blown through about fifteen hundred bucks in fuel and all we had to show for it was a little sunburn and six filets.

He agreed to come back on Saturday morning—weather permitting.

Later, I thought it strange he didn't say anything about our next trip also being dependent on Annie's condition.

Chapter Sixty-Two

Frank and his mother were curled up on the large leather sofa in front of the television. He'd brought a couple of DVDs with him from Boston, his mother's two favorite movies: "Arthur" and "Cool Hand Luke". The remains of some Chinese take-out were scattered on the coffee table in front of them. Annie had some egg drop soup and was doing a good job keeping it down. Dudley Moore was on the screen talking to his chauffer, Bidderman, and Frank was finishing the last of his beef with broccoli.

This was exactly the evening Annie had hoped for; she and her son, wrapped in a blanket watching television and catching up on each other's lives. She didn't have the energy to go out but didn't want to seem too frail in front of Frank. She was putting on a good show for him. She even suggested they go to a restaurant on Sixty-third, but fortunately Frank's preference was take-out.

She didn't tell him how sick she'd been just a few hours earlier, and dressed in a pair of jeans and a pink Bergdorf cashmere sweater she looked a lot better than she felt. This was her son. How could she let him go back to Boston worried about her? So far, she'd done a good job of faking it.

When the phone rang, Frank paused the DVD and jumped up to grab it.

"It's for you mom, a doctor Weber. Do you want to talk to her?"

Annie had no idea why Tomasue would be calling her at

nine-thirty on a Friday night. Maybe just checking on her. But she didn't want to be impolite and reached out from under the blanket for the phone.

"Hey Tomasue, what's up?"

"Hey Annie. How you feeling? More to the point, who's the handsome-sounding man who answers your phone?"

"Ah, that's my handsome son Frank. He came home from B.U. to take care of me this weekend."

"Oh, good for you. And how are you feeling?"

Frank had retreated to the kitchen to refill his ice tea so Annie had a moment to speak honestly with her friend and doctor. "Well, I've gotten very good at vomiting if that counts for anything. Otherwise, it's about as bad as everybody told me to expect."

"Some people have told me they developed quite the relationship with their toilets while going through chemo and actually missed the porcelain thrown when it was all over." Tomasue tried to make light of what she knew must have been a few bad days for her friend.

"Well, I'll be happy to get this over with. Only four weeks to go for round one."

"Make sure you keep the fluids up, Annie. Drink as much as you can."

"Thanks, as a matter of fact I just finished my third martini and decided to switch to beer."

"Very funny. No, no kidding. Hydration is the most important thing you can do for yourself right now. Lots of water, sweet ice tea or Gatorade."

"Thanks. Actually it's not so bad." Annie peaked around the corner to make sure her son was still out of ear-shot. "But, to tell you the truth, I'm not sure I could do another round."

"Well, let's take it one step at a time and see what your CEA count looks like in four weeks. Actually, Annie, that's why I called. I'm having dinner with a good friend of Jack's who lives in Minnesota and is here on a medical convention. He's one of the top oncologists at the Mayo and offered to take a look at your charts as a favor to me. He's done a lot of research on thyroid cancer. His name is Doug Langer, Doctor Doug Langer and he's only in town until Monday morning. So, I called John's office to see if he would send over your file and films but they said he's away until Tuesday. Obviously they won't release your file to me, so I called him on his cell a couple of hours ago but it went to voicemail and I haven't heard back from him. It would be a shame to miss this opportunity. Do you know how I can get in touch with John?"

Annie recalled John's story about his cell phone battery going down the elevator shaft and explained it to Tomasue. "He went fishing with some friends out on the island and isn't coming back until Monday. I have no way to get a hold of him because we already turned off the phone at the house for the season." Then she said, "Let me think." And she went through, in her mind, any other way to reach her husband. She didn't have Hank's cell number and there were no neighbors that would still be out there this time of year.

The only way to get in touch with John would be to call Doc and ask him to go over to her house and tell John to call Tomasue. But John had taken the directory with Doc's phone number with him so how could she explain that she knew his number without it? That could lead to an uncomfortable discussion.

"No Tomasue, I can't get in touch with him unless he calls home, but I doubt he will because he knows Frank's here. He knows I'm OK."

"That's a shame. Doug said he'd be happy to take a look for me. Well, maybe next week, when John's back, you can have him send a copy of the file to Doug in Minnesota. I'm sure he…Oh no, wait. He's going on to another conference in San Francisco so he won't be back to his office until the following week."

"How about if I pick up my file at John's office tomorrow and have Frank drop it off to you in the morning? Would that work?" Annie really didn't want to have to call Doc.

"Well, technically, they're not supposed to release it without John's OK, but if you've got a good relationship with the girls at his office, they probably won't mind. Great Idea, just make sure to tell them you need all the films and radiology reports too. Doug can take a look tomorrow afternoon. We're meeting him and his wife for dinner at Po."

"Oh, I love that place. Have the fresh mozzarella for me."

"Listen Annie. Doug is really good. He's the guy that everyone west of the Mississippi goes to when they have thyroid problems. And he's always on the cutting edge of new technologies so I'm glad we can do this. He might see something we all missed."

"Wouldn't that be nice." Annie said as Frank came back into the room. Then she added, "I'll call the office first thing in the morning and have Frank bring the reports to you by ten. Is that OK?"

"Great. I haven't seen your son since he was about twelve. He sounds so grown up on the phone."

Annie could hear restaurant noises in the background and didn't want to detain Tomasue any longer than necessary, although she would have been happy to talk about Frank for hours. "Listen, I'll let you get back to dinner. Thanks so much Tomasue, and Frank will come over by ten. Thanks again. Bye."

She looked up at her son who'd overheard his name being used. "Where am I going at ten?" He asked looking at his watch.

"No, not tonight honey. I need you to pick up my file at John's office and bring it over to my GP tomorrow morning. She has a thyroid specialist in town staying with her who offered to take a look. He's a friend of hers."

"Excellent!" He said as he pushed 'play' and Arthur resumed.

CHAPTER SIXTY-THREE

Miranda carried a tray full of beers onto the aft deck. She and her friend Lacy, who was to be Hank's entertainment, arrived at the dock about an hour after Doc departed. Lacy, a fourth year nursing student at NYU, drove them from Manhattan in her mother's BMW. She'd worked with Miranda before but never for John and she was amply impressed by his boat.

They'd taken the '*Annie's Pleasure*' through the canal and into the calm Peconic Bay where they anchored a hundred yards off shore and planned to spend the night. The Hampton Bays Elks club was putting on a modest fireworks display in town that evening and they had a clear view of the aerial display from their anchorage.

As the colorful lights reflected off the still water, Miranda wondered if Hank was satisfied with Lacy. John hadn't specified exactly what sort of second girl he needed tonight, just that she be gorgeous and of course, willing to work for the regular fee. Before agreeing to bring Lacy, Miranda made sure there would be a second man; she wanted no part of a three-way.

"Do you have limes for the beer, Jack?" Lacy asked. Tonight, John and Hank were Jack and Gabe.

"Yeah, honey. They're in the fridge."

They lounged around drinking and listening to a Van Morrison CD John had on board. Lacy and Hank were sitting on the swim platform with their feet dangling in the warm black water. It was Miranda who first suggested they go for a swim, and before anyone could respond, Lacy was pulling her tee shirt over her head and stepping out of her shorts.

Her slim naked body cut through the water like a knife, barely making a splash. She emerged fifteen feet behind the boat calling out for the rest to follow. "The water's so warm. This feels great."

Miranda quickly followed, dropping her clothes in a neat pile at John's feet and letting her hard nipples brush against his chest as she maneuvered past him over the transom. "Come on Jack. Don't be a party pooper." And in she went.

You two have fun in there. We're very comfortable up here." Hank called to them as the young girls splashed and swam away from the boat.

"Hey, don't go far. The current's not strong but it can take you further than you'd like to swim back." John didn't want to have to weigh anchor to go rescue them. He called out again, "Miranda, really. Don't go too far from the boat. I have big plans for you tonight."

"I'll bet you do." Hank said to his host. "That is some beautiful piece of ass you've got there. What is she, Mexican?"

But John never took his eyes off the girls. He wanted to be sure they could get back to the boat and was about to throw them a life preserver when they both began swimming towards him. "Good, stay here at the back of the boat where we can keep an eye on you." Somehow, he felt a sense of responsibility for the young call girls. Maybe it was just because they were so young and he felt some kind of fatherly obligation. He didn't understand it or try to think much about it. He just knew he wouldn't be comfortable until they were back on board.

Like he said, he had big plans for Miranda tonight. And the last thing he needed was some stupid coed hooker drowning.

CHAPTER SIXTY-FOUR

Frank Dunn awoke to the wonderful smell of bacon frying. Annie had been up for two hours before he stirred. She showered, dressed and had made her son's favorite breakfast; pancakes and bacon. She ate a banana and some Cheerios for breakfast; the first solid food in three days. But it was Frank's presence that made her feel better than she had in a while. She wasn't ready for anything strenuous but she felt strong enough to maybe take a walk in the park later. Maybe.

They sat together in the sunny kitchen while he wolfed down six pancakes and enough bacon to start another pig. She marveled at his wonderfully healthy appetite. It seemed like just yesterday, the two of them, Frank and his twin brother Nick, would be horsing around at the breakfast table, each trying to get the other to laugh with funny faces and noises. How fast twenty-two years goes by.

Frank insisted on doing the dishes, including the ones piled in the sink from the previous evening. While he did, Annie sat and admired her wonderful young man. He really was becoming a lot like his father she thought. The broad shoulders and sandy-blond hair reminded her of Peter. He would have been so proud of his sons; he always was.

"What's the matter Mom?" Frank asked when he noticed Annie drifting off.

"Nothing. I was just thinking about dad and how proud he'd be to see you today and to know you're going to graduate from BU in a few months."

"Hopefully."

"You'd better. I plan to be sitting in the front row at your graduation."

"Hey, that reminds me. We need to check and see when Nick's graduation is. I bet it's before mine and I want to fly down to Florida for it, but I may need to work around finals."

"I already checked. Gainesville graduates on the Saturday before you. I think it's the ninth of May and you're the sixteenth, right."

As she was speaking, Annie noticed her medicine over the sink, just beyond Frank. She kept the bottle of Synthroid there to remind herself to take it every morning, but today she was out of her normal routine and had forgotten. "Frank, could you hand me my medicine; I forgot to take it this morning." She pointed to the small bottle on the shelf. "And can you get me a glass of water, please?"

"Sure, Mom. How many of these do you take?"

"Just one each morning, but I'm supposed to take it first thing."

And then, the first of two accidents that would save Annie's life happened.

As he opened the bottle of pills, Frank's wet hands slipped and the bottle fell onto the countertop. Many of the pills were lost into the soapy water in the sink.

"Oh, shit! I'm sorry Mom."

"It's OK, Frank. Don't worry about it. There weren't too many left anyway." She lied.

"I can get it refilled when we go out."

After retrieving the open bottle Frank noticed there were two pills still in the container. "Well, you've got two left."

"Good. I'll take one now, please. And careful with that glass of water honey. I've already had my shower this morning." She teased.

Her son wanted to make up for his clumsiness and said, "I'm going to get a newspaper anyway. I'll get it refilled for you. Do you still go to Philips?"

"Of course. I've been using that pharmacy since you were a baby. Dad used to carry boxes of formula home from Philips for me. Diapers too. And he made a lot of late night runs for that pink medicine you needed when you got your ear aches. Did you know Mr. Philips, the father, died? Now his son James is the pharmacist and runs the store with his wife. I think her name is Bonnie."

"That's too bad but he must have been over eighty, right?"

"Yeah, like the rest of us, he just got old."

"You're not old Mom." And for the first time, Annie could see the boyish concern on her son's face. He was a college senior, but he was also a little boy who wasn't ready to lose his mommy.

"Thanks honey."

"So what are we going to do today?"

"Well, after you pick up my file at John's office and drop it off at my doctor, how about we walk through the park to that pizza place you love over on the west side?"

"That's a long walk mom. Are you sure you're up for it?" His concern was sincere and she was touched.

"Sure. And if I get tired, we'll take a cab home. Then maybe, if you're up for it, I thought we'd have an early dinner at home and go see a movie."

"Sounds great."

After finishing the dishes he disappeared into the bathroom and emerged as a well—groomed young Manhattanite. Frank almost always wore kakis, so that didn't surprise her, but today he had on a well pressed powder blue button-down shirt with a Brooks Brother's logo. That hadn't been his style when he left for Boston.

"Where'd you get that shirt honey?" She thought she already knew the answer.

"It was one of Dad's. He never even wore it. I took a couple of them when I left for school." He was obviously proud of his choice.

"It looks great on you." Annie was on the verge of an emotional collapse. A mixture of joy—at having her son home, and sorrow—at the thought of her first husband's death and the pain that caused her sons, and pride—at the wonderful young man standing before her in a shirt she remembered buying for Peter.

"Thanks mom. I'll be back in less than an hour. I need your doctor's address. I want to grab a paper and I'll get your prescription." He was on his way out the door.

Annie called to him, "I'll phone James at Philips and tell him you're coming."

She dried the dishes then remembered she needed to call John's office to release the charts to Tomasue. She made that call and one to the pharmacy and before she knew it, fifty minutes had passed and Frank was back with a copy of the Saturday Times under his arm.

"The pharmacist said I could pick up the prescription for you after three. He even remembered me, but I think he's got me mixed up with Nick because he was talking about something I did as a kid with his son. It must have been Nick. And I dropped your file off at your doctor's office. She seems really nice. She said she remembers me but I don't remember ever meeting her before."

"You were too young to remember. How about a slow walk across the park? You can bring your paper because I'll probably need to take a rest halfway there anyway. We'll see what's playing at the Lowes."

While they strolled through Central Park they talked.

People on rollerblades and bikes whizzed by. Joggers passed them like they were standing still, but the slow pace didn't bother Frank. He was enjoying his time with his mother. He rarely got to spend time alone with her anymore. He and Nick made a point of coordinating their visits in order to maximize time with Annie and minimize exposure to their step-father. So, when he did get to see her, usually Nick was there too. As a result, one-on-one time with Annie was rare, and he was drinking it in and loving it.

And Annie was experiencing a pleasant nostalgia as well. All her memories of her boys were wonderful collages of happy faces and little-boy shenanigans. In twenty-two years she couldn't recall a bad memory. Well, just one—she could never erase the image of her sixteen year-old sons looking down into the casket of their father.

Frank sensed their pace slowing a bit and suggested they rest for a few minutes on a bench near the rowboat house. They were about half way to the pizza shop anyway.

"How about we stop for a while and let me take a look at the paper?"

"Sounds good to me."

Frank sorted the Times into sections, handing Annie the entertainment portion and keeping the rest. "See what's playing at the Lowes, Mom. I bet that new one with Jim Carrey is there. It just came out. Looks funny. We could use a good chuckle."

He spent several minutes pouring through the paper. It reminded Annie of the way his father would read the paper on Sunday mornings; always spread out on the table and folded in halves. The apple doesn't fall far she thought.

Frank was looking through the business section when he said, "Hey, this reminds me Mom. Frank Montague, your lawyer, sent me an email about a week ago. He said he wanted to arrange a meeting with Nick and me when we're home for Christmas vacation. He said you knew about it. What's that all about?"

Annie recalled the conversation she had with Franklin about the trust funds. "I think he wants to talk to you about your trust funds from poppa. You guys turn twenty-three in January and the trusts change then. He probably wants to make sure you understand what's going on. It's a lot of money, you know."

Frank understood little about his trust fund other than the fact that he had no access to it yet. But his entire life had been a privileged one, and access to enough money to do the things he wanted had never been an issue. There was always money. As a consequence, he rarely thought about it.

"So, what happens when I'm twenty-three?"

"It's complicated, but basically the trusts, all of them, change, and most of what's in mine transfers to yours. You still can't get at it but I think poppa did it that way to save inheritance taxes somehow. Anyway, that must be what Franklin wants to talk about." And then she remembered the letter.

A month before he died, her father, knowing his end was near, wrote a letter to his two grandsons. Annie didn't know its contents but assumed it had to do with how proud he was of them and the responsibility that comes with wealth, especially inherited wealth. Burt often spoke of that in his last days. He wanted the fruits of his life's work used prudently, perhaps even philanthropically. Most important, he didn't want Annie's second husband to have unbridled use of the money. Burt feared John's motives from the start and had often counseled Annie about it.

"I think also, he might have a letter for you that poppa wrote. You know how much he loved you boys."

"Well, I'll email him and set up the meeting when we're

home in December. I was worried it might have something to do with you, you know, with your illness."

"No honey. I'm sure it's about the trusts."

The rest of their afternoon together was all enjoyment. They stopped for pizza at Frank's favorite place. Annie had half a bagel and a cup of soup and was grateful that she felt well afterwards. She didn't feel ready for pizza yet.

She was in such a positive mood, after lunch she suggested they walk back to her apartment rather than taking a cab. Though the return walk tired her out, she felt invigorated by Frank's company. She didn't want the day to end.

When they arrived back at the apartment, there was a voicemail message for Annie from James at the pharmacy. He asked that she call him back before coming in to pick up her prescription. She was about to return the call when Frank announced he was going for a jog in the park.

"It's such a beautiful day, I hate to waste it." He'd already changed into running attire. "I'll be back in an hour. Maybe less if I'm as out of shape as I think."

"OK honey. I may take a nap so take a key with you."

"Way ahead of you," he said, showing her the keys in his hand as he left.

Annie put a kettle of water on the stove for a cup of tea she planned to enjoy before her nap, then dialed the number for the pharmacy.

"Hello, this is Annie Dunn." She still used her old name for most of the neighborhood people who knew her the longest. "I'm returning James' call. Is he there please?"

A moment later the familiar deep voice came on the line. "Hello Mrs. Dunn. How are you today?" He was unaware of Annie's cancer so she didn't feel the need to say anything other than, "Good, James. How are you?"

"Well, I'm a little concerned about you, to tell the truth."

Annie didn't understand. How could he have known about her illness? She hadn't told anyone in the neighborhood and John rarely spoke to any of their neighbors anyway. The only explanation she could come up with was that perhaps Frank had told him this morning when he dropped of the empty bottle of Synthroid.

"Well…I'm OK, really. But thanks for asking James."

"Well, the reason I'm concerned is because you really shouldn't keep your medications in anything but their proper container. That's how accidents happen."

"What do you mean?"

"Putting one medicine in the container of another medicine is dangerous."

"I still don't understand. Why are you telling me that? I wouldn't do that." Annie was genuinely confused.

Mr. Philips could hear the confusion in her voice and started over. "Annie, your son came in this morning to renew your Synthroid. He brought in the old Synthroid bottle but I noticed there was one pill still in the bottle. When I went to fill your prescription I could see the pill wasn't Synthroid. He'd told me how he accidently knocked over the bottle and all the other pills went down the sink. He felt bad about it. But you really shouldn't keep your Carisoprodol in the Synthroid bottle. You could make a mistake. That's very dangerous."

"What's Carisoprodol?"

"It's the little blue pill you had in your Synthroid bottle. Actually, it looks just like your thyroid medicine, just a little bit bigger pill. That's why you could easily confuse them. I suggest you keep the Carisoprodol in its properly marked container. This is a powerful depressant."

"Mr. Philips, I don't know what you're talking about. The only medicine I take is Synthroid; one pill a day, in the morning. I never heard of Carisoprodol."

"I'm glad to hear that Mrs. Dunn. And that's why I wanted to talk to you. Do you think it's possible that the Carisoprodol belongs to your son? Why would he have put it in your bottle? I'm a little confused myself."

When a parent first hears the word "DRUGS" used in the same sentence as the name of their child, their first reaction is usually, "Not my kid." And in this case, Annie would have bet her life Frank had nothing to do with drugs. He and Nick had both been open with her about some casual pot use, but the thought of him using depressants was absurd. Why would he need depressants?

"Mr. Philips, there has to be a mistake. Are you sure you didn't mix my last pill up with something else?"

"Mrs. Dunn, you've known me for almost thirty years. This is not a mistake. There was a Carisoprodol pill in your Synthroid bottle. I checked the label on the bottle. I personally filled your last prescription on September 16th. I wouldn't make that sort of mistake. We don't even stock Carisoprodol. It's usually only prescribed by psychiatrists and I have to special order it when a prescription comes in. I haven't had it in my store in a couple of months. Frankly, it's too expensive to stock."

Now Annie was a little less certain about her son. The thought of him using any sort of drug made her weak in the knees. Why would he do that? Could it be the pressure at school?

"Well, I'm glad to hear it's not yours, anyway. I've filled your prescription. Shall I have it sent over? Oh, by the way, your insurance company won't cover the prescription because you had it filled just two weeks ago. They'll only pay every thirty days. Sorry about that. So I only gave you fifteen pills. That should hold you, and then I can refill the full prescription later. Is that OK?"

Annie was still distracted with the thought of her son taking dangerous drugs, but she heard enough to answer, "Yes, thanks. Please send them up."

"I guess I'll just toss this Carisoprodol then?"

"Fine. Like I said, it's certainly not mine." She knew that sounded like she was somehow implicating her son, so she added, "It's got to be a mistake."

She hung up. Then waited for Frank to come home to the conversation no parent wants to have.

Chapter Sixty-Five

A nap was out of the question. She was way too upset. While she waited for her son to get back she went online and Googled Carisoprodol. She quickly learned from Wikipedia:

> *Carisoprodol is a centrally acting skeletal muscle relaxant. It was developed in 1959, is colorless and soluble in water, and is has limited marketing in the U.S. under the brand name Soma. It's been banned in Sweden because of the tendency for abuse.*

She still couldn't believe her son would take drugs. He was an athlete. He always seemed so concerned about his health and worked out at a gym several times a week. This had to be a mistake.

The messenger from the pharmacy arrived just as Frank was returning from his jog.

"Hey, I would have picked that up for you. I just ran right past Philips."

Annie tipped the deliveryman and closed the apartment door. She dreaded this conversation and didn't know how to begin.

"I'm going to jump in the shower, Mom. Are you still up for a movie tonight?"

She couldn't wait for him to take a shower. She needed to know if her son was taking drugs, and she needed to know now. So, she just asked.

"Frank, I need to ask you something and I need you to tell me the absolute truth."

Her serious tone caught him off guard. He leaned on the kitchen counter and took a sip from his water bottle, then said, "Sure Mom, what's up?"

"Mr. Philips called me earlier. He said the bottle you brought him this morning had a pill in it that wasn't my medication. It was some form of depressant called Carisoprodol." She paused and watched for a reaction. There was only a confused look on his face; exactly the look she was hoping for.

"How'd that happen?" He wanted to know.

"I'm not sure. In fact, I have no idea. Synthroid is the only medicine I take." She emphasized the word "I".

Frank caught her implication immediately. "You think it was mine?"

Shaking her head, she admitted, "I don't know what to think."

"Mom, you think I take drugs!" He was laughing. "I don't even take aspirin. Are you crazy? Why would I take depressants?"

"I'm sorry honey. I didn't know what else to think. Who else would have put that in my bottle?"

"My guess is someone at the drug store screwed up. But what a strange coincidence."

"What do you mean?" Annie sat down. Relieved and convinced her son was telling her the truth.

"I mean, that was the only pill that didn't go down the drain. If someone at Philips screwed up, and gave you…How many pills do you get at a time?"

"Thirty, enough for a month."

"So, someone puts twenty-nine of the right pills and one wrong one in your bottle, and the one that's left when the rest go down the drain is the wrong one. What are the odds?"

"Actually, they'd be one-in-thirty." Annie was always good at math. Then she remembered the second pill that didn't go down the drain—the one she took this morning.

"No, there were two pills that didn't get wet. Remember? I took one."

"Right. Hey, it's a good thing you took the right one. What would the other one have done to you?"

"I'm glad I didn't have to find out. I'm even more glad that it was a mistake. I was freaking out thinking it was yours." After witnessing her son's honest concern for her, she was a bit ashamed she'd jumped to the conclusion she had.

"Well maybe you'd better think about a different pharmacy. That kind of carelessness could get somebody killed. What if it was something that could have killed you? Jeez mom, you really dodged a bullet here." And as he spoke the words, he realized the irony of his statement; a woman, in the fight of her life with cancer, almost gets accidentally poisoned to death!

Chapter Sixty-Six

Doc

I don't remember the day when I first realized I'd lost my faith, but I remember the exact moment I was certain of it. It was the day after my fishing trip with Annie's husband and I was scheduled to fly to Boston to meet an old friend for a Red Sox game. We made the plans months before; long before I retired from the real world. I was in my seat on the plane waiting for the Boeing 737 to pull away from the terminal at MacArthur Airport.

Now, I've flown a lot in my life; over forty trips to London alone, and hundreds of flights around the states visiting clients everywhere from Miami to Seattle. Flying never bothered me. In fact, once in the air, I usually took advantage of the temporary serenity to catch up on reading or watching movies I'd missed in the theater.

But before take-off, I had a ritual that I never failed to go through. It went back to my childhood and the thought of flying without doing it was unthinkable. I'd been doing it religiously (for lack of a better word) since the fourth grade. That's when I took my first class trip on a bus.

It was a beautiful June day, one of the last of the school year, and everyone from my class waited for the huge coach bus to turn the corner so we could file on and be chauffeured to the Museum of Natural History in Manhattan—an unbelievable thirty-four miles away. As was customary at our school, the nuns had us assembled in straight lines, in height order. When the shiny silver bus finally arrived we took our seats according to our position on line, meaning we couldn't sit with our best friends. Worse yet, I was stuck sitting next to Mary Ann Quigley, a girl!

But the real trauma began when Sister Helen Angela boarded the bus. Standing in the front, just next to the driver, she explained that a bus ride of this sort, particularly one that would need to travel on highways and over a bridge, was very dangerous, and required all the divine assistance we could muster. So, before the doors closed, she led us in an entire decade of the rosary. The driver wasn't quite sure what to make of the delay but I guess he was Catholic because, although I couldn't see if his lips were moving, I definitely saw him make the sign of the cross at the beginning and end of the prayers.

Sister explained to us that the Hail Mary was a particularly appropriate prayer for two reasons: first, it was a direct appeal to God's mother, and second because it ends with the phrase, *"Pray for us sinners, now, and at the hour of our death. Amen."* She told us, in no uncertain terms, that if those were the last words we said before the bus drove off the bridge into the East River, that we would instantly go to heaven. No questions asked. Why? Because we'd just asked Mary, the mother of God, to pray for us at the hour of our death. And since Mary had considerable pull with her son, should our driver have a heart attack behind the wheel and send us all into the river, we were assured eternal bliss.

Better yet, we were told that by saying the Hail Mary before any major travel, you were pretty much assured a safe trip. And since we got safely over the bridge twice that day, I was convinced it worked. From that day forward, any time I got on a bus, train or plane, but especially planes, I said a silent Hail Mary. For some reason Sister didn't think the Hail Mary had the same effect on car rides—or at least she never mentioned it.

Once I started taking a bus to high school the habit sort of died off and when I was commuting on the Long Island Railroad as an adult, I never thought to begin the journey with a prayer. But I never stopped the ritual when flying. It had always worked. Logic told me that since I'd never been in a plane crash, it must be the Hail Mary's that were saving me. And the great thing about Hail Mary's is that, by saying one, I not only saved myself, but everyone else on the otherwise doomed flight as well.

This went on for over forty years of flying. I would always say a silent Hail Mary just as the plane was about to begin its acceleration down the runway. That way, I figured if we crashed on take-off, the most dangerous time in air travel, I would have muttered those fateful words, "...*and at the hour of our death*," just in time, and certainly before I had a chance to screw up the effect by committing some other sin.

And I wasn't alone. A lot of other passengers must have gone to Catholic elementary school as well because I would see other people's lips moving as the plane raced down the runway. Once, I was traveling to Chicago with the CEO of the biggest construction company in New York and we were sitting next to each other in business class when the Braniff flight started to take off. I noticed he put down his magazine and gazed out the window. I could see his lips moving, silently mouthing the words, "*Hail Mary, full of grace.*"

After realizing other people believed in the power of the Hail Mary as well, I was afraid to ever not say it. Call it superstition or whatever, but I was not about to tempt fate. This gimmick of Sister Helen Angela worked. After hundreds of flights, I was proof. And, although the skeptical side of me wanted to see what would happen if just once I didn't say it, the little boy in me was afraid to rock the boat—or in this case, the plane. After all, if you think about the words, it's the perfect prayer when you're trying to curry favor with the big guy.

"*Hail Mary, full of grace. The Lord is with thee.*" This is a direct kiss-up to the mother of God.

"*Blessed are thou among women and blessed is the fruit of thy womb, Jesus.*" Again, more kissing-up to Mary and a direct reference to her son, the big guy. What mother doesn't like to hear about her successful son?

"*Holy Mary, mother of God...*" Another reminder of her special place in the cosmos.

And then the clincher, "*Pray for us sinners, now and at the hour of our death.*" Like I said, it's the perfect prayer as you hurdle down the runway in two hundred tons of steal that's about to defy gravity.

So, there I was in seat 8E on a commuter flight to Boston. The plane was making its final turn onto the runway and I was facing the moment of truth. I'd come to the conclusion, months earlier, that I no longer believed in god. I'd denied myself the comfort of our friendship and his protection. I was certain I no longer believed and doubted that I ever should have.

But this would be the first time I was flying since my loss of faith. This would be the first flight in my life I didn't say the prayer. If nothing else, that just seemed like asking for trouble. Was I that convinced of my convictions, or lack of convictions?

If I was to be true to myself, I knew I had to refrain. I couldn't say it. You don't just believe in god when you need help. Either you believe or you don't, and I don't.

The engines roared and the plane began to speed down the runway. It was the moment of truth. I was taking a stand. I decided that if I was going to die, I would do so thinking, not about Mary and her son, but of my own children. So I conjured an image of Kitty and Peggy when they were young, swinging on the swing set I built them.

As the plane lifted off the ground and began to climb, I realized how stupid I'd feel if the engines stalled and we began to fall from the sky. I'd realize that I'd been wrong. That there is a god and that I needed him.

But the plane didn't fall. It continued to climb and as we leveled off over the Long Island Sound, I felt triumphant. I'd been brave enough to back my conviction. I knew I'd never feel the need to say the prayer again and that it had just been a stupid superstition all along. I felt good about myself.

But I felt extraordinarily lonely.

Chapter Sixty-Seven

"I feel better than I've felt in a long time." Annie said to her son. "I know it's too early to hope for any improvement from the chemo but this is the best I've felt since…" She paused to think. "Maybe since Labor Day."

Annie wasn't just reassuring her worried son. She really did feel good today. She assumed her high spirits were a result of his visit. Annie thoroughly enjoyed her time with Frank in a way she hadn't focused on before. It occurred to her that an ironic benefit of cancer was clarity about the preciously few hours we have with those we love. Until now, time wasn't a commodity; it just was.

So as Frank stood in the doorway with his suitcase in hand, she thought about the possibility that she might never see him again. Saying good-bye after a great weekend was one thing, and emotionally draining enough, but to think she might be hugging her precious son for the last time, well, that was more than she could take. She couldn't think that way. She had to focus on the positive. Frank would be back in four weeks and that was that. She'd see him then. They'd go for pizza again.

"Are you sure you don't want me to ride in the cab with you to Penn Station?" She was hoping for a few more minutes with him.

"No mom. That's silly. I'm not five years old. I need to get going. My train leaves at eleven fifty. It's almost eleven now." He was checking his pockets for his dorm keys and cell phone as he spoke. "I think I've got everything."

"Well, I really loved having you home. You made me feel so much better. Really."

"I had fun. I can't remember the last time we walked across the park. That was nice." Frank was equally aware of the possibility this could be the last time he got to spend "good" time with his mother. He realized the next time her saw her, she could be much worse; maybe bed-ridden. He secretly wiped a tear from his cheek as he came in for a final hug. "I love you Mom." He said as he squeezed her. "Make sure you continue to get better. I want to walk in the park again."

"I will, baby. You have a safe ride back to school."

And then he was gone. Annie was left standing in her doorway watching the elevator doors close in front of her son. With all the walking they'd done over the weekend, she should have been exhausted. But she felt good. She knew it was because of Frank. He was good medicine.

With nothing on her calendar for the day and John not due home until dinner, Annie thought about sending a long email to Nick in Florida, letting him know about the great visit she and his brother just had. Nick would be happy to hear Frank was keeping an eye on their mom. She knew he felt guilty about not coming himself and she wanted to let him know she was feeling a little better.

As she settled into her favorite chair and pulled her laptop in front of her, the phone rang. But it wasn't the house phone, it was the cell phone in her purse, and by the time she dug it from the bottom of the bag, she'd missed the call.

Annie pressed the sequence of buttons to see the number she'd just missed. It was a 212 area code but an unfamiliar number. She considered not returning the call until after finishing the email to Nick, but the chime sounded indicating a voicemail. It was from Tomasue.

"Hi Annie, it's Tomasue. Please call me as soon as you get this and don't tell John I called or that you're calling me back.

It's about eleven on Monday morning. Call me on my cell at 212-721-8365. It's important."

Tomasue sounded upset, which was unlike her usually professional demeanor. It took Annie a moment to remember that Tomasue had taken her medical records to have her associate review the films. It must be even more bad news, she thought. Why else would she say it's important? But why wouldn't she want John to know? How bad could the news be that she wouldn't want her husband to know?

Suddenly, she no longer felt so great. Frank wasn't even in his cab yet and the positive effect of his visit had been wiped out by Tomasue's onerous message. Panic surged through Annie when she considered, *maybe that really was the last chance I'll ever have to hug my son. What if I have much less time than I thought?*

A flood of negative thoughts overtook her. Each one led to the same conclusion; *it must be worse than everyone thought.* It occurred to her that the doctors at John's office may have been sugar-coating her diagnosis because she was John's wife. Perhaps even Dr. Cox, who seemed so sincere, was trying to spare her the pain of the truth at John's request. And now, a disinterested doctor from Minnesota, had reviewed her test results and gave Tomasue an honest evaluation; one that probably meant less time for Annie.

She dialed Tomasue's number. Her doctor and friend picked up on the first ring.

"Annie?"

"Yes. I'm afraid to ask."

"Annie, I need to speak with you right away. It's about your test results. Can you get to my office in about thirty minutes? This is really important."

Annie wondered what could be so urgent about more bad news. "I assume your friend found more bad news?"

There was a brief silence. Then Tomasue said, "No, Doug

confirmed the findings you were given by the people at John's office; stage four cancer—thyroid, lung and lymph nodes on both sides. He agreed with the treatment plan." Another pause, then, "But that's not what I need to talk to you about. I don't want to do this on the phone. Can you come in?"

Chapter Sixty-Eight

Annie stepped out of the cab in front of Dr. Tomasue Weber's office. It had taken just six minutes for the taxi to travel the twelve blocks down Fifth Avenue. Annie was hoping for more time to figure out what was going on. The phone conversation had left her wondering what could be so important, so urgent, that she needed to see Tomasue now?

Emotionally, she was torn. She expected the findings of Dr. Langer to bring more dire news but Tomasue said he simply confirmed the previous findings and agreed with the treatment plan. In the scheme of things, that could be interpreted as good news. Then why the clandestine and urgent meeting?

When she opened the door to Tomasue's office Annie was, at first, surprised to find the waiting area completely empty. Then she remembered that Tomasue normally didn't have office hours on Mondays because she liked having two consecutive days off each week.

"Hey stranger." Tomasue appeared from an inner office wearing jeans and a white Polo shirt with the collar turned up. She sounded more relaxed than she had on the phone. Both her demeanor and her attire helped bring Annie's anxiety down a notch.

"Come on in." She motioned for Annie to follow her into her office.

Before they sat down, Annie began. "OK, Tomasue, you've really got me spooked. First I thought you had some horrible news, then you tell me your friend found nothing new. I don't get it."

"Sit down Annie. What I have to tell you is very difficult for me. So, I'll just get to it."

Annie took a seat on the sofa next to her doctor, her friend.

"Annie, it's true that Doug looked at the films and found nothing new. He's one of the best and he spent a solid half hour going over the reports, the blood work, the films, everything. His diagnosis is exactly the same as John's and Dr. Cox. I'm sorry you didn't get to meet him. He left for a meeting about an hour before I called you. Needless to say I was really disappointed he didn't have better news.

"I was preparing to return your file to John's office this morning and I decided to take a look at the films myself. I don't know why. I guess just because you're my friend and I love you. It just seemed like the right thing to do I guess."

"And?" Annie prompted.

"Annie, remember about fifteen years ago when you separated your shoulder skiing with Peter in Colorado?"

"Yeah…?"

"Remember you had surgery and they put a suture-anchor strap on your left shoulder. That little piece of plastic is all that holds your ligaments and tendons to the bone at the socket of your shoulder. Without it you couldn't lift your arm. Now-a-days they use titanium because it lasts longer and it's lighter, but in 1993 all they had was plastic. You've got a two inch piece of it inside you."

"So…?" Annie had no idea what this had to do with her cancer.

"The thing is, it should show up on both your x-rays and the MRI. But when I looked at your films this morning, it's not there. It's a heavy plastic; it would show up just like a bone, but it's not there."

"What are you saying? That it dissolved or something?"

"When I didn't see the strap, I took a closer look at your films and compared them to other records I have in your file like your last three chest x-rays and a CAT scan I had from when you hurt your neck."

"Tomasue, I'm lost. What are you trying to tell me?"

"That the films and reports in your file, the one I got from John's office, are not yours."

"You mean they sent over the wrong reports?"

"No, what I'm saying is that the films I reviewed, the ones I had Doug review, had your name on them, but they're not yours. Somebody deliberately changed the name plate on the films. They belong to another woman, probably someone about your size and height, but definitely, not you."

"So they sent the wrong reports." Annie still couldn't understand why Tomasue was belaboring the issue of a clerical error.

"Annie, look at this film." Tomasue held out one of the large x-rays from the file on her desk. "It has your name and date-of-birth on the plate up here in the corner. Right? But it was changed." She pointed to the edge of the film. "See here? You can see that someone put your name over the plate that was there before. I'm not sure how or why but I can tell because I can see a corner of the old plate here. You'd never notice it if you weren't looking for it but when I didn't see the plastic strap on the films, I knew they couldn't be yours."

"So whose are they?"

"I don't know. But they belong to someone who's got stage four lung cancer, advanced thyroid cancer and significant lymph node..." Annie cut her off.

"You mean...wait, I don't know what you mean."

"I'm not sure either. But I want you to go over to Sloan Kettering and have these tests done again. I've already set it up. I'm going with you."

Annie leaned back in the sofa still not grasping the significance of her doctor's message. "Why? Why do I have to do all those tests again?"

"Annie, the diagnosis you were given was based on the radiologists reports which were based on these films—someone else's films! Someone else's cancer! John, Dr. Cox, Dr. Langer, anyone who read those reports would have come to the same conclusion, but they were basing their conclusions on someone else's medical file."

For the first time, Annie understood. "You mean I might not have cancer?"

"All I'm saying is that so far, I haven't seen any films or reports about Annie Dunn. But let's not get ahead of ourselves. The blood work I did on you two weeks ago definitely showed unusually high levels of calcitonin. That's for sure. That's not good and would be consistent with certain carcinomas but let's get the tests run again and find out for sure."

Annie sat completely still for several moments. She wasn't able to process all the information coming at her quickly enough and needed to sit back and think. But all she really heard echoing in her head was the sound of her own voice saying, "*I might not have cancer.*"

"My car is in the garage downstairs but it would be easier to just take a cab out front. When you called me back I called over there and set up the MRI for noon. We'll be a little late but that's OK. I play tennis with the radiologist on duty. She'll squeeze us in. Then we can do the ultrasound right after." Tomasue was speaking as she prepared to close up her office. "Let's go Annie."

CHAPTER SIXTY-NINE

Doc

The Red Sox beat Cleveland in the bottom of the ninth on a two-run single by their catcher. My old friend, Vick and I had a great time and a great dinner at a little place just around the corner from Fenway on Commonwealth. It was good to see Vick. I guess you could say he was going through a rough patch lately. His wife left him for another man after twenty-two years. Vick, who was always very involved in his parish, sought comfort and guidance from their pastor, pouring his soul out to him on several occasions, before his wife told him that their pastor was the 'other man.'

So, in the course of a few short months, poor Vick lost his wife, his home, his children and his church. I thought that while he was furious at organized religion, I would tell him about my new-found atheism, but it didn't seem like the right time. Vick was too focused on his own misery to care about mine.

But, going on the theory that 'misery loves miserable company', I did tell him about Annie and the fact that I'd lost her just as I was realizing how much I loved her. I must say, he was very sympathetic, especially for a guy who'd just lost so much more. But that's Vick. He was always a great guy. I wish we lived closer.

The flight back to Long Island was uneventful. I didn't say a Hail Mary and the plane didn't crash. Figuring I'm now two-for-two, I guess I'm done with the prayer thing.

I hadn't seen Annie in over a week but her scent still

lingered in my mind and I could see her face everywhere I looked. I really missed her. It's not that we were together so long, it's just that I was so hopeful about our future together. I was already planning trips to Italy and Ireland for us. It would have been a wonderful life. The two of us were good together.

And that's the hardest part for me. I'm not sure if I lost her to cancer or if I lost her to John, her husband. I don't know if the illness swallowed her or if the illness simply caused her to rethink a crazy summer fling. I wish I knew, although knowing probably wouldn't make me feel any better.

When I got home, there was a voicemail from John Weaver on my machine. A chill ran through me as I thought something might have happened to Annie. Then I remembered the fishing trip.

"Hey buddy, it's John Weaver. Just wanted to make sure we're still on for fishing this Saturday. I cleared my calendar. I was going to suggest we take my boat though. Hope that's OK. I'd just feel more comfortable. Anyway, give me a call when you have a chance. My cell is 212-566-1110. Talk to you soon."

CHAPTER SEVENTY

Jenny, the little girl in the Toy Story tee shirt was running around the waiting room while her father read the New York Post. Annie had already been waiting when the black family arrived and watched as the man kissed his wife good-bye. She was here for MRI that would probably determine whether Jenny would be needing a new mommy anytime soon. The man had explained to Annie that his wife's mother and grandmother had both died of breast cancer.

Although Tomasue had been sitting with Annie in the hospital waiting room for most of the afternoon, neither woman said much. There wasn't much to say. All focus was on the door leading to the radiology department. The tests hadn't taken long. It took Annie longer to complete all the hospital's insurance forms than it did to do the MRI and chest x-rays. Thanks to Tomasue's relationship with the staff, they'd been told they would have the results by four o'clock. The last time Annie glanced at her watch, it was 4:35. All they could do was wait.

"This really sucks. I'm going in to find out what's going on. They should have at least been able to review the MRI by now. What the hell is the hold up?" Tomasue was losing her patience.

"Take it easy." Annie whispered. "We'll know soon enough."

"How can you be so calm about this? This could turn out to be the best day of your life."

"Or just another bad one on the way down the drain. Anyway, even if it's great news, it's not even close to the best day of my life. That was the day the twins were born." Annie reflected. "I thought I had everything. I had Peter, Frank and Nick. I did have everything."

"You were always good at keeping things in perspective, Annie."

"I get that from my dad. He was the most grounded person I ever met. I can remember one time, just before I got married, dad and I had just come from a lunch at the Plaza. We had lunch with the mayor and Governor Carey because dad had just donated ten million dollars to build a playground in Central park. It was a big deal. I had never met either of them before. So we walk out of the Plaza and we're standing on the front steps. Right after the governor and mayor leave, dad runs into this real estate guy he hadn't seen in a few years. The guy asks him what he's doing at the Plaza and my dad says, *'I was just having lunch with my beautiful daughter.'*"

Tomasue was just about to mention that she had once met Annie's dad, when the swinging doors to radiology opened and Dr. Chavda walked towards them.

"Dr. Weber, we should have the reports in five more minutes, but may I have a word with you for a moment?" He motioned with his eyes for them to move to the other side of the waiting area; out of earshot of Annie and the other people sitting nearby.

Tomasue looked to Annie for approval. "You OK for a minute?"

"Sure. Go do your doctor thing."

Dr. Vivek Chavda was a senior member of Sloan Kettering's radiological staff. His Indian ancestry gave him handsome dark features and his eight years at Oxford produced a classic

British accent and flawless diction. He and Tomasue had worked together several times in the past. She had complete confidence in his attention to medical details. If he had a short suit it was his patient bedside manner. He was all business—medical business.

When they had walked to the far end of the waiting area, next to a water fountain and a window overlooking the East River, he asked Tomasue, "What's your interest in Mrs. Dunn"s case?"

"She's a patient and a good friend. Why?"

"Well, you said you wanted us to look for any sign of medullary thyroid carcinoma. I checked all the films. I saw nothing more onerous than some arthritis in the left shoulder. Lungs are clear, thyroid and surrounding nodes, all clear. I'd say your friend's in good shape. Ultrasounds were all clear too. Why the cancer concern?"

Tomasue Weber let out a long breath. "Thanks Vivek. That's what I wanted to hear." She glanced around to be sure no one was within earshot. "There was a misdiagnosis based on the previous films. The poor thing's already been through two weeks of chemo, and for nothing."

"Jesus! Sounds like a malpractice case. Who's the lucky doctor?"

Not wanting to get into a story she didn't know how to finish, Tomasue sidestepped the question. "It's not that simple. But thanks again Vivek. I really appreciate you pushing this to the front of the line." She reached up and gave him a kiss on the cheek. "You're the best."

"That's why you came to me." He winked. "You'd better tell your patient the good news. It looks like she's going to strain her neck trying to read our lips from over there."

When Tomasue returned to Annie she wasn't sure how to

break the news so she just said, "You're great. All the tests were negative!" She tried to sound professional but her excitement was obvious, even to the little girl in the Toy Story shirt.

Annie had prepared herself for some other cruel twist of fate, so when she heard the words, *"All the tests were negative,"* she fell back on the sofa in disbelief. She was mentally prepared for another disappointment and didn't know how to react to the news that she was going to live; that she might get to play with her grandchildren and do all the things she was afraid she was going to miss.

"You mean no more chemo?" Her face lit up as she spoke the words.

"No. You're fine. No more chemo!"

"You saved my life Tomasue!" She leaped up. "If you hadn't noticed the mistake on the x-rays, oh God, I don't know what would have happened!"

The realization that she'd just been handed back her life was overwhelming. Annie could feel her legs turning to rubber and she became lightheaded. If she hadn't been hugging her friend, she would have collapsed to the floor. "I need to sit down."

Tomasue helped her back to the sofa then got her a cup of water from the nearby fountain. "Here, drink this. Relax a minute. Then I'll take you across the street and buy you a real drink to celebrate."

≈

Fifteen minutes later, the two women were sitting at the far end of the bar in Clancy's, a place neither Tomasue nor Annie would normally have frequented, but in this case, both were willing to overlook its shortcomings. The afternoon crowd was thin. Most of the scattered patrons were watching a Sarah

Palin press conference on the flat screen at the end of the bar.

"To a long and happy life." Tomasue offered a toast and clinked her martini against Annie's Grey Goose and tonic.

"Amen." Annie threw back almost half her drink.

"I'll bet, when you got up this morning, you didn't think you'd have much to celebrate today."

"I still can't believe what's happened. It's like a dream I'm afraid I'll wake up from."

"I'm so happy for you Annie."

Annie asked Carmen, the bartender, for another round. "Carmen, do you have a family?"

"Yes, a boy six and a little girl two and a half." She answered through a heavy Ecuadorian accent. "My boy, Simone is very smart. He already go to school."

The mention of school caused Annie to think of her own son, who, by now, had arrived back in Boston. She turned to Tomasue. "I need to call the boys and tell them the news!" For the first time since they left the hospital, Tomasue could see the pure joy on Annie's face. The very mention of her sons caused her to light up. She was so happy for her friend.

But she knew there was still one delicate conversation she needed to have with Annie. Those x-rays and MRIs didn't change themselves. The films and reports that convinced Annie and her doctors she had cancer were sabotaged. Someone deliberately put Annie's name on the films of a very sick woman. Of this, Tomasue was sure. This couldn't be an accident. Radiology just didn't work that way. No one would ever accidentally do what had been done. The technology would have to be manipulated several times to achieve the results she'd seen.

Tomasue knew the original tests were done at John Weaver's offices. She also knew his practice had a fabulous reputation in the field of oncology, especially juvenile oncology, a field often sidestepped by physicians due to the high incidence of malpractice suits. John's practice had its own radiology capabilities. They, like many other multi-doctor practices, had invested heavily in the costly equipment necessary to maintain state-of-the-art technology. When a practice could generate enough volume, such equipment could become a major revenue source for the practice and its owners, the doctors. Tomasue knew that in John's case, not only did his own practice utilize the pricey machinery, but several other doctors on the east side of Manhattan also referred to his labs. When used to capacity, an MRI device alone, could generate close to a million dollars a year in revenues.

So why then, would someone in John's office tamper with Annie's films? Such a blunder could jeopardize the licensing of the practice. Could it be someone who had a grudge against John? Could someone be so twisted that they would want him to think his wife was dying of cancer, just to punish him? Or maybe Annie wasn't the only person this happen to. Maybe, the sicko who tampered with Annie's films had done it to others as well in an attempt to ruin John or his partners. Perhaps a disgruntled employee at the office? Maybe one of John's own partners trying to destroy the practice for some reason Tomasue couldn't imagine.

There was so much she didn't understand. But there was one fear she hadn't yet confronted, either with Annie or with herself.

"Annie, I need to ask you something. It's important."

The smile that had lit up her face, faded quickly. "Sure doctor. What can I do for you?" She was already beginning to enjoy the effects of the vodka, but she could tell by Tomasue's expression, that the celebrating was over.

Tomasue took another long sip of her martini, straitened

herself on the stool, and leaned toward her friend. "Annie, did John know about your shoulder surgery?"

"What do you mean?"

"I mean, did you ever tell John that you had shoulder surgery fifteen years ago?"

Annie thought for a moment. She thought about the first time John noticed the scar on her shoulder when they were lying in bed in a hotel in Rome. He'd asked what it was from and she explained the skiing injury many years before. Then he kissed the scar and promised that if she let him kiss it every night, for the rest of their lives, it would disappear.

"Yeah, I told him about the surgery a long time ago. Why is that important?"

Tomasue looked away from Annie and focused on the drink in her hand. "Because I can't understand how he didn't notice the very same thing I did. That those films couldn't be yours. There was no plastic buckle on those films. How could he not notice that?"

CHAPTER SEVENTY-ONE

All the way home in the cab, Annie thought about Tomasue's dire question; "*How could John have not known?*"

In defense of her husband, Annie suggested that she probably never told John about the buckle, just that she needed surgery. That seemed to satisfy Tomasue. But it didn't satisfy Annie. She was certain they'd discussed it once at a dinner party with an associate of John's who frequently used the same procedure on his patients to repair dislocated clavicles. She recalled him saying they now used titanium and that she may someday need to have another surgery to make the change over to the more durable material. John joked that he expected a professional discount if his friend did the replacement.

And on another occasion, while they were sitting on the beach in Southampton, John came across an article in the Sunday Times, about the advantages of titanium, and reminded Annie about her buckle. "Maybe you should think about doing this honey. I mean, before the plastic starts to give you any trouble."

So, back to Tomasue's question; how could he not notice?

"I'm his wife for Christ's sake!" She heard herself say out loud as the taxi pulled up to her building.

But she decided that even John's lack of concern for her wasn't going to spoil the day. She'd been given a "Get-out-of-jail-free" card, a reprieve from the governor. She was snatched from the tracks as the oncoming train whizzed by. She got her life back today! And even if her husband had screwed up, so what? The important thing was that she was alive and hopefully going to stay that way for a long time. John's lackadaisical approach to her wellbeing shouldn't completely surprise her. And it shouldn't spoil her excitement about telling Nick and Frank the good news. She couldn't wait to call them both.

It was already dark when she got home but she noticed from the street, the light coming from her apartment window above. "John's home," she thought. And the elevator couldn't rise fast enough.

He was sitting in the living room with a large glass of scotch. He'd just begun looking through the mail that accumulated during his short absence, when Annie came through the door.

"Where have you been? I was beginning to worry about you. How are you feeling?"

She gave him a huge hug. "John, I have wonderful news!"

"I could use some wonderful news. Tell me."

Without taking a breath, she relayed the events of the past several hours including the trip to Sloan Kettering and Dr. Langer, Tomasue's weekend guest who agreed to review her file. She told him all about the new tests and the fantastic results from Dr. Chavda. She showed him the reports from Sloan Kettering that gave her back her life, the new x-rays and MRI, and explained how Tomasue noticed the mistake on the original films.

"Isn't that wonderful?" She said as she wrapped her arms around his neck.

To her complete surprise, John grabbed both her arms and pushed her back. "Wait a minute. You mean all the tests we did were mismarked? How can that be?"

Still in his grasp, she said, "It seems someone at your office screwed up big-time. I hope…"

He cut her off. "How the hell did Weber get your folder in the first place?"

"Gee John, I thought you'd be happy to hear I'm not full of

cancer. I don't really care how the mistake happened. I'm more concerned about the outcome."

At that moment, he seemed to come to the realization that he was still holding her. "I'm sorry," he said. "I just don't understand how this all happened." As he said this, he released his hold on her wrists.

"I don't understand it either, but isn't it wonderful? I owe Tomasue my life. Christ, if her friend hadn't been in town for that medical convention…I hate to think about it."

"You're right, honey. It is wonderful news. Have you told your sons yet?"

"I'm going to call them right now."

"Good, you do that and I'll call Marano's and see if I can get us a reservation for dinner. We need to celebrate." He gave her a kiss on the forehead.

"Use your cell. I want to use the house phone to call the boys." She said as she picked up the phone and walked into the kitchen. "And make the reservation for eight. I need to shower and wash my hair first."

She caught Frank as he was leaving his apartment on the way to a class, but the news brought him to tears. Annie hadn't heard her son cry since he broke his arm in the sixth grade. It made her feel wonderful. Frank promised to call her back as soon as he got out of class. "Just call me tomorrow when you can talk. John and I are going out to dinner to celebrate."

The call to Nick was equally fulfilling. Nick tried hard not to show his emotions but Annie sounded so full of life on the phone and, being in Gainesville, he felt so far from home, by the time she finished the story, he broke down as well. But when he heard about the mistaken x-rays, and realized his mother had been put through hell for two weeks because of someone's carelessness, he became unusually angry. "John's got to find out who did this. I mean, this could have killed you Mom."

"I only *thought* I had cancer, Nick. I didn't really have it."

"Yeah, but the chemo and radiation treatments could have killed you. Over time, they'd make you so weak, you'd be susceptible to all kinds of things. I hate to think what could have happened. And for nothing!"

"Well, I'm just grateful we found out as soon as we did. Except for a little nausea and fatigue, no real harm done. It just feels so great to get my life back."

After she hung up, Annie thought about Nick's concerns. True, a prolonged program of chemo therapy would have dramatically weakened her immune system, but she had only gone for two treatments. She'd be fine. She made a mental note to ask John about it over dinner. He'd know what to do. Maybe some extra vitamins for a while until she got her strength back.

In the shower she sensed a new awareness of her body. As she soaped her shoulders and undercarms, Annie reveled in the knowledge she'd survived this threat; not because of any tenacity on her part but because of her friend. Tomasue probably saved her life. At a minimum, she saved her a lot of pain and suffering over the next few weeks. The next round of tests, would have uncovered the mistaken first tests, but she wasn't due for more testing until the first program of chemo was finished—about four weeks from now. There would have been a lot of puking between now and then.

Instead, she was already feeling better. She knew it was probably more psychological than physical but that didn't matter. *What's perceived as real, is real in its consequence.* She remembered that line from her Intro to Psych class in college. It was sure true today. Whatever pixies were dancing around in her head, sure made her body feel better.

As was her usual routine, she shaved her legs in the shower. When she was finished, Annie admired her naked body in the mirror. She'd lost a few pounds since this all began, but other than that, she saw no other damage from the ordeal. Her legs and butt looked as firm as ever. Her breasts weren't as perky as they were twenty years ago, but hey, she was almost fifty-two. They looked pretty good. Maybe she'd even get back to running soon.

And that's when she thought about Doc.

CHAPTER SEVENTY-THREE

Kelly Mastro had never gotten such a tongue lashing from her boss. In the six years she'd worked as Dr. Tomasue Weber's receptionist, she couldn't remember the doctor getting even a little angry. But this morning was a different story. The twenty-nine year old mother of two, had endured a verbal barrage for the last ten minutes and didn't understand why.

Kelly opened up the office, as usual, around seven. The doctor came in, as usual, around seven-thirty. She seemed to be in a good mood at that point. She was happy her first appointment wasn't until eight because she said she had paperwork to do before disappearing into her office. A few minutes later, all hell broke loose.

"Kelly, what happened to the medical file we got from Dr. Weaver's office on Saturday? It was on my desk when I left yesterday afternoon and now I can't find it."

"I returned it to Dr. Weaver's office yesterday on my way home. You told me on Saturday, that it had to be back on Monday, so I dropped it off."

And that's what triggered the fireworks. Kelly had no way to know about Tomasue's plans. She didn't know Tomasue intended to make a copy of everything in Annie's medical file before returning it. She was unaware of Tomasue's suspicions. And when Tomasue went ballistic on her, it seemed completely unreasonable. After all, she'd done what she was told to do.

But Tomasue had had time to think about the events of the previous day. The more she reflected on the films and the manner in which they'd been compromised, the more her suspicions kept coming back to John Weaver. She believed there was no way he wouldn't have noticed the mistake. You don't look at a picture of your wife's chest and upper torso and not notice the differences. She didn't know why, but Tomasue suspected deliberate foul play by John Weaver. For some reason, he wanted to hurt his wife—to make her think she was suffering from a lethal dose of lung cancer. That's why she intended to take the films, or copies of the films, to the board of medical inquiry at Sloan Kettering.

But now, without the films, there was nothing she could do.

CHAPTER SEVENTY-FOUR

Minutes after John left for work, Annie was up and dressed. She made herself a bowl of Cheerios and banana, one of her favorites. Now she was watching the clock on the microwave, waiting for the digits to read 8:00. She was filled with enthusiasm. In fifteen minutes, she was going to call Doc. She had so much to tell him.

It happened during dinner the previous evening. She and John were sharing a bottle of champagne, celebrating her new lease on life. They were seated at a small table along the front window of one of their favorite places. Dinner plates had just been cleared away and they were finishing the last drops of the champagne when Annie had her epiphany.

Maybe it was the adrenaline that rushes through you after a close encounter with death or maybe it was just the collective effect of the day's alcohol, but sitting at the table, across from the man she'd married, the man who'd abused her countless times, Annie suddenly had a burst of clarity. The statement came from nowhere.

"John, I have to tell you something."

John leaned back in his chair and tilted his head. "Sounds serious."

"It is." Annie swallowed the last of her champagne. "John, before this all happened, I mean the cancer scare, I wanted to talk to you. I was going to talk to you two weeks ago, the day we found out about the cancer. And then everything changed. But nothing really changed."

"Talk to me about what?"

"About divorce." There. She said the word out loud, probably for the first time.

"Divorce!" He said it a little too loud for the nearby diners. "Annie, you're just reacting to the events of the last few weeks. After you…"

"No! John, I've thought about this a lot. I've been thinking about it all summer. We weren't meant for each other. There are times when you treat me like a queen, but there are times you mistreat me. You know what I'm talking about."

"Annie, you just…"

"John, listen to me. This isn't about cancer. This is what I'd decided to do before all that. I'll move out of the apartment later this week. I'm not going to tolerate any more abuse from you. It's not right." Her thoughts drifted to the embarrassing positions he'd put her in. It made her angry. But she was resolved not to speak out of anger.

"Look John. We're just not right for each other. I'm not happy and I know you're looking for things from me that I just can't give you. This doesn't have to be ugly. We can do this like adults. Look, we have no children together. This doesn't have to get complicated."

"Sounds like your mind's made up." John said in a monotone voice. "Do I get a vote here?"

"Oh John. Please don't make this difficult. I already feel like a failure. Don't fight me on this. Please."

For several minutes, the silence hung over the table like a heavy cloud. The waiter brought the check and John put two hundred-dollar bills in the leather folder without saying a word. Then he took a long drink of water. It looked to Annie, as if he was thinking. Finally he said, "Let's go home."

Annie didn't move when John stood up.

"John, we need to finish this conversation. Please."

Looking down at her, he said, "It sounds to me like you're done talking about it, Annie. What do you want me to say?" Then, without waiting for an answer, he added, "I'll tell you one thing. You're not going to toss me away like some other toy in your endless life of privilege. Getting rid of me isn't going to be easy and it's not going to be cheap. That, I promise you. Now let's go home, honey."

―――

The next morning, John left for work without saying a word. Annie had slept in the guest room. The sheets still smelled of her son, Frank's aftershave. The smell of her son gave her the inner strength she needed once the alcohol began to wear off. Although she'd locked the guestroom door, she knew, if he wanted to, John could force his way in. He'd done it before.

Annie's decision to be with Doc had made the discussion with John inevitable. And once she'd made up her mind, there was no point in delaying the conversation. Actually, she was mildly surprised how smoothly it went. Aside from his brief outburst in the restaurant, John's reaction had been relatively civil. She expected the threats about making the divorce difficult and expensive, but she was certain her pre-nup, the one Franklin had put together before they were married, was airtight. She didn't expect any money trouble; just the discomfort of actually moving out.

But the exhilaration she felt about telling Doc her great news, more than offset any worries about separating from her husband. Her plan was to call Doc as soon as it was a reasonable hour (she'd decided 8:00 AM was reasonable enough), to book herself a suite at the Essex House again, and then to head out to Southampton for a few days. She could get her clothing packed in a few hours and have a service deliver it to the hotel later in the week. Annie kept most of her summer and fall wardrobe in the Southampton house anyway. She'd leave John all the furnishings in the apartment, most were there before she moved in anyway. The move would be frighteningly simple; almost as if she'd been visiting a friend for the past three years and never really moved in. That's what it had been like living with John.

At 8:02 she dialed Doc's number, but he didn't answer. When his voicemail recording picked up, Annie decided to keep it short. *"Hey Doc. It's me. I was feeling pretty lighthearted today and was thinking about taking a drive out east. I hope you're around. I have some great news. Well, hopefully I'll see you later today."* Then, just in case he was away, she added, *"It's about eight o'clock on Tuesday morning. I miss you."*

Annie was determined to be packed and out of the house by ten. After calling Doc, she called the Essex House and reserved a one-bedroom suite for the rest of the month and all of October. She knew she'd be spending a lot of time at her Southampton house but anticipated the need to be in New York a lot to deal with Franklin on the divorce issues. She made a mental note to get the locks changed in Southampton. After all, that was her house, or more correctly, her father's house, left in trust to her sons. John had no claim to it. She'd have his personal things packed by tomorrow and FedExed to him by the end of the week. Purging her personal space of everything 'John' would be a healthy exercise.

She knew she was moving quickly but it felt right. After all, she was just picking up where she left off three weeks before; before her plans to leave her husband were abruptly interrupted by a few medical tests gone wild. Back then, she had it all planned out. At least she thought she did. Actually, she knew her plans only extended a few weeks into the future. The divorce she was sure about. That was the right thing to do for a hundred reasons. It just took the strength she gathered from Doc, for her to realize it. And as for her relationship with Doc, well, that would take whatever course it was meant to take. If he turned out to be as sensational as she first thought, they might live happily ever after. If not...well, she'd cross that bridge when she got to it. Today was the first day of the rest of her new life.

Annie was determined to limit her packing to two small pieces of luggage. She'd take those with her today. The rest she'd pack into three boxes from the storage closet and have the doorman send them over to the Essex House. It was while she was sorting through a drawer of socks, trying decide which ones were worthy of the journey, that it happened. A pair of new sweat socks fell behind the drawer and into the drawer below, one that John used to keep his winter sweaters.

To get to the sweat socks Annie needed to take the lower drawer out of the dresser and reach in behind it. When she removed the drawer it slipped from her grasp and fell to the bedroom floor, its contents tumbling onto the carpet. When Annie began to refold the fallen sweaters she noticed a thin panel of wood had come loose from the drawer. It had served as a false bottom to the drawer. Below the panel was another two inches of drawer depth which had been hidden by the cover. Annie removed the panel and found several vials of prescription drugs. She was about to replace the panel and sweaters, assuming this to be just another one of John's nefarious secrets he kept from her. But as she picked up the first vial of small blue pills, her eye caught the name on the label: CARISOPRODOL!

She felt as though a cold damp hand had just rested on her shoulder. A chill went through her. She checked the other three bottles; MEPROBAMATE, EQUANIL, and OXYCODONE, names that meant nothing to her. But what frightened her most was that all four bottles contained small blues pills that were almost identical in appearance to her thyroid medicine.

Annie sat back on the floor; socks, sweaters and Rx bottles all around her. She couldn't breathe. Her mind raced from one disconnected thought to another. Pieces of a complicated puzzle swirled in her head. Why all these pills that look the same? Why hide them? And then it hit her.

"The bastard was trying to kill me!"

Chapter Seventy-Five

The daylight at the east end of the midtown tunnel couldn't come fast enough for Annie. As the tunnel lights swished by her car she thought about the symbolic significance of her exodus from New York and her life with John. In a way, it felt like the end of one part of her life and the beginning of another; the one with Doc, the life that waited on the other side of the tunnel. The life in the light.

She'd been unable to reach Doc before leaving the apartment so she left another voicemail: "*Hey, it's me again. It's about noon on Tuesday and I'm driving out to Southampton for a few days. I hope you're around. Call my cell if you get this.*"

She tried to remember the last time she saw Doc and exactly what was said. Unfortunately, her memory of their last conversation was a little fuzzy. But she did remember making it clear she was going back to Manhattan to try to get better under the watchful eyes of her loving husband; the same husband who was trying to kill her. She also remembered saying something about her intentions if she was able to beat the cancer, but her recollection of the words was blurred. Was she going to stay with John or run back to Doc? How could she not remember something so critical?

As the Long Island Expressway straightened out before her, Annie could feel the excitement and tension. This truly was to be the first day of the rest of her life. Was it to be a life with Doc or was he so hurt by her that she'd have to start over alone? Had she said things she couldn't undo? Did Doc feel betrayed by her in some way? She'd know in a couple of hours.

Annie remembered a quote attributed to Winston Churchill that went something like, *"There is nothing so exhilarating as surviving a gun shot directly at your face."* She now understood the exhilaration Churchill spoke of. Her husband tried to kill her and she survived.

As best she could piece it together, John must have started switching her Synthroid with the other, more diabolical blue pills sometime in August; probably around the same time she began to feel weak and tired. The pills looked so much alike, she never noticed the slight difference in size. Her morning internet research revealed the nature of the impostors: all barbiturates with the potential for hallucinogenic episodes and severe depression. Taken together, they were a lethal cocktail.

Judging by the number of pills remaining in each of the vials, and assuming each vial started with thirty pills, Annie calculated John had used a mixture of the four drugs, probably seven or eight of each. Sometime in mid August, he probably replaced her Synthroid with a like number of the depressants. Since then, each morning Annie had been playing Russian roulette, taking whichever of the potential poisons came out of the bottle.

By themselves, the barbiturates could have taken many months to render the desired effect, but in combination with massive doses of unnecessary chemotherapy weakening her immune system, the spiral downward would have been accelerated. That's why he switched the MRI and x-ray results. Her death would have seemed like a natural occurrence; something that you'd expect from a fifty-two year old woman diagnosed with terminal lung cancer. Pneumonia or some other parasite would have sucked the final life from her as she became too weak to fight.

Annie had to admit, it was a clever plan. John, the grieving husband, would be at her bedside as she slipped from this world to the next. No one would suspect foul play because she was so sick. People don't blame cancer on other people, they blame it on God, or lifestyle, or tobacco companies, but seldom on any one person. She was certain it would have worked had it not been for Tomasue remembering her ski injury and Frank knocking her pills into the sink.

What she was less certain of was John's motive. He was well aware of their pre-nuptial agreement. She didn't see how he could profit from her death. So if it wasn't financial motivation, what was it? Could he have despised her so much that divorce wasn't enough? Was he that much of a monster? Perhaps he feared a divorce trial might have revealed his abusive sexual exploits. That could be embarrassing for him professionally. Better to be the grieving widower.

She was passing exit # 41, about an hour from Manhattan, when it occurred to her she should have taken the four vials of pills from John's drawer. At the time, her first thought was to replace them so he'd never know she'd discovered them. Now she could see that was a mistake. His anger, upon learning that her medical file had been sent to Tomasue's office, was now understandable and he would probably destroy anything that connected him to her illness. The vials would likely be gone by the end of the day. She briefly considered going back to retrieve them, but decided against it. She was heading east; towards a new life. She didn't want to look back.

CHAPTER SEVENTY-SIX

"I think you'll like Dr. Kelly. He's very good with young children and one of the best surgeons on the east coast. I'll have Beth set up an appointment for you." John Weaver was ushering his first patients of the morning back out to the receptionist. "Beth, set up an appointment for Peter and Mrs. Buonono with Dr. Kelly."

Based on the tests he'd done, John knew Peter Buonono had a good chance of a complete recovery if Kelly could get to the seven year-old boy's liver without finding any more cancer in the surrounding tissue. The kid would be back in school before Halloween.

Once the boy and his mother had left the receptionist's area, John asked, "Beth, what's my morning look like?"

"You're booked straight through till noon, then you have lunch with doctors Klein and Rubin at the Seagrill. Your afternoon's not as bad."

"OK, try to keep my afternoon light. I need to get home for an hour at some point."

It had been a busy morning. John had already destroyed the duplicate set of x-rays, MRIs and corresponding radiology reports for Annie. He couldn't believe his good fortune when he found they'd been returned the day before from Dr. Weber's office. When her assistant called this morning to request a copy of the reports, John was happy to promise he'd have them sent over. Of course, the reports he would eventually send would be Annie's actual tests showing her to be a perfectly healthy woman. At least something had gone well.

But he needed to get rid of the pills he kept at home. In the unlikely event Dr. Weber did pursue this, there would be nothing linking him to his wife's condition. He planned to replace her Synthroid tonight, after Annie was asleep. Everything would be as it had been. And if Annie was serious about divorcing him, well then he missed his chance. So be it.

He sat at his desk and thought about the events of the last few months. Ever since he saw the notation in Annie's calendar about her meeting with Franklin Montague, he knew he didn't have much more time. If Annie was already discussing divorce with her attorney, he needed to act fast. Once her sons turned twenty-three in December, he knew most of Annie's fortune would move to trusts in their names. That bastard had seen to it before he died. Burt Dunn had taken all the right steps to keep his money out of John's hands. He'd established trusts to hold the money for Annie and the boys and once they reached twenty-three, he'd arranged to reach out from the grave and transfer most of it directly to the twins as a way for Annie to avoid considerable estate taxes.

It was sound financial planning. John ought to know. He had enough accountants and forensic tax specialists review it, without Annie's knowledge of course, to understand its workings better than the people who drafted it. And that's how he became aware of its Achilles' heel; the single way John could benefit from the lifetime work of Burt Dunn. And the best part was that it was probably Burt's own blindness that opened the door for John, for as tight as the document language was concerning the trusts and what would happen in the event of Annie's divorce, it was silent in the event of her death prior to the boys turning twenty-three; an eventuality, the old man just couldn't imagine. He was too focused on his own mortality to think of hers.

And, according to New York State law, and some loose language in his own pre-nup, *any assets acquired during the marriage, irrespective of the source of the assets, becomes marital property*, by-passes the pre-nup provisions, and is governed by state matrimony law. Burt died after John and Annie were married. Therefore, the trust he left directly to Annie, about sixty million dollars at the time, could be considered marital property until it passed to the boys. After that, a giant steal door slammed shut on John's chances of ever seeing a penny of Burt's money.

So his plan had been to arrange the tragic, but completely natural death of his wife shortly before the boys turned twenty-three. Cancer, since it had also taken her beloved father, seemed like the perfect villain. After several weeks of fighting gallantly and saying tearful goodbyes to her useless sons, Annie would succumb to the ravages of mega-doses of chemo and barbiturates. Because of her diagnosis and medical history, there'd be no inquiries, no autopsy, just the tragic death of a cancer-ridden woman.

Well, that plan had blown up. And to his surprise, John wasn't as disappointed as he would have expected to be. After all, he didn't hate Annie. He just resented her easy life. If there was another way he could have separated her from her father's money, he would have taken that route. He didn't need to see her suffer, but neither was her suffering to be an obstacle to his plans.

Now it was all over. After this, and the suspicions his actions must have raised with Annie and her pain-in-the-ass doctor/friend, he had no chance of getting rid of her. Certainly not before December, and if not by then, there was no point.

The money would be in the airtight trust funds of those two snot-nosed, elitist sons of hers. Divorce was a distant second, but still had advantages over marriage to a person who didn't want to be with him.

The way he saw it, he could probably threaten an ugly fight, contesting the pre-nup. He could threaten to make their sexual activities seem like her preferences rather than his, thus causing Annie considerable embarrassment in her social circles. She wouldn't want to see the tabloids' stories about the "*Socialite's Anal Sex-capades*". She'd pay to make it go away. And he wouldn't ask for much; maybe...three million. He could pay Zucker the $85,000 he owed and get him off his back for good. And the boat. Yeah, he wanted the boat. That would really piss off the old man.

Yeah, plan A had gone in the crapper but at least plan B would give him his freedom and a few bucks. And the boat, "*Annie's Pleasure*." It wasn't a total loss.

"Beth, send in my next patient."

Chapter Seventy-Seven

Doc

I'd been on the bay taking pictures from my boat all morning.
I wanted to get some shots of the beachfront homes with
the morning sun over my shoulder but the sun didn't break
through the cloud cover until almost eleven-thirty. Still, I got
some great black and white shots, and while I was waiting for
the proper light, I did a little fishing. But the tide was slack and
the only bites I got were from some black flies.

It doesn't usually work out this way, but today I had the
foresight to bring along a sandwich for lunch. And I was glad
I did, because by the time I finished trolling up and down the
shoreline taking pictures, it was after four. My fifty-five year
old stomach doesn't take kindly to being fed after the clock
strikes twelve.

I was just about to start the engine for the short trip back to
the pond when I noticed something along the shore that hadn't
been there before. I was less than 200 yards from the shoreline
and the houses that lined the beachfront when I noticed a light
in one of the houses. But not just any house; Annie's house. It
hadn't been there fifteen minutes ago when I took some shots
of her roofline with my telephoto lens.

My first thought was that John must still be out here.
When I left him at the marina on Saturday he said he was
going back to the city on Monday. Maybe he changed his
mind and hung out for another day. Or maybe he planned to
stay out all week. After all, we did agree to fish together again

on Saturday, although I was still questioning the wisdom of that decision.

But then my eyes glanced left and saw Annie's car in their driveway. Based on my last conversation with that part of the Weaver family, I didn't expect to see her out here again until the spring. If ever. I mean, she made it clear she wanted to go for the chemo treatments and lean on her husband to get her through her illness. She also made it clear, she didn't want me to be a part of this chapter in her life.

So you can imagine my joyful confusion when I spotted her standing on her deck, looking through a pair of binoculars and waving to me! She was wearing jeans and a white sweatshirt and I don't think I've ever been happier to see another person than at that moment. Maybe what made the moment so perfect was that we were so far apart; she on her deck and me 200 yards off shore, so we saw each other in complete silence. All we could do was wave our enthusiasm

That wasn't enough for me. I wanted to know why she was here but when I reached into my jacket for my cell phone, I came up with nothing but lint. I must have left it at the shack. "Shit!"

So I motioned with my arms that I was going to bring the boat back through the inlet and to my dock. And it's a good thing no one's out here this time of year because I ignored the "No Wake" signs posted all along the inlet and was back at my dock in five minutes. Annie had walked from her house to mine in the same time and was standing on my bulkhead with some sort of bottle in her hand. We were now close enough that I could yell, "What are you doing here?"

She went up on her toes as if to project her voice out to me. "I came to meet my man returning from the sea."

This was one of those special moments. My boat and I were

only a few yards from the dock but I wasn't sure if I should do a Forrest Gump off the side and swim to her, or if it would seem more dignified if I smoothly slipped the boat around to the dock and stepped off into her arms. I opted for dignity.

She came down the gangplank onto the dock and just stood there looking at me. I got one line on a cleat and stood facing her from the cockpit. I shut the engine and silence took over. We stood there, staring at each other for almost a full minute, or, at least it seemed that long. I still had the dock line in my hand.

"Well sailor, you going to invite me on board?"

CHAPTER SEVENTY-EIGHT

Doc

When she told me I wasn't going to believe what she had to say, like anyone else, I assumed it to be hyperbole. Boy, was I wrong!

We sat on the dock with our feet in the water, sipping the Chateau du Pape from colorful flutes Annie found in my kitchen. The two hundred dollar bottle of wine, she brought. The cheesy flutes I got in Macy's. By the time the bottle was empty, we were staring into a beautiful sunset and I'd heard the incredible story of the pills, the x-rays and Annie's miraculous sidestep around cancer. In some ways, it was like being a three year-old kid on Christmas morning. There were just so many packages of good news, I didn't know where to start. I decided to begin with Annie's decision to be here.

"Maybe this isn't a fair question, but I'm going to ask it anyway." I put my glass on the dock and looked directly into her fabulously deep eyes. "I need to know if I'm going to get my heart broken again. I don't think I could take it. You don't understand how I felt when you drove away two weeks ago. I can't do that again." I was afraid to stop talking because I knew when I did, she'd answer the question.

"No. It's a fair question Doc." She paused way too long. So I started to say something but she cut me off.

"Here's what I know for sure. Forty-eight hours ago, I thought I was dying of cancer. All I wanted to do was live. Twenty-four hours ago I found out I would. It was as if I was handed another life to live; a new one with endless possibilities and no script. That's when I knew for certain, I couldn't have John in that life. If I am to walk through a new door with no restrictions on the path I take, I want to be standing next to you. Of that, I am certain." She touched my chin with her glass to emphasize the point.

"Then this morning, when I found the other pills, I figured out my husband was probably trying to kill me. That's a lot to take. So, you'll have to excuse me but I've had a lot of significant life events the last few days. Isn't that what they call them, significant life events?"

I'm not sure I heard anything after, *"I want to be standing next to you."* This really was Christmas morning!

"What have you told the boys?"

"Just the good news. I just told them there had been a terrible mistake with the tests and when they were redone, the error was caught. They already hate John enough. They don't need any more reasons."

"I understand that, but you can't just sweep it under the rug. I mean, the guy tried to poison you! You've got to do something. You've got to go to the police, right?"

"And tell them what? That my pharmacist found one pill in my bottle that he already thinks belongs to my son? Or that the medical profession made a mistake with my x-rays and the second time they got it right? Big whoop! It happens every day. Without proof, I'm just a raving socialite. At least a dozen people heard us in the restaurant. They heard me tell John I want a divorce. The newspapers would have a field day with this."

"You told him you wanted a divorce before you found the pills?" I emphasized the word BEFORE as much as I could.

Annie paused for a moment, as if to mentally retrace her steps and be sure of the timeline. "Yes, I already told you. I told John I wanted a divorce last night. I found the fake drawer bottom this morning. Try to keep up will you Doc? This is kind of important. Her sarcasm stung a bit but she still looked beautiful sitting there with her feet dangling in the water.

There was so much I wanted to say, but the moment felt so right, just the way it was. I didn't want to change anything. The cool darkness had swallowed us as we sat on the dock talking and although I was getting hungry, there was no place else I wanted to be. In a way, I think I was afraid I'd break the magical Christmas-morning spell that seemed to surround us.

She seemed so strong for such a little thing. Her tiny frame was lost in the soft white sweatshirt, yet her words were those of a woman. Maybe I was just so happy to have her here with me. Or, maybe I was just so glad she was alive. Whatever it was, the words came out before I could stop them.

"Annie. I want you to stay here with me."

"That was sort of what I had in mind Doc."

"No, I mean for good. I don't want you to go back to New York at all. I don't even want you to stay at your beach house. I don't trust him. He might come out looking for you. He tried to kill you. He might try again. You have to stay away from him."

"My plan was to stay at the Essex House while we worked out the details of the divorce. My lawyer's in the city. It would be easier to…" I cut her off in mid sentence.

"I think you're missing the point!" I said a little too loudly. "He tried to kill you. Just because it was with slow acting poisons doesn't mean he won't be more direct the next time."

"There's not going to be a next time. His little plan didn't work. He had his shot at getting rid of me and he blew it. He knows it. I don't think he…"

"Annie, you've got to see this. Your husband wanted you dead. He put a lot of planning into this. There's got to be a very good reason for him to want you dead. And that reason hasn't gone away." I felt like my words weren't getting through to her; that I couldn't make her see the danger she was still in.

"Doc, relax. Tonight, let's just deal with tonight. OK? One day at a time. I don't want to think about John anymore tonight. I want to think about what you're going to make me for dinner." She turned towards me and ran her hand through my hair. "Then I want to think about how it's going to feel to be next to you in bed with my legs tangled around yours. How about we just focus on us for tonight?"

When I hear a beautiful woman say the words "legs" and "tangled" I become very attentive. It seemed like a good time to lean in for a kiss, which I did. We held the kiss for several seconds, then I felt Annie's hand on my shoulder. She wanted me to lie back on the dock. My feet were still in the water but I found myself lying on the cool wood looking up at her as she moved around and straddled me. Her hands massaged my chest; her pelvis pushed hard against me. Before I knew what was happening, she reached down and pulled her sweatshirt over her head and dropped it on the dock planks, just next to the empty bottle.

The faint moonlight peaked through the clouds and cast a muted glow on her bare breasts. Even with my head flat against the dock I could see she her face and her smile. As if the pelvic thrusts weren't enough, her smile told me she was getting into this. I obliged in any way I could and before long, we were both naked and flopping around on the decking like a couple of flounder, gasping for air. It's a good thing Tom and Marion can't see my dock from their kitchen window.

When we were both spent and trying to catch our breath, she leaned on one elbow and looked into me. I don't mean she looked at me. I mean—she looked into me. As if she could see the thoughts in my head and understand me more than

I understood myself. She said nothing, but stared for a long time. Finally, when I had my breath again, I said in a whisper, "Please don't ever leave me again."

"Are you kidding? I'm never leaving this dock! This place is great!"

That's what you gotta love about a girl like Annie.

Chapter Seventy-Nine

Doc

The next two days were heaven. Annie and I spent hours in bed, making love and just watching old movies. We had two straight days of cold September rains so my bedroom seemed like a great place to hide out. We listened to the rain falling against the skylights and decided that someday we'd build a house with a huge skylight directly over the bed. That way we could watch the rain and snow hit the glass from under the warmth of our blankets. It seemed like a good idea. I was pretty agreeable.

We went into town one night for dinner and made pasta fagiole at home the other. Beyond that, we lived on coffee and orange juice, the two staples I've always got in the fridge. Food didn't seem like a priority. We were busy talking and planning our futures. Neither of us focused on the reality that I was in bed with a married woman who still needed to work out a touchy divorce. We were just happy to be together and healthy and able to make long term plans that were wrapped around each other.

When it came time to talk about our children, we decided to wait another couple of weeks before springing the depth of our relationship on them. Although I was certain Peggy and Kelly would be thrilled at the idea of their father being in love, Annie was a little less certain about her sons. Not that they cared at all about John; they'd both be overjoyed upon hearing of Annie's decision to divorce the creep. She just wanted to take it a little slow breaking the news that mom had been sleeping atop another man while she was technically still married. I understood. There was no hurry. The boys weren't due back in New York until Thanksgiving, almost two months away.

Despite the weather, the last forty-eight hours were some of the best in my life. We just genuinely enjoyed each other. It was wonderful getting to learn more about Annie and her sons from the stories she told about their vacations. I learned a lot more about her father too. She seemed to have an exceptional relationship with him and still grieved his death some two years later. He was a lucky man to have accumulated so much wealth and still have the love and respect of his family. He had everything.

Last night, I got up around midnight to take a leak. Annie was sound asleep and the rain had stopped so I walked out on the deck to look for stars in the vast darkness and stillness surrounding the pond. I could make out the outline of the moon trying to shine through the lingering clouds, but no stars. It was a beautiful cool night. It occurred to me that, in the old days, before I became godless, this would have been one of those times I would have talked to him. Whenever wonderful things happened to me, like the last few days and the news from Annie, I would have said thanks. It only seemed right to thank him for all the good stuff because I sure bitched whenever bad stuff happened. So I might have said, *"Thanks for all the wonderful things you did for me today and all the great things I have. I don't deserve such gifts, especially when so many others have so much less."* I used to think it was a nice touch to mention others.

Thanking God for the terrific things in my life just seemed to make sense; sort of as if he were a friend who'd done me a favor. You've got to thank a friend like that, don't you? And I enjoyed the one-way conversations. They always made me feel close to my friend.

And so tonight, with all the wonderful things that had happened the last few days, I wanted to talk to him and say thanks. But I didn't. I couldn't. As I stood there leaning on the deck railing gazing up at the shadowy sky, I realized I'd closed that door already. In denying his existence, I had no right to hope any more. I didn't believe. And if I didn't believe, I had to go it alone. But I'll tell you, it was a very lonely feeling. In fact, the loneliness of the moment was a bit overwhelming. I felt like I was the only person left alive on earth with no one to talk to. Atheism is a lot tougher than just being a lousy Catholic. It's very isolating.

Then I remembered the adorable naked Catholic lying in my bed, so I went back upstairs and got over my loneliness. Annie didn't stir when I slipped back under the covers so I tried not to wake her. I lied awake for almost an hour just looking up at the ceiling and the skylight and thinking about all the great times ahead. I really wanted to take Annie to Italy. We'd already spoken about going in December, around the time of my birthday. And after Italy, maybe South America. I always wanted to take a trip on the Amazon. Annie seemed like the adventurous type. Maybe I'd found my life-long playmate.

Which brought me back to the reality of lying next to a beautiful but still married woman. From her rhetoric over the last few days, I was pretty sure there was no chance Annie was interested in anything other than a quick and painless divorce. The more she spoke about it, the more I understood this was something she'd been thinking about for a long time. But I wasn't as sure about John. Except for a brief phone conversation to say she had moved out and would be talking to her lawyer later in the week, Annie hadn't spoken to John since Tuesday morning. And he hadn't tried to call her cell.

For all I knew, he could be furious that she'd left. He might try to make the divorce as painful as possible. He could be professionally embarrassed. Hell, he could even want her back. How would I know? I couldn't know, and frankly I didn't care. The only thing I did care about was that he didn't try to hurt her again. That's why I insisted Annie tell him she was in the city. I didn't want him to think she'd come out to stay at her place in Southampton. We didn't need a jealous husband mucking up our good time this week. As long as he didn't know where she was, she was safe and that's what I cared most about.

Annie stirred beneath the sheets and flipped onto her stomach. Her naked back shined in the dim moonlight coming through the skylight. It looked so soft and delicate. The few freckles that dotted the arch of her back looked like a handful of tiny black pebbles scattered on an otherwise perfectly white sandy beach. I rolled on my side and put my hand on her back. It was cool and dry.

I made a silent pledge to myself that my first priority was to keep this lovely lady healthy and happy. That seemed to be a goal I would enjoy pursuing. At the time, I had no idea how difficult a job it was going to be.

CHAPTER EIGHTY

Benny had been selling pretzels on the corner of Sixty-first and Fifth for more than seven years. He'd seen the guy before but never really paid him much attention. But today, the elderly white dude in the Armani suit was hanging around his corner, as if he was waiting for someone. He seemed nervous, as if something was about to happen. He just kept walking back and forth in front of Benny's stand.

"You want a pretzel boss?"

"No thanks. Just waiting for a fiend." Eric Kaplan wasn't exactly telling the truth. He'd been told to meet Arnie Zucker on this corner at 10:15 AM and it was now a quarter to eleven. He was getting nervous. Zucker had called Eric himself and set up the meeting.

Just then, two young, well-dressed black guys came across the street. Eric had never met Felix and Levon before and wasn't expecting anyone but Mr. Zucker himself, so he was caught off guard when Felix said, "You must be Mr. Kaplan. I apologize for being late. Mr. Zucker asked me to apologize for him too. He couldn't make it."

Levon stepped closer to Eric and motioned for him to move back toward the brick wall so they could talk without being overheard. The shear size of him made Eric comply without question. Levon was intimidating, sure. But what could happen on a busy street corner in broad daylight? Fifth Avenue was crowded with shoppers and tourists stopping to look in all the finely decorated windows. At the moment, Eric was leaning against a window displaying Italian shoes for women.

"Am I to assume Mr. Keller will not be joining us today?" Felix asked in a polite but slightly sarcastic tone.

Eric tried to remain calm. "No, someone's got to stay home and run the fort. Herb asked me to speak for both of us."

"O.K. then. Speak."

"We need a little more time. Just a few more weeks. I've got this week's money but the balance we need to let ride for a few more weeks. Same interest rate." Eric Kaplan was talking fast. This wasn't his circle of comfort. The money he, Herb Keller and John Weaver had borrowed from Arnie Zucker was due and they didn't have it. Actually, John was completely unaware of his partner's business with Mr. Zucker. Herb and Eric had taken it on themselves to use Zucker to finance the most recent technology upgrades to their practice. He had no idea Eric and Herb didn't go to Citibank as they'd agreed. Instead, in order to get the machine faster than traditional forms of financing would have permitted, they borrowed the entire $600,000 from Arnie Zucker, expecting to repay it within weeks when the Citibank loan came through. Zucker's weekly interest of nearly $12,000 didn't seem like a problem at the time. Herb and Eric only expected to need his money for a few weeks; three at the most.

But the banking industry was just beginning to climb out of its own financial woes, and the wheels of high finance turned slowly for a loan to a medical practice, secured only by the equipment itself. Herb and Eric found themselves in the uncomfortable position of having promised Arnie Zucker something, they could not deliver. And although Arnie was happy to take their vig every week, he really needed to get his money back and get it out on the street where it could earn some real return.

Eric did his best to explain his banking consternation to Felix and Levon but they neither understood nor cared. Their job was to drive the point home that Arnie wanted to start seeing sizable chunks of his money soon. And in the meantime, the vig keeps rolling in each week. Their intimidating physical presence was probably enough to convey Arnie's message: "*Pay da man or deal with these two savages.*"

The curbside meeting lasted less than five minutes. That's all Felix needed. He thanked Eric for his time and closed with the phrase, "Don't make us come up to Scarsdale to see you again."

When the two thugs were across the street, Eric pulled his cell phone from his pocket and dialed Herb Keller's cell number. "Herb, we need to bring John in on this. This schmuck's not going to wait another few weeks for his god-damned money."

Chapter Eighty-One

Doc

"Is that Alec Baldwin?" Annie whispered across the breakfast table at the Driver's Seat.

I turned around just in time to see the "30 Rock" star wearing a Yankee cap and walking out the revolving door at the front of the restaurant. He was with two younger men.

"Sure looks like him." I said as if spotting famous people was so commonplace for me that I barely lifted my attention from my French toast. "Let's see if he's wearing a Yankee hat tonight when we watch his show."

The sun had finally come out and it looked like the rest of the week was going to be one of those fabulous Indian summers Long Island is famous for. Dry, warm sunny days; probably the last we'll have before October's frosts start. I love this weather.

Annie was in the mood for pancakes when we awoke and I didn't have the fixings at the house so we came into town and walked around until we found ourselves conveniently in front of my favorite place, the Driver's Seat. After breakfast we walked down Main Street all the way to the beach, probably a good two miles. Then we walked along the beach for another couple of miles taking in the sun and gentle ocean breeze. The ocean was unusually calm, almost still. Its tiny waves seemed to be softly licking the shore line rather than crashing down upon it.

While we walked, Annie took a call on her cell phone from her lawyer and agreed to meet him for lunch on Friday to discuss her divorce. In less than five minutes she brought him up to date on the cancer thing and even a mention of me. When she wanted to be, Annie could be callously all-business. For a second, I almost felt sorry for her adversary, her husband. Then I recalled that the prick tried to kill her.

We walked all the way to the Shinnecock Inlet, as far as you can walk west without getting wet. Annie sat on the jetty for a few minutes watching sea gulls dive for bunker in the swift-moving waters of the inlet, while I tossed shells into the sea. She was wearing a pink cable-knit sweater with a deep v-neck and some designer logo I didn't recognize. Her hair was pulled back in a ponytail. She looked beautiful. How could anyone want to hurt this beautiful little lady?

We didn't talk much that morning. Maybe we were all talked out from the last few days of constant companionship. But that was OK. We each seemed to be comfortable with our own thoughts as we walked back toward town. We'd left our shoes back at the dune cross-over where we entered the beach so the warm September sea felt good on our feet and Annie kicked water on me once. But other than that we didn't really say much. I assumed she was miles away, working out the details of her meeting tomorrow. But it's hard to get into the head of someone who just got their life back; someone who, a few days ago, thought she'd be dead before Christmas.

Or she might have been thinking about us and the years of blissful happiness that I intended to shower on her. Annie was basically a positive person so maybe she was lost in thoughts about our life together and how great it was going to be. Or maybe she was thinking about her sons and the fact that now she'd get to see them graduate from college, get married, have children and all the other life events she thought she'd miss.

Like I said, I don't know what Annie was thinking about on that quiet walk that day. But now that some time has gone by, I'll tell you what I was thinking about that day. I was thinking about how close I came to losing her. I was thinking about the fact that, but for a couple of chance events, her husband's plan to kill her might have worked. I was thinking about the notion that neither of us were really sure he wouldn't try again. I couldn't let that happen. I had to protect her.

I found myself thinking about murder.

It wasn't about revenge or vengeance. I just had to be sure John Weaver, a man who had already attempted to kill Annie, never got another chance. She'd already decided not to go to the police, which I still thought was a mistake if, for no other reason than to put John on notice that others knew about his failed plot and were watching him like hawks now. But I also understood her reasons for not involving the police. The media would turn her life, and probably mine, into a front-page circus. When you're the daughter of an ultra-wealthy guy like Burt Dunn, you tend to attract a lot of unwanted attention. The tabloids would have a field-day with stories about their failed marriage, her sons distaste for John, the money, the excesses, and her relationship with me.

And for what? There wasn't any real evidence to put John away. The media frenzy would only serve to make the divorce more painful, public, and expensive. Her children and mine would all learn of our relationship in the worst possible light and it would be difficult to have them see it in any other way. After all, she was carrying on an affair with me. It would be impossible to spin that any other way once the newspapers did their thing.

So, in the interest of our future peace and happiness, I reluctantly agreed that going to the police would be a mistake. But I didn't agree to put it behind us. Annie, the eternal optimist, believed she was no longer in any danger from John. I wasn't as sure. Someone who is willing to kill for callously financial gain is demented and shouldn't be trusted. I tried to put myself in his position. If I were motivated enough to try to kill my wife once, why not try again. The same pot of gold was out there, just outside his reach. John was an intelligent guy. He could come up with something that, to others, might look like an accident or another tragic illness.

Or maybe, precisely because he was intelligent, he'd wait. Maybe the bastard would settle the divorce in a seemingly upright way, and then come after Annie again later, out of pure vindictiveness. He could wait months or even years to settle the score. Someone with access to the cornucopia of narcotics he had could do a lot of damage without ever being suspected. I'd always be worried about that. Every time Annie caught a cold, I'd be worried that the medicines she'd be taking hadn't been tampered with. Every time she left my sight, I'd be worried that he'd corner her in the elevator at Bloomingdale's and pump a syringe full of something lethal into her heart.

I didn't want to live that way. I wasn't even comfortable with Annie driving back to the city tomorrow to meet with her lawyer. I imagined John waiting behind every lamppost as she walked back to her room at the Essex.

We'd just about walked back to my Jeep in town when Annie surprised me with her own concerns.

"Doc, do you think it's possible that John might have poisoned anything else? I mean, something I'm not even aware of yet like my make-up or toothpaste or my cloths. He could have put some sort of anthrax-like shit in my closet and every time I put on something from the closet it's rubbing against my skin and making me sick."

Wow! I guess I'm not the only one having macabre thoughts this afternoon. Maybe Annie's not really telling me how concerned she is. Maybe she's a lot more scared than she wants me to think.

"I'll tell you what. Let's stop at CVS and get you some

new make-up and toothpaste, just to be sure. And don't even think about going back to the apartment to get anything tomorrow."

"You're the best Carafa. I'm going to keep you around for a while."

"Good, because I intend to do the same for you."

CHAPTER EIGHTY-TWO

As they drove back to Cold Spring Pond, Annie and Doc talked about the upcoming weekend. It was Annie's intention to drive back to Manhattan tomorrow for her dinner/meeting with Franklin Montague, stay at her room at the Essex House, and maybe do a little shopping on Saturday and Sunday. She'd check out of the Essex on Sunday and drive back to start her new life with Doc. He insisted she not go back to her apartment for even a minute and, although she protested, she finally agreed whatever cloths she'd left behind could easily be replaced. Most of her jewelry was in the safe deposit box at Chase and she kept all her really personal stuff at the Southampton house anyway, so she wasn't leaving much behind.

As they drove down Cold Spring Point Road, Annie's beach house came into view. It was the tallest house on the beach and could been seen from the Sabonac Road turnoff. She thought about all the times, as a child, she'd traveled from the city with her parents for a long weekend "*at the beach*" as her father used to say. She remembered so many times they'd driven down this same road and she'd spot the house for the first time and scream, "*We're here!*" Between her childhood and her years with Peter and the boys, some of her best memories were tied to the rooms in that house. It was her home and if you asked her sons where they were from, they'd probably say Southampton, New York, even though they grew up in Manhattan.

Since they'd been sequestered away on their love-fest for a few days, Annie and Doc took turns catching up on emails on Doc's laptop. Annie had one from Tomasue Weber just asking how she was feeling and trying to arrange a lunch next week. She also had one from each of the boys letting her know how happy they were about her "miraculous" recovery. She knew that both her sons found it easier to speak from the heart via email than in person or on the phone. She assumed most men were the same. And there was an email from Franklin Montague confirming their dinner tomorrow.

Doc had a weeks worth of financial reports from Fidelity and Vanguard as well as notes from Kelly and Peggy. Both had been trying to get him on his cell for two days and were concerned that he hadn't returned their voicemails. It was then that he realized he'd never recovered his phone since the day Annie came. It had been in the pocket of a pair of pants he'd thrown in the corner of his bedroom just before taking the boat out two days ago. The battery had long since gone dead and with his focus on Annie the last few days, he never thought about it.

After replying to his daughter's emails, assuring them he was fine, he retrieved his phone from the jeans and stuck it on the charger. Doc was just going into the outdoor shower to get rinsed off when Annie said, "I'm going over to my house to pick up some clothes for the weekend. I'll be back in an hour. Do we need anything for dinner?"

"Only if we want to eat."

"Well then how about you go to Schmidt's while I do my thing and I'll meet you back here for cocktails and dinner? How 'bout some fish?

"I'm on it babe." Came the words from under the shower.

Annie drove the quarter mile back to her house because she expected to pack a suitcase full of cloths for her trip into the city. When she pulled into the driveway she was surprised to see she'd left several lights and the kitchen TV on when she left to meet Doc at his dock on Tuesday. She'd only been back once since then and that was just to pick up some clean cloths and some toiletries. She hadn't noticed the TV and lights then.

As she stood at the kitchen sink, overlooking the expansive deck and the rolling bay beyond, her thoughts drifted back to simpler times. She thought about all the meals she'd cooked for the boys and Peter in this kitchen. She thought too about her mom and dad standing in this very place the night they hosted a party for her engagement to Peter. And then the place next to the table where the twin's highchairs used to stand. She could hear the happy laughter that used to flow from this sun-filled room over the years.

Then her eye caught the caulk board next to the wall phone. The push-pins that used to hold drawings from school or soccer practice schedules were empty now. All that remained was a painful memory of the night John smashed her head against the board before he viciously raped her against the kitchen table. They'd been married less than a year. She hadn't realized he was as drunk as he was when she confronted him with a pair of pink panties she found while cleaning her father's boat that afternoon. It was the last time she challenged him. He'd nearly broken her cheekbone.

Knowing she'd be in the city for a few days, Annie closed all the windows and was careful to turn off all the lights when she left. She'd only packed a small bag so rather than cluttering up Doc's driveway with two cars, she decided to leave hers and walk back to Doc's house. She'd already decided to take the train back to Manhattan so she wouldn't need her car for a few days anyway.

The sun was already low on the horizon when she walked back to Doc's carrying her small green Hermes bag. As she turned the corner to his street she could smell the smoke drifting from his chimney. It smelled wonderful. Somehow, it smelled like home. He greeted her in the driveway.

"Where's your car?"

"I figured I'd just leave it in my driveway so it's not in your way while I'm in New York." Then she added, "You don't think I want your creepy Jeepy hands on my finely tuned German machinery while I'm away, do you?"

"Hey, don't be maligning my automobile. I love that piece of shit."

"What did you come up with for dinner?"

"Blackfish, wild rice, asparagus, and a tomato and goat cheese salad. I also sprang for the big bucks, since you're leaving for a few days, and got two bottles of that Barolo you like. We drank the last of Bobby's on Tuesday."

After dinner they sat in the hammock and finished the second bottle of wine while looking for shooting stars. They found the bottom of the bottle before any stars began to move. Although neither spoke the words, they were both thinking about the first night they spent in his hammock on Labor Day. It seemed like so long ago. So much had happened in those few weeks. Being in the same place again made them both aware of how fast everything had been moving.

"You got any more of that Sambuca you like to lick off unsuspecting women's breasts?"

"No, but I hear red wine works just as well."

"No don't! It will stain my shirt."

Doc stood from the hammock with his wine glass in hand and mocked, "Boy, we seem to have lost that playfulness that once was. How about this?"

He slide down to the end of the hammock on his knees and poured a few drops of his wine on her naked feet. Then he began to gently lick her toes. When she didn't object, he poured a little wine on her ankles and licked both clean, then kissed them softly. This time he thought he heard a low moan so he flicked a few drops of the red liquid on her left calf and ran his tongue up her leg, kissing and licking all the way.

"Oooooh, that feels so nice." She whispered to the sky.

He repeated the seductive dance on her right toes, ankles and calf and by the time he had worked his way up to her right knee, he heard the sound of her enthusiastically unzipping her shorts.

"Have you got enough wine left to make it up to my lips? If not, feel free to linger wherever you run out." The words were barely a whisper.

They'd been asleep for several hours. Doc couldn't remember leaving the hammock and walking up the stairs to his bed, but—there they were, entangled in each other's nakedness and lying on top of the sheets. The digits on the cable box said it was 4:45 A.M. Doc woke up really thirsty and needing to pee at the same time. Wine usually had that effect on him. So did good sex.

He slipped back into bed and gently pulled the sheet up over Annie. She must have sensed the change and rolled onto her side without opening her eyes. Doc lied on his back with his hands behind his head, gazing up. He didn't expect to fall back to sleep anytime soon so his eyes were wide open, tracing the shadows that colored the ceiling.

It often happened, when he awoke after several hours sleep, that he couldn't get back to sleep for hours, sometimes after sunrise. Usually, he'd use the time to think.

But tonight something was different. The ceiling had an odd hue. There were faint streaks of red and yellow mixed with a white haze from the far window. He'd never noticed it before. Then he realized the red and yellow fog was moving, sort of dancing in a circle on the center of his ceiling. The motion was familiar but he couldn't place what it reminded him of. The faint colors seemed to be flashing at the same time they were circling each other.

Then it hit him. Police car lights!

He bolted up in bed and could see through the window at the far end of the bedroom. Somewhere in the distance there were definitely police car strobe lights, lots of them. He stumbled out of bed and before he even got to the window he could see the lights were coming not from police cars but from fire trucks parked on Cold Spring Point Road. And he could see a fire.

"Holy shit!" He fell back into the room groping for a pair of pants to pull on.

"Annie! Annie wake up. I think your house is on fire!"

Chapter Eighty-Three

Doc

By the time I threw on a pair of boat shoes, Annie grabbed one of my sweatshirts and was running barefoot down Lynton Lane towards her house and the flashing lights. I was a hundred feet behind her, so I had a good view of Annie when she turned the corner onto Cold Spring Point Road and came to a sudden stop. It was as if she'd hit a wall.

There must have been twenty volunteer firemen in the streets running around the four fire trucks, three police cars and two SUVs that said SHERIFF on the hood. The night seemed like day from all the bright lights. It looked as though they were already in 'clean-up' mode because only one fireman was still spraying water on the front porch while most others were either rolling up hose or dealing with the charred debris they'd hauled from the house. There was already a pile of burnt furniture in the driveway that was still smoldering as the junior-most firefighters picked at it with long poles.

The house itself seemed to have survived. At least that's how it looked to me in the middle of the night. One side looked to be badly burned and the wooden porch and Annie's beautiful deck were just about gone, but the rest of the house was still standing with most windows still in tact.

"My house." I heard her say in a weak voice. "My beautiful house."

On the other side of the biggest fire truck I spotted an elderly woman waving at us. It was the woman who lived to the right of Annie, Marge Wilson. She motioned for us to join her in the middle of the road, away from the smoke and spray.

"Oh, thank God, Annie. I thought you were in your bedroom. I told the firemen you must be in there because I saw your car in the driveway." She was nearly hysterical as she hugged Annie.

Well, so much for our keeping our little affair a secret. Now that Mrs. Wilson and the other dozen neighbors standing around saw us come running down the street in the middle of the night, wearing one piece of clothing each, I guess we've been outted.

"Marge, what happened?" Annie was almost sobbing the words.

"I don't know. I woke up about an hour ago and heard the flames on the deck. It was really crackling. Your whole deck was on fire, then it spread to the house. I called 911 and they were here in minutes." She pointed to the firemen. "Jimmy tried spraying this side down with our garden hose but the fire was too hot." I found out later that the eighty-six year old geezer in the red-plaid bathrobe was her husband Jimmy.

While Annie was getting the story from Marge, I noticed another one of the spectator—neighbors talking to a fireman in a white hat and pointing in our direction. I assumed he'd just pointed Annie out as the homeowner because the white hat was walking toward us. He introduced himself as Chief Bridgeman. I guessed that referred to his position within the fire department and not his status as a Native American.

"Are you the owner of the home?" The chief asked me. But before I could respond, Annie stepped in.

"It's my house. I'm Annie Dunn." Her voice was still weak and shaky.

"Well Mrs. Dunn, we're going to get things cleaned up in

another half hour, then we'll get plywood up on all the doors and windows that have been compromised."

He could have just said "burned".

"We were told that you may have been in the house so we needed to break in the front door to check the bedrooms as soon as the first engine arrived. I'm sorry about the door but glad to see you weren't home." He gave me and my pajama bottoms a disapproving glance.

"What happened? What started the fire?" Annie wanted to know.

"We're not sure. Someone from the department will be out here in the morning to have a closer look. But to me, it definitely appears to have begun outside the house; probably on the deck." He pointed to what was left of the stairs to the deck. "See this? This looks to be the origin of the fire. You can tell because the damage is so severe. As you go around the house, the fire seems to follow the easy source of fuel; the wood on the deck, then the porch and the porch roof, also dry wood. We're lucky your neighbor called when she did or you probably would have lost the whole house. These cedar shakes would have been the next thing to go." He pointed to the siding on the house. "That's why I don't like cedar shakes on house near the beach. They just get too dry."

"How much damage was done inside?" I asked

"Looks like just the area on this side of the house was fully involved." He motioned to what had been the living room. "You can go in and take a look. In fact, I'd suggest you remove any valuables before the guys with the plywood get here. It's safe to walk in there. We got all the hot spots taken care of. But after the plywood's up you really won't be able to get in there until after your insurance people come and inspect. So take any important papers or valuables now."

Annie and I walked through the first floor of her house

and were surprised to see that the Chief had been right. Except for the living room, there was almost no damage from the fire; just a lot of smoke in the air. The pile of charred furniture we'd seen in the driveway was what they'd pulled from the living room; Annie's two sofas, a couple of wooden end tables, a bookcase filled with what used to be her dad's collection of classics, and a couple of rugs.

But other than that, the house was pretty much OK. The second floor was untouched. We gathered a few pieces of jewelry from Annie's bedroom and a couple of pairs of shoes. Other than that, she really didn't need anything else. Her homeowner's policy was in a cabinet in the kitchen. In ten minutes we had everything we needed.

The Chief told us they needed to turn the power off because the fire had damaged the wires leading from the street to the house, so we may want to clear out the frig. He seemed like a very practical guy. Why waste a half a jar of Mayo if you don't have to? But, since she hadn't been out here much, Annie kept almost nothing in the frig anyway.

The crowd of concerned neighbors had begun to disperse. I'm sure there would be plenty of breakfast chat about Annie and the new guy from the Mauro's house. Oh well.

Annie and I walked back to my place to get properly dressed and by the time we returned, all but one fire truck had gone and the sun was beginning to creep up in the eastern sky. The Chief and his fancy truck were still there. He was filling out some paperwork. A crew of men had begun to put up the plywood. I was totally surprised at how fast a bunch of volunteers can get things done in the middle of the night. But I could tell the Chief was right. If Mrs. Wilson wasn't such a light sleeper, we'd be looking at a pile of ash instead of a boarded up house.

After Annie signed some forms for the Chief and thanked him several times, he drove off into the rising sun. I never did figure out who sends the plywood guys. They just seemed to appear, do their work, and disappear. Soon Annie and I were the only people on the street. We were both staring at the soggy pile of debris in her driveway.

"I know what you're thinking." She said without looking at me.

"No you don't."

"You're thinking John did this."

"You're good."

"You're thinking he tried to burn my house down just because he knows how much it means to me and because it was my father's."

Actually, she was close. I figured the bastard drove out to torch the house out of sheer vengeance, but when he saw Annie's car in the driveway, he thought he could kill two birds with one stone. If she was asleep in the house maybe this was his last best chance to get rid of her. Worse case, the fire would scare the hell out of her and send the message that he was not to be fucked with in the upcoming divorce negotiations. If he drove fast enough, he could be back in Manhattan quickly enough to set up a solid alibi.

That's what I really thought. What I said was, "I don't know. But I'm glad you were sleeping next to me last night."

CHAPTER EIGHTY-FOUR

Doc

We drove into town and had an early breakfast at McDonald's. There's nothing like an Egg McMuffin after a house fire. Annie had pancakes.

I convinced her to keep her appointment with her lawyer later today. All she really needed to do was call her insurance guy. I could take care of everything else out here. Since it was a Friday, there was a good chance the insurance guy would come today anyway. I could meet him at the house for her. The meeting with her lawyer should come first.

She agreed. Since the house was boarded up, there was nothing we could do anyway. So I dropped her off at the Southampton train station just before noon. This way, when she got back to the city, she'd have time to check in at the Essex House and take a nap before dinner with the lawyer.

I stopped at Schmidt's to grab a few things I'd need to sustain myself for the weekend. As I was driving back to the pond, my cell phone made that funny sound it makes when you have a voicemail. It never rang, but someone's message must have gone straight to voicemail as usually happens when I'm driving through an area AT&T has decided to ignore. I dialed my voice mailbox and listened:

"Hello Doc. This is John Weaver. I just wanted to check with you to be sure we're still on for fishing Saturday morning. I invited a buddy of mine but he can't make it so it's just the two of us. I can meet you at my boat at ten if that works for you. Just give me a call back to confirm and so we can discuss what type

of bait you want me to pick up. My buddy says they're doing well with live eels. I'll be in the office all day Friday so give me a call here. The number is 212-697-6325."

I was so enraged at hearing his voice, I almost drove into the back of the black Bentley in front of me on Jobs Lane. The balls on this guy! I actually had to pull over and calm down. I was crazy with rage.

As I sat parked on the side of the road, I realized he has no idea I know about him trying to kill his wife, once with poison, and potentially once with fire. He doesn't even know I know about his impending divorce or even his estrangement from Annie. On the other hand, and to be totally fair, he also doesn't know I'm sleeping with his wife. I guess, all things considered, we both have our little secrets.

It was actually kind of creepy listening to his message. I mean, I don't think I've ever actually spoken to a murderer, or in this case, someone who has attempted murder. What I found creepy was that he sounded so normal; just like anyone else who planned to go fishing. His voice was clear and calm. He actually sounded very friendly. But this prick had tried to kill my Annie.

My first thought was to not call him back at all. But when I thought that through, from his point of view, why wouldn't I? For all he knew, I had no reason not to call or to want the guy dead. After all, we had made plans to go fishing together. I even invited him on to my boat. Why would I suddenly blow him off unless I knew something about his activities over the last few days? No, ignoring him wasn't the right answer.

Then I thought about calling him back with an excuse about why I couldn't make it on Saturday. *"Because you tried to kill your wife you cocksucker!"* I could probably come up with a better excuse or, at least one that didn't indicate I knew as much as I did. Something like, *"I have to go out of town,"* or

"I forgot all about it and made other plans," or, and I liked this one best, *"I hurt my back fucking your wife you son of a bitch!"*

None of those seemed quite right. I was still very upset.

I decided not to think about it for a while and finished my drive back to the house. Maybe I should talk to Annie first and see what her take is on it. I could call her later in the afternoon. For now, I wanted to forget about John Weaver and how much I wanted to kill the prick.

My cell phone rang again and I was almost afraid to answer. Just in case it was him, I pulled over again to save myself the discomfort of driving into a tree.

"Hello."

"Hey honey, it's me. I'm on the train and got through to my insurance guy. He said the claims adjuster can be at the house at three today. Can you meet him there?"

I was so relieved to hear Annie's voice I almost didn't hear what she said.

"Yeah, sure. Three o'clock. I'm on it. What's his name?"

"I think he said his name was Williams, but I forgot his first name if he even gave it to me."

"OK, I'll take care of it. Hey listen to this. Guess who called me a few minutes ago. I'll give you a hint. He tried to burn your house down last night."

"Are you shitting me? Why was he calling you?" She was flabbergasted.

I reminded her of our fishing excursion the previous weekend and of our plans to meet again this Saturday. I couldn't explain why I'd made such plans because I really didn't understand my motivation myself. Maybe, at the time, I saw it as the only way to stay in contact with someone who was actually in contact with Annie.

"Remember, this time last week I thought I'd never see you again."

"Well you're not thinking about going fishing with him, are you?"

"Only if I can use him for chum."

"I don't think you...can't...it will be..." The phone reception was starting to break up. Thanks again AT&T. I did hear her say "...call you later." So I hung up and continued home figuring I'd hear from her when she got to the hotel.

CHAPTER EIGHTY-FIVE

Doc

T he bright red SUV was sticking out onto the road. I guess when you're the Sheriff, you can park wherever you want. I'd just turned onto Cold Spring Pond Road, Annie's street, when I noticed the huge Denali in front of her house. A uniformed cop was putting up yellow crime-scene tape all around her property and a grey-haired guy in jeans and a Suffolk County sweatshirt was walking around talking notes. I pulled in behind the SUV to see what was going on.

The older guy must have recognized me from last night. "You're the boyfriend, right? I'm Sheriff White, Ed White."

It hadn't occurred to me that just by being seen with Annie last night, everyone made the assumption I was the "boyfriend". Then again, we were in our pajamas.

"Yeah, I'm Doc Cafara. I was here last night with Annie, the owner." I pointed in the direction of the house. "What's going on?" I was glad to see someone else thought a crime had been committed.

Sheriff White explained to me that, in addition to being one of the town's sheriffs, he was also the only fire marshal and arson investigator in eastern Suffolk county. Apparently, Chief Bridgeman thought he'd seen enough damage to the decking last night to suspect an accelerant of some kind had been used to start the fire. He'd called for the arson investigation.

"I just finished my investigation of the property. I'll send a copy to the owner but if you talk to her first, tell her to have her insurance people give me a call." He handed me one of his cards.

"Can you tell me what you think?" I wanted to know.

He pulled off his SCPD hat and wiped his forehead. "Technically, I'm supposed to discuss my findings only with the owner and the insurance company. However, since I'm still conducting my investigation, how about I ask you a few questions?" He gave me a wink and smiled.

"What sort of questions?" I asked.

"Well, for starters, do you know any reason why someone might pour gasoline all around the perimeter of the deck along the house here?" He pointed to the scorched decking closest to the house.

"Are you saying someone started this fire on purpose?"

"I don't know what the purpose was, but I'm saying pressure-treated lumber, even as old as this is, doesn't burn that easily unless either there is a heat source beneath it or some form of accelerant poured on top. I looked for a source of heat under the deck but found nothing. I even crawled under there at the low side."

It was clear the Sheriff liked his work and enjoyed talking about it to someone eager to listen. I was eager to listen. He made a point of showing me how he got under the shallow end of the deck and used his flashlight to search for any signs of faulty wiring or combustible material stored under the deck. He'd found none.

"So if the wood is this damaged and there was no source of heat coming from below, there had to be some form of accelerant on top. In this case, gasoline. You can always tell when gasoline has been used because the arsonist usually splashes it all around instead of just pouring it. When you splash it, the gas leaves singe marks on the surface of the wood planks that don't have enough fuel to burn through. So you get these sorts of black marks at the edges of the fire zone." He pointed out several black marks on the edges of the deck. "But whoever it was, was an amateur. He made no attempt to disguise his work."

I spent another fifteen minutes talking to the Sheriff about the fire and his views on the likely points of entry, the places where the flames penetrated into the house. He was pretty sure it was probably local kids who started the fire thinking it was just another summer house that had been abandoned for the winter. "Happens more than you'd think."

I told him the insurance guy was coming later this afternoon but the Sheriff couldn't come back today and said he was really supposed to wait for the insurance information to come from the owner. I gave him Annie's cell phone number.

What I didn't give him was the name of the guy who'd started the fire and tried to kill Annie.

<hr/>

A few hours later I found myself back at Annie's house waiting for the insurance adjuster to show up. Annie left me a key so I could show him the damage on the inside. I was waiting in her kitchen when the phone on the wall rang. It scared the hell out of me, and I wasn't sure if I should be answering the phone in the home of the woman I'm having an affair with. Then I thought it might be Annie so I picked up after the fourth ring.

"Hey sweety. It's me. Did the insurance guy come yet?" Annie sounded great.

I told her about the arson investigation and my chat with the Sheriff. She didn't seem all that surprised. I thought that was odd. I mean, even in the very darkest days during my divorce, if my ex had tried to kill me, I would have found it pretty upsetting. But Annie just didn't see it. Maybe, she just didn't want to see it. Or maybe, on some level she couldn't deny the facts, but didn't want to believe her husband was still trying to kill her.

"Look Annie. Whatever you do, do not make any contact with John while you're in New York. I mean don't talk to him, don't go anywhere near the apartment, and don't tell anyone where you're staying."

"You're over reacting. But I promise to behave. I just checked in to my room and I'm going to get a massage and get my nails done before I meet Franklin. I'm meeting him at the restaurant in the lobby."

"Great. Call me when you get back to your room tonight. I'll let you know what the insurance adjuster has to say." Then I added, "I miss you."

"I love you Doc. I'll call you later."

I hung the phone back on the wall and could see a noticeably attractive red-head standing at the back door about to knock. She couldn't have been more than twenty-five and was wearing a tightly fitted black sweater over a cream colored skirt. She was a knockout.

"Are you mister Dunn? I'm Katie DaRin from Chubb." She handed me a card.

I explained I was standing in for the owner, Mrs. Dunn, who had to go back to New York. "I'm a neighbor. She asked me to meet you here, but she said a mister Williams was coming."

"I work for Jack Williams out of the Riverhead office. He asked me to handle this." She handed me another card, this time with the name John T. Williams, Licensed Insurance Adjuster on the front. I was glad old Jack couldn't make it.

I gave her the background about the fire, when we first heard the fire engines, the approximate time the last fire truck left, the names of any firemen we'd spoken to and a hundred other facts; I couldn't see how they'd help estimate the damage.

But Katie had her method and was walking around taking notes as we spoke. I really couldn't help her with the age of the furniture that was destroyed, but she got a good look at it in the driveway pile of scorched upholstery and wood.

"So you and Mrs. Dunn weren't at home at the time of the fire?" She said it without looking up from her notes but I could hear the sarcasm in her voice.

"No. We were staying at my house, just down the block. No one was home at the time of the fire." That's all I planned to say about that. Her prurient curiosity would get no more from me.

"I understand from the Southampton Fire Department report that the fire is under suspicion and an arson investigator will be around to do a further evaluation." She kept making notes and walking as she spoke. Katie was gorgeous but all business.

"Actually, he was here this afternoon. Just a few minutes ago." That's all I had to say about that too.

When she got to the back of the house and looked out at the Peconic Bay, I could tell she was impressed. It was, after all, a very impressive view.

Just to make small talk, I asked, "How long have you been doing this Katie?"

"About four years now. I started doing claims work part-time while I was going to NYU, then I got a full-time job when I graduated. My dad's a big shot at Chubb and got me the job."

"I'm sure you would have gotten it on your own." I wasn't kidding.

After a thorough inspection of the interior, Katie handed me three sheets of paper and instructions for Annie to fill out the claim forms and include any receipts for unusually valuable items that were destroyed. "I can have a check for her forty-eight hours after we get the paperwork back. You're free to use whatever contractors you choose or we can make recommendations for local tradesmen. It's up to you. Actually, it's up to Mrs. Dunn."

And that was that. I guess when you're rich, you can afford the class-A insurance company and they send class-A type people who give class-A type service. Anyway, Katie with the tight sweater was on her way and I locked up Annie's house and walked back to mine.

When I got home I made a phone call.

"Hello, John? We still on for that fishing trip tomorrow?"

Chapter Eighty-Six

Doc

Friday night was tough. I spent a lot of time trying to form a visual picture of John Weaver switching Annie's medicine for the poisons. I thought if I could see the image, it would validate my nefarious plans. I needed to picture him pouring gasoline on her deck and lighting it. I wanted to imagine him switching Annie's X-rays. I needed to hate him. I needed to hate him enough to kill him.

I had no trouble justifying my plan. This lunatic had tried to kill Annie; not once, but twice. Was I supposed to wait around for him to try again? I tried to imagine a scenario where the lines were clear; where anyone would come to the same conclusion. I imagined the three of us standing in an empty room; John, Annie and me. Annie is standing against one wall with her back to us. I'm standing at the other end of the room, right next to John, who is standing next to the only furniture in the room; a table full of very sharp butcher knives. John picks up one knife and, before I know what's happening, he throws it at Annie. The knife misses her by inches as she turns towards us in horror. I'm so stunned I am frozen. Before I can react, he picks up another knife and throws it at Annie. This one misses by less than an inch.

Now you tell me. Am I supposed to wait and see if he picks up another knife before I say or do anything? Am I supposed to call the cops? Am I supposed to reason with him? Or am I supposed to take the bastard out?

I vote for taking the bastard out and, given those circumstances, which loosely mirror what's happened so far, I think most people would agree. The question is, could most people actually do it? Can I do it?

A year ago, I'm not sure how I would have answered that question. I'm not sure that a year ago I could have killed someone. I'm just not sure. I always believed that human life was somehow sacred. It had to be, or we would degenerate into a bunch of ruthless animals. A year ago, I was firmly against capital punishment, even for the most horrific crimes. It just didn't seem right, when you had time to rationally think it through, to deliberately end the life of another person who was no longer a danger to anyone.

But that was how I felt when I believed in God. When I thought there was an all-knowing God, taking a human life just didn't seem like a right we could assume. If he didn't pass judgment on them, who are we to do so? That's what I was taught in school. It's not our place to judge, right? Bullshit.

For the first time since I turned my back on God, I felt, not lonely but liberated. Free to think analytically and rationally without the haze of faith clouding my decisions. With no risk of eternal damnation hanging over my head, I could do what seemed right for me. I could make decisions based on things I could see and feel: science, nature, natural laws like gravity and physics. Survival of the fittest. These things all made sense to me. I could believe in them, if that's the right term.

I think Napoleon was right. Religion must have been invented by the rich to keep the poor from killing them in their sleep. Without the threat of some higher authority sitting in judgment of me, I am free to think logically. Religious beliefs no longer enslave me. For the first time, I could empathize with the dichotomies facing Galileo, Copernicus, and daVinci;

men who saw science in conflict with the spiritual mandates of their time. Men who just wanted to act rationally.

I guess that's the way I saw it. Killing John Weaver would be a rational act because it could save the life of someone I cared deeply about. My only conflict was the subtle distinction between 'could' and 'would.' How could I be one hundred percent sure he intended to try again? How could anybody be sure? What odds would justify murder?

If someone told me there was a ninety percent chance he would try to kill Annie again, I wouldn't hesitate. If the odds were fifty percent; a toss of the coin, I wouldn't hesitate. But if someone assured me the odds of him trying again were less than ten percent; one in ten, I'm not so sure anymore. That's the grey area for me.

There's a part of me that sees John Weaver as a damaged human being, someone's child who went wrong along the jagged path of life. Maybe he is what he is because of things that happened to him in his life, maybe in his childhood. Maybe his father beat him. Would knowing that make a difference? I wish I knew.

On the other hand, we're all what we are because of the genes we were dealt and the experiences we encounter along the way. That can't be a valid excuse for trying to murder someone. Not when the motive is money or revenge.

But is it any more valid when the motive is love? I love Annie and want to protect her. Of that, I'm certain and I feel comfortable that my motives are genuine. But would murdering John Weaver be justified by my love? Would I be acting out of love or out of some basic form of self-preservation? If I didn't love Annie, would I be justified killing John? More to the point, if I didn't love Annie, would I do it?

I tortured myself with these doubts until after midnight.

Eventually, I came to the conclusion that I am an animal like any other walking the surface of the earth or swimming in the oceans. We kill to survive. Let the fittest among us survive. If I was a lion and another animal threatened my pride of cubs, I would kill without hesitation. I would attack without provocation. I would not let the attacker have his chance to spoil the life I am entitled to. I would not let faith in some higher being dissuade me. I would kill. I would bite down into the neck of the threat and rip the veins and muscles from him until his blood splattered on my face and I could taste his death.

Yeah, I could do it.

I had to do it.

And I'd already figured out how to do it. John Weaver himself had given me the perfect opportunity.

CHAPTER EIGHTY-SEVEN

Doc

Saturday looked like it was going to be a beautiful day. The air was clear and dry. It was a perfect day for the end of September. I wasn't yet sure if it was the perfect day to kill someone.

I woke up early, around 5:30 A.M., and couldn't get back to sleep. I had a lot on my mind and a lot of serious thinking yet to do. So I just stayed in bed and waited for the sunrise while I put together my plan to take John Weaver out of our lives. I'd decided last night that I couldn't dwell on the moral issue any longer. It wasn't getting me anywhere and I knew I'd come to the same conclusion even if I thought about it for another ten years. So, with the ethical questions off to the side, and not to be disturbed again, I conceived and polished my plan.

John had offered me the perfect opportunity when he invited me on to his boat instead of mine. The arrogant prick said he'd be more comfortable on his boat. Well, maybe for a while anyway.

I was supposed to meet him at the marina at ten o'clock. He said don't bring anything, but I told him I'd bring a cooler with beer and ice. However, instead of beer, I planned to bring about eight water bottles filled with gasoline. And instead of ice rumbling around in my cooler there would be about twenty feet of heavy chain and a small auxiliary anchor I had in my garage. Those two items plus a book of matches and the aluminum bat, which I noticed on his boat last week, were all I needed. I already had the gas in my garage. I keep a five gallon plastic container for my lawn mower. And the chain and anchor came with the house. I found them, and a lot of other crap, in the crawl space after the closing. So I wouldn't be creating a trail of recent purchases with any of the murder weaponry, not that anyone was ever going to find it.

We'll fish for about an hour then I'll direct John to take us out to the ledge, the place where the Atlantic bottom drops off to about two hundred feet of water. We'll drift. When the opportunity presents itself, I'll sneak up from behind him and use the bat to knock him unconscious. I need to be careful not to leave any blood on the deck from the blow, just in case some fragment of the boat is later found and analyzed.

Then I'll securely wrap the prick in the chain and toss him, the chain, and the anchor off the side. In two hundred feet of water, nobody's going to find him. But just to be sure, I'll drive the boat back closer to shore, maybe a mile or so off the coast. That's where the terrible accident is going to occur. I'll use the gasoline to start a significant fire in the cabin. I will slip over the side with a life jacket and start swimming away from the boat. If all goes well, and I think it will, the fire will consume the interior of the cabin. Directly below the cabin sits about six hundred gallons of diesel fuel, which will not burn or explode on its own. Diesel needs to be heated to over one hundred twenty degrees before it is combustible. I remember that from my early days in commercial real estate when I asked someone why oil was considered a safer fuel than gas for heating a building.

But the cabin fire will set off the propane tanks in the galley which should give us all the heat we'll need to get that diesel burning. After the explosion, which will be visible from miles away, they'll be very little left of the boat. Nearby vessels will respond to the explosion and find me in the water clutching the life jacket and screaming that there's another man in the water. I just won't mention that he's twenty miles away and under two hundred feet of water.

So I'll make a fuss about how we need to look for John because we were both knocked off the stern and into the water when the explosion occurred. We noticed the fire in the cabin but before we could do anything, kaaboom! The boat blew up.

The Coast Guard will search for John but they'll be looking on the surface and in the wrong place. I'll insist on staying with the search team but the dizziness and pain I plan to feign will make them insist on getting me to the hospital. They'll search until the sun goes down and then maybe again the next day, but that will be it. Everyone will assume he drowned about a mile off shore in less than thirty feet of water. They'll wait to see his decomposing and fish-ravaged body wash up on West Hampton Beach in a few days. I suppose it might, if the chains come loose someday.

Because I'll be in the hospital, someone from the Suffolk County Police will call Annie to tell her the tragic news. That's the only part of this I feel bad about. Annie will be shocked and worried and hurt by this. Initially, she won't suspect I had a sinister role in this, but at some point the doubt will cross her mind. It will cross everyone's mind because at least a dozen of my neighbors saw us running from my house in our underwear a few nights ago. The "boyfriend" of the grieving widow will certainly be a suspect but there'll be no evidence of a crime.

I suppose I'm taking a big gamble here, but it's one I'm willing to take to protect Annie. Something could go wrong. Some small piece of incriminating evidence that I overlooked could wash ashore and I'd be fucked. Or maybe John's body does wash up someday and someone notices the bruise on the back of his skull from my batting practice. It could happen. And I suppose, for the next six months, I'll worry about that every day.

But I won't regret it. I need to do this.

So, I emptied four two-liter bottles of diet Coke and four bottles of seltzer down my kitchen sink. I carefully poured the gasoline from the plastic container in my garage into the eight empty plastic bottles. I was very careful not to spill any on the garage floor. Then I put the bottles into my white Igloo cooler along with the chain and anchor. The anchor just about fit with the top closed. I just had to hope John didn't want a beer before I went to bat.

I stopped at McDonald's for an Egg McMuffin and a cup of coffee. Something about doing normal things on the day I was going to kill someone just didn't seem right. But I guess most killers eat breakfast. I'll bet if you did a survey of all murderers, ninety-five percent of them had breakfast the morning of their murder.

I arrived at the marina a few minutes late, grabbed a book of matches from my glove compartment, and carried the cooler down the gangway to the floating dock. I could already see John on his boat. He was taking down the side canvas. The twin diesel engines were already purring and I looked around to see if anyone else was aboard. No one. Excellent.

I also glanced around the marina to see if anyone was around. I wasn't sure if I wanted someone to witness me getting on the boat or not. I suppose, if it ever came down to witnesses, it might be helpful to have some bystander say that he noticed John and I seemed to be joking and pleasant to each other and looking forward to our fishing trip. On the other hand, maybe my paranoia was getting the best of me.

I was determined not to let him handle the cooler. I needed

to carry it all the way onto the boat and put it down softly. The chain was making more noise than I'd expected and it really didn't sound much like ice.

John noticed me walking down the dock. "Hey buddy. Right on time."

"My name's not Buddy. I'm not on time. I'm fifteen minutes late and I'm going to kill you, you miserable son of a bitch." That's what I thought. What I said was more like, "Morning. Permission to come aboard?"

He offered to take one handle on the cooler as I stepped onto the swim platform but I said, "No, no. I've got it. Where should I put it?" First disaster averted.

It occurred to me that I hadn't thought through a workable plan "B" in case something goes wrong. What if he opens the cooler? What if he doesn't want to go out to the ledge? What if he confronts me about Annie? For all I know, he could be totally aware of my relationship with her. Maybe he was infuriated when he learned of our affair and is looking for payback. Shit, he could have invited me to go fishing so he could kill me! What if he has a gun? What if the bat's not there?

We hadn't even left the dock yet and I was losing it. I was beginning to doubt my resolve. Could I really do this? How could I not have a plan "B"? My heart was pounding so loud I could hear it over the noise of the engines. Pull yourself together Doc.

"I got a dozen live eels already and Mark's going to bring us down some frozen squid in a minute," he said.

Mark? Who the hell is Mark? Oh shit. If he invited someone else along, I'm screwed.

Maybe the best thing to do would be to feign a sudden stomach ache, take my cooler and be on my way.

Then I heard him say, "Here he comes now."

I saw Mark, the kid who pumps gas and runs the bait station at Jackson's Marina carrying a bucket and coming toward us along the dock.

"I gave you two bags doctor Weaver. They're still frozen so I put some water in the bucket. Should be thawed out by the time you're rigged up." It seemed like the kid was bucking for a tip.

John took the bucket from him but I didn't see any tip change hands. The kid stood on the dock trying to hide his disappointment. I figured I'd just found my bystander, so I tried to think of something to ask the kid while I reached into my pocket.

"So where are they running, Mark?" It was the best I could come up with.

He was happy to oblige. "One eighty, straight out of the inlet—about fifteen minutes south. Yesterday they were getting them on eels but you never can tell. A guy from Montauk said he got his limit on Wednesday with twelve-inch spoons. I think Stripers will eat just about anything, but you got to know what they want today."

I handed him a folded-up twenty without John noticing and said, "Thanks for the advice. We'll bring you back a forty pounder. See you later Mark." There, I used his name twice, asked his advice, and over-tipped him by fifteen bucks. The kid's got to remember seeing us. But hopefully, it will never come to that.

John was all business up on the flying bridge. He called down to me to cast off the stern lines and pull up the fenders. We were on our way out of the marina and into the channel that led through the locks and out to the ocean. As soon as we separated the boat from the land, I felt a separation from the rest of the world. Now it was just the two of us. This boat was our world. There was nothing else. No one else. Just the two of us. And I noticed the aluminum bat was right where it was last week—hanging on the back of the cockpit wall, next to the gaff.

I joined John up on the flying bridge and took the seat next to his. I was curious to see if he mentioned anything about his wife leaving him, or for that matter, about his wife's sudden return to good health. But he just fiddled with his GPS screen and maneuvered the yacht through the canal and toward the inlet. The water was calm and we made good time going through the Shinnecock Inlet. We were in the ocean by eleven o'clock. Everything was going well so far.

I noticed his GPS system was very sophisticated and had an enormous flat screen that showed our exact location. The problem was that John had the tracker on. The tracker leaves a trail of little white marks on the screen that shows were you've been. It's helpful if you go somewhere new then need to find your way home in the fog or in the dark. It's like leaving a trail of breadcrumbs to find your way home. But in this case I didn't want anyone to know where we'd been. If, by some bad luck, the boat isn't completely destroyed and the coast guard is able to use the GPS to see where we've been, they'll know where to look for old John. That's wouldn't be good and I started to realize maybe I hadn't thought this through well enough.

So I made a mental note that after I send John to the bottom, I need to disable the GPS. Unplugging it from its power source will do the trick. OK, problem solved, but I started to wonder what else I hadn't thought about.

While we traveled south, John started a conversation about the upcoming presidential election. *Too bad you're not going to get to vote, scumbag.* Seems like he didn't approve of either candidate but he did want to nail one of the candidates for Vice President. And it wasn't Joe Biden.

Later, the conversation elevated to the Yankee's chances of

making it through the playoffs. Apparently he had a big bet that they'd win the pennant. I came to learn John liked to bet. He talked about his most recent trip to Atlantic City and playing poker for three straight days. It sounded like he'd lost more money in one weekend than I paid for my first apartment. I realized we lived in completely different worlds. And yet, we'd both fallen in love with the same woman. Odd.

I told John to throttle back the engines and we fished our first spot, drifting with live eels for bait. This was pretty much the spot I planned to take the boat back to later when I set my fire and jumped in the water. I noticed two large jellyfish drifting by in the still water and wondered how long I'd be in the water before someone rescued me. An hour? Four hours? After five hours it would be getting dark. The thought of bobbing around out here in the dark made me realize I'd come across another loose end I hadn't completely thought through.

We were just about in sight of land so I suppose I could swim towards shore while I waited to be found and rescued. But it would be a more convincing show if I stayed close to the explosion. Then there were the jellyfish. I've been stung by them many times before but, on those occasions, I was able to jump out of the water and rinse off, leaving just a painful welt on my skin. If I was in the water for several hours and got stung a lot, I'm not sure what would happen. I was wearing jeans and a short-sleeve shirt so I guess the biggest danger was to my arms and head. Hopefully the lifejacket would keep my head out of the water.

The sun glistened on the still water. Not much was happening with our eels and we both just stood on the deck of the boat with our legs braced against the transom, holding our rods and waiting for a bite. Neither of us spoke for several minutes. My mind was racing with thoughts of what I was about to do.

I wonder what he was thinking about. He still hadn't said a word about Annie and I was wondering if he was waiting for me to say something about the fire. After all, I had to notice that Annie's house had yellow tape all around it, didn't I?

Now I had a dilemma. If John hadn't set the fire, he'd have no reason to be aware of it. If that was the case, his silence on the subject made perfect sense. But if he had set the fire, as I suspected he had, then he still couldn't ask about it. To do so would beg the question of how he knew of it.

So we were both keeping many grave dark secrets from each other. He just seemed to be better at it than me. All the lies and cover-stories I had swirling around in my head were beginning to make me a little crazy; a little paranoid. John on the other hand, seemed to have no problem living with the secret that he'd tried to kill his wife and that she was planning to divorce him. He just seemed so cool. Like lying wasn't something new for him.

"How about trying another spot?"

"Sounds good. Let's work our way out toward the ledge. Maybe the fish are running a little deeper today." I realized I was having trouble looking him in the eyes when I spoke, but I decided to send up my trial balloon just to see his reaction. So as we reeled in our lines I said, "Hey, what's going on at your house? I saw the yellow tape this morning. Everything OK?"

And that's when I saw it. That's when I knew I'd been right about him. As I said the words, *"I saw the yellow tape"* I saw him look straight out at the ocean and his mouth opened a bit. He rolled his tongue along his top teeth while he thought about his response and a tiny smile seemed to take over his mouth. He didn't see me watching.

A four-foot swell rolled by and we both had to steady ourselves for a moment. John used it as an opportunity to turn his back to me while he said, "Yellow tape? What yellow tape?

What are you talking about?" He should have been a professional actor. He was good.

"It looked like there was a small fire or something." I left it at that and waited for a response.

"I don't know. I'll ask my wife when I get home. I haven't been out there since last week and I don't think…" He stopped before finishing the sentence that was probably going to end with "…my wife was either."

You piece of shit. You tried to poison her then you tried to burn her to death. If you really didn't know anything about it, you'd be on your cell phone right now dialing her number. Oh, that's right. You can't call her. She dumped your sorry murdering ass.

I realize now that by mentioning the yellow tape in sort of a casual way, I let him know his short career as an arsonist had failed to accomplish his goal. He hadn't burned the house down and he hadn't succeeded in toasting his wife. Until then he probably didn't know how unsuccessful he'd been. Maybe he thought he was already a widower and just hadn't gotten the call yet.

Then I realized that didn't make sense. If Annie had been killed or even seriously injured, he would have gotten a call from the Suffolk County police on Friday morning. When that didn't happen, he must have figured the fire didn't do as much damage as he'd planned. Or…

Maybe after setting the fire, he remained in the area somewhere to watch from a safe distance. If that was the case, he might have spotted Annie and me running around in our underwear that night. In which case, he knows I've been doing his wife and that I know all about the pills and bogus x-rays. And that brings me right back to my paranoia that maybe he's planning to do me in instead of the other way around. Or…

Maybe he just drove past the house this morning on his

way to the marina; just to take a peak at what damage he'd done. Yeah, I'm going with that one.

We traveled further south, to an area where his chart showed about ninety feet of water. "Let's try here."

By now it was after noon and my fear of him asking for one of the beers I supposedly had in the cooler, was growing. I needed to make my move soon. I just didn't have a plan "B". Fortunately, we landed two stripers, each over twenty ponds, and that kept his mind off food and beer, at least for now. But that wouldn't last forever, so I surprised John when I suggested we leave the spot we'd successfully fished for only a few minutes, and move out to deeper waters. Water that would hide my crime.

"If we want the big fish, we need to be in deep water." I made it sound like I was getting really psyched about going after the "big ones".

"All right! Let's do it." The poor bastard was actually enthusiastic about driving me out to the deep, dark waters that would be his grave. After stowing the two fish on ice, he pushed the throttle near full and we were on our way. The mighty Bertram engines lifted us atop the waves and cut through the increasingly deep-blue sea like a hot knife through butter. I stayed in the aft cockpit and watched as the passing water grew darker and darker, in stark contrast to the bright white foam in the boat's wake.

I went into the galley and grabbed two beers from his refrigerator. I figured the condemned man should have one last beer. I also figured this would keep me from having to open my cooler until I needed to. I brought them up to the flying bridge, handed him the beer and took the seat next to him on the bridge. I quickly opened mine and took a long drink before the prick wanted to clink bottles in mock celebration of our friendship. It just didn't seem right to drink with a guy you're about to kill. I'd never be able to look at a beer the same way again.

As we headed further away from land and closer to the ledge, I had one last chance to reflect on my decision. My rationalization was that there was just no other way. No other way to be completely sure he wouldn't again try to kill the woman I wanted to spend my life with. He was obviously either deranged or just a complete sociopath. If he could murder for money or revenge he needed to be stopped. I, on the other hand, was about to murder for a more noble cause. I was doing it to protect Annie. Or, was I doing it so I could have what I wanted—a life with Annie. Either way, I felt justified.

I wondered how I would feel a week from now, a year from now. Would I have nightmares about it? Would I see John's decomposing corpse floating in my dreams? Would I ever be able to look at the ocean in the same way again? Would I be able to look at myself in the mirror and be a hundred percent certain I'd done the right thing?

Yes. God damn it. Yes! I almost said it out loud.

This was it. I told John we'd gone far enough when I saw the depth chart blinking two hundred and fifteen feet. From here we'd drift into even deeper water. "Let's try here," I heard myself say.

I knew that the more I thought about it the more freaked out I'd become. I needed to just do it. I needed to move quickly, before my resolve faded. There was no time for indecision. I decided as soon as we got down to the deck and he turned his back to me to let his line out, I'd grab the bat and strike. One really hard blow to the back of the head—that's all it should take. I can do this.

I can.

I have to.

John went down the ladder first and already had his rod in

hand. He was determined to get his eel in the water first. His back was to me.

"Let out about a hundred feet of line then slowly start reeling up," I instructed. Then I reached for the bat. I remember hesitating briefly to look down at the bat in my hand. Then I focused all my attention on the back of his skull.

CHAPTER EIGHTY-EIGHT

By Sunday morning Annie had checked off everything on her to-do list. Her meeting on Friday night with Franklin Montague gave her the confidence she was hoping for. Franklin usually had that fatherly effect on her. He always had her best interests at heart.

He'd been flabbergasted to hear about the x-ray mix-up but delighted to learn Annie was cancer free. She hadn't mentioned anything about the pills to Franklin. Annie was determined to put this all behind her and the fewer people who knew John tried to kill her, the easier that would be.

His advice about the divorce was what she'd expected. Don't go back to the apartment, assemble good records about bank accounts, assets and liabilities, and let Franklin handle the rest. He was confident her pre-nup was solid so this should just be a matter for the lawyers to hash out. Annie would have very little to do. Because their marriage had produced no children and no commonly owned assets, the terms of the pre-nup were clear: everybody go home with what you came with. That was about it.

Annie had told Franklin about Doc. She explained he had nothing to do with her decision to leave John, but she wasn't even sure she believed that. Franklin advised her to keep a low profile with Doc for the time being. He was afraid such info could enrage John and make whatever negotiations were necessary more emotional than they needed to be. Too many times he'd seen a smooth divorce turn ugly when one spouse found out the other had a new squeeze. "People are jealous and possessive creatures by nature," he told her.

As she stood in front of the Essex House waiting for her car service, she glanced north, through the park's treetops toward the upper reaches of Fifth Avenue where their apartment stretched up over the golden autumn colors. She knew another chapter in her life was coming to a close. It seemed unlikely she'd be living in Manhattan again anytime soon. If there was a life ahead for her and Doc, it wouldn't be here.

The black Town Car arrived and the driver helped her load her bags and the fruits of two days shopping, into the truck. During the ride back to Southampton she called both her sons for her usual Sunday call. They were both extremely supportive of her decision to leave John and move out to Southampton. She still hadn't mentioned Doc to them. It was better this way. When they come home at Thanksgiving—that will be a good time to talk about her new love.

She also tried to call Doc but he didn't pick up. She'd tried twice on Saturday and left him two voicemails but she hadn't heard back from him. This time she left him a message saying she was on her way back to Southampton and would probably be there by three o'clock. She assumed he lost his cell phone again. Why can't men be more responsible?

CHAPTER EIGHTY-NINE

Doc

I woke up around noon. Someone was knocking on my door. My head was pounding from the eight shots of bourbon I'd washed down with beer the previous night. I hated myself for what I'd done. I felt like shit.

"Hold on. I'll be right there," I yelled down toward the thumping door. Oh, this was going to be one brutal hangover.

As I staggered toward my dresser to grab a pair of shorts I caught a glimpse of myself in the wall mirror. I squinted and looked closely to be sure the reflected creature was really someone I used to know. "You look like shit." I said out loud, both hands resting on the dresser, supporting me. To say my head was foggy would be a gross injustice to fog.

The knocking at the door persisted.

"I'm coming!" The sound of my own yelling echoed through my skull and actually hurt my eyes. Everything was sort of a blur. Then, as the image in the mirror came into focus, the events of the previous day began to come back to me. Here's what I remember:

John had his back to me and was busy working his reel to let out line. I looked down at the bat in my hand and then at the back of his head, my target. I took a step closer. The bat felt like it weighed a hundred pounds and my hand was squeezing it so tightly I was beginning to cut off the flow of blood to my fingers.

Another step closer. From this distance I could take a full

swing with both hands. My eyes were glued to the back of his head. This was it. This was my chance.

But I couldn't do it.

I couldn't bring myself to kill a man. I don't know why. I just wasn't strong enough to do it. Later, sitting alone at the bar, I guessed maybe I just hadn't become the hunter I thought I was. All my self-rhetoric about the animal kingdom preying on the weak failed me. My survival of the fittest theory didn't make sense when I held the weapon of death in my own hands. Perhaps some men are born to be the lions and others, like me, are born to be the lambs.

So I spent the night hanging on the bar at Tide-runners, a great place to forget who you are. I felt like a complete failure; not just because I'd failed to protect my woman from the asshole who'd tried to kill her, but more because my convictions weren't strong enough to see me through this. At the end of the day, I guess I still believed there was something special about life, even his life.

I staggered down the steps, through the kitchen and opened the thumping door. Three large men awaited me on the other side of the screen door. One was dressed in a suit with a black trench coat protecting him from the morning drizzle, the other two were uniformed Suffolk County cops. They were getting wet.

The trench coat introduced himself as Detective Peterson. "Are you Jerome Cafara?"

"I usually am when I don't feel this sick. What can I do for you?" My first thought was that it had something to do with the fire at Annie's house and I was tempted just to tell them Annie wasn't here. If they wanted to continue their arson investigation it would have to wait until she got back later today. But, like many things recently, I was wrong.

"May we come in?" Detective Peterson looked sarcastically skyward as if to say, "*Come on asshole, it's raining out here.*"

I was hanging on the refrigerator handle which had been supporting me nicely and was about to tell them that if they were looking for Annie, she wasn't here. I really wanted to get back to the darkness and quiet of my bedroom. But before I could open my mouth, the three cops were standing in my kitchen.

"I'd like to ask you a few questions if you have a moment Mr. Cafara." He didn't seem to care that he'd woken me from a sound sleep, but then I realized it was after noon. It appeared the best way to get rid of them would be to answer their questions. Hopefully, I'd be back in bed in ten minutes and my head would stop pounding. Wrong again.

"OK. What can I do for you?" I said as I leaned against my kitchen counter more for support than comfort.

The two uniformed cops were standing directly behind the detective but their eyes were taking in the whole room. They seemed to be looking for something or someone. I'm usually the last guy to criticize a cop, but these guys just seemed rude.

"Mr. Cafara, can you tell us where you were last night?"

Oops. I guess this wasn't about Annie's fire. I must have done something stupid last night. I don't remember pissing on anyone's lawn or puking on Main Street. And I'm sure I didn't drive myself home. I remember getting out of a cab and falling onto the pebbles in my driveway.

"Did I do something wrong last night? I had a little too much to drink at Tide-runners." I said sheepishly.

"Can you tell us where you were between six and twelve last night?"

"I just did. I was at Tide-runners in Hampton Bays. I'm not

sure what time I left but I'd guess it was after twelve. I got there around six I'd say."

"Were you with anyone else that can verify that?"

"Why would I need to verify that? I was sitting at a bar."

Detective Peterson intended to be the only one asking questions this afternoon. He didn't seem too friendly and I was beginning to wonder just why these guys were here. I mean you don't send three cops to investigate an act of public drunkenness, or whatever it was.

"Can anyone verify that you were at Tide-runners last night?" He said matter-of-factly.

I thought back through the fog. "I don't remember much about last night. I don't think I saw anyone I knew but I was talking to the two bartenders about the Met game that was on the TV over the bar. One was a cute kid. She said she went to Stony Brook. The other was a guy. I don't know their names."

The detective made a few notes in his composition book. "And where were you prior to Tide-runners?"

"I'd been out fishing with a friend. He keeps his boat at Jackson's Marina, just down the street from Tide-runners. When we got back I drove over to the bar. I guess I left my car there. I hope I did."

"Did your friend go to the bar with you?"

"No."

"What's the name of your fishing friend?"

"John Weaver. It's his boat."

"And what time would you say you left the marina for Tide-runners?"

"I'd guess around five-thirty or six. It was already getting dark so probably closer to six. Why? What's this about?" Now I was hung over and confused. But mostly I was hung over. And I really needed to pee. But these guys weren't going anywhere.

"Mr. Cafara, we're just doing some preliminary investigative work into a situation that occurred last night at the marina. Can you tell us anything about that?"

"At the marina? I told you. I was at the bar all night. How would I know what happened at the marina?"

"That's what we're trying to find out. Mr. Cafara, your friend, Mr. Weaver, was found this morning at seven A.M. with a knife sticking out of his neck. It appears he was murdered sometime during the night."

Even in my fog, the words hit me like a baseball bat. Poor choice of words.

"Somebody killed John?" Was all I could gasp. I fell back and probably would have hit the floor if the detective hadn't grabbed me. He set me down for a gentle landing on a chair.

"He's dead?" Was my next super-intelligent question.

"Yes, Mr. Cafara. Can you tell us anything that might help us? How did you know Mr. Weaver?"

What was I supposed to say? It really didn't matter. Turns out, the detective and two uniforms had been walking around the neighborhood before coming to see me. Along the way, they ran into a few neighbors who told them about Annie and me running around in our underwear the night of the fire. By now, the quiet little hamlet of Cold Spring Pond must be ablaze with rumors. More to the point, I had three cops who knew I was having sleepovers with the dead guy's wife.

"It's a long story."

"I've got all day," said the detective.

I was surprised I hadn't pissed my pants when he told me John had been murdered. I needed to go that bad. "I need to take a wiz. Give me a minute to go to the bathroom and get some clothes on. OK?"

"Sure. Try to be quick though."

When I got back up stairs I dealt with nature's calling, then brushed my teeth and threw on a pair of jeans and a South Park tee shirt. It was only later I realized the shirt said *"Oh my God, somebody's killed Kenny!"* Another poor choice in a growing list.

When I came back downstairs the three cops were sitting at my kitchen counter and had left the forth seat for me. I guess I was supposed to sit down and I did, but mostly because I still felt like shit.

"So, how do you know Mr. Weaver?" The trench coat still wanted to know.

I thought about it for a few seconds. I didn't want my answer to sound trite or insensitive but I had no reason to bullshit them either. While I was thinking, the detective was scribbling in his notebook. Finally, I said, "He was a neighbor. He and his wife lived just down the street. You probably noticed the yellow tape around their house. They had a fire a few nights ago."

"That's it?"

"What else do you want to know?"

"What was your relationship with Mrs. Weaver?"

At the sound of Annie's name a flood of emotions ran through me. Poor Annie probably got a call this morning telling her John had been murdered. Even if you're in the process of divorcing the son-of-a-bitch, that's got to hurt. She was, after all, married to the guy for a few years and must have loved him at one time. This must be so painful for her. I felt badly that I wasn't with her.

It took another question from Detective Peterson to snap me from my daydream.

"Mr. Cafara, what was your relationship with Mrs. Weaver?"

"We were very close friends." There. That should do it. Wrong again.

"Were you romantically involved with Mrs. Weaver?"

I decided that other than the embarrassment of being caught diddling another man's wife, I had no reason to lie to these guys. They were trying to find out who killed John. I don't think I could help but I certainly didn't want to get in their way.

"Yes, actually we were. We are. Annie was in the process of getting a divorce and we've been romantically involved, as you put it, for a few weeks now."

"You say they were in the process of a divorce?"

"Yes. She didn't tell you that?" I asked.

"We haven't been able to contact her yet. We were hoping you could help us find her."

"So, Annie doesn't know yet?"

"No. We only have a phone number and address in Manhattan and we've tried both. We were hoping you'd know where she is or have another phone number for us. I'm sure you do." He said the last part with a really nasty inflection. I was beginning to dislike these guys. But to be fair, the two guys in uniform hadn't opened their mouths but to breathe so I guess I just disliked their looks.

"I have her cell number in my cell phone, but this isn't the sort of news you give a woman on the phone." I protested.

"Let us worry about that. We'd just like to get the number please."

I hesitated just a few seconds but it was long enough to piss off the detective. Suddenly he had a very condescending approach to all this, as if I was some sort of low-life for having an affair with a married woman. He seemed very judgmental. He ran his hand through his short black hair and then pounded it on my table.

"Mr. Cafara, are you going to help us or not?" He was a few notches louder than before.

I'm not accustomed to dealing with the police. Bottom line is—I'm intimidated by them, or more to the point, I'm intimidated by their guns. So I started looking for my cell phone. It occurred to me that I hadn't seen it in a while. I didn't bring it on the fishing trip because I expected that trip to end with me getting wet. So I searched the places I might have left it on Friday night. Sure enough, it was in the pocket of the jacket I wore when I met the insurance lady.

I retrieved Annie's number for the cops and the detective wrote it in his notebook. I wondered what they would say when they called her. I was worried about her reaction and tried to picture where she would be. Then it occurred to me that she was probably already on her way back to Southampton. She'd said she'd be back Sunday afternoon, and despite what my body thought, it was already Sunday afternoon. I remembered she'd left her car in her driveway so she's either on a train or taking a limo. That's when I noticed I had several voicemails waiting for me.

I asked the policemen to excuse me for a moment and I went back upstairs to listen to the voicemails. They were all from Annie and the most recent one was left about an hour ago saying she'd be here by three. She didn't say how she was coming but since she didn't ask me to pick her up at the train station, I figured she took a limo. I wondered if I should share this with the cops in my kitchen.

When I came back down, Detective Peterson was alone at the table. I was glad to see the two silent thugs had left. Unfortunately they'd only gone outside to take a call on their radio. When they came back the short one asked to speak to the detective outside for a minute. The tall one stayed with me, as if I needed company.

When Detective Peterson came back in the house he looked like he'd just swallowed the canary. He couldn't wait to tell me his good news. "Mr. Cafara, we found your car at the Tide-runner."

Since I'd already told them that's where I thought I'd left it, I didn't see this as brilliant police work. Although, I must say I was impressed at how fast they found it. Still, that was an easy one. Then the detective asked me a tough one.

"Do you mind telling us about the contents of your cooler?"

CHAPTER NINETY

Doc

I spent the rest of Sunday afternoon at the police station in Southampton. Apparently I was their prime suspect in the murder of Dr. John Weaver. How ironic. The guy I wanted to kill winds up murdered and I'm blamed for it.

The best explanation I could whip up for the bottles of gas, chain and anchor in my cooler, was that it was an extra anchor I used to keep on my boat and the gas was some extra gas I was going to put in my boat's tank but left it in the cooler in case it spilled before I got around to getting to my boat. It was pretty lame but I defy you to come up with something better when you've got three cops in your kitchen who think you're a murderer.

After my lame explanation, they invited me to come with them to the police station. They said I wasn't under arrest, they just had a lot more questions to ask me, but I'm pretty sure they just wanted to be able to look through my place with no one home. Anyway, as I said before, I'm pretty much a whimp when it comes to cops, so I did as I was told. They took finger prints and a DNA sample. I just kept telling myself, "*You didn't do anything. You have nothing to worry about.*" But I wasn't sure if I believed myself.

Besides, once detective *know-it-all* realizes he's been busting my chops for nothing, I figured I'd get a big apology and a ride back home. My greatest concern was for Annie. The poor thing was on her way to my house and she was about to learn her husband is dead and her lover is suspected of having killed him. I wondered how she'd react to the news of John's murder. As much as she wanted him out of her life, she wasn't the sort of person to wish anyone harm. Even the prick who tried to kill her a few days before.

And then I wondered how she'd react when she heard they think I did it. Would she, even for a moment, think it's true? I would, if I were her. After all, she knows I love her and that I freaked out when I learned of John's attempts to kill her. She also knew I blamed John for the fire and that we spoke about her still being in danger from him. Actually, now that I think about it, if she knows me at all, she should think it was me. And it would have been except that I chickened out.

For most of the afternoon, I was confined to a small but comfortable room and barraged with questions from several different cops, each with their own style but basically all asking the same things. I guess they don't get too many murders in Southampton so this was big doings. There were even two reporters waiting on the steps to the police station. I didn't see anyone snap a picture, but I'll bet this is a page one story in the local paper on Monday.

I was asked if I wanted an attorney but since I knew I'd done nothing illegal, and because I put lawyers in the same basket with used car salesmen and other parasitic organisms, I said no thanks. Besides, I figured I'd be home by dinner time. Well, that didn't happen, and I suppose it was around dinner time that they left me alone in the room for almost an hour. I assumed there was some form of surveillance device or one-way mirror but if there was, I couldn't find it.

When the door finally opened, Annie was standing there.

It was obvious she'd been crying. Her face was puffy and her eyes were red. The kind Suffolk County Police were nice enough to wait for her at my house and ambush her with the news about John. I guess they wanted to see her reaction, just in case she was in on his demise. They probably figured if the boyfriend killed the guy then the wife was probably part of the equation. She might have even set the whole thing up.

But, of course, that wasn't what happened. When Annie heard the news about John she fainted, right in my driveway. After she'd come to, they were sweet enough to question her for over an hour in my kitchen. Mostly they asked about her relationship with me. At that point she didn't know I was suspect number one and she told them the truth—that we'd been lovers for about a month and that she and John were preparing for a divorce. I'm not sure the truth helped my cause. Actually, the truth made it look like I had all the motive in the world to kill her husband. And they didn't even know about John's attempts to kill his wife.

Annie stepped into the room and I stood, thinking we would embrace. She looked like she needed a hug. But she stopped after one step and just stared at me. Her eyes were watery and I could see an enormous sadness in them. She looked down to avoid my gaze. Then she turned to one of the detectives standing in the doorway and said, "Yes, that's him."

My mouth hung open. I didn't know what to say. It felt like someone had just kicked me in the stomach and I'd lost all the air in my body. I can't remember ever having an emotional pain like that.

I suppose the cops wanted to see what sort of exchange was going to occur between us because they gave us all the time in the world to stand there facing each other. Finally, I mustered enough air to say, "Annie, you don't think I did this do you?" But the words sounded weak, almost as if I didn't believe them myself. And why should I? This time yesterday, I held a bat in my hand, ready to do it. I wanted to kill him. I'd planned to kill him. I tried to kill him, but I couldn't.

"You told me you weren't going fishing with him." She said it in a near whisper. "Why would you go?"

She had a good point. Why would I go fishing with the prick who tried to kill her unless I planned some sort of revenge? It was another good point that wasn't helping my social standing with law enforcement. I had no good answer other than the truth, which was that I had planned to kill him. I decided not to mention that. Neither Annie nor the cops needed to know that.

"Annie, I can't explain it. But you have to believe me. I didn't kill John."

She turned away and walked out of the room with one of the female cops holding her by the shoulders. She'd identified the boyfriend, now she had to go down the hall and identify the victim. Poor Annie.

I tried to think of something I could tell my captors that would make them understand I hadn't done it. Something that would make them believe me. But everything I came up with would only make me seem guilty. I was sleeping with the guy's wife. I was seen with her two nights before the murder by a dozen neighbors. I had suspicious materials in my trunk and really couldn't account for my whereabouts when John was killed. And if I told them about John's attempts to kill his wife it would only look worse. Revenge would seem like a reasonable motive.

After Annie turned her back on me, I realized this may not be as simple to work my way out of as I'd originally thought. I asked one of the uniformed guys what do I do about getting a lawyer. Without Annie on my side, I had no one. I suddenly felt like I needed some help. I wanted to pray, but that ship had sailed too.

CHAPTER NINETY-ONE

The investigation into the death of Dr. John Weaver was the biggest thing in Southampton since the Ted Ammon, Generosa, Danny Pelosi triangle that resulted in the murder of Ammon and sent Pelosi to Elmira Correctional facility until 2031. Like the former case, the local papers had a field day with the murder of John Weaver, exploiting the love triangle end of it, thereby causing Annie much embarrassment. And like the former case, the media made it difficult for anyone to form an unbiased view of the suspected killer. There were even media rumors that linked Annie to the plot to knock off her husband.

In the five days since the murder, the media had created its own hypothetical crime; one in which the retired businessman seduced the wealthy beauty in an attempt to gain the family fortune by conspiring to kill her husband, the dedicated doctor. The local TV channel went so far as to fabricate a story wherein Annie and Doc planned to kill the doctor on his boat and throw his body overboard using the chain and anchor found in the killer's car. Allegedly, there was a two million dollar life insurance policy involved. By Thursday, the running rumor was Doc and Annie had planned to hide out at the Essex House after the murder, then fly to Europe until things quieted down. Ambitious reporters had pieced this together based on conversations with the reservation clerk at the Essex House and sales people who'd assisted Annie with her shopping in Manhattan.

"Jerome Cafara, a retired real estate tycoon who moved to Southampton only a few months before, has retained Byron Munson, Esq. to represent him. Mr. Cafara has been charged with the murder of Doctor John Weaver and is being held at the County correctional facility in Riverhead. A preliminary hearing to set bail is scheduled for October 6th." Or so the media would have us think. Actually, Doc had not yet been to the grand jury, so he was not yet formally charged with anything. But he was being held on suspicion of murder charges pending the results of the DNA analysis and medical examiner's report. Both were due tomorrow and everyone expected a trip to the grand jury after that.

In the meantime, Annie had a quiet one-night funeral service for her husband in Manhattan near their apartment. He was buried next to his mother in a family plot in Pinelawn Cemetery. About a hundred people associated with his medical practice attended. By the Thursday after the murder, Annie was back in her apartment, piecing together her life and sorting John's clothes into boxes for the Salvation Army. Both her son's had flown in and were staying with her, helping her rid her apartment of John's worldly possessions. The media coverage forced her to have a difficult conversation with her boys about Doc. She had hoped to put off telling them about him for several more weeks.

Annie hadn't seen Doc since Sunday afternoon at the police station. Although the media had her involved in the plot to kill her husband, the police didn't see it that way. Once they unraveled the forensic accounting and realized it was Annie who came from family money, not her husband, there was no credible motive connecting her to the murder. But Franklin Montague, the dedicated family attorney, advised her not to talk to Doc for the time being for fear it would only fuel the media fires.

Like everyone else, Annie couldn't help but hear the stories circulating around her husband's murder. All of them pointed squarely at Doc as the murderer. Her own theory was that they must have fought that day on the boat, probably after Doc confronted him with the knowledge he'd tried to kill her. John's temper got the better of him and their argument turned violent. Either in the act of fighting or as a measure of self defense, Doc must have stabbed John. She couldn't imagine Doc had done anything premeditated. The initial coroner's report said the neck wound, although not deep, had hit the jugular vein and John bled to death in under a minute.

Because Annie didn't believe Doc had planned to murder her husband, she couldn't reconcile the gasoline and chain in his trunk. The only explanation she could conceive was that after the fight, Doc panicked, went home to get things that would help him either conceal the body or destroy the body and boat together. Both were gruesome images for her. They just didn't mesh with the man she thought she knew and loved.

But there were inconsistencies. If Doc had fought with John there should be evidence of that. There was no blood found anywhere Doc had been or anywhere in his car or home. There was also no evidence he'd cleaned the blood off himself. In fact, all three policemen who went to Doc's home said his hands still smelled of fish from the day before. Apparently, Doc hadn't showered since the fishing trip, something a murderer would do immediately.

She hated the thought that Doc had killed John. She was repulsed by the idea that he may have done it for her. But worst of all was the thought that Doc was innocent and could still be convicted of a murder he didn't actually commit based on a lot of circumstantial evidence. And most of that evidence dealt with Doc's relationship with Annie.

But, if she believed it had been self defense in the course of a struggle, why had she abandoned Doc so quickly at the police station? Just when he needed her most, she'd turned her back to him. The thought of him sitting in a jail cell in Riverhead broke her heart, and she wondered if anyone had been to see him. Had he even called his daughters? She doubted it. It would be like him not to have them worry and unless they saw local news, they would be unlikely to hear about it.

The image of Doc in an orange jumpsuit, sitting alone in jail with no one visiting him was more than she could bear. She told her sons that tomorrow morning she planned to drive out to Riverhead and see him even though Franklin had advised against it. Both Nick and Frank would be on their way back to Gainesville and Boston by noon anyway. To her great surprise, they thought it was a good idea. They could see the pain she was in and knew it wasn't from losing her husband. It was from having her lover taken from her.

The next morning she made the boys a hearty breakfast. Frank needed to make a train at eleven-thirty from Penn station and Nick had a car picking him up for the drive to JFK around the same time. For the second time in their young lives they were saying good-bye to their mother—leaving her alone and widowed.

She packed a small bag and began the two hour drive to Riverhead. Along the way she called Franklin to tell him what she was doing. She wanted to make sure he understood her motive and how strongly she felt about it. She'd decided if his objections were purely in defense of her reputation, she'd go anyway.

"I know this guy is very important to you Annie. But haven't the events of the last few days caused you to see a side of him you hadn't seen before?"

"I don't know Franklin. I just can't believe he would deliberately kill someone. Even someone like John."

"Well then, do what your heart tells you is right. You always were a softy for anyone in distress."

———

About the same time Annie was on the phone with her friend and lawyer, Doc had been taken back to the police station in Southampton. He had expected to be taken to the courthouse in Riverhead for the grand jury. His lawyer, Byron, had told him he would meet him there. But when the uniformed Suffolk County cops put him in the back of their Crown Victoria, they drove past the Riverhead court and back to Southampton.

His mood, after five nights in the county facility, was morose. He hadn't shaved since the day before the fishing trip and his gaunt face and stubble made him look a bit maniacal. The photographers ate it up and were waiting at the station when the car pulled up. Questions were screamed out from the small crowd.

"Why did you do it, Jerome?"

"How were you treated in Riverhead?"

How does it feel to be facing life in prison?"

Doc lowered his head and followed the uniforms through the crowd to the front door of the modern police station. He was led back to the same room he was interrogated in five days earlier. He expected they'd want to talk to him about the DNA evidence and M.E.'s report before taking it to the grand jury, but by now he knew he wasn't supposed to talk to anyone without Byron at his side. He'd seen enough Law and Order to have an idea about what was about to happen and he couldn't believe it was happening to him.

One of the uniformed cops took the handcuffs off Doc's wrists and he was left alone in the room for fifteen minutes. For the first time in his life, he was scared. Scared that a blind justice was going to be applied and he'd be one of the *one-in-a thousand* innocent guys that gets sent away for life for a murder they scream they didn't commit. Other than his lawyer, no one was on his side. Worst of all, because the police were convinced they had their man, they were spending all their energies building a case to prove he'd killed John Weaver instead of looking for the guy who really did.

Once again, abject loneliness was his only companion. He'd been embarrassed to call anyone, not even his daughters or Bobby. And ironically, the embarrassment flowed not from being paraded around like Charles Manson for the media's benefit, but from the self-understanding and guilt that he actually had planned to kill the man who was murdered.

And then there was Annie. Oh, how wonderful things could have been. Seeing her walk away was painful in ways he didn't fully understand. He knew she was in shock the day she walked into the room and said, "*Yes, that's him.*" But how could she turn her back on him? How could she give up on him without even hearing what he was trying to get everyone to understand? Yet, he felt no anger. He loved her. He was ashamed that he'd disappointed her. He could see that disappointment on her face and it cut him deeply.

And then everything changed.

CHAPTER NINETY-TWO

Detective Peterson was the first of two cops to enter the room. The other was a stocky black woman in a police uniform that looked to be two sizes too small for her substantial frame. But something was different about her uniform. It wasn't like all the others he'd seen the last few days. This one was dark blue and had an NYPD emblem on the sleeve. Why would New York City cops be out here? Doc's first thought was that something had happened to Annie. He froze in his chair.

Detective Peterson was the first to speak and when he did there was no longer contempt in his voice. "Mr. Cafara, this is Sergeant Roberta Pullman from the NYPD. I think you're going to want to hear what she has to say."

"Is everything OK with Annie?" He had to know.

The tall detective and the pudgy sergeant looked at each other. They seemed to have no idea what Doc was talking about.

"Mr. Cafara, as far as I know, we haven't been in contact with Mrs. Weaver since she claimed her husband's body. What makes you think something's wrong?"

Doc was relieved to hear the NYPD's presence had nothing to do with Annie. Other than that, he almost didn't have the energy to care why she was here. He was tired. His back was sore from the thin mattress at the county jail, and he hadn't eaten a good meal in over a week. He just shrugged.

"Mr. Cafara, Sgt. Pullman is here because yesterday... well why don't you explain, sergeant?" He stepped back and made room for the portly woman to sit across from Doc at the table.

When she was comfortable on the small stool, she began to explain the reason she was there. "Mr. Cafara, yesterday afternoon, a woman named Miranda Pavida walked into the 43rd precinct house in Manhattan, where I was on the desk, and told us she was the one who stabbed John Weaver to death. She said it was in self defense and once the public defender was appointed, she gave us all the details."

Doc slumped in his chair and let out a long sigh.

"We spent the rest of the day and night working this and here's what we know. It seems about an hour after you left Mr. Weaver at his boat, he was paid a visit by a couple of thugs who do collection work for a guy Weaver and his business partners owed money to. We later collaborated Ms. Pavida's story with the dock hand at the marina, a kid named Mark Vecchio, who said he saw you leaving the marina before the two large collection agents arrived. They actually asked the kid which boat belonged to the victim so he got a good look at them. Based on the descriptions, we picked up the two guys, a Felix Brown and his cousin, a Levon Whitman. It seems the victim owed their boss quite a bit of money and had been dodging them for a while, so they must have roughed him up."

Detective Peterson added, "It couldn't have been too bad because the M.E.'s report didn't show much in the way of bruising, but they probably pushed him around and threatened him enough to get him pissed off."

Sergeant Pullman looked over her shoulder at the detective and seemed to be annoyed by the interruption. She continued her monolog and made a point of looking at Doc. "The kid at the dock confirmed that the two men left the marina about ten minutes later. Then an hour after that, he sees Miranda Pavida get onto the victim's boat. Apparently she was a regular visitor and knew the kid by name. She's a call girl, a high-end escort I guess if you're trying to be diplomatic about it. She told us she'd been with Weaver several times before, usually meeting him on his boat. He'd called her a few days before and requested her company Saturday night. She's a college kid from New York, probably not more than twenty years old if I had to guess. She took the train out from the city.

"Anyway, it seems when she arrived that night, Weaver was still really pissed off about his visit from Felix and Levon and the way they treated him. She said he wouldn't let it go although he hadn't explained to her who they were. She wanted him to take the boat out for a ride. He didn't want to.

According to Ms. Pavida, the victim had a history of roughing up his playmates, sometimes during sex and some-times after. But this night, they never got around to jumping in the hay because he's raving about the two niggers; his words, not mine—who had been there earlier. Her side of the story is that she and Weaver got into a pretty nasty argument which turned into a one-sided fight, with him kicking the shit out of her. When I saw her yesterday, she still had some bruises and black and blue marks on her face and arms; all hundred and five pounds of her."

It was clear to both men in the room, Doc and the detec-tive, that Sergeant Pullman had no patience for men who beat up women.

"Her story is that they were fighting in the cabin of the boat and she picked up the knife to get him to stop hitting her. But this just makes him crazier and he comes at her swinging both fists. She claims he got stabbed when she held the knife up to defend herself. According to the Suffolk County police, the stab wound on the victim's neck would be consistent with a backward movement, but that's not for us to decide.

"She says that she ran from the boat with him still yelling

obscenities at her and a knife in his neck. She claims he was very much alive when she left. Again, that's not for us to decide. She says she got a cab at the marina back to the Hampton Bays train station and took a train back to the city around nine o'clock. She says she didn't know he died until she read about it in the paper a few days later. After twenty-four hours of soul searching, she came to see us and confessed. My guess is she figured since the kid at the marina knew who she was, that the police would be looking for her anyway. Apparently that wasn't the case." She glanced toward detective Peterson for the first time.

Doc was incredulous. "You mean I'm not going to the grand jury?"

Detective Peterson stepped forward. "No, Mr. Cafara, you're not. You're going home. I will personally apologize on behalf of Suffolk County for all you've been through, and I will be happy to drive you home or anyplace you'd like to go."

CHAPTER NINETY-THREE

Doc

I said nothing on the way home in the detective's car. At least, I don't remember saying anything. I just wanted to get home, take a shower and sleep. I guess Detective Peterson was feeling a little foolish because he didn't offer much conversation either. To his credit, when I got out of the car, he made a point of saying, "Mr. Cafara, I was doing my job. I'm sorry we got it wrong this time."

I felt an urge to reply, "*You were closer to right than you think*." But I kept my mouth shut. He drove away not seeing the irony. They arrested the person who had killed John Weaver unintentionally, and released the person who intended to kill him.

I checked my refrigerator but everything was at least a week old. My hunger would have to wait until I found the energy to drive into town. The Suffolk P.D. had been nice enough to drop my car off in my drive way.

I called Kitty and Peggy and told them about my ordeal; the ordeal of being falsely arrested, not the ordeal of trying to kill my lover's husband. Neither of them had heard anything about it. Thankfully, it was just local news. I agreed to meet Peggy for a long overdue dinner in the city next week and Kitty promised to fly home at the end of October for a long weekend.

Then I called Bobby. He hadn't heard anything either and was astounded when I gave him the details. Again, not the entire story, but enough to make the cop in him pretty angry that his counterparts in Suffolk had failed to question the kid at the marina.

I thought about calling Annie. I wanted to call her. I just didn't know how to start the conversation. Or maybe I was afraid she wouldn't take my call. When I finally got up the guts to dial her number, I realized my cell phone was going dead from a week of neglect and the three calls I'd already made. I really need to get a land line.

As I stood in the outdoor shower gazing up at the cloudy sky, the steamy hot water hit my shoulders and seemed to wash away the memory of jail. I soaped, rinsed and re-soaped several times until I felt new again. Using the mirror in the shower and the last of my Noxzema, I shaved clean and was going under for a final rinse when I heard someone walking on my deck toward the shower stall.

I hurried to rinse the last studs from around my eyes when I heard the shower door latch click open. I squinted through the water in my eyes and saw Annie standing there holding the wooden shower door open.

"I hear you busted out." Her voice was as soft as I remembered.

Before I could respond, she was standing next to me. Her clothes were getting soaked by the shower spray. The door slammed shut behind her.

"Learn any new tricks in prison?" She teased as she wrapped her hands around the back of my neck.

———

It seems Annie had gone to the Suffolk County Correctional facility expecting to pay me a visit. When she was told I was no longer living there, she called her lawyer who made a few calls, and found out what I'd been told a few hours ago. The cop at the Southampton station said a detective had dropped me off at home.

So as not to completely disappoint her, we had sort of a conjugal visit in the shower. Afterwards, we wrapped ourselves in terrycloth robes and sat in the white wicker rocking chairs sipping Drambuie from red plastic cups.

"I'm so sorry I doubted you Doc." She said as we both stared out at the dusk-lit pond.

"You didn't doubt me. You were given a set of facts and you responded like anyone would," I assured her. Then for fun, I added, "You threw me under the bus!"

"I'm so sorry."

Maybe it was because I love having beautiful women in terrycloth robes apologizing to me, or maybe I just wasn't ready to tell Annie the truth. I would someday.

Just not now.

Actually, we didn't say much. We sat together, like two old people rocking, staring out at the eerie stillness of the pond. I felt like I'd been given a new lease on life; a second chance much the same way Annie had. I should have felt guilty about what I'd planned to do, but instead, I felt a calmness. I'd walked to the brink and turned back. I don't know why, but I felt good about not having what it takes to kill a man.

I thought for a moment about the loneliness I'd been feeling since walking away from God. It's like being an orphan in a world filled with willing parents and deciding I don't need them. I can figure out the puzzle for myself.

Maybe.

"I'm sorry too," I said. But I wasn't sure if I was apologizing to Annie or to the wisp of clouds hanging over the pond.